I0780531

FEEDING BEAUTY

HOLLY ROBERDS

BOOKS BY HOLLY ROBERDS

To my own coven of Lost Girls
Emily, Bree, and Nicole
*You are the inspiration and reality for the fantasy friendships I
write*

CHAPTER I
BEST SEAT IN THE HOUSE
TALON

urora's face twists into an expression of concentrated ecstasy as he licks up her dripping sex with the fervor of a starving man.

Through the slats of the viewing screen, I watch him spit on the pink petals of her slit before guiding two fingers inside her. Aurora cries out, hips bucking as her eyes glaze over. I swallow hard and try to focus on my duty instead of wrapping my hand around my rock-hard cock. There's time enough later to run my aching dick in my palm as I replay every micro expression the princess makes as her thighs shake and quiver under the man's onslaught.

She reaches up to pluck her pert pink nipples, desperate to give herself relief.

As always, the sight of her burns into my brain, adding to the never-ending catalogue of these moments.

If it were me, I'd make sure my fingers were slightly curled. That evokes the most delicious sounds from her.

Her long waves of cotton candy pink hair fan about her head. Her golden skin glistens from the sheen of sweat covering her, turning her luminescent. Thin ropes of diamonds glitter in the low light and drape her body. The deliberate way they gather at the curve of her hips and slide down the slopes of her thighs creates an illusion of luxury. They might as well be chains.

When she first stepped out from behind the curtains and invited the John to her bed, she appeared like a goddess bestowing a gift upon a mere mortal. Touching her, tasting her, is a prize he doesn't deserve but is given anyway.

He'll pay the price for it though.

"I still can't believe it," the John says, shaking his head, staring down to watch his fingers slide in and out of her perfect body. "I can't believe I finally killed my bitch wife and here I am. I thought I was going to be taken to the monster of the castle everyone whispers about." A half-hiccup, half-laugh of disbelief jerks his ribcage. "But I'm about to have sex with the untouchable Princess of the Realm of Roses. If I'd known this would be the prize, I would have killed that useless whore years ago."

Behind the partition, I don't have to hide the sneer that spreads across my face.

You fucking idiot.

Aurora's lashes flutter, a languid blink that could be mistaken for pleasure as he climbs up her body. Too wrapped up in his own need, the John doesn't notice the unsettling cold beneath her inviting smile as she meets his gaze.

I know her sense of justice wars with her disgust every time we have to do this. Her feelings knot and tangle within her until they're an impossible boulder crushing her chest.

I feel it too.

Pushing her legs up, he slides his hard dick into the princess as he begins pumping furiously. She cries out louder and louder.

His ass cheeks ripple from the continued impact into her perfect body.

Aurora claws at the back of his head as he kisses her fiercely. Little whimpers and moans emit from her throat.

My fingers unconsciously tighten through the slats.

It's going to take more than that for her to come.

He doesn't have the right angle to do the job. She's going to need to change position if she wants to finish this.

The princess uses her knees to push him out of her and guides him onto his back. She crawls over to straddle him on the massive silk covered bed. The many candelabras flicker with innocent warmth all around them.

"Look at me," she says to the John, spearing her own fingers through those glistening lips. She spreads her fingers apart, putting herself on display.

I lick my lips, mouth suddenly dry. My tongue is sandpaper as I focus on her visible clit. It's red, aching, and so very needy. If I could just. . .

Both hands now gripping the slats, I watch, fixated on her with a familiar hunger so deep I sometimes think it will kill me.

"Fae fucks, that's hot," the John breathes, taking in the salacious view.

Teasing them always makes it more delicious.

It's been nearly an hour of teasing. This one has a lot of fortitude for being a scumbag murderer.

"Tell me you want this," she says in a whisper, her gaze lowered.

Oh, Aurora.

Something in my chest twists with extreme violence.

"More than anything, princess." His thumbs rub along her hips as he gulps.

With a slight nod to herself, she slides down, impaling herself.

They both let out a shout as he fills her again. Aurora leans over to kiss him deeply before sitting up. Bracing her palms on his chest, she sets the perfect rhythm.

Those gray eyes turn up, colliding almost violently with mine. Despite the slats, I know she sees me.

My breath freezes in my chest. Her irises are the color of light passing through smoky quartz, and I know them better than my own. My heart swells and beats so hard it threatens to break my ribs so it can fall at her feet.

Aurora bites her lip, and I know that means she found the angle where she can repeatedly rub her clit roughly against his pelvic bone.

Her pink hair is wild and tousled, a waterfall down her back, making her look all the more a sex goddess. The John curls up to capture one of her nipples in his mouth.

Fae fucking hell. What it would be like to know how they taste...

Her pace picks up as she rides him harder, faster. Her gaze never leaves mine, and I don't look away.

I'm with you.

I'll always be with you.

It's okay.

I don't say the words out loud, but I know she hears me all the same.

Her breath hitches and her rhythm stutters.

"Wait, what?" The John has finally noticed the glow around her body.

He must feel it now. Maybe he even knows what's coming, but I doubt it.

Those gray eyes begin to glow pink, several shades more intense and vibrant than her hair.

"Wait, stop," he begs. His voice has already turned thready as she feeds on him.

She's *been* feeding on him. He just hasn't noticed. Like taking sips from a glass of water before she downs the rest of her cup's contents in one go.

Her expression glazes over as she sucks in her fill, feeding off the John's lust, the sexual energy crackling between them, circling like static.

He only now understands he's dying. Fingers claw weakly at her shoulders, but his hips still move in tandem with her like he can't help himself.

"*Ungh.*" Aurora cries out, throwing her head back, coming with a burst of invisible energy. Gooseflesh rises along the nape of my neck as it washes over me.

And then it's done.

The silence presses in, the room's color drained to gray. Only the candles flicker.

Aurora rises, careful not to look at the John's face as she steps down from the dais. I move from my place in the shadows, her robe in my hand. Black claws extend from my fingers and pierce the fabric.

When had that happened?

Aurora turns away from me, and I help her into the silk garment. I'm careful not to touch her as I drop it onto her shoulders.

"Does it help?" I ask. "Asking them if they want it?"

There's no answer for a long beat. I wish she'd face me.

Aurora finally twists to catch my eye. There's an unnatural coldness in her gaze. A hardness she's constructed and keeps reinforcing, just to stay sane. A spark of resentment in her expression at my question.

"I'm just saying, he deserved it. They all deserve it. I make sure of that, Aura."

I'm not sure if it's my words, or my nickname for her that does it, but that cold resentment cracks. I see the deep grief that's plagued her since the day I met her.

The arousal still coursing through my body is immediately extinguished.

"I know you do," she says quietly. Her gaze slides over to the John's corpse.

I step in the way, blocking her view. "Hey. Don't."

Suddenly we are inches away. She smells like sex and candy, and shamefully my dick twitches as blood rushes south again.

Those impossibly long, dark lashes sweep down as she takes in my bare chest. Obsidian black scales cover half my shoulder and sweep down over the front of my body, fissures of bright red heat cracking through them.

"I'm not sure how much longer I can do this. I'm not sure how much longer they can keep me in this castle." She says it to my sternum, not looking up.

"Your parents care about you. *I* care about you."

Her lashes sweep up at that, brows snapping together. "Don't say that. I can't hear that right now."

Aurora jerks away to storm off. On instinct I tug her robe, and she twirls around. Too late I've realized my mistake. She loses her balance and trips. My throat closes off as my muscles tighten, bracing for impact. Helplessly I watch as her hands land on my bare chest.

The startled animalistic scream of pain she releases lodges itself between my ears in a way that will forever haunt me.

She scrambles away and pulls her hands into her body.

I move toward her, overwhelmed by the need to soothe her pain. She jerks, and I freeze.

"Let me see." It comes out a desperate rasp.

"It's fine, Talon. I'm fine," she says hurriedly.

"Aurora." Her full name bursts out of me with equal parts command and fear.

With a sigh, she unfurls her trembling hands from her chest. She winces. Violent red blisters mar her burned palms from where she made contact with my flesh and scales.

I'm a fae fucking idiot. Self-reproach hammers my brain and body until I'm almost forced to my knees.

"I'm sorry." I retreat on shaky legs, raking my hands through my shaggy hair. "Fae lords, I'm so sorry, Aura."

Tears gleam in her eyes, but they don't fall. Her robe has fallen open, revealing the glittering threads adorning her naked body. I know they are as much decoration as they are symbolic of chains holding her down, holding her back.

For a moment I'm struck by how we are both imprisoned by our forms. The awareness that neither of us can change our nature is too bitter of a pill to swallow at times.

This is one of those times.

She's a Succubus who has no choice but to feed to stay alive. And she can't feed without killing.

I'm a Dragon—perhaps the last of my kind—and my flesh burns all who touch it.

We are each one of a kind. Alone. Together.

Most of the time, we find consolation in that, but moments like now make it nearly impossible to bear.

My molars clench so hard they threaten to crack under the force. The internal pressure threatens to blow me apart.

"Shh," she hushes in a soothing tone. "I'm okay, Talon. It was an accident."

She shouldn't be comforting me. Something snaps tight in me as I focus on my job and become what she needs me to be. "As soon as I clean up here, I'll call a handmaiden to help tend to that," I say, with a jerky nod toward her hands.

Aurora licks her lips, and I swear she wants to say something, but she holds back.

A long pause beats between us again as I give her the space to say it. My heart falls in that space every time. Then she shakes her head ever so slightly.

"Thank you," she mutters before disappearing to the bathroom.

There is a finality to her words tonight. Like her frustration is boiling over into something dangerous. For the first time, I wonder if the endless cycle we have built, feeding, surviving, pretending it is enough, is hurting her as much as it's helping.

If I could fix it, I would. I would go to hell and back for her, even if it was simply to make her smile. But I don't know how to help her more than I am.

I stalk toward the shriveled body of the John, ripping off my leather jacket. His desiccated cheeks are sunken in his head.

He weighs next to nothing as I grab him and throw him over my shoulder and head to the balcony.

I can't call the handmaiden until I get rid of the body because no one knows about Aurora's condition. Her curse. Only her parents and I know, and it's my job to keep it that way. It's been that way for six years. It will be this way for as long as we both live.

No matter how much the tension sizzles between us more with each passing year, cranking tighter and tighter, putting us under more pressure to cross an impossible boundary.

No matter how much she wishes she didn't have to

feed, I'll be here to make sure she does, to make sure no one hurts her, and to clean up the mess so no one finds out.

I step onto the railing and look out on the moonlit expanse of the Rosari Kingdom. The village is quiet and dark below. Tomorrow the sun will rise. The residents will wake up and open the market, converse and drink in the tavern, and never put together that their whispered conspiracies about the monster lurking in the castle are actually about the Princess of the Realm of Roses.

I'm not sure how much longer they can keep me in this castle.

What could she mean by that? There is nowhere else for her to go. This is her life, *our* life, and there is no changing that.

No matter how either of us wishes we could.

My foot falls off the ledge, and my body plummets as I keep hold of the body on my shoulder. I wait dangerously long before my wings snap out and I catch air, gliding upward.

We'll love each other till the day we die and never once be able to touch.

I tell myself that's enough.

Because the only thing worse than wanting her...is the thought of losing her.

CHAPTER 2

MS. POUTY RUNAWAY PRINCESS

AURORA

I did it. Oh my fae lords, I *actually did it*.

I left home. I'm going to be a new person. I'm starting a new life.

Facing the prospect of actual independence and a fresh slate feels like being dunked in a crisp, chilled river and coming out to stand in the sunshine. Goosebumps rush along my arms and legs, and my chest hitches with excitement.

I'm not sure what's more impressive. Sneaking out of my parents' castle, getting through the border that leads to the Common World without raising so much as an eyebrow, or slipping by Talon.

The smells of hot foods, diesel fumes, and the frosty night air of Boston assault my senses. Vapor hisses from underground grates, rolling over my boots and curling around my legs, as if the city itself is exhaling in the cold. My vision blurs as I struggle to take in the lights of the city and the constant supply of cars and people streaming by.

I walked away from the cage I'd been lovingly locked away in. Once a month I would be fed, like clockwork. A system my parents and Talon agreed to, and we never veered from the schedule in all these years.

They loved me the only way they knew how, by keeping me safe. Even now, my chest aches thinking of them waking to find my room empty, just that letter on my pillow. But I can't continue to suffocate under their care, no matter how well-intentioned.

After so many feedings and killings, and having it called survival like it's my right, when it is carving me apart piece by bloody piece. After feeding on that man who bragged about killing his wife, I felt nothing. Not even a flicker of remorse or regret. And that terrifies me more than anything else ever has. Even more than when my terrible power was made to manifest.

I had to leave before that emptiness swallows me whole, before I stop caring entirely.

Others enjoy the Realm of Roses for the simpler living, but it already feels like the electric current of this new world is running through my veins. My heart quickly pumps and skips as I take it all in, adjusting the backpack over my shoulder.

A shakiness thrums through me, as the backs of my eyes prickle with the threat of tears. I'm not sure if I'm more overwhelmed by the sensory onslaught or by the sense of freedom that has me on the verge of screaming or falling to my knees. It's all too much.

And it's witchtitting wonderful.

This is what it is to be alive.

I hadn't even realized how numb I'd been until now, how curated and silent my life had been. As if I'd been living in a museum exhibit.

Back in the Rosari court, the women always smiled at me as though I were a statue—pretty, priceless, and entirely irrelevant to the real world. Their compliments were syrupy, their conversations rehearsed. They'd praise my gowns and mimic my hair, then keep talking, shutting me out of their world.

I still remember the acute pain of trying to share in a joke about kissing tutors.

"How come the boys get all the handsome tutors?" one of the girls had complained. "Ours were either ancient or mean."

"Mine had three teeth and smelled like boiled cabbage," another had laughed.

I saw an opening and took it, sidling up to the girls. "You're lucky. Mine was so sour I would've rather kissed a stable horse, *with* tongue."

They both blinked at me in surprise. When they recovered, their tones turned polite and formal. "Oh, we are so very sorry to hear it, Your Highness. You are truly the most beautiful of all of us and should only be surrounded by beauty."

I had no idea what my looks had to do with it. I was only trying to make them laugh.

They offered too-bright smiles, curtsied, and made excuses to retreat from my company.

Whether it was because of my looks, my status, or both, everyone watched me. No one ever *saw* me.

My life as a royal was too boringly perfect to have anything real to say, so no one expected me to try. When I laughed too loudly or asked questions I wasn't supposed to, people got that frozen smile—like I'd stepped off-script.

I was so tired of being just a symbol.

I used to watch other girls whisper and shriek and storm off and cry and make up with their beaus or each other, then do it all over again. I hated how much I wanted to be in it. That messy chaos of girlhood. I wanted to be someone you had a pillow fight with during a sleepover and shared secrets with, not someone you bowed to.

Not that I could ever share my secret with anyone.

Still, a girl could dream.

The people of Boston slow their gait as they walk by and try to study me.

Even covered in a cloak, I know my pink hair sets me apart. Or maybe it's the cloak itself, and the dress beneath it, with its laced bodice and heavy skirts. Perfectly ordinary back home. But here, it makes people stare.

Well, that, and the way every detail of me, down to my bone structure and nail beds, is shaped to be a sexual lure.

My physical form is that of a predator designed to draw in prey for survival.

My stomach twists with a sick feeling of self-disgust.

I ignore the gleam of interest sparking in the eye of nearly every passerby.

Some things don't change.

But I am.

Changing, that is.

As I saunter down the busy walkway, I remind myself I'm not going to spend the rest of my life feeding in that castle. I'm going to show my parents, and more importantly, myself, that I am more than my curse.

Here, I'm just a girl.

A girl who has no fucking idea where or how she is going to live. I'm going to figure it out. All on my own.

"Aura."

The bark cuts through the street noise. My shoulders snap tight, a shiver racing to my ears.

Closing my eyes, I pause for three long beats before turning around.

My skipping delighted heart drops to my stomach, weighed by the same feelings I always have whenever I see him.

Talon.

My protector stands, staring me down as people walk by us on either side as if we are rocks in a moving stream. Dark, shaggy hair hangs in his eyes. He wears his usual fae leather jacket and pants, and he's blending in no better than I am. People slow as they pass, their gazes falling to the black scales creeping out from under the jacket covering one pec before morphing into the sculpted flesh of a man.

Even though his back and arms are covered, I know exactly where those scales start and stop on his body. The heat seeps between their glowing fissures as a warning. *Touch, and you'll burn.*

The people here shoot glances at him the way people in our Fae Realm do. With fear and awe. The words I always heard whispered were "*dangerously gorgeous.*"

The dangerous part is true in more ways than they know.

His dark, imposing figure seems to suck all the energy of the city to him, and an orange glow flashes in the depths of his eyes as he takes me in. Exasperation? Annoyance? Maybe both.

A stab of guilt goes through me.

"What do you think you are doing, Aura?"

My shoulders drop as I let out a heavy sigh. "Talon."

His name is a complaint, my voice filled with irritation, submission, and longing.

Every part of me aches at the sight of him. My heart resumes its usual attempt to break its way past my ribs so it can fall at his feet.

A tingle sweeps across my lips as my body and soul are stricken with a fierce need.

A need neither of us will ever see satisfied.

No matter how many hands touch me, they will never be his. Every day it kills me. Just as I know it kills him.

"I'm taking control of my life," I say, proud that the words come out steadier than I feel.

He shakes his head. "We have to get you home."

My lip curls. "No."

Talon's jaw flexes as if he's grinding down something unspoken. He scans the city, nostrils flaring at the unfamiliar scents, then mutters, "At least tell me you're not planning to start eating from sketchy food trucks like the one over there. Looks like it hasn't seen a health inspection since the Realm Wars." He keeps staring at the truck with hand-painted letters that announce it to be The Salty Bastard. "Smells like lobster and grease." Then he shakes his head.

"Aura. You don't belong here." As he steps toward me, his words are a whip snapping against a familiar sore spot, leaving a harsh sting in its wake.

"I don't belong anywhere." The hurt is raw, but I can't hide it. I could never hide anything from him.

Talon's expression softens. *Pity.*

Anger bubbles up in me. I am not to be pitied. Or feared. Or admired. No one ever sees past princess, Succubus, or unearthly beauty to realize I'm a person.

I cross my arms over my chest, tightening my jaw. "Besides, it's not like you can force me to go home."

He suddenly stands in front of me. The pitying expression is erased, his dark glower bearing down on me.

My mouth parts as his comforting smoky scent snakes

over my senses in ghostly whisps, blocking out everything but him.

"This is a bad idea. You could get hurt."

I shrug, schooling my expression into icy indifference. "No, I won't. You're here to protect me," I say, ignoring the fact that he isn't supposed to be here.

"Aura. . ."

"I made a vow to myself. I'm not going to feed anymore." My words come out in a hushed tone as I drop my arms.

Not that anyone overhearing would understand. Not even in my own Realm do the people understand. My curse is a secret that has kept me isolated since I was a teenager.

The first awakening of my power still haunts my dreams.

Talon's expression snaps taut with disbelief.

"Maybe everyone is wrong. Maybe I can control it. But no one will give me a chance." My voice cracks. Desperation is plain on my face, and I don't even try to hide it. I need him to see it, to understand. "I want a chance to build a life of my own. I want to be more than what this curse has made me."

Those deep, molten brown eyes search mine, and I melt a little.

Come on, Talon. You've always given me what I wanted. Don't stop now.

Pushing my lip out in a slight pout, my pathetic big eyes are an absolute ploy.

Talon's gaze drops to my mouth. And there it is. His hunger. The open desire. A fire kicks up in my belly.

Then it's gone. He stiffens, emotion sucked back the way the tide abandons the sand.

"No." Talon's eyes are hard and commanding with his final decision.

"W-what?" The abrupt turn leaves me reeling, my chest lurching at the speed of it.

"We are going home."

Irritation spikes in me, as I push my tongue against the inside of my cheek. "You can't make me."

He startles, flinching just enough for me to notice. "What?"

"You. Can't. Make. Me." I enunciate each word with all the petulance of a child. I've never stood against him like this, and despite my exasperation with his unyielding nature, a little thrill goes through me. "What are you going to do? Drag me back?" I hold open my arms, as if waiting for him to grab me and pull me away from this place.

He won't. He can't.

Not without burning me.

Talon's brows drop as his expression darkens. His hands flex uselessly at his sides.

Part of me recognizes my taunt is cruel, but the reality of our situation is never far from my mind. How could it be?

This is the first time I've been able to use the thing that keeps us apart to my advantage.

"The way I see it," I say, adjusting the pack over my shoulder, "you can go back without me and explain to my parents why you can't make me go home, or. . ." I draw the word out. "You can stay here and make sure nothing bad happens to me."

Conflicting emotions churn inside me, tangling like restless serpents.

You're desperately trying to keep him by your side. It's foolish, knowing you can't be together. You should break away and forge a new path on your own. Stop torturing yourself.

Yet an overwhelming part of me dreads facing this alone. He's my only true friend, the one person who truly sees and cares for the real me.

Talon never treated me the way everyone else always has. He always talked to me like I was a person. Not a princess. Not a symbol. Just. . .me.

When his square jaw flexes with barely restrained violence, I know I've won.

"Perfect." I clap my hands together. "Let's go."

I turn and start back down the street.

"Where are we going?" Talon growls. His displeasure is like a cape sweeping behind me.

"I'm going to get a job." I don't even try to hide my excitement. "We are going to a bar called Poison Apple."

CHAPTER 3
WHERE LOST GIRLS LIVE
TALON

As I follow Aura along the city streets, I can't stop thinking this is a terrible idea. Why am I going along with this?

Because you can't do anything about it.

The princess has never thrown that in my face before, and I don't like the taste of what she served me.

Oh, if I could touch you, Aura, I'd do more than drag you home. I'd do everything you ever wanted and more.

But my angry, desire-fueled thoughts burn away the second we step inside Poison Apple.

The bar is nothing like what we have at home.

Back in the Realm of Roses, taverns are built for lingering. Heavy wooden beams, crackling hearths, ale served in earthenware mugs. Everything is slow, rich and warm. You don't drink to forget. You drink to remember.

This place? This place isn't for remembering. It's for getting lost in the haze of lust, liquor, and dance.

A massive tree stretches overhead, its thick branches decorated with fairy lights that throw a magical warmth over the sleek black tables and the packed dance floor.

Behind the bar is a rising tower of glass and gold, glowing from within, a beacon, each bottle catching the light in molten amber and rich crimson. A backlit shrine to vice.

The floor thrums beneath my boots, the bass so deep it thrums with the pulse of some great beast. It surges through bodies dancing in tandem. Unlike the songs of home—ballads of heroes, sorrow, and victory—this music is made for sex. Hands on hips, teeth on throats, lips parted for things that have nothing to do with words.

Aura stares, mouth slightly agape, eyes wide, catching the shifting light, the sheen of sweat-slicked skin, the golden gleam of liquor being poured.

"This is. . ." She breathes in, nearly laughing. "Fae lords, Talon, look at it."

I *am* looking.

At her.

Her eyes gleam in the low, golden light, drinking in the flickers of motion, the pulse of sound, each glint of glass and temptation.

I'd spent every step here trying to scheme a way to drag her back. Reinforcements, an order from the crown, someone who could put hands on her and force her home. But seeing her like this, lit from the inside, eyes wide with wonder, I know I can't.

But I'm sure as fae fucks not going anywhere.

I made an oath to protect the princess. Where she goes, I go.

I'm not here to enjoy myself. I'm here to keep her alive. That's all I am to be. She is mine to guard, no matter where she runs. Even if it means watching her stumble through a dangerous world I cannot control.

A dozen sets of eyes slide to her, some curious, some predatory, all drawn in like moths to flame.

I shift closer, instinct tightening my muscles, my senses sharpening.

Aura turns in a slow circle, taking in the bodies pressed together on the dance floor, the glittering chandeliers overhead, the way sweat and perfume and alcohol swirl into something heady and intoxicating in the air.

"This is amazing," she whispers.

I exhale slowly. "That's one word for it."

She grins at me then, a smile of pure excitement, pure energy, something innocent despite the decadence surrounding her.

I shake my head. No good can come from this. Aura thinks her curse is something she can outrun, but we can't pin so much on a baseless theory. I should drag her out of here before something bad happens.

But I don't.

Because against all my instincts, I want to see what she does next.

And that is dangerous.

The lights in the bar pulse, then vanish.

Darkness swallows the room, cutting through the heat and noise like a blade.

Adrenaline surges through my muscles, instincts roaring to the surface as I prepare myself to fight, to rip through whatever danger is about to emerge from the dark.

Next to me, Aura steps closer. Her hands close around my jacket-clad arm as her breath hitches.

A *whumpf* sound cracks through the silence, as a single spotlight explodes to life.

A blast of shimmering cobalt-blue powder explodes in the air, a storm of enchanted stardust. The air clears, leaving a figure standing on the platform beneath the lantern-lit tree.

The spotlight expands, revealing a man with a strong, heavy jaw in a top hat, his sapphire coattails draped over a bare chest.

"Good evening, my wicked little deviants!" The man's voice is velvet-laced. "Tonight, I am your host and emcee, Geanie. Welcome to the *only* bar in Boston where the drinks are potent, the women are deadly, and inhibitions are checked at the door."

This Geanie character strikes me as a ringmaster of some wicked circus.

"We all know why you're here," he continues with a sly smile. "To drink. To forget. To sin." A ripple of cheers surges through the crowd. "And no one serves up sin better than our *Lost Girls*."

The bass *drops*.

A light hits the other side of the bar, revealing a petite girl with twilight-colored skin that gleams under the blue light. Her white hair is braided through with countless tiny silver hoops.

The girl is ethereal beneath the shifting lights, with tattoos winding like frost patterns up her slender arms and down the exposed length of her abdomen. Leather clings tight to her hips, hugging her curves as she moves forward, her fishnet-covered legs stepping with choreographed ease.

"Our girl Snow is happy to help you reprobates with your boozing needs." A cheer goes up. "This Lost Girl might seem as sweet as freshly driven snow, but don't let appearances fool you."

Snow flicks her electric blue gaze around the bar, then reaches casually to scoop up a bottle. She spins it expertly between her fingers before tossing it high into the air, not bothering to watch its twirling descent. She catches it effortlessly behind her back, one delicate brow lifting in silent challenge.

"Petite as a pixie and twice as wicked, Snow will freeze your heart with a glance and coat your throat with an equally cold cocktail."

The entire crowd is hers now, their collective breath suspended in awe, the air thick with anticipation.

Geanie's voice lowers into something conspiratorial. "But beware, my friends. She can set fire in the most unexpected of places."

She pours a glittering stream of liquor into her mouth straight from the bottle, head tilted back, eyes closed. With a teasing smirk, she swallows and raises the bottle again, this time tipping it toward the cheering crowd, a shimmering cascade of liquid raining down like an offering. They all open their mouths, welcoming the free pour passing by.

Snow tosses the bottle upward again in a high, spinning arc. It soars through the air, tumbling toward a waiting hand.

It lands effortlessly in the grasp of another woman poised high on a platform. The spotlight illuminates the new Lost Girl in a turquoise glow.

"Our next Lost Girl came to Boston a fish out of water," Geanie says, now lying on his side on one of the heavy tree branches, fingers running along the bark suggestively.

Long copper hair cascades around the Lost Girl's slender shoulders, catching fire in the lights as she rolls forward in a sleek black-and-chrome wheelchair. Tattoos swirl over one arm, intricate ink against porcelain skin, a striking contrast. Piercings glitter subtly along her ears and nose, silver accents on sharp edges.

"But oh," Geanie continues, eyes sparking with mischief, "how quickly our girl Ariel learned to swim."

As if answering his call, Ariel pivots her wheelchair into a tight, lightning-fast spin, her copper hair whipping outward in a dazzling arc. The crowd gasps, completely enthralled as she slows to a flawless halt, aquamarine eyes simmering with quiet challenge beneath smoky lashes.

"Don't let Ariel's quiet fool you," Geanie warns warmly. "Still waters run deepest, and in hers, you just might drown."

With deliberate ease, Ariel lays the bottle horizontally across her tattooed forearm, letting it roll elegantly along the intricate patterns before flicking it upright into her hand. Without looking away from the crowd, she lifts the bottle to her lips, taking a slow, deliberate drink.

Lowering it again, she extends the bottle out over the bar, allowing it to slip casually from her fingertips, tumbling gracefully downward into another waiting grasp.

Another spotlight hits, bathing a third woman in golden light.

Geanie's voice rolls through the room again, vibrant and teasing. "And finally, our fearless leader, the original Lost Girl herself—the boss lady who built this den of sin brick by wicked brick. She's the queen of this court, and she makes her own rules. I give you, *Rap*."

The woman named Rap instantly captivates, owning the space behind the bar without needing theatrics. She catches the falling bottle effortlessly.

Her lean, muscular frame is draped in intentionally shredded clothing. Rap's short platinum hair is braided back on either side to create a Viking mohawk that is streaked in pastel colors. Sharp eyes survey the crowd from beneath heavy, smudged black eyeliner. She's older than the others, though not by much, and authority radiates from her like heat off a flame.

Poison Apple belongs to her.

She places the bottle on the bar with calm authority, as she scans the crowd in silent command.

When Rap's gaze hits us, it jerks to a halt.

I tense under the quick but targeted scrutiny, but then she continues surveying the crowd.

The emcee turns, leaps off the tree, and lands easily on the floor. He sweeps an arm toward the bar. "Drink up, darlings. Because what happens at Poison Apple stays with *us*."

The spotlight vanishes as the house lights lift.

The dance music blares and the bar roars to life again, bodies moving, glasses clinking, bottles flying between skilled hands. The Lost Girls keep the energy high, pouring drinks, teasing the crowd, their control absolute as they dance to the heavy, quick beat of the music.

"That was fantastic," Aura breathes, her fingers still gripping my arm.

Never before did we engage in casual touching like this. I tighten my jaw, liking it too much. Wanting her to never let go. Yet it's not nearly enough.

A creeping, uneasy feeling travels up my spine. "Aura, why are we here?"

"I want to be a Lost Girl," she says, smiling at me. Then she's off like a shot.

Oh. *Oh fae lords.*

She's going to give this Dragon a heart attack.

CHAPTER 4

A SUCCUBUS AND DRAGON ON RUMSPRINGA

AURORA

"What'll you have?" Rap asks me without looking up. She's busy removing dirty glasses from the bar top, pulling fresh glasses, and mixing multiple cocktails at once.

A lump rises in my throat, pumping in time with my heartbeat. "A job."

The woman's eyes barely flick up at me, and she doesn't even pause what she's doing.

"You're not from around here."

"I'm not." I swallow, but nothing moves. My throat scrapes raw. Maybe I should order a drink. "But I'd still like a job."

Rap slings three cocktail glasses on the bar and pushes them over to the guy waiting next to me, taking his credit card in turn. "Why? You have money. Lots of money from the looks of it."

A jolt goes through me, but I try not to let my surprise show.

The sting of guilt and confusion over leaving home

snakes in, winding around me for the first time since I left. "I want independence. I want to live my own life, without being under anybody's control."

Rap stops cold. One hand is poised with a scoop of ice hovering over an empty glass, but she doesn't pour for one...two...three beats.

It's as if I've said something that struck a gong at her center, hitting a mark so hard it's reverberating through her entire body.

I don't say anything as she processes...whatever it is that she is processing.

The ice clinks into the glass. Suddenly, she's back to swift movements and harried execution as if nothing happened at all. She takes orders from more patrons who've pushed in next to me. The place is packed, and despite her fluid movements, she is barely keeping up with the crowd.

I bounce on the balls of my feet, becoming restless and impatient. I want this job. I want it bad.

Ever since I overheard that human woman talking about this place, I knew, just knew I needed to be here. I don't know if it was the way she described the cozy lights and the delicious concoctions, where the entire place is a sultry haven, or if it was because of the rebellious badass Lost Girls who worked here. I just knew I wanted to be one of them. It lit up inside me like a beacon I followed all the way here.

"What about the Dragon?" Rap asks, continuing to work without pause. "Is he bothering you?"

Yet again, I swallow back my surprise. "No." I twist to look over my shoulder.

My tall, dark sentry several feet away watches me and the bar, scanning for trouble. A girl with short blonde hair sidles up to him, running her fingers over his jacket. An inch off and she'd get a hot shock. From the tilt of her head, I can tell she's flirting.

His lips barely move as he responds with something I can't hear. The girl's hand drops as she leaves with a vague look of disappointment on her face.

"He, uh, he's helping me." *Against his will, but let's count it.*

"Be here when we close at two. Both of you," Rap says before taking off to get orders from another group of thirsty patrons.

Giddiness gallops in my chest again.

It wasn't a yes, but she'll find out I won't accept a "no."

"I DON'T SUPPOSE you have a resume," Rap says, fingers interlaced on her heavy desk. Unlike the warm, sensual maximalist style of the bar, her office is devoid of personality with only a tall file cabinet, a desk, and the couple chairs across from it. Talon chooses to remain standing.

He studies the one semi-decorative item on the wall. A calendar with a picture of an unamused looking cat strapped with a pair of bunny ears, with the caption *You'll Pay For This.*

Despite the woman's commanding force, there are circles under her eyes. While Talon and I got drinks and retreated to a corner to people-watch, the crowd didn't let up until the lights went up at closing time, forcing everyone to spill out on the streets of Boston.

"No resume." My voice is quiet to my own ears. To compensate, I sit up straighter. "But I'm willing to learn."

Even as I say it, I'm mentally preparing counterarguments for whatever objection she might raise. It's a stubborn streak I can't seem to shake, even when I know I'm out of my depth.

Those emerald eyes study me for a long time, and I bite back the urge to fill the silence. I'm sure Talon has no difficulty with the tense quiet. As I've told him on many occasions, brooding is his superpower.

"You got people after you?" she asks casually, as if it's a normal interview question.

I think about it for a minute. My parents could send more people after me, but they don't know where I went. The letter I left behind said I needed some time to myself, and I asked them not to follow.

I shake my head.

"What are you to her?" Rap barks at Talon.

To his credit, he doesn't even flinch at the command in her tone. Rap can't be much older than me, but she carries a steely confidence that I'm in absolute awe of.

"Her brother." The lie is smooth off his tongue.

Rap snorts, lips twitching up at the corner, as she leans back in her chair. "Yeah, that's not gonna fly, hot boy. Anyone who even so much as glances at the two of you will suspect you of harboring some intense incestuous feelings."

Talon visibly stiffens. I'm not sure if it's because she sees straight through him, or because of the vulgar suggestion.

She opens her hands. "You might want to change your story."

"He's my boyfriend," I blurt.

"I'm her protector," Talon says, his voice hard.

That's not going to work. Normal people don't have protectors. I'm supposed to be normal now.

"My overly protective boyfriend," I rush to add.

Rap chuckles quietly, a wry smile twisting her lips. "You two haven't thought this out at all, have you?"

I squirm in the chair, realizing how true what she says is. I crossed the border and came straight here, believing I'd figure out the rest later.

Rap's eyes narrow, one brow arched as she pins me with a look. "Don't tell anyone he's your boyfriend. My girls will figure out in a heartbeat that's not true."

"Okay." Excitement flutters in my belly. I'm getting the job.

"I'm not sure what kind of rumspringa you're on, but you don't leave without giving notice. Understand me?"

I nod eagerly, though I don't know what a *rumspringa* is.

"You steal from me, you're out. Being a Lost Girl means more than just swinging bottles and mixing drinks. You need to bring attitude and there is a certain dress code you have to adhere to."

The mirth falls from her face, and Rap suddenly looks tired. "I don't know your story, and I don't have to. But don't lie to me." Her gaze falls to Talon. "You want to stay near her?" Rap jerks her chin in my direction. "You're gonna have to work here too. I'm in need of some more bodies on my security team. Don't touch my patrons unless you absolutely have to. I'm counting on you to menace people in line."

Talon simply grunts. Rap seems to also understand that is assent to her terms.

"Do you have a place to stay?"

"I—" my voice falters. The urge to look to Talon is strong, but I hadn't planned on him coming along. I don't plan on leaning on him. Otherwise, I might as well have stayed right where I was. "No."

My hands fist as I grip the material of my dress. I was

taking things one step at a time, but Rap makes me painfully aware of how foolishly I've approached this.

She hums. "I know of a sublet opening. It's not glamorous, but it's available now and you won't have to worry about background checks."

"Th-thank you," I stutter. Gratitude grows in my chest, warming me up from the inside out.

Rap opens her laptop, and I've lost her attention. We're being dismissed. I rise on unsteady legs and head toward the door, followed by Talon.

"One last thing, Aurora."

I turn.

"Don't fuck with my staff or my patrons."

"I wouldn't. . ."

That sharp gaze meets mine. "You feed far away from here, if you have to."

All my excitement burns away at the realization this bar owner knows exactly who and what I am.

"Rosari may have a soothing effect on people with high emotions, but I don't want my patrons mellowing out. This is a human city, or it was..." she finishes on a mumble.

Relief sweeps through me. She only knows where I'm from and my people. She doesn't know the truth about how I have to feed.

Talon nudges me in my back, pushing me out the door.

CHAPTER 5

AN UNEXPECTED ROOMMATE NAILS THE TESTICLES

TALON

The petite Black girl with white hair turns the lock and we follow her into the apartment.

"It's not much," Snow announces, letting us file past her into the tiny two-bedroom space.

She's not wrong. The place is clean but far from new or polished. The lumpy red couch in the living room is flanked by mismatched end tables and crowned with a crooked painting of a mountain landscape. The kitchenette has beat-up oak cabinets and a mini fridge that hums ominously. The hallway is too short, the ceilings too low. I could burn this entire apartment to ash just by breathing too hard.

The earthy smell of mold tickles my nose, but is beaten back by layers of vanilla, lavender, and something that smells vaguely like sugar cookies. Dozens of candles line every flat surface. Some are melted nearly to the wick to combat the mildew. It's a weird combo.

Still, Aurora beams, wonder lighting her face.

Snow tosses a set of keys onto the coffee table and jerks

her chin toward the hallway. "Bathroom's through there. I appreciate y'all subletting from me. I moved to the ground floor with Ariel. The landlord is a bit of a dick and wouldn't let me out of my lease here. Subletting isn't exactly allowed, so if you see that tubby guy with the stained shirt, act like you're visiting someone."

Oh great. Just what we need. An illegal squatting situation.

Snow opens the first bedroom door with a flourish.

"This is yours." She winks at Aurora.

Aurora clutches her chest. "It's perfect."

Snow throws a look at me, a silent sanity check on my companion.

It's. . .really not. The room is maybe six-by-four feet, and the only furniture is a full bed, a scratched vanity table, and a plastic drawer set being used as a dresser. Still, it has a window, though it's covered in poorly hung black gauzy curtains shot through with glitter. Aurora rests her palm on the peeling paint on the wall, and exhales like she's found her sanctuary.

Snow gestures but doesn't open the door. "That's the second bedroom," she says, turning to me. "But there's a situation. Shower leak from the apartment upstairs. There is no flooring and one of the walls has been stripped down to its foundation, and the maintenance guy is on vacation until next week. So..."

"I'll take the couch," I say.

"Figured you would." She spins on her heel. "There are spare blankets in the hall closet."

"Noted."

Snow crosses her arms and eyes us both with renewed interest. "So where exactly are you two from?" Her gaze flicks between Aurora's long dress and cloak and my scorched leather boots. "Because you look like you walked out of a Renaissance fair."

Aurora's mouth opens, then closes.

"And you could be part of a motorcycle gang with all that leather. Wait, are you? 'Cause I can't afford one myself, but I'd totally knock some off your rent for a ride. Though you are a Dragon, right? I didn't know any of those really existed anymore. Do you have wings underneath your jacket? I feel like that would be cramped. You probably don't need a motorcycle when you can fly. Oh shit, I'd take a ride like that too. But like, would you hold me in your clawed feet—if you have clawed feet—or I could ride on your back? Oh, there's the thing where your skin is too hot though, right? But that doesn't mean you don't have a motorcycle either. You could be into both."

Snow's quick barrage of words hammers into my head with little order or sense. My brows furrow deeply, an attempt to protect my brain.

"No." The word comes out flat. It's a no to everything she just said. "And we're...not from here." There is an underlying warning in my tone. *Don't dig.*

Snow studies us a second longer, then shrugs. "It's not like I'm proud of where I'm from either." She yanks open the fridge and grabs a half-empty bottle of pink wine, then opens it and drinks from it directly. "You got cash, right?"

I pull a stack of folded bills from my inner pocket and hand them over. "Two weeks in advance."

Snow whistles. "Fae's tits, that slaps." She recaps the bottle and takes the money. "Alright then, you're good."

A black blur streaks across the apartment and launches itself directly at Snow's chest.

"What the—?!"

The bottle of rosé slips from her hand and rolls across

the floor, while a cat digs in with its claws, yowling with outrage.

Snow tries to pry him off, and I step back as fur and fury erupt around her head. I clench my fists to keep from grabbing the animal. I have to shove down my urge to intervene. I don't want to burn the creature.

Aurora rushes to help, which leads to more of a struggle.

"Come on, sweetheart. Let go. Good kitty," she attempts to coo, but the cat is having none of it.

That is *not* a good kitty.

At last, the cat launches off poor Snow, landing on the coffee table with a disdainful *mrrreow*.

Its fur sticks out at odd angles, as if electrocuted or bathed against its will. Maybe both. Hackles up, it hisses at all of us before darting under the couch.

"Lucifer! You absolute asshole," Snow yells, arms flailing. "You ruined my shirt."

The black band tee she changed into after her shift is now ripped in several places, though I have to say it looks rather deliberate and matches her torn black jeans.

Snow stalks over to the mirror hanging in the hallway to investigate the damage. Red welts have risen along her skin, and there are a few scratches mark her cheek.

"I swear I'm going to kill that cat," she screeches.

Aurora kneels down to peer under the couch. "I don't think your cat is going to come out."

Snow's nostrils flare as she whips around, stabbing an accusatory finger in the direction of the feline's hiding place. "*That* is not my cat. That little monster terrorized me and my former roommate for months, uninvited. He kept breaking in here to piss in her boots and attack me at random. Last I knew, the little demon had gotten himself trapped in the Midnight Realm, and I hadn't seen claw nor fang of this little fucker for six blissful months." She smooths her hair in an attempt to compose herself. "But I guess the little guy still has a hard-on for this apartment."

"Lovely," I say flatly. "You're saying our new accommodations come with the cat."

"'Fraid so, big fella," Snow says, patting my leather clad shoulder. "Whoa, you really do run on the warm side, don'tcha, hot boy?"

Aurora climbs to her feet and mouths *hot boy* at me, her lips twitching with barely suppressed amusement.

Apparently, Rap's nickname for me is going to stick.

No one in the Realm of Roses even dares bring their gaze up to meet mine. Now I'm getting pats on the shoulder, inappropriate nicknames, and new furry roommates. All in barely acceptable living conditions for a princess.

A wave of exasperation washes over me, and I suppress a sigh.

Aurora's eyes sparkle with amusement in response.

"You," Snow says, nodding at Aurora, "are officially one of us now. Meet me outside Poison Apple at eleven a.m. We're goth-glamming your ass before your first shift. You need combat boots and a choker, stat."

"It's already three a.m.," Aurora points out, voice soft with suppressed laughter.

"Exactly. Sleep while you can." Snow picks the wine bottle back up then makes her way to the door, throwing a middle finger toward the couch where the furry monstrosity still hides.

"Welcome to the club, new friends."

～

I PRETEND NOT to notice the fabric of Aurora's dress sliding down her body in the bedroom as I peel off my jacket, letting my bare chest and shoulders breathe.

I've seen Aura naked thousands of times, and in far more compromising positions, but something about the new environment makes everything feel more intimate. New.

Aura dons a silk sleep dress she brought in her pack, and we turn out the lights.

The couch is a lump beneath me. My shoulders are too wide for it, my body already overheating the cheap fabric. Thankfully, it's fae made materials, otherwise I'd set it aflame.

Aura's bedroom door remains open.

Of course it does.

I wait for the familiar rhythmic, grinding sound of her snores. A habit I've grown oddly accustomed to over the years. Though how such a small woman produces those sounds...

But she's not asleep. I can hear her shifting. The bedsprings creak. After a while, the window clicks as she slides it open. The hush of traffic, so far below, creeps in like a new kind of lullaby.

Then her voice cuts through the quiet.

"You hate this place, don't you?"

I don't answer at first. Not because I don't have words, but because I have too many.

"I guess I have a hard time believing you find this...place," I try to choose my words carefully, "perfect."

"Okay, so it's not a castle and it's got a funny smell. But it's exactly where I want to be. Perfect is overrated."

Just when I think I know Aurora inside and out, she surprises me.

"I don't hate this place." I sit up, elbows on my knees. "I hate that you ran away in the middle of the night with no plan. No allies. No understanding of this world. You act like you've just made some grand choice, but it's a child's rebellion."

Her lips part in the low light, her golden skin flushing with rising heat.

"That's what you think?" she breathes. "You think I'm being childish because I finally wanted something that wasn't handed to me? Because I no longer want to be locked in a cage? Because I want to be more than my curse?"

"I think you're gambling with your safety just to prove a point." I stand slowly, unable to remain on the couch.

She surges to her feet, stepping over the creaking threshold of her room and into my space. Her sweet scent envelops me, washing out the strange, moldy vanilla mixture of the room. We're inches apart. My heat stirs the air between us. Her breath catches, but she doesn't step back.

"Have you ever thought that maybe I don't need to feed?" Her words snap out, tight and fierce. "I was seventeen the first time. I lost control and someone died. After that, everything changed."

That's when her family paid a fortune to have a Dragon tracked down. The only one who could resist her power. Even her own parents weren't safe around her hunger.

"Since then, I've been on a schedule," she goes on. "Tightly managed. Tightly watched. Between my parents and you, I've never had a chance to question it. You...you all treat me like a bomb on a countdown, and maybe that's why I've never tried to stop. Everyone made me too afraid to even try." Her hands ball into tight fists, and I vaguely wonder if she wants to take a swing at me.

I shake my head, heart pounding in my throat.

"What if I don't need it anymore, Talon? What if I only ever needed it because I was taught to fear the alternative? What if I've just been...kept in a cycle?" She pauses. "Like an addict who was never given the chance to get clean."

"Aura," I warn. "You don't want to know what happens if you're wrong. If the hunger takes over—"

"I *know* what happens," she cuts me off. "I know better than anyone what it feels like to take someone's last breath and still want more. I live with that every day. You think I want to hurt people? I think I'd rather die than lose control." She swipes at her eyes, blinking hard. "But I've been dying a little every day because I haven't ever been allowed to try."

Everything in me coils tight as I force myself to stay steady. Her grief, her pain—I've always known it. She carries it so close she's had to befriend it, but she's never shared *this* with me. This haunting suspicion that she may be able to rise above her curse, that we are forcing her to be a monster.

I see it in her eyes now and I don't know how I could have missed it. The resentment is clear as day. My stomach gives a sickening lurch.

"Your family and I have only ever tried to protect you, Aura." I need her to understand.

"I'm tired of being protected." The admission splinters from her, raw and unsteady. "I want to live. And I'm starting right now." She lifts her chin in stubborn defiance.

"And what about you, Talon?" The words lash out, sharp and clean. "Aren't you tired of your duty? Chained to me all these years?" Her lip curls as if she's disgusted by the idea. "You don't have to stay, but I am. I'm doing this."

"Chained?" Offense rocks through me, though I'm not

sure if it's on her behalf or mine. "No, Aura, I've never been chained. But I *am* bound to you."

I made a vow of fealty. Of the few things I know about my own kind, a Dragon's loyalty isn't something that can be severed. Once earned, it runs deeper than bone. It *is* bone. Unbreakable. Absolute.

"You're not. You can *go*." The hallway seems to flinch at the whipcrack of her words. "If you hate this so much, if you think I'm being reckless and foolish and pathetic...go back. Or wherever you like. You're not a prisoner. You never have been."

She is the prisoner.

She leaves it unsaid but it radiates around us as if she screamed it.

"Aura—"

But she's already turned, that storm of silken hair lashing behind her as she stalks toward her room.

I follow.

I don't think. I just move. Like she's a magnet I can't resist.

She stops in the doorway. Her fingers grip the frame.

The room in front of her glows softly from the city lights filtering through the blinds. The sheets on the bed are rumpled. Her backpack leans half-unpacked against the wall. It's not much. But it's hers.

"And I like it here," she says, her back still to me. "I like the mess. The weird smells. The tiny fridge. I like the fact that no one here knows who I am or what I've done or what I'll always have to do to survive."

Her fingers grip the doorframe harder.

"I like knowing that tomorrow I won't wake up to silk curtains or be treated like I'm made of porcelain. Or worse," she swallows hard, "like I'm something to be feared. And you, standing here, judging it—judging *me*—makes you no better than the rest of them."

For a second, I think she's going to slam the door.

But she doesn't. She simply goes to bed. Slipping between the sheets, she turns away from me.

The door is left open.

Always open.

Leaving me here.

Burning.

I want to tell her she's right. That this can be a new start for her. That she can forget where she came from, and what she is.

But I know better.

She thinks if she changes the scenery, she can change the story. But no matter how far she runs, she's still carrying the very thing she wants to escape.

Her hunger. Her magic. Her curse.

This isn't a place that will make her dreams come true simply because she wants it.

I see now my words won't reach her—not when she's this determined. But I'm not going anywhere. Even if I wasn't bound by a vow of fealty, I wouldn't leave her out here, exposed and alone.

I return to the lumpy couch, positioning myself as comfortably as I can. I fold my arms across my chest as I stare up at the stained ceiling.

She wants a life here. A future. Something beyond survival. I see it in the way she smiles at the mess of this place.

How long has she been letting these ideas stew and boil inside her? Too long to be subdued by logic.

Some things can't be told. They need to be lived.

Aurora is going to have to find out for herself that this

dream can only end a nightmare. And it very well might leave her shattered.

All I can do is be here to help her gather the pieces.

Even if she never lets me hold them.

An intense feeling of being watched suddenly cuts through me. I slowly turn my head and meet the glowing feline eyes of Lucifer. The cat is sitting there on the coffee table, tail twitching, watching me with unnerving intensity. Then his body tenses and coils into itself.

"Claw me, and you'll be medium-rare and full of regret."

In one leap, he lands on my lap, nailing my balls with unholy precision. I jerk underneath the painful impact, and Lucifer lets out a pissed off sound over his landing spot moving. He scrambles up on the back of the couch, hisses at me, then disappears somewhere into the apartment.

I'm left clutching my boys and wondering who will break me first. Aurora or the damn devil cat.

CHAPTER 6

FROM KISS TO CURSE

TALON

6 Years Ago

The girl with pink hair sits on a boulder in the middle of the creek with her back to me. The sun shines through the rustling leaves of the massive trees overhead, throwing dappled rays on the soft cotton candy curls trailing to her waist. The water glitters under the same light, rushing loudly so she can't hear me approach.

I sigh heavily as I stalk toward the girl.

I don't want to get involved. I just want to be left alone.

But the Rosari King and Queen had me tracked down at great expense and effort, so they could plead with me to hear their case. Their daughter needs protection they can't give her. Protection and help only I can provide.

I told them I wasn't interested and that they'd wasted their time.

I'd been ready to turn and fly off to continue traveling the Realms, always alone, never staying in one place.

"Just meet her. Please." The queen's eyes had been glassy with unshed tears, her knuckles white from her fingers inter-

lacing too tightly. The king held her shoulder with what looked like a vise grip. As if I were the last thread of hope they were clinging to.

My insides pinched, and something itched under my skin at all the exposed emotion, until I heard myself agree to the Queen's request.

Making my way along the bankside, I try to make sure the princess sees me long before I get to her. The teenager's shoulders tense when she catches me in her peripheral vision. Something about the movement strikes something inside me. The same soft spot her mother hit with her pleas.

I pause several yards away, sticking my hands in my pockets. It's too hot to be wearing my jacket, but it's a shield I need to keep wrapped around myself so I can extract myself as soon as possible.

"Who are you?"

Her shout is a challenge, a warning. She's so painfully seventeen. I've only got a couple of years on her, but I've never had the luxury of being a teenager. The entitled, fiery defensive-ness that wards off everyone with a silent dare is clear. Yet beneath the surface, there is a desperate plea.

Don't leave me.

I shouldn't be here. I don't belong with others. I'm meant to be by myself, always alone. Or at least that's what makes sense when you are the only one of your kind.

"Your parents sent me." I yell out over the rushing water. "They wanted me to talk to you."

The tenseness in her posture slips away. "Oh," I see rather than hear her say. "You're the Dragon," she says, raising her voice enough for me to hear this time.

As she twists to get a better look at me, I also see her fully for the first time. My heart stops in my chest as one of the fae lords reaches down into my lungs and rips the breath right out of me.

She's beautiful.

No, beautiful doesn't begin to describe this girl. Eyes that remind me of the pale shimmer of snow over stone are set against skin that shimmers faintly, as if dusted in powdered gold. Her lips are full and perfect. Even her eyebrows are perfect, a feature I'd never given any thought to before.

Under the perfect angles of her face and her full strawberry-tinted lips, there's a low thrum of energy I can almost see, like heat rising off pavement. It warps the air at her edges, but I know it's not visible to anyone else.

There's a tug in my chest. A sharp awareness in my spine. Her magic doesn't just shimmer—it reaches. Not aggressively. Just...enough to pull you closer if you're not careful.

My Dragon sees the sexual draw of her energy clashing with the awkward teenage self-consciousness that is wrapped around her bones. It's likely to remain that way for several more seasons.

The princesses' face tightens with a stricken expression, and she draws her arms in tight, shielding herself. Some of my admiration or surprise must have slipped through.

I instantly shutter my expression. "Don't worry. It doesn't work on me."

Her shoulders relax a fraction as she waits for me to do something, or for my expression to change. "Because you're a Dragon," *she finally says.*

"Because I'm a Dragon."

Most shifters can sense magic in others, and can sometimes even nullify it. But they are never fully immune to its effects the way Dragons are. Though my body is young, my blood remembers wars before the Realms even existed. You can't fool it. You can't twist it.

I'm the only one she can't manipulate with her power.

Her magic doesn't care if the warmth it senses comes from a stranger or the ones who raised her. It doesn't recognize family.

Only need. And that's why the King and Queen found me. That's why they begged. Even they need to keep a certain distance from their own daughter or risk being consumed.

I scan the water rushing between us, no longer content to yell this conversation. "Mind if I join you?"

She shrugs.

I easily step from rock to rock until I've made my way over to a boulder next to hers and settle down.

"They want me to be your protector," I say, cutting through the bullshit.

The princess shakes her head before wiping away a tear. "No. They want you to protect other people from me." Then her face whips toward mine with a sudden fury. "I killed him. Did they tell you that?"

They told me. A boy died.

"I've always been well-liked in school, but recently I've been dodging crushes like it's my job." She launches into the account as if she's going to explode if she doesn't tell someone. She likely hasn't been able to. From what I understand, her parents covered things up quickly and efficiently.

"But this one boy, Ike, had been obsessed with me for years. I'd always ignored it, but then the last couple months I started to, well, notice him too. I left him a note to meet me in the stables. I wanted to—" Her voice breaks, and her long lashes turn wet as she blinks rapidly. "—kiss him." She says the words like it's an unforgivable crime for a teen girl to want to kiss someone.

She swallows a couple times, keeping her gaze on the water. "We did it. We kissed and it was..." She swallows again, the next words no louder than a breath, wistfulness tightening my chest again. Without another word, I know it was everything she dreamed it would be. "So, we kissed again. And then I...I started to feel hungry. Like really hungry, and the more we kissed, the hungrier I got. We kissed more and more, and we...touched." She digs the heels of her hands into her eyes. "It got out of control. Everything just felt so good, nothing else existed. It was all so delicious." Her words break as her shoulders rock in silent sobs. "I couldn't stop. I didn't even think to stop and now he's...he's—"

Dead.

Her power, her curse, made a rather dramatic entrance. Especially considering how long ago it was cast upon her.

The boy's death was staged as some kind of horse-riding accident.

When the princess looks up at me, her eyes are owlishly big with dark circles under them like she's haunted. "And worst yet," she whispers so I can barely hear, "I'm still so hungry." It comes out in a whine before she bursts into full, body shaking sobs.

I don't know what to do. Someone else might pat her on the back or offer a hug. I can't do either of those things.

Maybe tell her it's going to be okay?

It probably isn't. She's the first Succubus in centuries. And she's going to have to keep feeding to survive.

I could tell her it was an accident.

It doesn't change the fact she killed the boy she had a crush on.

So, I just sit there with her. I let her cry. I let her be swept away by all the grief as she sits with her confession. I don't offer empty assurances or condemn her with judgement.

After some time, she dips a hand into the cool, clear water and uses it to wash off her face.

"I'm a monster," she says in a much calmer tone.

"You're not a monster."

"Yes, I am. All other Rosari may be energy vampires, but they don't kill anyone. They feed off people's anxieties and actually help those they feed from."

"It's not your fault you're like this," I point out.

"Oh, I know it's not my fault," she says darkly.

Someone snuck into her nursery when she was a baby. The King walked in, in time to hear the curse spoken over Aurora's crib before the culprit fled.

Let love's first prick sow despair in its bloom.

The princess looks at me for the first time since she confessed her sins and scans my features with interest. "You're different too."

My throat tightens even as I nod. "I am."

"Is it true? That your skin...burns?"

A wry smile briefly pulls at my lips. Then I dip my hand into the cool water. Steam rises off the creek where I touch it.

"My leathers are special, but most things burn if I touch them. Mainly organic materials. I have to be careful not to touch certain things, like plastics and some fabrics." It's the reason I often traverse the Fae Realms. Here, the fae favor stone and metal. Their fabrics are also often resistant to my heat.

"If you touched me, would you burn me?" The shimmering air around her intensifies, and her beauty both sharpens and softens at the same time. Her hunger is reaching out to me. Her curse wants to feed.

I stand, leveling her with a heavy look. "I wouldn't touch you. And I am not tempted."

Even as the princess scrambles to her feet, she recoils with what I recognize as rejection. Good. She needs to know she can't affect everyone.

"I didn't mean to...I didn't think you thought I was..." she stammers.

I lift a hand to stop her from spiraling. "I'm just clarifying."

She follows as I step from rock to rock and head back to the riverbank.

"What about other Dragons?" she asks.

I can't help the heavy sigh that leaves me. It's my turn to cast my gaze to the water. "I don't know if there are any other Drag-

ons." I don't know why I have the sudden urge to walk, but she trails alongside me.

"What? What about your family? Your parents?"

"I don't remember my father, and I was very young when my mom left. One day she just left and didn't come back. Later, I learned Dragons are solitary, and it's normal to leave their young to fend for themselves as soon as they're able." She might be alive, but I've searched far and wide for her. If she is alive, she doesn't want to be found. As I grew older, I began to understand. I started to feel an intrinsic need to keep moving. To never form attachments. To live a solitary life.

Her brows knit. "How old were you?"

"Six."

She gasps in horror.

I shrug. "It's fine. This is how my kind is supposed to live."

"From what I know," she says after a beat, "I'm the only Succubus too. Succubae and Incubi were killed off two centuries ago. Too dangerous to let live." She frowns and kicks a rock out of her way. Then a hopeful smile springs to her lips. "Guess we're kind of alone together."

"Alone together," I echo.

The moment I say it, something shifts inside me.

The restless part of me—the part that always itches to move on, to avoid connections, to keep from getting tethered to anyone or anything—goes still. Like it's been waiting for this. For her.

I don't feel trapped.

I feel...anchored.

A weighted silence falls between us, as if something invisible has locked into place beneath the surface of the world.

Aurora rubs her palms down the sides of her simple skirts, eyes darting around. "I don't mind being around you," she says, then rushes on before I can react. "Not because you're a Dragon or because you're supposed to be here, or whatever."

She swallows. Her gaze flicks toward the trees, trying to focus on anything but me.

"It's just...people don't really see me. They see some weird idea of me. Because I'm a princess. Or because I'm too..." She makes air quotes. "'Pretty.' Even to other kids my age, I'm not real. I'm more a symbol they'd rather talk about than talk to. They'd rather make up stories about me instead of bothering to find out who I am."

Her voice drops. "You're the only one who hasn't done that. You make me feel real. So, uh...thanks. I guess."

An odd sensation presses deep into my chest. No, deeper than that. Into my bones. A knowing. A recognition that defies reason.

She takes a breath, almost bracing herself. "So. Are you going to stay?"

THE CEILING above me is water-stained and cracked. The blinds rattle faintly in the air from the heater, casting slivers of neon city light across the floor like prison bars.

Sleep evades me as the memories return.

Six years ago, I made a vow. To the King. To the Queen. To *her*.

I vowed fealty and protection to the princess for as long as my services were needed. I'll help keep her secret, make sure she feeds, and dispose of the evidence.

I'll stay with the princess until the day I die. I'm not entirely sure that part of me wouldn't rise from the ashes of my own corpse and rejoin her.

Because while that vow connected us, I didn't expect to fall for her. Being with her hurled me down an endless staircase, the ground never arriving, not after months, of even years.

Despite my feelings, I force myself to focus only on what I do. I protect her. I contain her curse. I clean up the mess.

I turn on my side, trying, and failing, to get comfortable.

Because nothing else will ever be possible.

CHAPTER 7

HOT GIRL JAIL

AURORA

"So, what's the deal with you and hot boy?" Snow asks, as she and Ariel lead me out of yet another clothing store.

I brought enough cash to cover getting started here, but I'm quickly running out. Hefting several bulging bags, I'm realizing how much these Lost Girls spend on clothes and accessories. Oh, and the shoes. My fae lords, the shoes.

The tendons in my shoulder pull painfully from holding up the bag with not one, but two pairs of combat boots. If Talon were here, he wouldn't let me carry these heavy bags. He'd take on the weight like it was nothing.

I bristle at the thought. I don't need him. I don't need anyone to carry my bags. I'm a normal girl, going shopping and getting ready for her first day of work.

"We..." I pause, remembering how Rap said they'd catch onto any lie. "We grew up together."

Ariel rolls the wheels of her chair along the Boston side-walk without so much as a strained breath. "There is a lot of chemistry between you two."

Despite her fantastic show of popping wheelies in

provocative clothing, I find Ariel is rather careful with her words. It seems to me as if half her mind is always somewhere else. She pauses to lift a camera from the strap around her neck and snaps a picture of the city street. She's always taking pictures. Like she wants to collect every single moment she can.

"Like scalding hot chemistry. Why haven't you tapped that?" Snow adds. Unlike Ariel, Snow has zero filter and tosses out whatever is in her mind at any given moment.

"It's...complicated." Not a lie.

"Is it because his dick could roast you from the inside out, or is there something else?" Snow asks.

They both watch me expectantly as my mouth flaps open and closed a few times before I break out into a grin. "Yeah, that pretty much covers the issue."

"That'll do it," Ariel breathes.

"Major bummer." Snow shakes her head.

"Do you think we should put him out of his misery and invite him in?" Ariel asks, as Snow holds the door of our next destination open for us.

The urge to turn my head to try and catch a glimpse of him trailing us is strong, but I push down the impulse. The girls caught on early that we were being followed. My ever-present shadow. I can't tell right now if I feel grateful for the familiar support or annoyed that I can't escape our old patterns.

"No, I think not." It comes out a little haughty. I still feel raw from last night's fight.

A child's rebellion. Hmph.

He doesn't understand how I feel. Talon thrives on solitude and compartmentalization. I tried to be like him, *really tried*, but the loneliness ate at me until I couldn't stand it. And I can never escape what I am, or what I've done.

Talon doesn't wake up in a cold sweat, stomach churning over who he is or what he's had to do to survive. He simply views his job as serving my basic needs, and his feelings end there.

Mine keep twisting and tightening until I think I'll break out screaming and never stop.

"For the best," Snow says, interrupting my morbid thoughts. "I get the sense hot boy won't care for what we've got next on the agenda."

It's only then I realize we've stepped into a tattoo shop with a big green neon sign behind the checkout counter that says *Inked by Tink*.

Instead of neon lights and sterile walls, the space is cozy chaos. A velvet loveseat, floral-print lamps, framed awards, and glittering magazine covers clutter one wall. The scent of antiseptic mingles with something floral— lilac, maybe—and ink. The black-and-white checkered floor is slick from the melting snow on my boots. Everything about this place feels lived-in and lit up from the inside.

A woman leans back on a stool, boots propped up on the reception desk, sketchpad balanced on one knee. Her long, wavy platinum hair is buzzed on one side.

She's pierced all over—ears glittering with rings and studs, silver hoops in her lip and brow. Her black tank top reads *Don't be a dick*. The tank clings to her bird-like frame, her low-waisted pants showing off a jeweled belly ring that catches the light.

And her tattoos...they're art. Blooming vines. Stardust and lush trees. A full skeleton of a phoenix crawling over one arm.

She's vintage pin-up collided with a punk witch and came out furious and fabulous.

"What's up, ladies," she asks without raising her head. I get the sense she knows it's Snow and Ariel without even looking. When she finally looks up, I am struck by the unusual color of her eyes. Green, lush fields of grass, with pupils rimmed in aquamarine. Like she's seen the ocean from both sides.

"Ah, fresh blood." She closes the sketchbook and stands, stretching the tension from her petite frame. Her wings—yes, *wings*—twitch and shimmer in the light. Boston isn't the human-only city I was led to believe, which is a bit of a relief. Having other fae around makes me feel a little safer.

"I'm Tink, and you must be the new Lost Girl." She reaches out to shake my hand. Her many rings are cold as she grips my hand in a firm shake before letting me go.

"H-how—"

She smirks as she pulls out a pair of thick black framed glasses. "You got that look about you."

I recoil on instinct, my stomach tightening uncomfortably. A realm away from home and I'm still being judged at first sight. "What look?"

"Like you're ready to burn down who you were to become who you really are," she says conspiratorially with a flash of white teeth.

My shoulders drop, releasing all tension. Her words drop into my gut. That's *exactly* how I feel.

A hand on my arm draws my attention to Ariel, and she gives me a reassuring smile. I see recognition and acknowledgement in the aquamarine depths of her eyes. They say, *"I've been there too."*

"Are you sure you're up for what it means to become a true Lost Girl?" Snow asks, easily jumping up to sit on the reception counter. She's far more athletic than I would have guessed.

"Hell yes." It comes out breathy because I have a feeling becoming a Lost Girl is an awful lot like being found.

Tink pushes up her glasses with the back of her gloved hand, continuing to focus on the design she's needling into my skin. It's almost like I'm not even in the room. The playlist of grungy indie covers has become the soundtrack to this new experience.

A single stud glints from my nose. A silver bar in my brow. Countless new piercings arc up my ears like constellations.

She noticed I kept admiring hers until she asked if I wanted the same. At first, I was worried I would be seen as copying, or that it would be weird, but with these girls, there are absolutely none of the passive-aggressive or combative undertones that I'm used to. No sizing me up. No testing if I deserve what I have.

Admittedly, I've only spent the afternoon with them, so my gut remains slightly clenched and on the defensive as I wait for the other combat boot to drop.

Combat boot?

Wow, they really have influenced me in the last couple of hours.

Tink is finishing the outline of a curling black vine of flaming roses with thorns winding around my arm. My throat went dry when I realized what she was designing. I never mentioned being from the Realm of Roses. The fire reminds me of Talon.

"Tink's talent is giving you the marking you need," Ariel says after snapping another picture.

Snow's sprawled across the couch, legs flung over

Ariel's lap as they sip iced coffees they got from The Magic Bean across the street. I nervously sucked mine down a while ago.

"Yeah, I got a handheld mirror that has the glass shattered," Snow says, showing off the beautiful ink design on the inside of her forearm. "Still not sure what that's about," she mutters.

"You'll know when you're meant to," Tink says without breaking her concentration.

"I can't believe how nice you've all been," I say, barely louder than a breath.

They all glance at me. Even Tink pauses for a moment.

Ariel raises a brow. "Why wouldn't we be?"

I stare at the ceiling for a second. "People usually...treat me different. Either they want something from me, or they treat me like I'm not real. Like I'm some...object. Pretty, maybe. But not really a person."

Snow lets out a low whistle. "Ah. Hot girl jail."

I blink. "What?"

"You've been in hot girl jail," she says, like it's obvious. "People think you've got it so good they feel entitled to hate you for it. Project their own shit. Blame you for being born lucky. Sucks."

That lands sharper than expected. Back home, no one had any concept of how difficult it was to be me. They just expected me to be grateful.

Grateful for the stares. Grateful for the silence they wanted from me. Grateful to be an ornament.

"That shit doesn't matter here," Ariel adds. "We all get judged when we walk in the door. Doesn't mean that's who we are."

"Don't you mean roll in the door?" Snow grins wickedly at her.

Ariel narrows her eyes in fake annoyance. "I'm going to steam*roll* right over you. And apparently no one would blame me, because I'm just a poor, helpless girl in a wheelchair." She says the last part in singsong.

I nearly choke on my own spit. My laugh escapes in heaving wheezes.

Ariel blinks. "Oh my gosh, that's how you laugh?"

"Be still," Tink murmurs, pausing until I calm down.

"Dammit," Snow gripes. "Well, Aurora knows better now. You'd avenge my death even against a seemingly defenseless girl, wouldn't you, Aurora—ow!" Snow's legs snap up as she rubs the part where Ariel gave her a wicked pinch.

"Thought you said I was defenseless?" Ariel bats her eyes at Snow.

I try to suppress my laugh so I don't move, but it comes out as a rough snort.

"Sometimes people judging you by what they think you are leaves them at a huge disadvantage," Ariel says with the first true grin I've seen from her. "I've learned to either prove them wrong as often as possible or," she says with a lofty shrug, "exploit their assumptions." Her face softens. "Really, Rap taught me that."

A solemn moment quiets the group, as they pay silent alms to the bar owner.

"They'll underestimate you. Let them," Tink says as if repeating some mantra.

"They'll want you to play nice. Don't," Snow continues, still holding on to her bruised leg.

"Because Lost Girls aren't made to fit in. We're made to find each other," Ariel finishes.

"And become unfuckable with." Snow pumps a fist, finally dropping her leg.

I get the feeling there'd be a clink of glasses, and everyone would take a drink if there had been a round present.

Tink wraps my fresh tattoo, assuring me the pixie dust she used will heal it in a matter of hours.

I glance toward the front of the shop where my reflection stares back from a vintage mirror half-covered in stickers, and barely recognize the girl looking at me. She's someone I might want to be—edgy, unpolished, self-assured. Dare I say, chaotic.

But something's still...off. Not unfinished, exactly, just....

"Hang on," I mutter.

Tink glances up, but I'm already heading for the front counter. There's a pair of hair scissors resting in a mason jar beside a comb and some latex gloves. I grab them without asking, stepping toward the mirror again.

"Uh," Snow says, sitting up straighter. "What are you doing?"

I sweep my pink hair over one shoulder. It falls past my waist, the same way it has for as long as I can remember.

And then I cut.

The first lock falls to the floor like a ribbon severed.

"Oh, witchtits," Ariel breathes, wheels whirring as she rolls forward to get a better view.

I cut again. And again. Until the ends lay just below my shoulders, jagged and wild.

When I'm done, I run my fingers through the shorn waves. It's lighter. It's freer. It's *mine.*

"I think I'm done being who I was." My breath comes quick with excitement. I feel I'm on the edge of everything.

There's a beat of stunned silence, then Snow lets out a whistle. "Hell yes."

Tink's smile is impish as golden motes float off her fluttering wings. "Respect."

A moment later, Snow practically springs to her feet. "OHHHH—we *have* to do blue tips."

"No, we *don't*," Ariel shoots back. "Her pink is iconic. You don't mess with iconic."

"She needs to be more punk!"

"The pink is *gorgeous as-is!*"

"Oh my fae lords," I laugh. "Are you two really going to fight about my hair?"

They both turn toward me, totally unrepentant.

"Yes," they say in perfect sync.

CHAPTER 8

DON'T COME IN YOUR PANTS, DRAGON

TALON

Rap doesn't say much when I enter the Poison Apple for my orientation.

She just hands me a staff security badge, a black comm earpiece that'll *probably* work, and goes over a few cursory rules and regulations any idiot would intuit.

Thankfully, I don't have to wear a uniform or shirt. Rap makes some joke about how no one fucks with a guy who wears leather over a bare chest.

The only reason I left Aura alone is because the shop they went to is right next door. And she is nowhere close to needing to feed. I can lengthen the leash...for now.

I can't deny I took advantage of it. Before coming here, I found myself called back to that disgusting-looking food truck I clocked the first night we arrived. The Salty Bastard.

After devouring one of their suspiciously inexpensive lobster rolls dripping in butter and sweet brine from a paper boat, I realize that by the end of the day I'll either be violently ill or have a food habit that will be very hard to kick. The fries were crisp and salted to perfection, and I already can't stop thinking about when I can go back.

I shouldn't develop a dependency on food here. We won't be staying.

Though a part of me hopes Aurora's right. Maybe she can go cold turkey. Maybe she knows her body and power better than anyone.

But the larger part of me knows. Her power is a curse. It is not to be controlled. It is only to be endured.

Shaking my head, I push my worries of the future out of my mind and focus on being shown around Poison Apple from front to back.

I don't need to ask questions. The work's familiar—stand still, look dangerous, end problems before they start.

It grounds me.

The bar isn't open yet, so I pitch in to help prepare, bringing out crates of booze from the back. I drop a stack of three crates when I hear the deliberate thud of heavy boots approaching. They strike the floor with real weight, not the dainty tap of someone trying to make an entrance.

Laughter spills down the hallway. "Five bucks says he walks into a wall," Snow sings.

"His pupils are gonna dilate so fast he'll blackout," Ariel adds, somewhere between amused and pitying.

I turn in time to see the two Lost Girls make space, and then she steps out.

Aurora.

Only this is not the princess I've guarded for years.

No glittering chains. No silks draped over curves to imply virtue or seduction. No crown of grief.

Hair hacked to her shoulders, pink, choppy, wild, as if cut on a dare. Blue streaks drip down the ends, inked rebellion in her hair. Her lips are stained a dark berry red, and her eyes are lined in sharp black. A bar pierces through her brow, complemented by a stud in her nose. Her ears glint with silver. She looks like sex and war had a baby and dared you to touch it.

She's wearing a grunge band tee that's cut in a crop so high, I can see the under swell of her breasts. The very thought of her lifting her arms to expand the view turns my throat dry.

A leather skirt hugs her to mid-thigh, over fishnets with one rip near the knee. Combat boots envelop her feet, and a black choker wraps her throat.

It's not an outfit for lust. It's not for me. It's not for anyone.

This? This is hers.

Aurora didn't dress to please. She got dressed to be. And fae fuck me, I've never wanted anything more.

My cock stirs before I can stop it. My skin tightens with heat. My teeth ache. I want to turn away but can't. She walks like a blade being unsheathed. Every step loud enough to drown my thoughts.

I know the girls are watching me.

My jaw clenched, chest rising and falling in jagged breaths.

But I don't care. She's radiant. And it's not magic. Not her curse. Not the energy that ensnares when she feeds. It's something wilder.

She's fire and steel and leather and skin, and I want— gods, I want to drag her to a back room and rip those fishnets with my teeth as I grip the collar at her throat. I want to bury my tongue between her thighs and make her forget every person she's ever had to feed on.

I want to hear her moan my name while I bite the place just below her ear that always made her shudder when she fed.

Snow elbows Ariel. "Yup. Hard as stone."

"He's gonna ruin his pants," Ariel mutters, while shaking her head.

Rap doesn't say anything. She just watches me, cataloging every move.

Aurora doesn't flinch at their teasing. She doesn't blink.

She's watching me. Not with mischief. Not with heat. Her eyes pin me in place. There's a furrow in her brow, a tight pull to her mouth. She's bracing for rejection. Like she thinks I'm going to tear her down. Like I'm still the person who gets to say what's right for her.

I hate that she's holding her breath on my opinion.

"You look..." I swallow, because my mouth's gone dry. "Good."

It's not nearly enough, but it's the only word I trust.

Her shoulders drop. The tightness in her face melts into something warmer.

She smiles.

I said the right thing. Thank the fae lords for that.

In a moment, she's swept away by the others, disappearing behind the bar so they can teach her the basics. Before long, it's time for me to open the doors and check the IDs of the masses lined up to get in.

The night rolls forward, and I lose sight of Aurora in the throng.

In less than an hour, the bar's packed shoulder to shoulder. Sweat and perfume hang thick in the air. The line still wraps down the block, but we've reached capacity. I nod to the outside guard to hold it up. That's when it hits—the familiar burst of powder-blue sparkle dust, an explosion of magic and flair.

Geanie.

He appears beneath the lantern-lit tree again, top hat

low, coat tails trailing. His voice pours over the mic, silk wrapped around sin.

"Alright, you wicked little deviants. You know the drill." His grin is all fangs and fanfare. "Drink deep. Touch soft. Sin hard."

The crowd roars.

I cross my arms and lean against the wall to watch.

Snow's up first—same routine, same flair. She smirks as she tosses bottles behind her back.

Then Ariel rolls into place, copper hair flashing fire as she spins in her chair, her tattooed arm steady as she pours shot after shot into a tower of glasses.

Geanie purrs into the mic. "And now..." He drags out the pause until the air buzzes. "Our newest temptation."

He saunters a slow circle around the bar, his voice deepening with every syllable.

And then—

A *pink* spotlight cuts the bar in half.

Aurora's boots connect with the wood in confident, measured strides. She lifts her arms.

Fae fuck me off a cliff into Kraken's arse.

The sight slams into me, every bit as I feared it would. The impact drops lower and stiffens my cock as her shirt lifts dangerously high, threatening to reveal more than the heavy swell of flesh.

Her skirt is tight enough to tempt, short enough to be dangerous. Her thighs gleam beneath the torn fishnets, golden and strong.

Aurora spins slowly with a dancer's grace sharpened into a weapon. Her piercings flash. Her hands trail over her hips, then up, up, until they're in her hair, fluffing, twisting, lifting. She bites her lip, and everyone in the place *loses it.*

She's a natural performer.

"She's not here to flirt," Geanie intones. "She's here to set the room on fire and let you beg for the burn."

She dips her body low into a roll, palms brushing the bar, then rises again, hips swaying. Her lips part. Her head tilts. She's flirting with the entire room, and no one can resist her. They aren't drawn to her curse. They can't resist Aurora, herself.

Suddenly, I'm not just stunned.

I'm jealous.

Ugly, *ravenous* jealousy claws up my throat as I watch the room devour her with their eyes. Hands reach. Voices howl. Someone yells, *"Marry me!"* and another slaps down a couple large bills.

Even when she's fucking and feeding, I don't feel a tinge of jealousy. As she takes whatever she needs, the other person doesn't get even a little piece of my Aura.

But the girl up on that bar isn't the same girl I've protected for years, and for the first time, I have to share her.

It's fucking *terrible*.

Because I suddenly realize this could be the beginning of losing her. And I can't do a damn thing about it.

The primal side of me wants to explode in wings and fury, pluck her off that bar, and hold her to me as I fly us to a far secluded cave and keep her. Hoard her the way Dragons guard their treasure. My treasure. My Aura. My everything.

But I can't touch her. Even in this new world, with this new Aurora, the rules remain the same.

"Her eyes promise trouble, her fingers spell sin, and her smile will send your soul packing."

The crowd screams. But I'm silent. Carved hollow by

want and fury and the ache of everything I can't have. My jaw clenches so hard it clicks.

Geanie lifts his hand.

"One more thing," he purrs, voice velvet dark. "If you're thinking about taking her home," he grins, "you better make peace with dying happy."

The bar *erupts*.

Aurora throws both hands in the air and *howls*, laughing as the pink light pulses around her in a flirtatious heartbeat. She belongs here. A Lost Girl.

And it guts me. Because I see now how right she was. Here she is alive and free.

Which is going to make the fall all the more brutal.

CHAPTER 9

GIRL, CLEAN YO'SELF UP

AURORA

The second my boots hit the floor behind the bar, the high rushes straight to my head.

It's not magic. Not feeding. It's the rush of being *seen*, not just watched. My breath comes fast, my skin flushes, my body sparks from the inside, lit on a live current.

The crowd is still screaming, but they're miles away and I'm floating above them. Golden, electric, and real.

I'm a crown jewel that's been gloriously smashed into a hundred dazzling pieces.

Here, I'm still a symbol, sure. A Lost Girl. A dare. A fantasy. But I'm not behind the glass anymore. I shattered it. Stepped through.

I danced. I laughed. I took up space. And no one recoiled.

No one offered tight smiles or curtsied before turning away.

They screamed. They roared. They reached for me. Not to cage me. To celebrate me.

For the first time, I'm not cursed. I'm alive.

And I don't ever want to go back.

Snow squeezes me so tight, I yelp. "That was so sexy, I'm mad about it."

My heart does a half-skip. "Mad?" I think she's joking, but she's touched a sensitive nerve.

She shakes my shoulders. "Oh, hell yeah! I'm jealous as all witchtits. I could keep it inside and let it fester and get all passive-aggressive or just call out my shitty response to your awesomeness." She gives me a gentle nudge. "Jealousy is normal, girl. I'd rather you take the compliment that I'm threatened, and we laugh it off, and then move on."

My brain can't wrap around that.

"She came out with the attitude of someone who's been doing this for years," Ariel nearly whines, rolling behind the bar. "Do you have any idea how long it took me to get comfortable doing this? Weeks."

"*Months,*" Snow mouths to me.

Rap doesn't say anything. She just flicks her eyes up and down me, then nods once. That means more than any applause. Her approval means I get to stay.

"Shot?" Snow offers, already holding up two mini glasses. She passes another to Ariel as Rap leaves, heading to her office.

I slam it. The liquor scorches down my throat with fire and honey. We clink the empty glasses.

"Hell yeah," Snow yells. "Let's get these thirsty people some drinks."

The crush of people at the bar nearly spills over with excitement at her words. I dive in, ready to slay the rest of this night.

This is my moment.

∽

THE MOMENT IS ON FIRE. Everything is on fire.

Not literally, but it starts with the very first drink order when I reach for the soda gun and press the wrong nozzle. A full stream of club soda hits a man square in the crotch.

He yelps, jumping back from the bar with a curse.

"Oh no…shit—" I fumble, hit another lever, and now I'm spraying something red and fizzy directly onto the bar top. It arcs into the air, raining down in a sticky fountain.

Snow doubles over, howling. Ariel claps once, slow and solemn.

I grab a bar towel and try to mop it up, but now I knock over someone's beer.

Chaos.

Pure, dripping, humiliating chaos.

"Damn," Snow wheezes. "Hot Girl can command a room but give her one button and it's a war crime."

I groan, already flushed, already laughing. "Why are there so many buttons? Is this thing powered by dark magic?"

"That's what I said when I started," Ariel deadpans. "Don't worry. We all baptized the bar in soda our first week."

I look down at the disaster I've created. A pool of sticky liquid, a grumpy wet patron, and a half-mopped mess.

Okay, this is fine. Apparently, this is normal. Things can only get better from here.

It does *not* get better.

I forget which liquor goes in a vodka soda and pour tequila instead. A guy asks for an old fashioned and I ask him what era that is. I can't work the tap without the handle jerking sideways and spraying foam all over my shirt.

Every time I try to ring something up, the register beeps at me, judging my whole existence.

Snow keeps yelling "STOP HITTING VOID!" while Ariel wheels by tossing coasters like ninja stars and mouthing, "*Don't panic,*" in slow motion.

Someone asks for a French 75, and I black out.

I break two full bottles of liquor, four glasses, burn myself on the espresso machine, and ruin someone's expensive whiskey pour by topping it with ginger ale. The guy doesn't even flinch—he just tips his head back and drinks it.

And the worst part?

I care.

I want to be good at this. I want to do it right without magic or manipulation.

But nothing works the way I want it to. There's no quick fix. No charming smile that rewinds time. No handmaiden or servant to call to come clean up my mess. And I have never been so infuriated in my life.

I used to hate being underestimated. Now I hate that I might deserve it.

At the end of the night, I'm left woefully scrubbing the bar top, sticky from head to toe and feeling I'm an utter failure.

My stomach is cramping with hunger. I was too nervous to eat before my shift and too busy screwing up drinks to grab anything during. The emptiness makes every small failure feel catastrophic.

Talon walks up, the entire place shut down for closing and clean up.

"How was your first night?" he asks.

Irritation flares in me. I can't tell if he's being glib. My lack of food also might be contributing to my ire.

From his position at the door, Talon likely had a good view of my disaster zone but every time I looked over, he was either ushering new patrons in or checking IDs. Maybe he didn't notice?

"I served exactly two drinks correctly. Two. Out of...okay, let's not count how many." I shut my eyes tight, rocked by the reality and resisting the urge to tally the exact numbers. "How was your night?" I ask, changing the subject.

He shrugs. "Nothing to it." He pushes a small dish of bar nuts in front of me.

Great. So much for a distraction. I instantly pop some of the snacks in my mouth even as I glare at him.

"Hey, hot boy," Snow calls from where she's replacing the bottles of liquor I broke earlier. "Take her home so she can get some rest and a shower."

A flash goes off in my face. Ariel has snapped yet another picture, with the benefit of extra light to capture the mess I am.

She grins at me from behind the camera. "You'll love that I captured this memory one day."

I doubt it.

I return to vigorously scrubbing the bar. "No, I need to help finish clean-up."

Ariel and Snow approach me from either direction. Snow shakes her head. "Nah, we got this. Right, Ariel?"

"Totally, go rest," Ariel says. "Tonight was...a lot."

My shoulders drop as I stop cleaning.

"It's okay if it takes you a couple weeks to get the hang of it," Ariel reassures me.

"Or months," Snow says, shooting a quick sideways glance at Ariel. "Months is okay too." Then with a genuine grin, she gives me a side hug. "You'll get it babe, hang in there."

I return a weak smile. "Thanks guys."

"And good job, big fella," Snow says, shooting a double thumbs up to Talon. "Way to stand there all night and look menacing."

"Ten out of ten," Ariel nods. "Very scary." They both give him a polite golf clap.

He narrows his eyes at them, clearly not sure what to say.

I throw on my cloak, hating the slide of it over my sticky arms despite trying to wipe them off in the bathroom earlier. Talon and I step out into the biting chill of the night, our breaths visible in the air.

Although spring is poised to arrive at any moment, winter stubbornly hangs on, much like a needy pet refusing to let go. The city streets are lined with a thin layer of frost that crunches under our feet. Despite the cold, I prefer the icy embrace of this urban landscape to the comforts of home, where the fields are already bursting with lush green grass and vibrant flowers.

"I can't believe they don't hate me," I mutter, shoving my hands in my pockets.

Talon nearly stops walking, brows furrowed. "Why would they hate you?"

"Because I was just awful." I scrub a hand over my face. "I made things so much worse. I'm supposed to be there to help, and Rap had to come out and cover the bar too. If I were them, I'd hate me."

Talon half-snorts, half-huffs. "No, you wouldn't. And they don't either. Besides, this is the first time you've ever had to try so hard."

I bristle at that, blood rushing to my cheeks. "I try

constantly. I had to work extra hard with my tutors to prove I'm more than just a face. The amount of effort it takes to look and act royal the way I'm expected to is staggering. So no, this is not the first time I've *tried,* Talon."

For as long as we've been together, I'm genuinely pissed he doesn't think I try. He thinks I'm a spoiled princess. Like everyone else.

He doesn't say anything for a couple of steps, allowing me to simmer in my self-righteous anger.

"You're right, I'm sorry," he says carefully. "I guess I lose sight of that because you've always made the difficult things look so easy. So maybe this might be the first time you've ever tried and failed?"

I open my mouth ready to shoot out some snappy retort, but I've got nothing. He's right. My gait slows.

The stickiness covering me is a coating that seems to crawl over my brain. I can't wait to get back to the apartment and shower it off. Maybe have a good cry. Definitely burrow like a little miserable slug under the covers.

I steal a look at Talon, tucking a hand under either arm to hug myself. "Aren't you going to say it?"

He turns to me, with an expression of surprised confusion. "Say what?"

"That this was a terrible fae fucking idea, and we should go home?" Misery wraps around my words. I deserve the recrimination. He should lay it on me.

Talon gently tugs at the back of my skirt, bringing me to a halt so we're both standing facing each other. The side street is deserted, creating a quiet, almost serene atmosphere. Overhead, the streetlamps cast their soft, yellow glow, illuminating the area with a warm light that contrasts with the brisk chill of the evening air sweeping through, sending a shiver down my spine.

Talon dips his head. Black shaggy hair falls further over his eyes, but they still pin me with their intensity. "You want me to tell you it was a terrible idea to get a job? That you shouldn't try something you've never done before, and then punish you for not being instantly good at it? I'm not going to do that, Aura." His deep, dark gaze latches on the piece of hair that's blown into my face, and I intuitively know he wants nothing more than to reach out and push it back. I quickly brush it behind my ear.

"I've always held you in high esteem, but I'm learning just how fearless and resilient you are." His jaw ticks as if something else is straining to come out. "Tonight, I've never seen you so happy. So connected."

"And then miserable, clumsy, messy, and an absolute wreck," I add.

One side of his lips lifts. "That too. And I didn't mind seeing that side of you either. You want to be new? You want to be free? This is what it entails, Aura. The safety rails are gone, and this is how it is. I do think pretending your curse is just going to go away is a bad idea and that we should go home. But..."

"But?" Hope rises in my chest.

"I would rather see you fail with your freedom a thousand times so you could taste a glimpse of the happiness I saw in you tonight." His words are thick with emotion, and it hits me in the chest like a physical blow.

I don't know when I stopped breathing. I don't know when I got so close that his heat wraps around me, protecting me from the cold. The spicy smokiness of him calls to me with a delicious invitation I always have to decline.

It's everything I didn't know I needed to hear.

"I would kiss you right now if I could."

I quickly bite down on my lip, wishing I could take the words back.

We don't give a voice to the obvious pulsating attraction between us, because it only makes things harder. Still, I couldn't help myself.

His fathomless dark eyes search mine for a moment, and his mouth tightens. "I would kiss you right back."

Coils of tension squeeze my chest from the inside until I think I'm about to explode or do something incredibly stupid, like try to press my lips against his, even knowing they'd blister and burn on contact.

I turn sharply and continue the route to our apartment. We walk in loaded silence all the way back.

By the time I've undressed in the bedroom, Talon has run a bath for me.

"You didn't have to do that," I say, staring at the bubble-filled tub.

"I know," he says. "I wanted to. I used one of the bottles left behind that smelled like lavender. I hope that's okay." His wings stretch slightly. He removed his jacket.

The way his words stumble betrays his nerves. He's never done something like this for me, I had handmaidens to do it. He's offering me one of my favorite creature comforts to make me feel better, and my heart is near bursting with love for him.

I slip into the tub and dunk my hair before sitting back up.

"How is the temperature?" he asks. I still detect a note of self-consciousness.

"It's, uh, great," I say.

He scowls.

"Okay, it's a little cold, but it's still lovely," I say,

sweeping up a handful of bubbles. I blow them at him with a grin.

Still scowling, he crosses over to me and crouches down. Meeting my eyes, he drops a hand into the water, careful not to touch me. Again, his face is so close to mine I'm tempted to do something tremendously dumb.

The water warms around my body as we are trapped in a stalemate of closeness. As I stare into his inky dark gaze, I imagine his hand drifts to my thigh and then slides over it to touch me between my legs. I bite my lower lip as my inner muscles contract.

The heat in his eyes tells me he's thinking an equally naughty thought.

I want him to pump into me until my knees shake and I break on his hand.

"Is that good?" he asks quietly. Again, his wings flex behind him in tandem with his round shoulder muscles.

It takes an impossibly long time for me to realize he's asking about the temperature of the water. It is now near scalding, but my skin has warmed and it's exactly how I like it. "It's good." My voice is raspy.

He pulls his hand out.

"Thank you." The words come out a bit strangled.

Talon swallows and nods, though he looks like he's in pain. He rises to leave, but I don't miss the way he adjusts himself as he goes.

Once I'm alone, I sink all the way into the tub with a long-suffering sigh. I still don't know if having Talon here is either the best safety net...or the most masochistic idea I've ever had.

My clothes are in a heap on the floor where I dropped them the last few days, while Talon's jacket hangs neatly on the door hook.

The bubbles close over my shoulders in a comforting shawl. The lavender envelops me, soft and familiar.

I stare up at the ceiling, water lapping gently at my skin, the heat doing nothing to ease the ache that's formed in my chest.

My mother would have swooped in to comfort me tonight, would have had the servants draw this bath with her favorite lavender oils. She'd stroke my hair and tell me I didn't have to worry about a thing. That it would all be taken care of for me.

My father would have already fired whoever let me struggle, replacing them before I could protest.

They never let me fail. Maybe that's why I'm so terrible at it now. The thought makes me miss them and resent them in equal measure.

I wanted a new life. One that was mine.

Turns out, it comes with shopping sprees, dance numbers, dropped drinks, and a healthy dose of humiliation. But some things don't change—like the temptation that cuts so deep it scrapes bone.

"No use," I whisper, eyes squeezing shut.

I can have a new life. A new me. But I'll never have *him*.

And after all these years, I still can't make peace with that.

I dunk my head beneath the water, trying to drown the voice saying I never will.

CHAPTER 10

HOW BIG DOES HE GET?

AURORA

The next two weeks are a blur. A messy, chaotic, blur of a learning curve.

Most of my time is spent working and learning at Poison Apple, but there are just as many nights in, sprawled on Ariel and Snow's couch watching *Hex Island*. The reality show disaster features a bunch of level two mages crammed into a beachside mansion for a million-dollar prize.

The catch? Every time they use their powers, they lose money. Which of course they do. Constantly. Because they're horny narcissists who can't stop flexing their magic to seduce each other. It's like watching magical Darwinism, and I'm beyond addicted.

Snow and Ariel cheer me on at work, insisting I'll get better behind the bar, but there are no empty platitudes. They're honest. Brutally so. Snow once called me a "hot mess with excellent tits and a tragic pour."

She's not wrong.

Despite Rap's hard exterior, she never comes down on me for my mistakes. She's sharp and direct with her feedback, but never cruel. And she always steps in to pick up the slack when I've created a disaster.

When I get caught in a spiral trying to apologize for it, she tells me not to bother. It's a waste of time. She says to just keep going and I'll get it.

Rap makes it so simple. No emotional recrimination required.

I don't love failing, or mixing up disgusting drinks, or dropping bottles that explode on impact, or getting so over-stimulated by lights and music and people yelling drink orders that words stop making sense. And the girls notice.

They see it on my face before I fully break, and they send me to the back to take a breath in the breakroom with bubblegum-pink lockers and a vending machine that always eats your coins.

I'm not used to this kind of care.

I've never had real girlfriends before.

They continue to tease me about Talon, about how he looks at me like he's two seconds from eating me alive (like one of those lobster rolls he's now obsessed with) or committing murder in my honor.

If they only knew...

I still keep the truth buried. What Talon really is to me. Who I was at home. I don't want to scare them. But also, it's not me anymore. That version of Aurora stayed behind in the Realm of Roses.

Here, I'm one of the Lost Girls. One of the reasons people show up to Poison Apple. The new addition. A little mystery with her own drink special and piercings. The pedestal I'm on isn't about decorum or being a marble statue. I work the crowd, and we feed each other with energy and excitement.

With Ariel and Snow, I'm just...a girl. Their girl.

Snow often rests her head on my shoulder because she rarely sleeps but is always tired. Ariel lets me help her push or maneuver her chair on the rare occasion she needs the help.

We gossip. We paint our nails. We argue about *Hex Island* like it's life or death.

It's messy, and sweet, and stupid, and everything I've always wanted. They're the kind of moments I've spent my whole life aching for, and now that I have them, I'm scared of how much they matter.

"So are Talon's abs just painted over cobblestones he glued to his stomach?" Snow asks while unwrapping another *Magic Morsel* snack pack. She pops the tiny chocolate cake into her mouth whole.

It's three AM and we are hunkered down in Snow and Ariel's apartment, decompressing from the wild frenetic night of work. Talon opts to decompress alone. Either he's gone to stretch his wings around the city, or he's just avoiding conversation. Likely both.

Snow and Ariel's apartment smells like toasted sugar and incense, with old wood floors that creak if you shift too hard. One lamp's missing its shade, and the TV's propped up on an uneven stack of books and board games. Snow is poised on the half-broken reading chair across from me.

Despite the decent money we make, a lot of that goes to clothes, tattoos, and well...rent. Downtown Boston ain't cheap, as Snow puts it.

"I mean, if his skin burns, why doesn't he wear a shirt?" Ariel chimes in, snapping a picture of Snow. Snow kindly obliges by opening her mouth so she can get a picture of the half-masticated sweet stuck to her teeth and tongue.

Half-grossed out, half-amused, I pick up one of the Magic Morsel boxes with the picture of the kindly grandma on the box. I've never seen Grandma's House products back in the Realm of Roses, but here her lifestyle brand is everywhere. The couch pillows are hers. The curtains. The throw blanket tangled around Snow's legs. But the Magic Morsels are definitely the bestsellers.

Because they can give non-magical beings a buzz of power that's light and fizzy, like soda in your stomach. You get maybe five to fifteen minutes of magic, depending on the flavor.

Evidenced by Snow now levitating her spoon from the pint of ice cream, shakily directing it to her mouth.

"Talon runs hot, so clothes are pretty uncomfortable," I explain. "The fae leathers are really protection for others, but he needs the ventilation."

"Lucky us then, huh?" Ariel says, shooting a wink at me.

Snow's spoon flops midair and splats ice cream onto the floor. She curses. "I wish I had real powers. Like Red or Goldie."

I've heard about the previous Lost Girls. Apparently, Red's grandma is the same little old lady on the box of our snacks and slipped the previous Lost Girls some cookies that turned them from human to level five mages.

"What about Cinder?" Ariel asks.

"Blood magic?" Snow wrinkles her nose. "I mean, if she hadn't been so involved with vampires, she might not even have known she had blood magic, and it doesn't seem very useful."

"You want to be like Goldie?" Ariel shudders as she puts her camera aside. "Have the attention of every single person whether you want it or not? Have people so obsessed they propose to you on the spot? No, thank you."

I stiffen, fear snaking through me. That sounds a little

too much like my own power, except I'm not a mage. My natural fae ability is cursed and twisted into a Succubus.

In another life, I could have fed off Snow's hyper energy, or Ariel's anxiety. They'd feel relaxed, I'd be full, and we all could be hunky dory.

"Is Goldie a…Succubus?" I ask, trying to keep my voice casual. My throat goes dry.

"No way," Snow says, busting out laughing. "Everyone knows people witch-hunted Succubae and Incubi and killed them all off by the end of The Great Culling. Goldie would probably be strung up if that's what she became."

My stomach twists like a wet rag drenched with fear and shame.

The thought of people stringing me up and setting me on fire, like they did in The Great Culling, flashes in my mind with vivid violence. It seemed like so long ago, but the attempted purge of fae and mage presence in the Common World was less than a hundred years ago.

I focus hard on the wrapper in my hands, but my fingers won't cooperate. Ariel notices, rolls her chair closer, and gently takes it from me. She peels it open, then lifts out of her chair to settle in beside me on the couch.

"Goldie is a level five mage," Snow explains, "but her power definitely has Siren-like qualities."

"I thought Sirens were fae," I say. "Or…are they Mermaids? Are Sirens and Mermaids the same?"

"They are *not*," Ariel says, more sharply than I expect.

Snow and I blink at her. As if realizing she came off a bit harsh, Ariel's shoulders slump as her pale cheeks turn bright pink. "I mean, Sirens are fae who want to lure sailors to their death, and Mermaids aren't murderous Harpies."

"Calm down there, tiger." Snow soothes. "No murderous Harpies here."

I place my uneaten morsel on the coffee table, growing increasingly queasy from the conversation.

Part of me thought I might tell them what I am. A secret part that hoped I'd be accepted. That part sinks into the pit of my stomach.

Who am I kidding? I'm a killer. Who would ever want to be friends with a Succubus?

Maybe I should go back to my apartment. With my murderous magic and all...

"We need to get back to the more important question," Snow says, turning her attention to me before I can excuse myself. "Why in the hell you aren't banging hot boy."

Ariel perks up at that. "Yeah, why haven't we talked about this before?"

Snow shoots her a dark look. "Because she dodged the question the first time, and *you* told me not to ambush her until after she'd gotten more used to our weirdness."

"Oh, right," Ariel nods before looking at me.

They're both looking at me, waiting for some kind of explanation.

"He's...and I..." I stammer. Sweat breaks out on my brow, and I feel as though I'm under a bright, hot spotlight. "We can't touch. He's a Dragon."

Snow adjusts herself so she is sitting on her knees now, clutching a pillow to her chest with barely restrained excitement. "Have you seen him turn into a Dragon? How big does he get?"

I shake my head. "I mean he's a Dragon with scales and wings, but he can't fully transform into Dragon form. That's something only the ancient ones could do."

"Oh. Have you seen his wings?" Ariel jumps on the question train.

"Um, yes," I say. "His back ones anyway."

They both tilt their heads in confusion.

"Does he have wings somewhere *else*?" Snow asks. Her eyes turn round with a curiosity that borders on hunger.

It's only then I realize how little they know about Dragon anatomy.

"Oh no, just on their backs," I rush to say. Talon would kill me if I told Snow where the extra set was. He would get no rest from the questions she'd hurl at him.

In fact, I doubt he even knows that I'm aware of the extra set. But being cooped up all day every day, I read a lot and found everything I could on Dragons after I became his charge.

"I don't know how he's held back this long," Snow says. "Hot boy is always looking like he'll eat you up like one of those nasty lobster rolls he's always chowing down on."

"Uh..." I can't tell if she was trying to compliment me or not.

"Listen, I know you can't touch, but why are you guys letting that stop you?" Snow asks.

I blink. "I don't understand."

"Well, fae leather doesn't burn," she goes on. "Otherwise, the boy would constantly be nude. I mean most of the fabrics even in the Common World are sourced by the fae nowadays. So why doesn't he slap on a pair of fae leather gloves and finger diddle you? Or you guys could get body suits? You could still rub all up in each other's business. Get a little creative and you two could be having lots of nasty fun." Snow grins wickedly.

My mouth falls open, then clicks closed.

"I guess...I guess I hadn't thought of that." I feel dumb. Truly and utterly dumb. Like someone pointed out an obvious plot hole in my favorite book. "Where we come from...we weren't allowed...I mean..." I stumble all over my words, over what to tell them. Over what not to tell them.

"He's my protector, and it'd be...wrong." It just pops out.

"Wrong?" Ariel echoes with evident disbelief. "I mean..." She clears her throat as if dealing with something delicate. "It seems he's not the only one with feelings."

"Maybe we should set you up with someone, then you can bang it out with them and forget about hot boy," Snow cheerfully adds.

I try to laugh. It comes out strained. "Sure, we've known each other a long time. I mean, I ran away from home and the clod had the nerve to follow me, and it's totally annoying, and he thinks I made a huge mistake coming here. I mean, he's always been there for me, even on the worst days of my life. Just letting me be whatever I need to be. And yeah, he's basically made of honor and grit." My words start to tumble, faster, looser.

"He checks every room before I walk into it. He knows how I take my coffee. He treats me like I'm the only one in the world who matters, and never makes me feel shitty about who I am. But he also holds me accountable for my behavior when no one else will, which is infuriating because by doing that he makes me a better person. And even though I'm completely and totally in love with him, I can't say it. It's just this scream I have to swallow down all day, every day. Because saying it won't change anything. Because with just a look, he already knows. He always knows."

When I stop talking, my chest heaves from the outburst.

Both girls stare at me in stunned silence.

I feel the slow, dawning horror of what I've just let out into the air. It's more than I've ever dared say before. The vulnerability is as raw as though I sliced through my stomach and let my guts fall out in front of them.

It's a wonder I didn't barrel on and jabber about how I've had to sleep with basically anyone *but* Talon since it's how I've survived. Oh yeah, and I've had to leave a trail of bodies behind as a secret Succubus princess.

Thank the fucking fae lords I didn't.

"Okay," Snow says slowly. "I'm thinking we *don't* set you up with someone else."

"Oh sweetie," Ariel says, rubbing my arm.

"It's fine," I say, trying to shrug it off even as my throat clogs up. My eyes sting, and my vision turns blurry. "I mean this is how it's always been. It's how it's always going to be." I quickly swipe at the stupid tears rolling down my cheeks.

Ariel puts her arms around me, before a second set joins in.

"Ugh," Snow says against the top of my head. "That sucks so bad."

I nod, sniffling. "It really does."

Despite all the raw, broken parts of me that long for Talon, I sink into the love and compassion of my friends. Real friends. I choke back another sob, thinking it's more than I deserve.

CHAPTER 11

THE DEVIL CAT WHO OWNS ME

TALON

The acrid yet sweet scent of burnt cinnamon fills the apartment. Butter sizzles faintly as it smokes around the charred French toast. Breakfast might be a lost cause, but the intention is there. That has to count for something.

I stand at the stove, shirtless and focused, a pair of tongs in one hand and a new scorch mark on the laminate counter beside me.

Lucifer watches from atop the counter. I'm sure now, he's a creature summoned straight from the pit. His tail flicks in malicious rhythm, yellow eyes trained on me, plotting the perfect murder.

He's jumped me three times this morning already, thus the ruined food. He only paused his harassment when I ditched my jacket. Now he's perched like a gargoyle on the leather, purring with possessive menace.

I hear the pad of bare feet, then her sleep roughened voice. "Hi sweetie."

My heart flips half a second before it realizes she's talking to the cat.

I reach for the dish soap to clean up and curse under my breath when it tips over—Aurora left the cap loose again. Soap pools across the counter, another small mess in the endless series of messes she leaves in her wake.

Yesterday it was the milk carton, creating a sour puddle in the fridge. And I'm still finding traces of that face makeup she spilled all over the bathroom counter last week.

Though I'm the one who's a disaster zone this morning.

Aurora stretches out a hand, slow and careful. Lucifer hisses and swipes his claws at her with the clear intent to disembowel.

She jerks back. "Well, that's rude," she mutters, then turns to me. "Did you know this little stinker peed in one of my drawers?"

Her pout is adorable. Distractingly so.

She rambles about the laundry. How she's just figured out the communal washer. How her clothes almost smelled musty. It's mundane and absolutely precious, but I don't let myself dwell on that.

"Shall we throw him out the window?" I ask.

She pauses, seriously considering my offer. Then she shakes her head. "He's probably been abused. That's why he's so distrusting. He probably needs extra love and patience."

I stare at her. At the sincerity in her face. The softness she hasn't let the world beat out of her. "He nested on my crotch last night. Claws out. I almost woke up neutered."

Lucifer, smug bastard that he is, starts kneading my jacket again, purring, certain the world—and me—belong to him.

"Okay, what is his deal with you?" Aurora points accusingly. "To him, I'm nothing more than a roach, but your dirty laundry is the best thing since canned sardines?"

"I have no idea," I mutter.

Lucifer leaps down, circles my legs, and makes a bold grab for my calf.

"Down, Satan," I growl, softly shaking my leg to get him off without hurting him. He clings, evil Velcro with claws.

Aurora steps closer. "I smell burning."

"French toast," I answer, finally freeing myself from the feline barnacle.

Lucifer leaps to the top of the fridge to glare from up high, giving loud scratchy meows of displeasure at not being allowed to treat me as his personal scratching post.

Aurora eyes the pan skeptically. "Was?"

I straighten, jaw tight. "It's salvageable."

She blinks down at the pan. It is not salvageable.

I take a moment to observe her. Her chopped hair is messy from sleep. She tucks the blue tips behind her ear, revealing rows of metal studs and rings adorning the shell of her ear. A bar cuts through her perfect eyebrow, only adding to her ire when she lifts at me in annoyance.

A black tank top clings to her frame, one strap slipping off her shoulder, leaving the ink on her arms bare to the warm kitchen light. She sports the same tattoo all the other Lost Girls have. A mix between a dripping poison apple and a skull and crossbones. But it's the roses on fire, etched in red and gold on the swell of her bicep, that burn into me every time I look.

She looks nothing like the royal she was brought up to be. Instead of the forced mask of stateliness she'd been trained to wear, a natural confidence has bloomed in her over the last couple of weeks. It radiates from her without trying.

And fae lords help me, I want her. I want her so badly the need cuts through me. I'm dying to melt her until she resembles the butter on that skillet, to feel her lips give way under mine, to taste her so deeply she's imprinted on my tongue. The desire pushes up against my skin until my fingers twitch and my forehead tingles from suppressing my urges.

I want to spread her legs and latch onto that perfect little clit with my lips until she's clawing at the counter and making those mewls of pleasure I've memorized. Or maybe given a chance, I'd inspire a new pitch of moan or scream from her.

Aurora steps forward as I discreetly attempt to adjust my thickening length.

"I can help," she says, reaching for the pan just as flames leap up the side.

She startles back, but I'm already moving.

I grab the pan barehanded. Fire licks over my skin, harmless to me. Smoke twists around my wrist. She gasps. I toss the pan into the sink and crank the faucet with my knuckles.

Steam erupts in a hiss, clouding everything.

When it clears, she's caged in. My arms are braced on either side, with her back to the counter. My body between her and the world.

"You okay?" I ask.

Aurora nods, slow and dazed. Her eyes are wide, her breath coming fast. Her lips...

She licks them, and their glistening plumpness becomes the center of my focus now that I know she's okay.

"I was just trying to help," she whispers.

"I know." My voice is rough. "I see you trying. Every day." I force my gaze back up to meet hers, no longer talking about breakfast. I'm in awe of how she tries, of how she's adapted, of how she's picked herself up after disappointment or embarrassment.

By the pink flooding her cheeks, I know she hears everything I'm not saying.

"Doesn't mean I think this plan of yours is smart," I add in a stern tone. "But you are so...impressive, Aura."

Her breath catches, but she doesn't move. Neither do I.

I know I should, but I can't force my muscles to budge. My body drinks up her nearness. It's as close as we'll ever get, but I revel in it.

Even with the few inches between us, my claws have sunk so deeply into her soul, entwined around her heart, that no one else could ever reach her core. No matter whose flesh invades or penetrates hers, they will never reach the profound depths I have claimed. I'll always be deeper, guarding her fiercely, adoring her with unbreakable devotion.

For so long, my life was about being alone and making the most of my solitude. Then it became about protecting Aurora, about following the rules, and cleaning up after the curse. But since we've been here, she hasn't needed my protection. Which has allowed me to become more than her guardian.

Sometimes I'm just a man, and she's just a woman.

The last few weeks have been full of these moments. Little domestic things, like going to work together then coming home. The paycheck is miniscule compared to the fortune she's entitled to, but the money feels so well earned. We pick out fresh produce at the farmer's market. She forces me to drink cheap boxed wine and watch crappy reality television which I claim not to care for, but I'm secretly invested in the drama. She banters with the Lost

Girls, who frequently poke fun at me, and she understands that I don't mind being the butt of the joke if it brings her joy.

And I'm constantly teased by the lot of them for visiting the sketchy lobster roll food truck at least once a day. Since they aren't convinced by the butter to lobster ratio as to why it's a perfect meal, I have to point out how reasonably priced they are. That I'm being frugal in a city that is insanely overpriced.

Snow and Ariel insist that the hospital bills will change my mind when I end up with botulism.

The line that's always separated us is blurring, and I'm struggling to maintain those boundaries.

Aurora laughs softly, nervous. "I'm starting to seriously resent my lack of culinary and domestic education."

I hum, a low throaty sound. "Even I've gotten soft after years of spoiled castle kitchens."

Aurora's lips twitch. "You, soft?"

Her gaze drifts down to my abs, as her tongue darts out.

My muscles tighten.

"I guess I should get out of the kitchen," she murmurs. "I'm not any help."

I meet her eyes. "I haven't known you to back down from a challenge."

Her breath catches again.

She tightly grips the counter behind her, chest pushing out. I swear I smell her arousal in the air. Judging by the tight buds pressing against her thin tank, it's more than wishful thinking.

In another life, I'd have her splayed out on this counter screaming my name. And then I'd finish making her breakfast, draw a bubble bath when she was done eating, and spend the rest of the day alternately washing her body, feeding her, and getting her filthy all over again.

"You never tell me to just sit down and do it for me," she says softly. "That's what everyone else always did."

My throat closes.

"You are *more* than capable." The words are no more than a whisper.

She licks her lips again and shifts a centimeter closer.

The words are there. Pressing into the air between us. The longing is a palpable thing, attracting and repelling us with its massive presence.

Even the continued angry chorus from Lucifer, still perched on the fridge, doesn't break the moment.

My throat works. I swallow then step back.

My stomach sinks even as I grab the tongs. Nothing can come of this. I have to remind myself of that before I hurt Aurora. Best to keep things light and easy.

I give her a lopsided smile. "Let's try pancakes. Maybe they don't catch fire as easily."

CHAPTER 12

FLIRTING WITH THE DRAGON

AURORA

The Poison Apple pulses, alive and thrumming. The music thrums low and dark, vibrating through the floorboards. Lights flash hot and fast. Every breath drags in sweet liquor and perfume, laced with sweat, magic, and lust.

A cheer goes up from the dance floor.

I glance over just in time to catch a mage conjuring a ribbon of glowing smoke between his fingers, twisting it into the shape of a snake. It slithers through the air before bursting in a harmless flash of gold sparks.

I've learned that Boston used to be a human city, but it's shifted in the last couple years. Fae, mages—they're pouring in. Poison Apple's becoming a hotbed for supernatural nightlife. And all that junk reality mage television has given me a knack for spotting the different levels of magic.

The mage on the dance floor is a level one—low power, high showmanship—but the girl he's trying to impress claps and giggles with an enthusiasm that guarantees he's going to get laid.

I shake my head, smiling to myself, and line up four shot glasses.

Pour. Pour. Pour. Pour.

My movements are quick, practiced, no longer plagued by clumsiness. The deep plum liquor catches the neon overhead, glowing with the shimmer of a potion. I swipe a napkin beneath one glass before it can drip, just as Snow whistles from across the bar. "Look at you, bartending and everything, babe." She throws up two thumbs of approval.

I grin and slide the tray to a table of bachelorettes already deep into the night. Their words are slurred, and their eyes are glassy from the night of drinking. One of them leans toward the bride, who is wearing a LED light up tiara, and yells to be heard.

"That's him, right? The Dragon at the door?"

"Seriously, I thought Dragons were extinct," the bride replies with wide eyes, her tone a mix of disbelief and intrigue. "He might even be the last one."

I pretend not to listen as I go about collecting the empty glasses littering the tables around them.

"I wonder if all of them were as hot as him though?" another chimes in, adjusting her glittering dress and flicking her hooded eyes toward the door with a smirk.

"Weren't they hunted for their scales?" the first woman asks, her brow furrowed in thought.

"No, you dumb-dumb," another laughs, playfully swatting her arm. "They were hunted for their treasures. Dragons are known to have amazing hoards they keep in like mountains and shit."

"No, no," the first woman insists, "I swear there is a thing about black market scales and Dragon wings."

The thought of anyone cutting off bits of Talon to sell makes me queasy.

Another woman, her cheeks flushed from laughter and champagne, giggles. "He looks like he'd split you in half. In the best way," she adds with a mischievous glint in her eye, glancing back at the doorway where the imposing figure stands.

Their laughter breaks like waves against my back. I don't flinch.

More people are coming to Poison Apple to see the Dragon. I often overhear people talk about *him*. The tall, dark Dragon shifter guarding the door. The girls flirt and swoon, half-joking about who could get him to crack a smile. Who could convince him to go home with them. How it would be to count how many scales he has and find out if there are any on his thighs or hips. No one has ever seen anyone like him.

I carry on like it doesn't bother me, like it doesn't produce the same ache I felt back home whenever someone mentioned him with a sigh.

When I glance up, I catch Talon watching me from across the room, half in shadow. Arms crossed. Expression unreadable.

But I know that look. Know the weight of it.

He hasn't looked at anyone else all night. And he won't.

Because he's mine. The same way I'm his.

I keep moving—pouring, wiping, garnishing—but it's harder now, because my chest is tight and my skin too sensitive.

Talon's presence is still the same steady force it's always been, a quiet, grounding weight in my chest I've come to rely on more than I should.

It's not healthy, needing that certainty. Not when we can never be. But some selfish part of me still clings to it, comforted by the one thing that bachelorette party doesn't know—they'll never touch him. Not because they'd blister if they tried, but because what Talon and I have is undeniable, unbreakable, and untouchable.

Literally.

I've tried to brush off Snow's out-of-the-box suggestions from the other night about how to get closer to Talon, but her words festered.

I hadn't thought of fireproof gloves or special bodysuits because it was never just the heat. It was also the history. The roles we were told to play. The boundaries we never crossed.

Six years of restraint. Of pretending we didn't feel what we felt. Of watching him stand beside me, behind me, never too close, never too far. Of being his mission. His responsibility.

But we're not in the palace. We're not being watched. We're not confined by duty or chained by decorum. Boston has cracked everything open—my fear, my independence, my hope.

And this morning, when he caged me in at the sink, smoke curling from his fingertips and his body heat wrapping around me, I felt it shift. Something old and forbidden turned fluid. Possible.

He didn't move right away. And I didn't ask him to.

Maybe I could find a way to touch him without pain. Maybe I could wear something special so I could climb on top of him. Let my hands roam over all that hard, blistering heat and not burn.

The thought makes my heart pound harder.

Maybe the old rules are shattering.

And maybe, just maybe, he'd let them.

I slide a cocktail to a girl who doesn't say thank you,

and a ribbon of syrup sticks to my knuckle. I lick it off without thinking, my gaze drifting back toward the door.

He's still watching. A shiver slides up my spine, vibrating through me at the possibilities.

That night, I go to bed thinking maybe, maybe, everything's changing.

Until morning.

I wake with a sharp, molten spark low in my belly.

Hunger.

CHAPTER 13
SNACK TIME AT WORK
AURORA

y hands push on my lower belly and the flame of arousal flares a little brighter as my throat turns dry. I squeeze my eyes shut tight.

No. *No no no no.*

"Aura?"

My eyes snap open as I jerk up in bed. Talon stands in the doorway in nothing but his black boxer briefs. His dark, deeply tanned muscles glisten with beads of water from the shower. They drip down the fine, dark trail of hair that disappears under his waistline, and I force myself not to focus on the bulge it leads to. Instead, my gaze catches on the striated muscle that flexes in his heavy thighs.

Hunger yawns in me. Then it cries out like a child about to descend into a tantrum.

Sex. Touch. Salty tasting skin.

I want it.

Catching myself in the ogle, my gaze snaps back up to Talon's face.

Though his wet black hair hangs even lower in his eyes than normal, they see straight through me.

"You okay?" Talon asks, voice low, as if he already knows the answer.

"I'm fine," I say too quickly. I jump up and run past him into the bathroom before setting the shower in a cold blast and dousing myself.

Shivering under the painful icy streams, it still pulses. The need. The hunger.

"No," I whisper to myself as I wrap my arms around my body. "I don't need it."

I'm a Lost Girl. I go to work. I craft cocktails. I hang with my friends. I feel all the bone deep satisfaction of the life I wanted.

I force myself to feel it so completely, so deeply, and eventually, the insidious spark dims.

When I come to my senses, I'm taking deep steadying breaths and rocking myself back and forth. A shocked laugh escapes me as I realize I've done it. I've muscled the need down.

"I can do this," I smile to myself.

In ten minutes, I'm dressed and ready to meet the girls for lunch before we go to work. With barely a goodbye to Talon, I'm out the door.

It's not the hunger, I insist to myself.

It's the attraction I have to Talon. Totally normal. Nothing to do with a feeding frenzy I need that leaves corpses in its wake.

But the spark persists. It grows. It throbs.

The next few days become a montage of increasingly desperate coping strategies.

Cold showers. Peppermint oil dabbed under my nose. Mental redirection. *Think about cocktails, think about the mundane errands, think about how horrible it would be to accidentally kill someone.*

Again.

Every morning starts the same. I wake up flushed, pulsing, too aware of the seam of my panties and the friction of the sheets. And every day, I shove it back.

The first thing I do is strip and blast myself with cold water until I'm shivering so hard, I can't think straight.

Then I suit up.

More eyeliner. Thick and jagged war paint.

More spikes. Necklaces, cuffs, rings with edges sharp enough to draw blood.

I raid Snow's wardrobe for anything that screams *look but don't touch*, because the truth is, I'm always looking. But I'm trying not to touch.

My hunger's not a magnet. It's a sniper scope. And every night, I'm aiming.

I clock the guy two booths down before he even opens his mouth. Tan, tatted, wearing a smug smirk like he's a gift to the world. His body language is loud, manspreading. Everything about him is a billboard that says *I know you want it.*

I overhear him as I pick up empty glasses nearby.

"She was begging for it," he brags to his friend. "I didn't even text her after."

My head tilts. My stomach tightens.

He's not my type. But he's a snack. A cocky, careless, disposable snack. And suddenly my mouth waters.

I don't walk away. I run.

Hours later, I'm coming back from the storeroom when all of me homes in on a different target.

The tall, gangly guy has been posted up at the bar all night with two friends and a bottle of bad decisions. Halfway through his second round of shots, I catch his voice, loud and brittle.

"She's not even worth it," he slurs, tossing another

drink. "I'm better off. Just need to get laid and move the fuck on." He pauses and then turns and staggers into the crowd.

He's the kind of guy who doesn't believe his own words. The kind of guy who's bleeding on the inside and hoping someone will lick it up.

And I'm ready to volunteer.

Unable to help myself, I follow after a few minutes.

I find him alone, returning from the bathroom. Slow. Swaggering. Vulnerable.

As we approach from opposite sides, we are suddenly on a collision course.

I tilt my chin and let him see me.

I flip the switch. Not passively. Not accidentally. I activate. My beauty goes sharp. Predatory. The energy around me tightens, until it's a precise and honed blade. Then I aim it straight at him.

I sway my hips just enough the leather of my skirt creaks. One hand lifts to tug the edge of my corset higher, fingers grazing the line of my cleavage.

Then I drop my eyes as if I'm letting him in on a secret.

I push my power toward him. My beauty. I wield it, cracking it right across his instincts.

His eyes go hazy, his jaw slack. He takes one step, then another. I've cast a reel, and he's hooked behind the ribs. His pupils are blown, his lips parted, his breath heavy.

He's so ripe with bitterness and need I can smell it— whiskey and want, sweat and grief, arousal tangled up in fury.

I back up until I'm against the wall, and he follows, crowding me, giving the illusion he is the pursuer.

I lean in close, just enough for his breath to catch. Just enough for my presence to wrap around his neck.

"Hi," I whisper, letting the sound kiss the space between us.

He shudders.

He's already mine.

My hand rises slowly. I trail two fingers down the center of his chest, over the tight pull of his shirt, the beat of his racing heart. Lower. Lower.

His cock stiffens instantly. Aggressively. I feel it straining at his zipper with a twitch that makes my thighs clench.

He groans, low and needy, his body strung so tight it might snap in half.

I flatten my palm just below his navel. My lips hover at the edge of his. And then I lean in—not all the way. Just enough for contact. Just enough for extraction.

I take a bite.

Not a full feed. Not even close.

A tiny, harmless nibble.

Just a flick of energy, a tap of power, a sip of the ache blooming behind his sternum.

And it's *delicious*.

Soaked in grief and bravado, sexual frustration laced with fresh heartbreak, his energy floods my tongue, hot and biting, laced with the sweetness of regret.

I don't even kiss him. My lips brush his skin at the hinge of his jaw as I pull. It's so good, a shuddering noise slips free.

His breath hitches. His hands fist at his sides. His entire body jerks once, then twice.

And he comes.

Fully clothed. Right there.

A strangled cry rips free as he stumbles, hand flying to the wall to steady himself. His cock visibly pulses in his jeans, damp spreading beneath his zipper.

When he opens his eyes, he blinks at me, stunned and glassy.

I blink back.

And for a second, I almost do it again.

I almost sink my teeth into all that anger and heartbreak and suck it straight from his booze coated mouth until he's truly empty and shaking and grateful and...dead.

He'd be dead.

I bolt. Heart hammering, breath ragged, I practically sprint through the throng of dancers, race around behind the bar, and plant my hands on the counter.

It's safer here. With polished wood between me and everyone else.

I try to steady my breath. My thighs are slick. My mouth is dry. My hunger claws at the walls of my chest, howling for more.

I almost fed.

I did feed.

Just a taste. But I feel even more unsatisfied than before.

The hunger isn't a whisper anymore. It's a scream.

And I'm not sure how much longer I can pretend I'm not listening.

With a quick glance, I confirm Talon is still working the overcrowded door, trying to keep everyone in line. He doesn't know I almost broke. I can still prove I can be more than my curse.

As I go back to work, the need is still all I can think of. Of what it would take to slake my thirst.

Fingertips brushing collarbones. A tongue dragging across my lower lips. A thigh slotting between mine in the back storeroom while my hands grip the shelves and...

I slam a glass down so hard it cracks.

Snow raises an eyebrow but doesn't say anything. Ariel watches me a little too long.

Snow nudges me as she passes behind the bar. "You good?" she asks, her tone light, but her eyes narrowed. She taps her temple. "You're buzzing like a goddamn wasps' nest."

Ariel rolls up next to us. "Whatever you're holding in, it looks like it's about to explode. Maybe you should talk about it?"

I want to lie.

I want to say I'm fine, but I can't trust the sound of my own voice anymore. I shake my head and dive back into work.

Glass. Pour. Smile. Repeat.

After a while, everything starts to blur. Voices melt into sound. Faces smear. I can't remember what drink I'm holding or which customer I'm bringing it to. My skin feels tight, my insides hollow.

I'm too aware of the way my corset presses my breasts. Of the sweat trailing down my spine.

Someone brushes my arm. My thighs clench so hard it hurts. I need...I need...fresh air.

The back door swings shut behind me, and I'm in the alley before fully realizing I've moved.

The jacked-up, tan fuckboy who doesn't text women back is out here, pulling on a cigarette with his tall, redheaded friend.

He startles when he sees me. I step closer. He doesn't move.

"Touch me," I say. Calm. Measured. Like I'm asking for the time.

Tan Fuckboy blinks. "What?"

"Touch me," I repeat, stepping into their space. My voice stays even, steady. A command disguised as a suggestion.

"Okay, whore," he chuckles derisively, and his buddy follows suit while continuing to suck smoke.

"Oh, *I'm* not the whore," I say, a sly predatory smile sliding up my face. "You are."

Their eyes go wide, they're dazed, unsure, but already in my hooks. Magic licks along their skin. My hunger prowls forward, impatient. Cigarettes fall from their fingers, forgotten before they hit the pavement.

"Service me," I instruct Tan Fuckboy.

He obeys, falling to his knees and dragging my panties down. His hand moves on its own, drawn by the heat between my thighs. He slides one thick finger along my slit. His finger sinks in, slow, deep. The pad of it presses against my walls like a promise.

"More," I bark.

Without another word of command, the redhead unzips his jeans and pulls himself free, already hard. He begins to pump furiously. Then he joins Tan Fuckboy on the ground. He pushes a finger up into me too. I gasp and claw at their heads as their digits pump in arrhythmic tandem, my arousal coating their hands. Their mouths join, as they lick frenetically at their fingers, hands, and my cunt, though it's a crowded mess. Still, I can't slow them down to sort out the choreography. Every cell inside me screams for more. Begs me to sip. To drink. To gorge myself on their sexual pulsating life force.

A half-whimper, half-desperate moan slips from me. It's too much. Not enough.

It feels like it's been forever.

My power coils, ready to pull. Just a sip. Just a taste...

Heat slams into my back as someone grabs me by the hips.

"Step away from her," Talon snarls over my shoulder at the men.

The hands fall away. Tan Fuckboy stumbles, blinking slowly, prey confused by its own survival.

The other freezes, caught mid-breath. None of them realize Talon isn't just being territorial. He's saving them.

Talon yanks me back with a snarl. The emptiness inside me grasps for them. For the hands. The mouths. The life I could've fed from.

"Now," Talon growls, voice low and dangerous.

Whatever they see on his face sends them scattering. Shoes slap the pavement as they hustle up the alley, vanishing into the night.

I'm panting. My underwear is around my ankles as I trip but Talon doesn't let me fall. His grip burns through my corset, but I can't tell if it's from his heat or mine. I break free from him to pull up my panties, then turn to face him.

His eyes sweep my face once. "We need to go. Now."

Guilt and shame wash over me, but my pride rears up ready to protect me from both even as I follow him into Poison Apple.

Talon steers me along the hallway, past the bathrooms, away from the crush of sound and scent and temptation. He pushes open the breakroom door and scans it. Empty.

The fluorescent light flickers above the row of bubblegum-pink lockers. It smells like dust and Ariel's lavender hand sanitizer.

He closes the door behind us and finally turns.

"You were about to feed," he growls, eyes flashing dark and furious. "On some strangers?"

My brows knit. "Wait. Are you upset you didn't get to pick the Johns out for me?"

Annoyance and what looks an awful lot like jealousy darken his face. "I'm upset you are losing control."

"I'm fine." I cross my arms. "I was just teaching those douchebags a lesson." That sounds lame even to my own ears.

"You're not fine," he growls. "You're starving, Aura. I can feel it coming off you in waves."

Talon doesn't wait for my answer. "You have to feed. We have to go home. We tried it your way. We tried to make this life work, but you were wrong, Aura. You can't outrun this. You can't fight it."

I flinch like he's slapped me.

"I'm not hungry," I snap, even though I'm shaking. Even though my thighs are clenched tight and my nails dig half-moons into my palms. "It's not that bad."

He doesn't move. Doesn't blink. Just watches me with those inky, molten eyes that see through every lie I've ever told myself.

"I can *see* it, Aura," he says, each word a hammer. "It's pouring off you, heat shimmering on pavement. You're lit up, Aura. Your power's broadcasting to everyone who breathes you in, and you don't know how to dim it. Because you can't. It's the curse."

My heart slams against my ribs.

He steps a little closer, still not touching me. "I see it in the way your skin glows, lightning caged beneath it. I see it in your eyes when you look at everyone as though they're a meal."

He steps closer.

"And I see what it's doing to you. How it hurts. How

you're trying to stand upright while your own body is screaming."

His words fray, going rough around the edges. "It's killing me to watch you like this. Do you get that? Every time you wince, every time I see that hunger clawing under your skin, and you pretend it's not there...it's tearing me apart."

I can't breathe.

Because it's not just the heat or the pressure or the ache. It's *him*. It's always been him.

We're too linked. Too wound together in a way I don't fully understand. He feels me when I unravel. I feel him every time I try to rethread myself. We don't have a bond. We *are* the bond.

And still, I can't touch him.

Still, I can't *have* him.

The unfairness of it punches through me like fire through glass, white-hot and blinding.

"Then don't watch," I snap. "Go work the front door. Go do whatever broody solitary thing it is you do. But I'm not going home."

"Aura—"

"No!" I whirl on him. "You don't get to make this choice for me. I finally have a life. I have friends. I *like* who I am here. I *choose* this."

His jaw tightens, nostrils flaring. "You can't pretend anymore that you aren't cursed."

"It's not *my* curse." Only when the words reverberate off the lockers do I realize I yelled them. Still, it doesn't stop the anger from pouring out. "It's my father's. *He* was the one who broke it off with a Midnight Fae princess and married my mother. Why should I be the one to pay the price? I don't deserve this. I didn't ask to be born. I didn't do anything. I was just a baby when she cursed me."

Chest heaving, eyes stinging with unshed tears, and the hunger still burrowing through me with relentless need, I register my own words. I've never openly blamed my parents until now. It feels like a betrayal. They love me and work so hard to take care of me, but finally tapping fully into the anger and blame feels good, freeing. But it doesn't change a fae fucking thing.

If Talon is surprised by my outburst, he doesn't show it. "You don't deserve it," he agrees. Behind his words is the same tidal wave of injustice I feel about the situation, but it comes out so even, so controlled. "But it doesn't change the fact you're hurting."

"I'm surviving," I yell back, needing to drown out his logic. I can't be composed anymore, not when I've finally cracked inside. "And that matters more than whatever version of myself you want to keep me locked inside."

He doesn't move. Doesn't stop me when I storm past him, my boots loud against the tile as I shove the locker room door open and disappear into the thump of the club beyond.

I know he's probably right.

But going back to who I was? I can't do it.

I *won't* do it.

CHAPTER 14

THE STARVING GIRL IN THE SHOWER

TALON

Aurora refused to talk to me, or even look at me, the rest of the night. She manages to steer clear of me when we get back to our impossibly small apartment, an impressive feat.

When she vanishes into the bedroom, she still leaves the door open. It never fully closes between us. It always stays slightly ajar. Like her heart. Like her pain.

I kick off my shoes and settle on the lumpy couch again, shifting every few minutes as the cushions dip too far to one side. I fixate on the stained ceiling that gives off a faint mildew smell I still haven't gotten used to.

The bedroom is patched up and I could sleep in there if I wanted, but I need to be within eye-shot of Aurora. Especially now. We don't fight often, and I feel like absolute shit.

Lucifer hops up onto the armrest and immediately begins purring like a possessed creature. I never pet him or feed him, so I'm still mystified by what the hell he wants from me. Still, his eyes track me as if I owe him something.

I stare into the next room at the lump of Aurora's body in bed.

My jaw clenches tight, a vise of frustration and help-lessness. She's thrust me into an impossible situation.

The princess wants a normal life. One without fear, without her curse dictating every move she makes. I want that for her. Fae lords, I want it more than anything.

But she's starving.

That agony is growing, a pressure cooker ready to explode. She's pretending she can manage it, acting as if this hunger is a test of willpower rather than a merciless compulsion.

She wants freedom. I want her safe. Two goals that shouldn't feel so far apart but do. A part of me seethes with anger that she won't return home where I can control the situation. Instead, I can only witness her suffering, para-lyzed and powerless. It's tearing me apart inside.

The couch digs into my spine while Lucifer curls up on my boots. Apparently, he owns them now. Eventually, exhaustion claims me, and I drift into a fitful sleep just before sunrise.

WHEN I WAKE, it's with a start.

Something's off.

The air carries the charged stillness of a summer storm. Still, yet vibrating with tension. Her magic—normally a faint hum beneath the surface—has changed. It pulses erratically, uneven as a heart that can't find its rhythm.

I push upright. My eyes snap to the bedroom door, open as always but the sheets are an empty pool.

Dread curls low in my gut, and I'm on my feet.

Lucifer leaps onto the spot I just vacated, tail twitching.

The erratic hum of power leads me to the bathroom. My

stomach knots. The door is closed, steam curling from beneath it, dense and unnatural.

"Aura?"

No answer.

Two steps take me across the hall, and I open the door. Her power billows into my face, carrying the chill of death itself. On the other side of the translucent curtain, her body is slumped in the tub, barely more than a silhouette. The sight hits me so hard my chest seizes, ribs refusing to expand.

I surge forward and yank the curtain back, the rings rattling against the metal bar. The icy stream of water is still pounding on her skin. I twist the knob off with more force than necessary, cursing under my breath.

"Aura," I say sharply, crouching down beside the tub. "Come on. Look at me. Say something."

She doesn't flinch. Her head remains bowed, hair plastered to her face, lips tinged with blue. Heavy magic leaks off her in thick, nauseating waves, the air bending and shuddering. Not pulsing with life—devouring it. As if her curse has turned inward, feeding on her own soul.

"Shit." I rip off my jacket, fast and clumsy, and cocoon her in it, a barrier between us. Even through the thick fabric, her skin is arctic. She shivers violently, a low moan rattling out of her, and for a terrifying second, I think she might slip under completely.

"Aura," I rasp, crouching lower, voice a fractured edge. "Stay with me. Move. Please, move." I give her a gentle shake.

Her head lolls to the side with a groan. "Talon."

My relief is short-lived. She's responsive, but she needs help.

I slide my arms under her and lift her out of the tub,

keeping the jacket between us. Her wet hair clings to her cheeks, her breath shallow. Each step toward the bedroom is a negotiation with balance as I try to make sure she doesn't brush against my bare chest.

We reach the bed, and I lay her down with more care than I've ever used in my life. I tuck the blankets around her, needing them to anchor her to this world. Looking down at her, the heat of my worry scorches my throat while I fight the urge to hold her closer than I should.

Fear coils through my body, taut bands tightening around every molecule. With each passing moment they squeeze tighter.

Aurora is starving. She won't go home and even if we did try to go back, it would take too much time. The obvious pain she is in compounds my helplessness as she groans and rocks back and forth.

But I'm not helpless. It's my duty to protect her. My princess. My Aura.

And I'll do whatever it takes.

I yank open a drawer in the kitchen and grab my phone. I got it quickly after we arrived, along with a special cover that ensures I won't melt the damn thing.

I hated the contraption at first. It may be a necessary evil to function in the Common World, but the learning curve is still too steep for my liking.

Now it's a lifeline.

The device is still unfamiliar to me, and it takes a frustratingly long time for me to use until I finally get what I want.

I planned for this. It felt like a betrayal at first, but all regret melts as I focus on what I need to do.

What Aura needs.

A sexual encounter.

The internet is a hub where most flock when they need the promise of touch or release. It takes almost no time at all to set up a rendezvous with someone. I wish I had more time to vet the situation, the target, but I don't.

I grab the pack I've stashed under the couch. All I need now is to collect Aurora.

This time, I find her on the bed, crumpled in a ball, rocking back and forth, eyes shut tight from the pain of starving.

"Come on. We're going." Even as I command it, I go to the dresser and pull out a few of her items.

Aura's eyes open, glossy and bloodshot. "What? Where?"

Thank fae lords she is up, but I still see her actively being eaten alive.

"You are going to do exactly what I tell you, when I tell you."

She sits up, her spine stiffening. "What's happening? What did you do?"

"What I always do." My words are harsh, not with anger but with stress, but she recoils all the same. "Take care of things. You are going to feed."

Aura stands, hands visibly trembling as she pulls on the baggy clothes I set out.

It kills me to see her like this, but I shove down those feelings. I will do what must be done.

Fifteen minutes later, we are in a motel room I paid for in cash, keeping Aura out of sight. Though the attendant seemed as though a bomb could go off around him, and he'd barely blink.

Once in the shabby room, Aura paces, rubbing her arms with growing agitation.

"I can't, Talon. I'll kill them. And we don't know this person. We don't know—"

"No. You won't." The words shoot out so firm, so commanding she stops dead in her tracks. "I won't let you. Now put this on."

I pull the crystal chains out of the small pack I brought and put them on the bed. Aura backs up quickly as she regards the familiar dress of jewels with a mixture of terror and revulsion.

She doesn't want to go back to this. She doesn't want to be what she's always been. It's why she ran.

But I can't let her be in this pain. No, fuck that. I won't *let* her be in this pain.

"Aura."

She lifts her tortured, miserable gaze to meet mine. My insides crack, but I don't let it show.

"Do you trust me?" I ask as if I have everything under control.

A beat, and then she nods slowly.

"Put it on," I say a little more gently this time.

Aura's shoulders slump as she walks to the bed, eyes glassy with unshed tears. As she touches the jeweled strands, her expression hardens.

She knows what she needs to do to survive.

Good girl.

I peel off my jacket the same time she strips down. Aura shivers as the glittering chains slide over her flesh, cold no doubt.

No matter how many times I've seen Aura's naked form, I am always in awe. I love every inch of her. I can't help but torture myself yet again with thoughts of all the things I would do if I were able to worship her body the way I dream of.

In this drab motel room of moss green and mustard colors, she is a jewel of vibrancy and seduction.

"Don't look at me like that," she says with sudden force.

I startle. "Like what?"

"Like everyone else does. Like I'm your wet dream come true. Like I'm some perfect untouchable *thing* you can only fantasize about. " The last words come out on a sneer.

I open my mouth and close it. I'm not sure if this new blatant way of speaking her feelings is because of the company she keeps now, or if she's always felt this way and has only now given herself permission to say it out loud.

Okay, it's probably the latter.

Fine. We're not at the castle anymore? The rules are different? We're saying what we're thinking now?

"You *are* my every dream come true, Aura. And it's not because you're perfect, because you're not."

Aura's shoulders tense as her chin lifts.

"Did you know you have a splotchy freckle on your ass?" I raise an eyebrow. "Very unsightly."

Her mouth drops open and then closes a few times like a fish out of water.

"You snore. You never put the cap back on anything. Jars, bottles, toothpaste. I've lost count of the number of times I've grabbed something only to have it spill all over me. It's infuriating. Your laugh? You start with this normal sound, but then it wheezes out like you're eighty years old and dying. It's horrifying. You're impossible when you're hungry. Worse than impossible. You become a nightmare gremlin. Snapping, pacing, biting people's heads off until someone throws food at you from a safe distance. You refuse to admit when you're wrong. I could *prove* something to you, have it written down, signed by the fae lords themselves, and you'd still argue with me out of pure, stubborn spite. You are messy. Not cute messy. Clothes *everywhere*, dishes left in the sink for eternity, your hair tangled in the drain like a horror show."

She glares daggers, and I want every one buried in me.

"See, princess? You're not perfect, and yes, you are *absolutely* my dream. You and I both know that I dream of making you scream, of being the one you feed on, because even with all of your many flaws, I'd let you suck the life out me through my dick, lips, or otherwise."

A knock on the door interrupts us before Aura can respond.

"Let me do the talking," I order.

She nods, but her eyes remain wide with astonishment, her mouth slightly agape, as if she's struggling to comprehend what I lay bare.

"One more thing." I grab another item from the bag. A jeweled collar with a long chain. I walk to her. "Lift your hair." The command comes out husky even though I don't mean it to. I could even let her put it on, but I do it myself anyway.

Never looking away from me, she lifts her hair, her breasts rising up toward me like an offering with the motion. I'm careful not to touch her as I fasten the collar around her long, elegant neck. My mouth turns dry with the need to run my tongue over the column of her throat. Warmth and energy crackle in the short space between our bodies.

Aura searches my eyes, though I'm not sure what she's looking for.

"I've got you," I say, giving the collar a short little double tug. A whimper escapes her, and I'm nearly undone. I step back, and she drops her hair.

Then I cross the distance to the door and open it.

"Thank you for coming," I say to the woman I've been expecting.

I promise. I won't let you die.

The promise is a silent vow to myself, to Aura, and to this woman.

I keep my promises.

LICKING MERRY
AURORA

A beautiful woman walks through the doorway in a tan trench coat. She's a little older than both Talon and I. Thick, curled dark hair falls over her shoulders, and her makeup is heavy, dramatic and sensual.

As Talon closes the door behind her, she takes me in, brows lifting in surprise.

There's no preamble. I'm naked and adorned.

"Aura, this is Merry."

"Hi." She waves a little shyly.

I do my best to give her a reassuring smile, but I'm out of my depth. Not only because this is a new playing field where the rules aren't as clear and it's an unfamiliar setting, but also because Talon just dropped his feelings on me like it was nothing.

Despite having an immunity to my power, sometimes I convince myself he lusts after me the way everyone else does. That he is victim to my power, and my actual self is a far distant being.

Well, he blew that out of the water.

My hot guardian made it completely clear that I am far

from perfect, and that he sees all my unattractive qualities, and he wants me just as I am. All that I am.

The volume on my screaming hunger dialed down as I took that in. Now I'm standing here, and I'm supposed to feed off this woman and not acknowledge my heart is in a vise grip, like he reached into my chest and gripped it with his fist and hasn't let go.

Some part of me doesn't want him to let go.

"You're..." Merry scans my form up and down before glancing back at Talon with uncertainty. Her gaze lingers on his scales.

"We're from the Realm of Roses. You said you didn't discriminate against race," Talon says, brows furrowing but he's already anticipating a problem. It's what he does. Assess and mitigate risk.

Half her mouth quirks up in a smile. "I was going to say you're *both* very pretty."

"Oh, uh, thank you." Talon says. His tone is gruff, and it occurs to me he rarely hears that. I certainly don't tell him. I figured he's always been painfully aware of how gorgeous he is, but maybe he's not. People seem to whisper it from a distance rather than have the courage to say it to his face.

"You're also beautiful," I tell Merry, meaning it.

I've always believed beauty lives in everyone, in the way creases of compassion line the face, or how desire can turn awkward limbs into poetry. But the truth is, most of the people I've been sent to feed on weren't just flawed. They were predators. Monsters with charming grins. Feeding off them didn't feel like stealing, it felt like justice.

Merry is different.

She's kind. Open. Eager, yes, but not desperate. Not dark. And that scares me more than anything. Because it means I can't hide behind morally gray lines or pretend I'm doing the world a favor.

This is for me. For survival.

And I don't want to ruin someone soft and good with my hunger.

"So, you like to watch?" Merry asks Talon.

"You said you were okay with that," he says. Always confirming the rules and boundaries.

"Oh, I am," she says, her hands fiddling with the belt of her trench coat. "Though if you decide to join in, I wouldn't be opposed either." A hunger deepens in her eyes, and she looks back and forth between us.

Talon and I exchange a look. She doesn't know what he is. With our silent exchange we agree there is no reason to elaborate more than is necessary.

"Thank you, but I prefer to remain an observer in this event." He's polite, but firm.

She nods, moving her attention to me. With seductive grace, she comes to stand before me. "Well, shall we get started?"

"Yes, please," I say. The hunger inside me roils and rips in excitement. "May I?" I ask, poising my hands over her coat ties.

"Please," she nods, openly eager.

My body clenches with anticipation.

I untie her coat and slide it over her shoulders, making sure the material scrapes against her skin, intentionally exciting her senses. My power catches a whiff of her arousal and it's like a delectable fruit sliding along my tongue with its sweetness.

The relief of a mere taste has tears springing to my eyes.

Don't cry. Don't cry. Don't be weird.

Merry is clad in a corset, panties, and stockings held up

by garters. "You smell good," I say. It's true, an inviting cherry blossom perfume emanates from her skin.

"So do you," she says. "Like a light, sweet candy."

My anxiety lessens slightly as I realize how well Talon chose for me, yet again. Women are lovely to be with in a different way from men, as there is often a genuine mutual admiration and complimentary nature to the exchange.

I lightly push her hair away from the smooth skin of her shoulders and lean in, slowly enough to give her time to move away. When she doesn't shy back, I press my lips to hers experimentally. They are soft and taste sweet, compelling me to deepen the kiss and slide my tongue past her teeth. When I gain entry, she moans.

I can't wait any longer.

I sip from her sexual energy. It's the barest trickle but the relief of knowing it is the first taste of a meal I desperately need is near overwhelming.

My hands skate teasingly over her arms and body, and she does the same in kind. Soon we are devouring each other, hands mussed in hair, limbs sliding and pressing against each other.

Oh fuck. Oh fuck. I need more.

Merry licks and sucks down my jaw as she plucks and pulls at my nipples. My eyes flutter and I meet Talon's hot, focused gaze.

Gratitude swirls and deepens my arousal, and I try to convey it to him with my eyes. We've spent more time speaking through our eyes than with our mouths, though that's been changing recently.

Still, I recognize his relief for me. He can't stand me in pain. Not from a splinter or a bruise. I'll be sure to point out how annoying that is to him later, since he was so generous to share all my faults.

And yet I want him too. Flaws and all. Deeply, forever.

For the thousandth time, I wish it was him touching me. I wish it was his fingers finding my slit the way Merry is, gently running his fingers along it, spreading my wetness and causing my stomach to coil tight with slow building anticipation.

I dream of it being his lips tugging at my aching nipples, pulling and teasing them, sending electric shocks down to my sex.

Talon's intense expression never changes but his stance shifts, and I know he hears my thoughts. I'm broadcasting them as loudly as I can.

I want you with me.

I want you in me.

I always want you.

A hunger pang strikes me in the gut, and I turn my attention back to Merry, kissing her thoroughly until she comes away panting.

Another sip. *Delicious.*

"Shall we?" she says, tilting her head toward the bed.

I nod.

"Wait." Talon stops me with a word. He picks up the long chain attached to the collar. It could extend across the length of the room, but he wraps a significant amount of it around his fist while giving me plenty of slack. He nods, signaling me to join Merry on the bed.

Again, we speak with our eyes.

I won't let you hurt her. You're safe.

I nod back.

Sliding between Merry's legs, we plunder each other's mouths, exhilarating in the soft supple skin of each other. I tear down the corset and tease and tug at her tight brown nipples with my teeth as my fingers rub at the lace panties.

I press the roughness of the material against her clit and lower lips until they're soaked.

Merry's head falls back, and she moans, surrendering to my touch. Another sip.

Fuck. Fae lords. Thank witchtitting gods.

The pain of starvation is slowly but surely being replaced by Merry's sexual energy. Soon her corset is gone, and she's bare from the waist up.

I already know this meal might be the best I've ever had since I've never been so hungry, and she is so very lovely.

Dropping down to my knees, I tug her panties to the side and swipe up her wet pussy with my tongue. Her hips jerk as she gives a pleasured shout. Oh lords, she tastes like honeyed lust, and I'm lost.

The cold crystal chain traces my spine, leading to where he has a hold on my collar. My mouth works harder against Merry, her taste coating my tongue, her moans vibrating down my throat. I spread for him anyway, ass high, offering him the view. The shame of it, the heat of it, the way I'm performing for both of them at once—it makes me wetter than I can stand.

Merry grabs the headboard behind her as my tongue quickly swipes and dips inside her honey. Then I'm suckling, attacking her clit, my hands pushing her thighs further apart, spreading her like a meal for me. And she is.

I take my first substantial drink of her energy.

Oh fuck.

It's so good, hot stinging prickles attack the backs of my eyes. I'm close to weeping with relief.

I need to go slow, but I can't stop myself. I drink her sexual energy in deeply a second time.

A harsh jerk, the crystal chain scraping between my ass cheeks as Talon yanks me out of it.

Too much.

This time I want to cry from frustration, but he's right. I was taking too much, too soon.

As if sensing the dynamic needs to change, Merry directs me up and turns me around so I'm facing Talon up on my knees. Pressed to my back, Merry plays with my breasts, dropping hot kisses over my shoulders. My hips jerk. The apex of my thighs is dripping wet.

Finally, her manicured hand finds my mound. I shout in relief as her fingers rub at my clit. I'd curve over if she weren't holding me up against her with the other hand, still playing with my breast.

"Do you want it slow or fast?" Her husky words send a shiver through me.

"Slow." My request is raspy.

I look directly into Talon's eyes as she rubs me with deliberate and steady strokes.

I'm trying so hard to be careful, to not lose focus. Grounding myself in Talon helps.

"Spread me so he can see," I tell her.

Surprise registers only slightly on Talon's dark expression, but I know he's rocked by me voicing that out loud.

It feels like we are putting on a show for him. He's always been privy to my sex life, but this time I'm deliberately involving him.

"Sit back." Merry directs, not even hesitating.

Sitting with my legs spread, knees up, Merry wraps her arms around me to pull my lower lips apart.

"You like that view?" Merry asks, directly addressing Talon.

His throat bobs and his weight shifts again. A hand brushes by the front of his pants as if he is resisting the urge to either rearrange himself or grab hold.

He never has. Not once.

I know he gets aroused. Every time. Despite his serious nature, he is affected. Every time he watches.

But we're out here in the Common World. New rules.

My tongue pushes against my teeth, hard. Can I ask him? This is a new line we'd be crossing. If we cross too many, someone will get hurt.

"Unzip your pants." My voice is hoarse. I'm not sure if it's from Merry dipping a finger into me even as she holds me open, or from the emotional weight of asking Talon for something so personal, for something I desperately want.

He stills. A form frozen by my words.

I can't breathe, anticipation wrapping around my ribcage in constricting straps.

Talon's brows lower in a near glower as he shakes his head no.

A tearing, ripping pain goes through me. A feeling I've never known before, it takes me a moment to identify it.

Rejection.

I've never experienced it before. And it hurts and tears at me like a bitch with razor sharp claws.

Is it this embarrassing and unbearable for everyone else? How do people bear it?

Anger rises in me. At him? At our situation? At myself for even voicing what I want?

I'm so stupid. Talon is always in control, and I'm just this pathetic uncontrollable curse he takes care of and cleans up after.

A weird flash of him accusing me of never putting the cap back on anything hits me.

Good. I hope everything he touches spills all over him. I want things to feel as messy and out of control for him as it does for me.

"More," I whisper to Merry, reaching up to fondle my own breast.

Merry slides a finger up into me, and I groan at the addictive sensation of being penetrated.

"Don't you wish you were touching her?" Merry addresses Talon as she pumps in and out of me.

He stiffens, still not used to being addressed.

"She's so wet. So tight." Merry's words are strained as if she's pained by how good it is. She seems to pick up on my need to torture him. A second finger joins the first, and she uses her other hand to rub my clit. I moan, and my hips buck for more.

A wicked smile curves my lips as Talon shifts again. We're pushing his buttons, but I want to slam down on them.

I writhe and roll my hips as if it were a dance for him to watch. The tension in my body swells higher, coiling tighter, sending hot tingles toward a place I'm desperate to go. I'm groaning and whimpering as I buck against Merry's skilled hands.

I turn my head and kiss her, putting on a show with a wide open, tongue fueled mating of the mouth.

When we break the kiss, she meets Talon's eye again. "Want me to tell you how she tastes?"

Talon's mouth parts then closes. Then he gives an almost imperceptible nod.

He wants it. He wants me.

The earlier rejection still hurts, but at least we are both being tortured.

She redirects me so I'm still on display for Talon. He has a perfect view of her spreading my legs and dipping down to swipe a tongue up my sex.

"Ungh." The sensation and need hit me so hard, my stomach flexes as my body curves, desperate for more.

"Mmm," Merry says, making a show of licking her lips before dropping between my legs and spearing her tongue into me. "She tastes like she smells. Like sex and sweet candies. I don't think I'll ever forget this delicious little cunt. You don't know what you're missing." Her wide, slow laps drag up my folds, each one forcing my knees higher. She sticks her own two fingers into her mouth until they are wet and glistening before sliding them into me, though I've been making a mess of the bed for the last fifteen minutes.

"Ah, please, yes." I arch my back, pushing into the sensation.

"Yours may be the prettiest pussy I've ever seen or tasted." Merry says it with near reverence, continuing to finger fuck me at a steady pace. She drops and suckles my clit, sending shooting pleasure skyrocketing even faster toward where I want to go.

The waves of sexual power we're creating practically roar in my ears, and I could drink it all and not leave a drop. I start to drink again, trying very hard to go slow. To not swallow it all. I don't want to hurt Merry, but oh gods, I need to feed. I need to come. I need everything and I need it right now.

My internal muscles flex along with my abdomen as I gasp. I'm so close. I'm so fucking close.

I drink deeply.

A painful yank at my throat stops me.

Too much, again.

I blink. Talon's glower is deeper, darker than usual, and I don't know if it's because I'm near losing control or because he is.

"You said you like toys." Talon's voice is gravelly.

Merry stops. "Yeah, in my purse. Would you be so kind?"

Again, he's being asked to participate. Talon does as she asks, grabbing her bag. He touches what's inside before pulling back. It's what he does to test if he can touch something without scorching it. Whatever it is passes the test, so he reaches in again only to pull out a sizable two-sided dildo. My throat goes dry seeing the size of it. I clench in need and anticipation.

Merry sits on her heels, creating space around me. "Why don't you just slide it on in there for her?" A wicked smile curves her lips as she gives Talon the go ahead.

Panic, fear, and need grip me all at once. We've never done this.

Talon watches. He protects. He doesn't get involved. I see the same mix of reactions in his eyes as he freezes, likely trying to figure out what he should do.

But I want it. Caution is long gone with him so near. I'm desperate to come, and with Merry right there, rhythmically fingering herself, stimulating herself and waiting for a little show. This is exciting her.

I widen my legs even farther, tilting my hips upward. "Please."

Blazing orange sparks flash in Talon's eyes which causes a shiver to roll through my body. His grip on the sex toy tightens and he steadies one palm on the bed, careful not to touch me as he presses it to my entrance.

It's not just a sex toy.

It's not just a regular feeding, even as I sip more of Merry's arousal.

This is *Talon*. This is the man I dream of every night, pushing a thick ribbed toy into me. To keep from instinctively reaching up and burying my fingers in his hair, I claw at the sheets under me. The magnetism I need to fight breaks my heart, but I also want this more than anything.

"Give her a couple pumps," Merry directs.

The fear in Talon's eyes is so real, it might as well be my own. Crouched over but not touching me, he drags the toy out before driving it in again, filling me almost to the point of pain.

It's so fucking damn good. It may be the best. Simply because it's him giving me this feeling. Of course, I don't feel even a drop of sexual energy from him to feed on. We are null and void to each other in that respect but in no other. He slides it in a second time.

A shuddering breath escapes him, and his skin and scales glisten with a sheen of sweat that wasn't there five minutes ago.

Then he's across the room. Distance spreading between us with a cold discomfort I instantly hate, because it feels like a rejection yet again.

The feeling is erased as soon as Merry maneuvers herself on the other end of the toy. We gyrate with push and pull, needing, wanting more. The room brims with sex, and I drink.

Merry rubs my clit with quick, jerky motions. I fly apart in bright hot sparks, coming hard and fast.

A waterfall of shudders grips my pussy, as I choke out a scream, the same time I drink Merry in, satiating myself on every level.

I ignore the yank at my throat. I keep coming. I keep feeding.

"Aura."

I vaguely register Talon's voice from far away.

The yank comes so hard this time I'm jerked off the bed and off the toy.

I cry out in pain, fingers flying up to the collar cutting into my neck.

"I'm sorry, I'm sorry," Talon rushes to say. "I'm so sorry." His words come out tortured.

A cold wash of fear goes over me as I find myself on the floor, looking at Merry's unmoving body on the bed. I cover my mouth as regret and fear choke its way down my throat.

"No. Oh no. Oh no, no, no." I chant the words, rocking back and forth.

I've killed Merry.

CHAPTER 16

JOLLY ROGER RUM WITH RAP

TALON

Aura rocks back and forth on the carpet, covering her mouth, but I still hear the stream of words from under her hand. "I couldn't have killed her. I'm still hungry. I'm still so very hungry. I couldn't have done that to her. I'm a fucking monster."

"Shh," I try to hush her. Not just to soothe her, but because I need to listen. I cross over to the bed and bend over to where Merry lays on her side, eyes closed. I hold my hand close to her open mouth. One, then two, then three little puffs of air hit my skin.

"She's alive." My shoulders sag in relief. I worried I didn't pull Aura back in time. She wouldn't stop until I literally dragged her away. I didn't want to be so rough, but I had to do it.

Aura still rocks back and forth, eyes wide, mouth covered. Something is very wrong.

I crouch down so I'm directly in front of her.

"Aurora, look at me." She still isn't responding. It's as if she's receded to some place far within her mind where I can't reach. I clench my fists to keep from grabbing her shoulders and giving her a shake.

"Aurora," I practically shout.

She blinks, finally focusing on me. "Merry is alive. She's just passed out. She's going to be okay. Take a couple deep breaths."

She does. First one, then two, then she bursts into sobs.

Driving her fists into her eyes, Aurora wails out with heart-wrenching cries of agony.

Oh fae lords, I can't stand to see her cry. Her cries rake through me, leaving my insides shredded and raw.

I can't stop it. I can't comfort her.

"Aura, please, Aura, tell me, what is it?" It could be anything, but I have to know what's torturing her. She's unresponsive again and my desperation grows. "Baby, please, tell me."

The pet name slips out before I can call it back. Another line crossed.

I've overstepped too many times, but I can't give a damn right now.

It does the trick though. Aura drops her hands so I can see her beautiful, blotchy tear-stained face.

"I'm still hungry," she sobs and hiccups. "It hurts to be hungry. And I was so scared I hurt her. I don't want to hurt her. I don't want to be like this. I don't want to be me. Oh fae lords, why can't I be anyone else? I almost can't bear it."

"I know," I say between more soothing hushes. "It's okay. Everything is okay. I know it hurts."

"Say it again," she says, squeezing her eyes shut tight and drawing her knees into her body.

I don't know what she means for a second. Then I realize. "I know it hurts, *baby*. It's going to be okay, sweetheart." With each pet name I let past my lips, she calms a bit more, though I immediately form an addiction to calling her every sweet thing I've always wanted to.

This is not good.

"If I could, I'd put my arms around you and never let you go," I say, unable to stop myself.

Aura looks up at me with a beautifully hopeful expression that makes every part of me feel alive.

"You could cry all over my shoulder and I'd just keep holding you."

"Even if I'm snotty and I get it on you?" she asks, wiping her nose with her arm at the same time.

I nod solemnly. "I wouldn't let you pull away or use a tissue, even if you tried."

The tiniest of smiles breaks through and it's like sunshine after a brutal winter.

"Help me make her comfortable, and we'll go home," I say.

"Home," she repeats, a wariness in her eye.

"To the apartment," I clarify. Aurora nods and gets up off the floor. She disappears to the restroom, leaving me for a moment. I scrub my fingers through my hair. I take a moment to process this shit show.

No. We did good.

Everything is okay.

I didn't touch Aurora.

She didn't kill Merry.

Though the hard boundaries that have always been there are no more than broken lines of sand now, and I don't know what that means or what the consequence will be, but things are changing. They are changing faster than I can control, and the worst part is I want them to.

I've regained my composure by the time Aurora returns. With her help, we reposition Merry in bed so she is comfortably tucked in. Aurora even rolled off the stockings and took off the constricting garter, saying it's not fun to wake up pinched.

We buy a couple water bottles and snacks from the vending machine and leave them on the bedside table for Merry when she wakes.

Then we're gone.

~

AFTER ASSURING MERRY WAS ALIVE, we rushed to the apartment to clean up and change for our shifts at Poison Apple.

The whiplash of it sits heavy in my chest. One moment, I'm dragging Aurora off the floor, her sobs ripping through the air. The next, we're stepping back into a bar lit up in neon and noise, pretending none of it happened. Pretending she didn't nearly drain someone dry.

But she does it. Slides behind the bar like nothing earth-shattering happened.

I take my usual post at the front, checking IDs and scanning for trouble, but my eyes are never far from her. At least I got her to eat. Granted she doesn't share the unhealthy obsession for The Salty Bastard food that I have, but I had to take control when she became barely responsive. She had half a lobster roll and some fries.

Every hour, I do a circuit. Bounce a belligerent drunk, clock the regulars, intervene just enough to keep order. But I always find my way back to the booth near the door, always keeping her in my sightline.

Aurora's still hungry. I can see it in the way her shoulders tighten when someone gets too close, in the way her laughter always ends a beat too soon. But the wildness in her power has dulled. She's sharper, focused. Pouring drinks and joking with the other girls.

She looks okay.

But I know better.

Earlier, Merry messaged me through the hookup app. Said the night was unreal, apologized for passing out, claimed that never happens. She offered to meet again.

That won't be happening. That kind of contact draws attention we can't afford.

~

HOURS LATER, the night has exhaled. The doors are locked. Music hums low through the speakers, meant only for the staff now. Chairs are flipped. The scent of lemon cleaner hangs in the air.

Aurora's still behind the bar, sleeves rolled up, practicing bottle flair with a half-filled plastic one. It slips mid-spin and clatters to the floor.

"Still not a flair master, huh?" Snow teases, perched on a barstool with a mop resting across her shoulders like a sword.

"It's the bottle," Aurora huffs, retrieving it. "She's a slippery little traitor. Betrayed me mid-spin."

Ariel, seated at the end of the bar with a bucket of clean towels in her lap, grins. "Maybe if you stop naming your bottles and forming emotional attachments, they won't betray you."

"I only name the ones I like," Aurora says with mock indignation. She lifts the bottle again, narrowing her eyes. "You get one more chance, Elena."

Snow snorts so hard she nearly drops her phone. "Elena?"

Ariel is there taking photo after photo with her camera.

From across the room, I sink back into my booth, elbows resting on the table, watching them. Letting the moment settle.

Aurora will need to feed again.

Moving here and pretending she could outrun her curse and deny her needs hasn't panned out. We haven't discussed it, but I doubt she'll submit to going home.

She was not fully satisfied today which means she'll likely need to feed sooner. A matter of weeks? Maybe even days?

Can we keep doing this? Keep going to seedy motels and arranging hookups that I need to constantly yank her back from the brink of killing?

Do we become vigilantes as I try to stalk the night and find bad people that the world would be better off without? I don't know this world. Not like our own. Back in the Realm of Roses I had contacts, I knew when things were amiss and where darkness went to nest. Here I lack the advantage and have no idea I would get it.

I rub my forehead as a tightness forms around my skull, signaling the beginning of a headache.

A couple glasses clank down hard in front of me, causing me to start.

"You look like you need a drink."

I look up to see Rap slide in the oversized booth, setting a bottle of brown liquor with an illustration of a ship being tossed on a tumultuous ocean next to the two glasses.

"Jolly Roger Rum," she says, doling out two healthy pours. "It's good shit."

I take her offering and clink glasses before giving it a healthy slug. It's sweet and smooth with a burn that only fans my inner fire. Rap kicks back the rest of hers and waits for me to do the same before pouring again.

This one slightly dulls my thoughts, and I feel a small sense of relief.

"Already better, huh?" she asks while looking at the glass she rolls between her fingers.

How does this woman seem to see into things so well?

"Yeah. Tough. . .week."

Rap nods as if in solidarity, though she has no idea what the past twenty-four hours have been.

"So...Dragons. They have a lot of interesting features." She pours another glass for both of us. This time I only sip it, wary of the bar owner.

"Their flesh burns flesh. They breathe fire. Very few of their kind left, or so we think. They are solitary creatures."

I don't know why she's listing all my traits to me. It's all very conversational, but the rum buzz is really kicking up in my stomach and loosening my muscles.

"You know a lot about my kind," I say. Perhaps she wants credit yet again for sussing me out? Though that doesn't seem right. This woman doesn't acquire information for vanity's sake. No, she gathers it for protection.

"I also know Dragons are immune to a lot of other fae powers." Her voice is low, casual, like we're just chatting after hours, but I know better. She's measuring me.

The bar owner swirls the rum in her glass. "Take the Rosari, for example. Most people think they move out to those lush, peaceful lands for the slower pace of life, but there's more to it." Her gaze flicks toward the darkened end of the bar where Aurora's laugh carries. "The Rosari are what some call energy vampires. Their regions attract people riddled with anxiety, emotional instability, burnout.

It's symbiotic—the Rosari feed off that excess energy, and in return, the humans feel lighter. More balanced."

She pauses long enough to refill both our glasses.

"But there's a rumor among the Rosari," she says more softly. "That there is a monster in the castle."

I'm careful not to look at Aurora. "Every place has rumors. Silly myths."

"True." She tips her glass toward me. "Some people say there is a leprechaun in the Boston gardens. That the ghost of a young motorcyclist haunts Route 44. That there is a literal underground network of information in Boston, a massive black market run by fae creatures."

"A leprechaun?" I ask with a snort.

Rap nods solemnly. Then she runs a finger around the rim of her glass. "The Rosari's myth of a monster includes the fact that this monster can feed on other fae. That humans, fae, and mage alike disappear, never to be found again."

"Sounds like your leprechaun," I say, taking a heavy draft.

When I put the glass down, Rap is studying me with her cutting green gaze.

"You're not the monster the Rosari speak of, are you?" It's not a question. "It's her, isn't it?" That one is a question.

CHAPTER 17

SLAP ON A PAIR OF FAE FABRIC GLOVES AND FINGER DIDDLE ME

TALON

Rap doesn't shoot a glance at Aurora, but she doesn't have to.

Every fiber of my being stiffens defensively. Fight or flight in my body is activated, and I'm not sure which mode is necessary.

"She's Rosari, but she's different from the others." Rap's voice is so low, only I can hear it. "What does she feed on, Talon?"

My lips pull tight. I force down the snarl climbing my throat.

If this woman so much as thinks about hurting or exploiting Aurora, I'll tear her apart. No one will ever find the body—or rather, the ash.

"You appear human," I say, echoing her earlier phrasing, "but you're different from the others?"

I've been watching her since the moment we met. She may run a bar in a human city, but Rap is anything but human. There are remnants of power in her, but it's been hacked off, like a limb. The absence of it leaves a bleeding, jagged edge to her.

"I've traveled a lot. Met a lot of different beings, Rapunzel." I use her full name deliberately. "I've seen another like you." My gaze drifts to her colorful braided mohawk with a pointed message. "Don't think for a second I won't use what I know to protect that girl over there."

To her credit, Rap barely flinches. Just the tiniest twitch under one eye.

My blood is ancient, and it is immune to her power, should she choose to access it.

Rap calmly sips her drink, her eyes lowered.

"Good," Rap says. "I may not know what she feeds on, but I know that girl has been locked up for far too long. I know all the signs." Something passes over her face. Something personal and painful. "No one should be locked away for what they are."

Then she looks over at Aura and Snow, who are bent over laughing so hard, tears are streaming down their eyes. Ariel has cast her head into her arm, shoulders heaving with laughter. Something about Aura practicing her bottle skills.

My heart tightens at seeing the unbridled, ridiculous joy Aura is experiencing.

"She's a good girl," Rap says, still watching.

"She is." The words come out rough, weighted with emotion.

When Rap meets my eye again, we are on a different playing ground. "I'm not going to hurt her, Talon. She's a Lost Girl now. She's one of mine. I protect my own."

Respect rises in me for this woman. There is so much more there than I could begin to guess, but I see enough.

I run a hand through my hair and throw back my fourth

glass she's poured, wondering if I'm about to yet again cross another line I shouldn't. "Succubus." The word is so quiet, I'm not even sure it passed my lips. "She was cursed to be a Succubus."

To Rap's credit, she doesn't react. She simply nods, eyes cast down as if thinking it through.

"I don't know how to help her," I say, in a rare moment of vulnerability fueled by the excellent liquor.

Rap jerks at that. "Don't be an idiot. You *are* helping her."

I rub my forehead.

"Hey."

Her "Hey," cracks like a whip, snapping my head up before I can stop it.

"Sometimes you can't fix it. Sometimes just showing up, being the one who stays, is the only thing that gets someone through."

It doesn't feel like enough. I'm her protector. I should force her to go home, to keep her in that safe bubble she hates.

More than that, I should be the one kissing her, touching her, feeding her. Instead, it's anyone but me.

It's always bothered me, but the rum allows me to admit to myself the pain of it has sharpened since we came to this place.

I'm back to holding my head in my hands. "It's complicated."

"You love her." Rap shrugs. "There's nothing complicated about that."

Her words strike me at the core.

It's not like I hide it, but there's something about having it so blatantly laid out. I'm hopelessly, madly, irreversibly in love with Aurora.

But Rap is wrong about one thing. Loving her is complicated because where I'll never get the satisfaction of expressing that love, she's taken away the one thing I clung to being able to provide. Safety.

As soon as Rap retreats to her office, Snow and Ariel insist Aurora and I head out for the night first, though we all live in the same building. They say we both look tired, and neither of us argue.

The girls are smart enough to know something is brewing, but they don't seem to push Aurora for answers. They give her space and encouragement as they can. Still, it's best we keep Aurora's...condition a secret, even from them.

As Aurora and I head down the street, the earlier events of the day begin to crowd in on us. The unspoken events become heavier with each step we take until I think she's going to avoid the whole thing.

"Thank you," she says finally. Contrary to how she was in the bar, she seems small, vulnerable now.

"You're welcome."

She gives me a weak smile.

"But we shouldn't be crossing all these lines. Involving me like that today is a bad idea. We can't do it again."

The smile disappears. Hurt flashes across her face, but it quickly turns into something else. "You didn't like it? You didn't like what you saw?"

They aren't questions, they are accusations.

I stop walking, forcing her to do the same. "Aura," I start as I scrub a hand over my face. "You know that's not it."

"Don't I? I'm constantly in a vulnerable position around you, and you couldn't give me a *little* vulnerability back?"

This is about me not undressing for her. Suddenly my temper flares too. "You *know* why. That path can only lead to pain. It's better not to entertain impossibilities. It will only hurt us both."

"Does it have to? Have we ever even tried, Talon? Snow asked me why you don't slap on a pair of fae fabric gloves and finger diddle me like you are always so clearly pining to do so."

"Finger diddle?" My brain short-circuits at the visual, equal parts horrified and tempted.

"Her words, not mine. Don't change the subject. The point is, I didn't have an answer for her, and I *should*. Because if two people love each other, they try to do everything they can to make it work, and we've never even given this thing," she waves a hand between us, "a real shot."

At that, I begin walking again. She has to scramble to catch up to my stride.

"Aura, I'm not entertaining this." I use my sternest tone to shut this down.

"But why?"

"Because," I roar, whirling on her. "You don't think I wanted to? You don't think I was affected, penetrating you? When I didn't keep fucking you with that toy like I wanted to, shoving and dragging it in and out until your legs collapsed and you gushed all over the damn sheets?"

My voice drops to a lethal rumble I've only ever used when I meant to kill someone. Never with her.

"It's because I want it so badly that I can't. We're crossing too many boundaries, acting as if I touch you, I won't sear your flesh off. It's only a matter of time before I forget myself, or you forget yourself and you get hurt, and I can't handle that. You think Snow came up with a revelation I've never considered? That I haven't already realized I could pull on a pair of gloves and finger fuck you until you convulse and come? Many, *many* times, Aurora."

Her eyes widen to saucers as she takes it all in. Some part of me can't believe she didn't know how much I've thought this through, tortured myself with ideas. "But all these scenarios end the same way. I hurt you, and neither of us get what we really want. Because unless it's *everything*, it won't be enough." The last word comes out on a hiss.

My spine stiffens as the night air is suddenly thick and charged, leaving my instincts prickling. Something is off.

"Talon, I—" Aurora starts.

A blur.

A *rush* of wind.

Something slams into my side with the force of a cannonball, throwing me into the brick wall so hard my vision sparks.

Aurora cries out, but before she can react, the shadow lunges for her, arms vise-tight around her body, *fangs bared* at her throat.

A vampire.

Not just *any* vampire. A hungry one. Desperate.

Aurora thrashes, snarling, but he grips her tight as his fangs pierce her throat.

For once, I don't hesitate to lay hands on someone. Roughly grabbing his bare arm, the vampire releases a loud cry of pain. I don't let go, not even after he's released Aurora and she stumbles back, covering her neck with a hand.

Despite the burning pain he must be suffering, the vampire throws a punch to my cheek. The contact throws me off-balance.

The second my grip slips, the vampire snarls and launches at me again—fangs bared, eyes wild.

I catch him by the throat mid-lunge and slam him against the opposite wall. Brick cracks behind him. My hand flares with heat.

"Bad choice," I growl.

Smoke curls between my fingers. His scream tears through the alley like a dying animal.

I hold him there, burning him from the inside out, until the stench of scorched flesh fills the air. It takes longer than it should, considering how desperate to feed he was.

Still, I don't let go until his thrashing turns to twitching. Until his body crumples to ash and bone at my feet.

Aurora stares, pale and wide-eyed. "Holy shit."

I shove down the shame and discomfort at her seeing how I've disposed of all the bodies. I'd been chosen by her parents because I'm unaffected by her power, but the sweet second benefit is no one can identify the ash I leave behind.

"We need to move," I bark, already ushering her toward the apartment, careful not to touch her. "Now."

We half-jog the remaining blocks, Aurora keeping pace beside me. Her breath is quick but even, the adrenaline still riding her hard. Mine isn't. I'm already doing the calculations. The questions. The *why*.

When we slam the door behind us and lock the deadbolt, the silence feels *too* loud.

Aurora paces, running a shaking hand through her pink hair. "What the hell was that? Was that random? Is that just what happens in the city? Like getting mugged?"

She knows that attack wasn't a coincidence.

Another sign she's too naive to be out here.

"No." I shake my head, still feeling the vampire's heat seared into my palm. "That was a Midnight Fae, Aura."

"He went straight for me," she says, pressing a palm to her throat, eyes unfocused. "He didn't hesitate."

"You've pulled a lot of attention lately," I say. "Being up on that stage every night. You've been recognized, and she knows who you are. Where you are."

Her eyes snap to mine. "You mean...Mal?" The name comes out a dry rasp.

I hesitate, then nod.

"She meant to kill you with that curse. She's sent a lackey to finish the job."

"Well..." her eyes are wide and glazed with fear, "fuck."

Couldn't have said it better myself.

CHAPTER 18

FOUND BY THE ENEMY

AURORA

Mal. The Midnight Fae who cursed me. She's trying to finish the job.

My parents caught her hovering over my crib, speaking a death curse onto me, but it didn't work out the way she wanted.

Then again, Midnight Fae aren't supposed to be able to wield magic.

After she was banished by her absolute asshole of a father, King Charming, she mysteriously developed a dark, unstable ability.

"Surely not," I protest. "It can't be her."

Talon looks at me with a flat expression, like he's talking to a child.

Maybe that's what I'm being. A child, trying to hide from the monster who doomed her.

Before I can react, Talon disappears into my bedroom. He grabs my bag and starts opening drawers, pulling out my clothes and shoving them in the pack.

I stop at the threshold, holding myself up by gripping the doorframe.

"What are you doing?" My voice sounds far away to my own ears.

"We're going back," he says without ceasing his motions.

Panic flares in me. I rush forward and grab the pack from him. Talon's gaze jerks up to meet mine, but he doesn't let go.

"No. No, we aren't going back."

His mouth opens then closes, and I can feel the frustration building in him. "Aura!" he finally bursts in exasperation. "We need to go back to where you'll be safe. You're starving here. You could hurt someone, or worse, you could get hurt. Do you know what finding you in the shower like that did to me?" His eyes blaze with orange embers.

"And now Mal is sending vampires to kill you?" He shakes his head. "No. We are leaving. Tonight."

The finality in his voice breaks my heart.

"No."

"No?" It's the most expression I've ever seen on his stupid, handsome, broody face and it's all exaggerated shock.

"No," I repeat, giving my backpack a little jerk, but he still won't let it go. "We aren't going back."

Talon's jaw locks. "You're being reckless."

"I'm being brave." My tone is sharper than I expect, but I don't back down. "For the first time in my entire life, I fed, and I didn't kill anyone. That's *never* happened before. Not once."

His grip tightens. "That doesn't mean it's safe to try again. You are still in pain. You're still *hungry*."

"I'm *changing*, Talon. You helped me change. Don't you get that? It wasn't just about surviving tonight. I did something *new*." I suck in a breath. "I didn't hurt her. That's groundbreaking for me."

He doesn't speak, but something flickers behind his eyes. He *knows* it matters. He just doesn't trust it to matter enough.

"I'm not running now," I continue. "Not because of some curse. Not because of Mal."

At the name, Talon flinches like I just lit a match under his skin. "She's *hunting* you."

"We don't even know that attack is connected to her," I protest.

His expression flattens and he blinks at me like I'm slow. "Vampire attacks rarely happen in the Common World, and even less in Boston, Aura. Not only is this a human city, but the coincidence is too uncanny."

I throw up my hands. "Well, she's been hunting me since I was born. She cursed me before I could *walk*. She's dictated every second of my life—what I could do, where I could go, who I could be."

His silence is suffocating, but I keep going.

"I'm done letting her rule me from the shadows. I won't be intimidated anymore. I won't run from everything I've wanted."

His hand is still on the pack. So is mine. The tension between us thrums with unspoken words and years of fear.

Then I glance at the window.

And our reflections are almost unrecognizable.

Me, in a torn band tee and fishnets, covered in spiky jewelry and tattoos, and holding my own like I never have before. Talon towering over me, carved from stone, but hesitating.

We're caught on opposite sides, holding my backpack

in a stalemate. But I don't see the princess I once was. I'm a Lost Girl now, and I decide my own fate.

I stare at that reflection and speak without looking at him.

"You think going back will keep me safe. But what's the point of being safe if I'm dead inside?"

His fingers don't loosen on the bag, but he stops pulling.

"You've seen it," I say, voice softer now. "Have you ever heard me laugh so much? I've never laughed like that in my life. Why would I want to go back to that castle, to rot in isolation with my secrets and shame?"

Talon doesn't answer, but his jaw ticks, like he's grinding down his resistance tooth by tooth.

"I've been in cages my whole life because I'm this dangerous creature," I whisper. "But today, you...you defused me. Not completely. But you showed me I could be more than what Mal made me. I could feed without killing. That's never happened before. Do you understand how groundbreaking that is?" My gaze locks on him with all the emotional weight I have. "If I leave now, I will lose all of this. I will lose *myself*."

We're frozen. Caught in this impasse. Both still holding the damn bag like it might anchor us to our sides of the argument.

THUMP.

Lucifer the cat jumps onto the bag with an angry yowl and lands full weight across the center, claws immediately sinking in.

"Shit," I gasp, letting go instinctively.

Talon curses and jerks his hand away at the same time. The bag drops to the floor with a dull *thunk*. Lucifer, unbothered, settles on top like a smug little goblin king.

We both stare at the devil cat who apparently thinks he's won the game we were playing.

Silence. Then I look at Talon. His gaze cuts to the bag, then to me.

He doesn't pick it up.

I've won at least one more night in Boston.

~

THE BLENDER SHRIEKS like it's possessed, a sticky mess of strawberry and something neon splattering across the counter. I hit the off switch too hard and curse under my breath, grabbing a rag to mop up the chaos.

Third time tonight.

I'm not usually this distracted on shift.

But then again, I'm not usually being *hunted*.

Talon's standing a few feet away, leaning at the end of the bar, sipping a glass of water. Always close. Always watching.

I told him we'd go back to the Realm of Roses if there was another attack. Swore it with a straight face and wide eyes and the tone I've perfected over the years—measured, believable, just desperate enough to be taken seriously.

He hasn't brought it up since. Instead, he hovers.

He's become my shadow. Not suffocating. Not controlling. Just...there. Always there.

When I pass too close, I feel the heat of him behind me, a quiet pressure against my back, gravity skewed by his presence. And at night, long after last call, I hear the thunderous flap of his wings above the building, circling the rooftop, a hellfire gargoyle in motion.

Protecting me.

Punishing himself.

The rag in my hand is soaked through. I toss it in the bucket and wipe my palms on my skirt, then rest my hands on the sticky edge of the bar. A pulsing, moody remix of something sad and sharp thrums under my feet. It suits my mood too well.

I scan the crowd but don't really *see* them. Just colors and motion and the occasional flare of a spark between lovers or enemies across the room.

Mal.

The name tastes like ash. It's been pounding in my skull since the vampire's fangs grazed my throat.

She's here. Or close enough to send her little monsters sniffing down alleys, trying to finish what she started.

And I'm supposed to go *home?*

Hide?

I'm not going back.

The blender shrieks again, and I whirl on the poor appliance like it insulted my boots. Ariel tosses me a look from down the bar, eyebrow raised in silent *"Are you okay?"*

I nod once. She doesn't press. None of them do. The girls seem to be giving me space, maybe even waiting for me to divulge why I've been acting so on edge. But I keep it to myself, even at our post shift hangouts in their apartment.

How are you doing?

Are you eating enough?

You look like shit—that one, courtesy of Snow.

The questions are careful, concerned, and though I want to spill my guts, I shove it all down deep. I give noncommittal answers and keep claiming that culture shock is a hell of a thing. I don't think they believe me though.

I thought I'd be afraid when Mal came back. I thought

I'd curl inward, collapse like I used to when I was little, and the curse burned too hot inside me, and no one knew how to help.

But I'm not scared now.

I'm angry.

So. Fucking. Angry.

She took my past. My future. My body. My choices. Turned me into a living curse and disappeared like a ghost, leaving me with death on my lips and guilt permanently lodged between my ribs.

And now she's sending assassins to finish the job?

No.

She doesn't get to choose how my story ends.

I grab another glass, fill it with ice, and slam the shaker lid on harder than necessary. The metal stings my palm. The rhythm of pouring and mixing helps keep the fury in check, but just barely.

This is my life now. Messy. Loud. *Mine.*

She can't have it.

"Cinder. Kai." Snow literally vaults over the counter to get to the two people approaching. An Asian woman with dark purple lipstick, and jet-black hair pulled into two ponytails framing her sharp cut bangs. The former Lost Girl has the expression of someone who has lived the goth lifestyle since emerging from the womb and has never smiled in her life.

Snow slows to give the woman she called Cinder a fist pump before turning to the taller, lean man next to her. Unlike his companion, he folds himself over to envelop Snow in a warm hug, sporting a devilish grin that stretches ear to ear.

I jolt when I register the fangs of a Midnight Fae.

Blood drinker. Vampire.

Alarm shoots through me, but no one else seems to be panicking.

"Steady," a low voice says from nearby. I forgot Talon was right beside me for a moment.

He's right to tell me to keep calm. No one else seems surprised this Kai person is here, and judging by Cinder's pallor, she's likely to be a vampire too. Or just...very goth.

There isn't much hope of her cracking a smile so I can gauge what enamel she's packing. I do remember Snow talking about Cinder's blood magic and consorting with vampires, but she didn't go into much more detail.

I curse myself for not asking more questions.

Giving in to my sudden bout of insecurity, I take a step closer to Talon.

As if knowing what I'm doing, he extends an arm on the bar, closer to me. Even without touching me, he calms me with his nearness.

Snow is practically bouncing off the walls at their visit, as Kai waves to Ariel behind the bar.

"Oh my gosh, I can't believe it's finally happening," Snow exclaims. "I thought for sure Goldie would lose patience and elope in Vegas like you guys did."

That's right. Snow, Ariel, Rap and even Geanie are going to Goldie's wedding, another former Lost Girl. This pair must be in town for the festivities.

"You kidding?" Kai jokes. "She's going for the full fairy-tale wedding."

"Goldie deserves it too," Cinder says, still straight-faced.

Despite the nice words, I'm not sure if Cinder means them. I guess you'd have to know her to get a real read on her emotions because she certainly doesn't wear them out in the open. I wonder whether she's also learned to wear a mask or is just naturally like that.

Kai nudges Cinder's arm. "I wouldn't be surprised if she released a flock of flutter buns as soon as they say I do."

The front doors of Poison Apple *explode* open in a cloud of shimmering gold and sapphire glitter.

A diva enters, strutting like the stage belongs to her. Rhinestones blaze on her heels, and a frosted swirl of powder-blue curls rises high enough to kiss the rafters.

Her skin gleams, all molten bronze under the lights. The sheer shimmer of a powder blue sequin jumpsuit wraps around her sculpted arms so tight it looks poured on. Long acrylic nails twinkle in the light with every dramatic gesture, iridescent and lethal. Her eyes are framed in glitter cut-crease shadow, lashes so thick they could double as brooms.

And she is smiling like the world's been waiting for her to show up and she's finally decided to bless it.

"Boston, my darlings!" she calls, her voice pours out smooth as butter, studded with rhinestone bite. "Did you miss your Fairy Godmother?" The deep tones along with the heavy makeup and extra muscular frame confirms this is a woman by choice, by design, by sheer audacity, and I instantly respect the energy she exudes.

The crowd cheers instinctively, even those who clearly don't know who the hell she is. Energy vibrates, the room's focus skews toward her, a current she bends with ease. I can't help being swept away with it too.

The woman struts toward the bar, the staccato crack of her heels cuts through the noise. Everyone parts for her to pass, as if they don't want to interfere with her red-carpet moment.

"Heya, Keeks," Rap says, pulling down a top shelf bottle

of some liquor I haven't touched since working here. "You pre-gaming already?

"I was on this side of town and all our lovelies are rolling in for the wedding, so I couldn't stay away." She waves to Cinder and Kai who wave back though they are still engaged talking to Snow.

"Who's that?" I ask Ariel.

"That's Dame Kiki Eleganza. She's the headline drag queen at the Pumpkin Coach Club. She's better known as the Fairy Godmother. She's also a *very* powerful healing mage. But, uh…" Ariel's aquamarine eyes search the room with wariness. "When she and Geanie are in the same room…"

She doesn't get a chance to finish.

A swirl of blue mist erupts from the center stage.

Geanie appears. His top hat shimmers, a night sky crammed with stars. His usual affable expression is dark as he approaches Dame Kiki.

"Is that a *second-rate Fairy* I smell in my bar?" Geanie sniffs. "Did your Pumpkin Coach break down, or are you just here to attempt to steal the spotlight?"

Kiki turns with the slow certainty of someone who owns the stage, and his interruption is a personal offense.

"Sweetheart," she says, hand to her chest, "if I wanted *your* spotlight, I'd take that tiny thing, tie a boa around it, and wear it to brunch."

The crowd *gasps* in delight.

Geanie saunters closer, every movement exaggerated elegance. "You always did confuse volume with talent."

"And you always confused charisma with shirtless desperation." Her massive lashes sweep up and down with disdain, and I wonder if Geanie feels a gust of wind from the motion.

A ripple of tension and glee rolls through the bar. Even Rap raises an eyebrow. Geanie and Kiki face off like diva-fueled demigods ready to rumble.

"They both have very big personalities," Ariel says to me and Talon, diplomatic as ever. "When they get in the same room, things tend to get...explosive."

"That shade deserves an apology for what you've done to it," Geanie snaps, "which is why you should stay away from *my* signature color."

"Honey, I am *crushing* this look." Kiki's pitch is scandalized. "You're just mad I wear it like royalty, and you wear it like a cheap cocktail napkin."

"It's always about the blue," Ariel adds in a murmur.

"Every single time," Rap mutters behind the bar. "You'd think the color wheel owed them royalties. Alright," Rap calls, louder this time, slicing through the tension with a tone that could crack glass. "This is *my* bar. No fighting unless it involves shots and generous tips."

Both Kiki and Geanie turn in unison and say, "Fine," with the same exact tone.

Geanie saunters dramatically back toward his stage, leaving Kiki to take the specially made cocktail from Rap. With a thank you and a flourish, Kiki turns to go mingle, but stops dead in front of me and Talon.

Her eyes, lined in glitter so sharp it should be classified as a weapon, flick from my face to his. She tilts her head, studying us both with an unnerving intensity as Ariel slides away with a tray of drinks.

And then Kiki smiles, slow and knowing.

"Well, well, well," she purrs, volume dropping to a level only the three of us can hear. "A Succubus...and a Dragon. Now isn't *this* a treat?"

My breath catches. Talon stiffens beside me. But Kiki

holds up one long, manicured finger and presses it to her lips.

"Don't worry, darlings. Your secret is as safe as my real age." She winks and somehow it contains both warmth and an ironclad promise. "But we need to have a *chat* later, hmm?"

Before I can respond, Snow interrupts.

"You guys want a drink?" Snow asks Cinder and Kai as she leads them over, volume rising as she approaches. "Oh, you need to meet our latest recruit. You are going to love her."

Both their attention swings toward me. As soon as his gaze lands on me, Kai's expression morphs. The warm, charming smile he sports evaporates as a cold hatred takes its place.

"*You*," he says quietly. It's fully loaded with accusation, and the blood freezes in my veins. I'm not sure why he's pissed, but I feel like I'm suddenly between crosshairs.

Cinder and Snow swivel their heads back and forth between us, noting the almost violent shift in his attitude. Confusion swirls in me too. I don't know this vampire, though a sneaking suspicion begins to form, and if proven true it would be very, *very* bad for me.

Before I can respond or process, he clarifies in one sentence.

"You ruined my sister."

OUTING THE PRINCESS

TALON

Kai's words cut through the noise of Poison Apple like a blade.

Everything slows.

Aurora's hand freezes mid-pour, and the glass in her other hand slips just enough to clink hard against the counter.

Muscles coil tight enough that my glass strains in my suddenly tight grip. I stare at the man through the hair that's fallen in my eyes. He hasn't noticed me yet. All of his open anger is pinned on Aurora.

Not just "Kai." This must be Kaison Charming, the new King of the Midnight Fae, and he's about to expose Aurora.

Snow's head whips toward Kai. "What did you just say?"

Ariel returns with an empty tray, looking between everyone, trying to gauge what's happened in the few minutes of her absence

Kai doesn't blink. Doesn't smile. Just stands there, impossibly tall in his tailored black coat, looking down his nose like Aurora is a stain he can't bleach off.

"I said," he repeats coolly, "she ruined my sister and broke up my family."

Aurora flinches.

Ariel is already rolling forward, voice tight. "Wait, what are you talking about? You have a sister?"

"I didn't know that," Snow adds, her face gobsmacked.

"Neither did I," Cinder says, all her focus on Kai now.

It's then I realize who his companion is. The human he took as his queen. She's since been turned into a vampire herself. I can see the cold energy pulse around them, along with a reddish aura. Hers is particularly strong, so strong I can smell it. She carries blood magic, which means she wasn't a human at all. She was a mage before she was turned.

Usually, the scent of a mage absolutely rankles my senses. They stink to high heaven to a shifter's nose. But this mage turned vampire smells more like winter air does when you breathe too deep. It stings my nose with cold. Beneath it, there's something old and metallic, like rusted iron under ice. Vampire and mage magic tangled together, frozen into something unnatural.

My hackles rise. I've got a thing against vampires with magic on account of the woman who cursed Aurora.

Though how Mal acquired mage abilities to curse a baby has always been a mystery. Mages don't typically retain their power when turned (on the rare occasion that happens), and Mal was a born vampire, not a mage. No one knows how she's acquired magic abilities beyond her fae race.

"We were forbidden to speak of Malixia," Kai goes on, full attention still on Aurora. "After she was banished from the Midnight Realm by my father."

Aurora recoils, taking a step away from the bar. Kai's eyes narrow.

Everyone watches the interaction like it's some kind of volleyball match, while I wait, ready to take any action necessary. If this bloodsucker even so much as thinks of hurting Aurora, I'll grab him by the throat and burn him to a crisp, Fae King or not.

Ariel's steady hand stops Aurora from retreating any further. "What does that have to do with Aurora?" There is a thread of defense in her tone.

"She's the Rosari princess." Kai's eyes flash red. "Her father was betrothed to my sister. It was supposed to be a political kinship between Midnight and Realm of the Roses. But a week before the wedding, Roland broke it off. A fortnight later, he married someone else. My sister was *humiliated*." A sneer appears on the vampire's face as he leans in to hiss at Aura. "My father was so livid, he exiled Malixia for not securing the marriage."

I stayed on the sidelines long enough. I'm up and next to him. "Take a step back." It comes out low, steady and even, but there is no mistaking the danger in my voice.

At first, he doesn't move. Then Cinder sets a hand on his shoulder. "Kai," she says in a low warning tone. He takes a step back.

"You're a princess?" Ariel asks, studying Aurora with new eyes.

"Explains the skillset," Snow adds, but wears an equally concerned expression.

Aurora grips one hand with the other, a sign she's nervous. "I-I wasn't even born yet when that happened."

"Your family broke mine apart, with no consideration. Because of your father, I haven't seen my sister in thirty years."

"Wait, how the hell old are you?" Snow asks, nose wrinkling in confusion.

"Vampires age slower," Cinder explains. "He's eighty err...something," she finishes uncertainly.

"Whoa, talk about cradle robbing," Snow says, glance flickering back and forth between Cinder and Kai.

"Or is she grave robbing?" Ariel adds, her grip still firm and comforting on Aurora's arm.

Despite the colorful commentary, Kai is still coiled as if ready to strike. Anger rolls off him in waves.

"Okay, let's break this up," Rap cuts in.

She sidles up from the other side of Kai to stand between him and the counter. Her eyes snap between all of us like she's already calculating how many bodies she's going to bury in the alley. "Kai, you need to chill," she adds in a hushed tone.

Kai's lip curls, eyes still locked on Aurora over Rap's mohawk. "I expected you to be better about what trash you pick up from the street and give the name Lost Girl. She should stay lost."

Heat rolls out of me as anger gets the best of me. "Apologize for that."

Kai doesn't even flinch but Cinder's grip on him tightens as she warily observes me.

"Talon," Rap warns sharply without looking at me. "You know I don't care what kind of teeth you have or what crown you wear," she says to Kai flatly. "If you're bringing this kind of energy into my house, I will kick your bony ass out myself."

A long tense moment passes before Kai's posture finally relaxes.

Cinder stares at Aurora a moment too long before

pulling Kai's elbow. He doesn't move at first, continuing to glare.

"How about we go visit Red, Brex, and the twins?" Cinder suggests.

His cutting gaze remains on Aurora even as he's drawn away.

Snow lets out a loud dramatic exhale. "Damn. Didn't know he had it in him. Normally, the dude is such a delight."

Ariel now looks at Aurora with new eyes.

Aurora's lips part slightly, her eyes still locked on the door like he might come back and do something worse.

I hate seeing her so stripped down, so vulnerable in front of everyone.

"Seriously, a princess?" Snow asks.

"Snow, Ariel," Rap barks. "Get back to work. Aurora, take five. Talon, go with her."

There is no arguing with the woman. Aurora only moves when I round the bar and press my fingers to her back. I gently lead her through the crowd back to the break room.

"Hey," I say when we are finally alone.

Aurora won't look at me.

"You don't have to tell them anything."

Her throat bobs. She blinks. "But they know now."

"Not everything, and it doesn't matter. They know *you*," I say. "They've watched you work as hard as any of them."

And they don't know about the curse, which is important. We can't afford for that secret to leak.

Even the emotionally stable Rosari people who live in a calm symbiosis with each other would not tolerate a Succubus in their land, much less as their princess. The Common World would likely react even less favorably.

They'd treat her as a dangerous entity. She would be scrutinized, and the razor-sharp point of fear could lead them to the trail of bodies I worked so hard to incinerate.

Aurora finally looks at me. There's panic in her gaze, but no fear. Humiliation. Guilt. The echo of a thousand things she's been forced to swallow. "I couldn't even defend myself. I couldn't say that his sister ruined *my* life." Anger spikes in her voice.

"I know it's not fair, but you did good, Aura."

"It's not fair," she adds with a sweep of her arms. "I didn't do anything, yet I'm the living embodiment of a drama that I had nothing to do with. Mal had me pay the price, but it's my dad's fault. *He* should pay." Aurora clapped a hand over her mouth, eyes wide with shock at her own words.

"You're not wrong," I reassure her. My hands itch to touch her, but I keep them at my sides.

Hand still covering her mouth, she shakes her head as her eyes turn glassy with unshed tears. "I shouldn't say that. I love my father."

"You can love him and hold him responsible for what happened."

Aurora digs her palms into her eyes as she groans in frustration. "It's so complicated. I hate how messy everything is. I hate Mal. I hate my parents for what they did, and I hate myself." Her arms open wide. "And Mal's brother hates me too. It's only fitting," she says with a dry laugh.

"He doesn't know you." I want to pull her hands away from her face and into mine, but I clench them into tight fists to keep from doing so.

She folds her arms over her body, shaking her head. "It doesn't matter. It's never mattered. I'm still judged for *what*

I am, not who I am. I'm a princess, a Succubus, a daughter to someone who hurt his family."

"Aura." I get her attention enough that her chin lifts toward me, defiant despite the tremor in her mouth. "King Charming was not a good man. The previous one," I clarify. "He was a cruel dictator, and he's responsible for hurting his own family. He didn't have to forsake his own daughter. That's not on you. That's not even on your parents."

"Yeah well, I still get blamed," she grumbles, rubbing at her face.

"Aura, I—"

"Break's over," she interrupts, whipping the door open and disappearing into the fray.

I take a breath before following her. I watch from the door as I go back to checking IDs. She keeps grabbing the wrong bottles, she breaks two glasses, and her confidence is a muted shadow of what she had.

She's right, it's not fair. Life isn't fair. But I would pay any price to give her what she really deserves.

I all but abandon my duties of policing Poison Apple, in favor of keeping near Aurora. Rap can cut my paycheck. I don't care. But the bar owner doesn't give me any flack.

Aurora is a flurry of movement as if nothing can touch her if she keeps going at a breakneck speed. But the second she slows down, the girls approach.

Snow leans in next to her, voice sharp enough that I can hear. "Kai was out of line, and he's lucky I didn't stab him with a straw."

Aurora huffs a single shaky laugh.

"I don't care what your last name is," Ariel says softly, rubbing Aurora's arm. "You're ours now."

Behind the bar, Aurora steadies. The next drink she

attempts to make comes out right on the first try, but her hands still shake.

She's desperate to cling to this new life—to the girl she's become, to the friends she's made in this loud, glittering place. But for the first time, I don't fear being the one who takes it from her.

I fear it will spit her out on its own.

CHAPTER 20

THE SECOND KNUCKLE AND A LITTLE FASTER

TALON

A couple nights later, Aurora is as right as rain again. I don't know what was said during her girls' nights, but I know Snow and Ariel were more than supportive after discovering Aurora's true identity. Though I confirmed she didn't reveal the Succubus part.

Thankfully, I don't have to convince Aurora why that would be a bad idea. I know she trusts her friends, but how they would react to a Succubus in their midst is an entirely different beast.

More people rolled in for Goldie and Ted's wedding through the week. The engaged couple even rented out the bar for their rehearsal dinner, and Aurora and I worked the event. I made sure Kai stayed far away from Aurora, though I didn't need to worry. Apparently, everyone else shared the same mission, and the most he did was shoot daggers at her from across the room.

The Vampire King's focus on her waned after a couple martinis, and he lost all interest when the dancing began.

Aurora doesn't speak as we walk home after our shift. We were invited to stay, but neither of us felt like it.

Though tomorrow is Friday, Poison Apple will be closed for the wedding, and we've been given the night off. The city is quieter than usual, and so is Aura. Despite her silence, I *feel* her.

I've been watching her hunger grow in intensity over the last few days, and tonight the spectral shimmer pulses.

It rises from her like heat off blacktop, distorting the air in waves I've come to recognize. A warning sign.

Her skin has gone pale. The vibrant flush that usually follows a feed is long gone, and in its place is a drawn, sallow exhaustion that no amount of sleep will cure.

She's starving.

In the apartment, Aurora moves through the space like a ghost—too quiet, too careful. I watch her from the kitchen as she sheds her boots, her bracelets, the outer layer of her armor.

I stay in the kitchen, nursing a drink I don't want, flipping through every possible solution in my head.

It's even less safe to go out seeking a meal for her with Mal's vampire lackeys crawling through alleyways, trying to sniff her out. Aurora's too visible now. Too vulnerable.

I don't know if I'll be able to stop her from killing this time. Without full feedings to satiate her, it's likely she'll gorge faster on instinct. And dealing with bodies and disappearances in Boston is going to be a lot tougher than in the Realm of Roses.

She needs someone disposable.

And I don't know a single damn person in Boston who checks that box.

The brief fantasy of having her feed on the Vampire King Charming comes to mind. But considering he's like family at Poison Apple, and he's royalty, he'd be missed.

So I lie awake while the city sleeps, Aurora's needs

clinging to my throat, the inside of my skull. The air in the apartment warps around it, too heavy, too saturated with my own worry.

Eventually, I grab my phone from the side table. I still don't like the damn thing, it's too slick, too bright, and too loud when I don't want it to be. But tonight, it's the only way I can chase a lead.

I open an app, careful with my thumbs as I'm still not used to typing such little characters. I pull up an option I considered a few nights back. It's an out of the box idea, but Aurora's been stomping on the box since we got here. Maybe it's time I do the same.

I haven't decided if my idea is a necessary risk or just...a risk.

Either way, I don't like it, but I might not have a choice.

Eventually, I pass out on the couch, no closer to an answer.

My sleep is shattered with a guttural moan, strained and sharp enough to twist my gut. My eyes snap open, body lurching off the couch before my mind can catch up.

"Aura?" I call in a panic as I cross the threshold to her room. Mid-morning light filters through the windows.

The memory of finding her in that shower on the brink of death turns my fire ice-cold.

But then, I see her.

Aurora lies on her back, knees drawn up, one hand gripping the sheets. The other is beneath the blanket, buried between her thighs, moving in slow, trembling strokes.

Her eyes are shut, her lips parted. Her brow is furrowed like she's fighting her own body.

She's glowing. Literally. That shimmer in the air around her is thicker than I've ever seen.

Her hips roll in slow, desperate circles. A moan slips out before she can stop it.

Fuck.

Maybe I should leave?

No. I've never left before, and I won't start now.

I step closer. "Aura?"

Her eyes snap open. She startles out a gasp but doesn't stop.

"It hurts. Talon," she pants.

My gut tightens. I move to stand at the foot of the bed. My heart twists at seeing her in pain, while my cock jerks against my boxer briefs, already thickening at the sight of her. Heat coils low in my spine like my own magic wants to spark. I clench my jaw and breathe through it, locking my hands at my sides to keep them from shaking.

"You should've woken me."

"I didn't want you to see me like this. I've never...not before..."

Her voice breaks as she looks away. And then her hips lift with another desperate grind. Her hunger is boiling over.

My fingers flex and then curl into fists. I can feel her need licking at my skin, making it hard to hold still. Every muscle in my body strains not to cross the line I'm sorely tempted to.

While all my sexual encounters have been limited to my own hand, this is the first time Aurora's ever touched herself. It's always been about feeding from someone else.

Even under the covers, I can tell her motions are jerky, rushed, and uncoordinated.

"Take off the sheet," I say.

Her motions slow as her eyes widen. "What?"

I lick my lips and swallow down the lump in my throat, already knowing how I can help. "Take it off. Let me see you. Show me that pretty little pussy, Aura."

Her mouth parts then shuts. She draws the sheet away slowly, baring herself to me, her thighs trembling and fingers slick and shaking where they rest between her legs. My breath catches like I've been punched in the chest.

Fae fucking witchtits.

My dick's hard now, full, aching, pinned against the line of my waistband. Every part of me screams to touch her, to crawl on top of her and finish what she started.

Her glowing, sun-kissed skin stretches over the curves I've mapped a hundred times with my eyes but never my hands. Her sweat glistens in the light like flecks of gold dust, like magic seeping from her pores. Her full, round breasts rise and fall with every sharp, uneven breath, nipples dark and tight from the strain of holding herself back.

Her gorgeous thighs tremble. I've watched them sway behind the bar, straddle a barstool, wrap around strangers, but now, they're parted, giving me a view that damn near brings me to my knees.

I shift my stance, trying to ease the pressure in my underwear. It's useless. I'm a goddamn furnace, barely contained. My pulse hammers in my ears as my eyes devour every inch of her.

No matter how many times I've seen her naked, no matter that she walks through this apartment with little to no clothes on, I'm always struck stupid by her. Awed.

"Touch yourself for me," I command. My throat is dry. My voice breaks at the edges. I feel wild with barely contained restraint.

Her breath catches.

"Go on," I murmur from the end of the bed. "Let me see how good you can make yourself feel."

She hesitates for just a moment, but then her fingers start to move again. Slow. Shaky.

"Don't think," I coach. "Just feel."

It's still awkward and rushed. She's too in her head.

"Circle your fingers near your clit, but don't touch it," I instruct, voice low and even. "Start slow, like this is fore-play. Like I'm kissing down your stomach, spreading your thighs, teasing you with my tongue just out of reach."

She gasps and obeys, her touch softer now. Her eyes flutter shut, jaw slack.

My cock throbs in time with every movement she makes. I shift my stance, grinding down the need to pull myself out and relieve the pressure building behind the fabric of my underwear. This isn't about me. This is for her.

"Now dip your finger in that tight, dripping cunt," I say in a silky tone, the words flowing out of me without thought. "Just one and only to the first knuckle, Aura. I want you to think of me teasing you with just the tip of my cock, just enough to feel that perfect heat."

Her lips part as she gasps.

She's wet. Silken. Glowing.

The scent of her, ripe and addictive, coats my throat. My pulse pounds in places I can't reach. I dig my nails into my palms and anchor my feet to the floor. One wrong move and I'll tear the bed apart just to get to her.

"You're so fucking beautiful," I rasp, voice sandpaper and heat.

Where most people stop at her body, at the pull of her curves, the arousal she inspires, I see more.

I've guarded this girl with the resolve of a soldier, but

I've also memorized every inch of her. I've memorized and categorized her glances, her moans, every stolen smile. I've watched her fight. Break. Rebuild herself from nothing but hope and stubbornness. I've watched her flirt and tease and feed.

She's far more than the sum of her parts, her hunger. She's *everything*.

In every sexual encounter, there's always been someone else. Some stranger at her lips. Her throat. Her thighs. Feeding her. Touching her. Taking something I wanted to give.

But now?

There is just the two of us in this room. No sharing. No buffering presence.

And it sinks into something primal. Something ancient. My Dragon wants to hoard her. Wants to lock the door, throw away the key, and never let her out of this room. Out of this moment. Out of my reach.

The greedy, fire-blooded part that doesn't understand reason or restraint wants to burn the whole world down just to keep this part of her all to myself.

She adds a second finger and dips into the second knuckle now, a little faster, finding a rhythm that wasn't there before.

My balls draw tight. I clench my jaw until it aches, every muscle in my body pulled taut like a bowstring. Every sound she makes feeds a beast I've caged for too long.

"You're doing so good," I whisper. "So fucking good for me, baby."

Her whole body shudders.

Then she opens her eyes to meet mine. "Say that again," she whispers.

"What? You mean call you baby?"

She nods, and her hand stutters, waiting.

"Baby," I say again, slower this time. Letting it land. "Sweetheart. *Mine.*"

A desperate sound between a moan and a warble escapes her when I call her by the little pet names. Her fingers plunge deeper, faster, but her untrained touch is moving her away from the edge of orgasm.

But she doesn't need to worry. I'll take her there. I can finish her from across the room with the lethal knowledge I have of this woman's body.

"You don't know what talking like that does to me," she whispers.

"I do," I growl. "I feel it in my fucking chest every time."

A broken whine tumbles from her lips. She tries to buck into her own touch, but I can tell she's losing the thread of feeling.

"Feel how wet you are? How silken and perfect? Now take those fingers and circle around your needy clit, *baby.*"

"This is harder by myself," she confesses with a little frustrated laugh even as she does what I say.

"Rub up and down with light pressure, then back to circles. Small ones, tighter now." I watch her hips twitch. "Right there. You feel that pulse?"

This time she moans, not from frustration but from satisfaction. Her hips chase the rhythm like she's been aching for this all night.

My cock pulses hard. My stomach clenches like I've been punched. I still don't touch myself—I won't—but every inch of me is strung so tight I could snap.

"You know why that feels so fucking good?" I ask. "Because I know everything about you."

Her fingers falter, her gaze meeting mine. I want to dive into those glassy, blown pupils.

"I know how your breath hitches when you're close. I know the way your thighs tremble when you want more, but don't want to ask," I say, my feet moving of their own accord. "I know that you always sleep curled on your right side, but when you've had a good feed, you roll to your back and let your legs fall open just like this."

She makes a strangled sound—half-laugh, half-moan—like no one's ever *seen* her this much.

Slowly, I stalk around the bed, nearing her from the side. "I know when a John's tongue isn't going deep enough. When they go too slow or go too fast. When they don't hit the right angle. I've watched them fumble through the motions while you lie back, silent, but your brow ticks just enough for me to know it's not right."

A shiver ripples down her legs. Her breath catches.

I drop to a crouch next to her, my face close, my voice soft but rough. "I know the exact second your lips part from real pleasure, not performance. I know the spot that makes your hips jolt—lower, harder pressure, just there," I gesture with my hand, and she obeys, biting her lip.

Her moan is all confirmation.

"I've memorized the sounds you make when it's working. And the ones you try to swallow when it's not."

Aurora's cheeks flush, her hand circling tighter.

"You think they ever saw you?" I whisper. "They fed you. Fucked you. But they didn't *see* you."

My hands tremble, caught between the pull of her and my own resistance. The urge to move closer is overwhelming, yet I force myself to stand, backing up two steps to put her out of reach.

"But I have, sweetheart. I've watched your body through every feed, memorized your tells, mapped out your need like it's sacred scripture. And not once, not *fucking* once, have I ever been the one inside you."

I clench my fists. Hard. My knuckles crack. I grind my teeth like it'll keep my hands from reaching for her, from ruining everything with one greedy grab.

The fire in my skin buzzes, desperate. Starved.

Is this what she feels like all the time? This ache? This madness? The yank in my gut, the burn in my spine—it makes me believe I could take her without hurting her. Makes me believe the rules don't matter anymore.

Her head falls back, fingers finding that spot to the left that makes her purr.

"I've never gotten to touch you. Never felt your skin under me. And still," I growl, chest tight, voice wrecked, "I know exactly what you need."

"And yet," I say, barely breathing now, "I fantasize about giving you even more."

Her smoky, crystalline eyes widen. She's hungry to feed, but she's also hungry for my words. I can see in every tense line of her face that she's addicted to everything I'm saying.

"I dream about inflicting new sensations on you." Standing over her, I scan her body. A vicious possessive little smirk ticks up the side of my face. This beautiful image is mine and no one else's. It sears into my memory like a brand.

"New rhythms. I fantasize about hunting down every spot they missed. Those little neglected places of pleasure, the ones no one's taken the time to uncover. I'd press my mouth to them, suck, lick, and prod until you give up a sound you've never made before. A pitch so sharp it'd live in the walls."

"T-Talon—" She cries out, the word breaking on her tongue, and her hand jerks faster, obedient to the picture

I'm painting, desperate to feel it for real. She whimpers like I've touched her, like my words have slid between her legs.

"I'd worship you, baby," I whisper. This time I can't help myself. I slip my hand under the waistband of my shorts, gripping my dick. I almost choke at the sensation. "Slow. Thorough. I'd keep pushing until you forgot every stranger who ever touched you, forgot your own name, forgot everything but *mine*." My fist moves up and down in unhurried strokes, and her eyes hungrily track the motion. I want this moment to last. I may never get another like it.

But what if this is all she needs?

Aurora's right. We've been so busy feeding her regularly, we've never thought outside the box. Maybe the sexual power from within can sustain her?

Maybe this could be us now? Me directing her every move, her every touch, confessing every filthy thing I've harbored for years. Things I know she'd adore. Things she'd beg to hear more of.

"Keep going," I tell her, as I grip the base of my dick. *Fuck*, my wings want to spread *so bad*. "Don't stop now. You're so close, sweetheart."

Maybe I would get a pair of special gloves? Maybe I could lay the sheet over her and rub her sweet little cunt until it wets the fabric? I'd have to pull away often so I didn't burn her, but maybe quick little touches?

Maybe we could make this work? Imperfectly perfect.

Aurora's body shakes, her thighs clenching around her hand. Her pink hair has darkened and matted against her forehead, dampened by the beads of sweat that trickle down from the intensity of her effort.

"If I could touch you," I say, words shaking now, "I'd kiss my way up your thighs so slow, you'd forget how to breathe. I'd part your lips with my tongue and learn the exact rhythm that makes you fall apart."

She cries out, bucking into her hand.

"I'd pin your hips with my hands, hold you down while I fucked you with my mouth, make you come so many times, your power would crack the fucking walls."

"Please—" she gasps.

I'm burning alive with the need to claim every sound spilling from her lips.

"I'd kiss you while I slid inside you. Hold your jaw in one hand, your hip in the other. You'd be begging for that massive dick, wouldn't you, baby?"

"Fuck," she chokes. "Talon, yes—please—"

My cock is aching, leaking, and I give into a little more speed as I devote my every word to her. What I would give for some of her wetness on my hand, around my dick.

"You'd ride my face like you were made for it," I growl. "You'd come on my tongue and cry my name. And I'd keep going just to see how many times you could break for me."

"Close." Her lashes flutter. "*I'm so close.*"

I step forward again and crouch down, leaning in. I can smell the sweet, addictive scent of her slick heat.

"I'd spread you open with my fingers," I whisper into her ear, still jerking off. "Slow and deep until you're dripping for it. Then I'd slide in, inch by inch, and ruin you for anyone else. I'd fuck you like I've waited a thousand years," I murmur. "Because I have. Every day I've held back, I was dreaming of this. Of *you.*"

Her moan fractures into a sob. Her hand moves faster. Her thighs shake. The glow spreads, thickening the air around us. Her power spikes, bright and coiled and teetering.

"Say it, baby," I whisper, knowing exactly how to push her over the edge. "Say you're mine."

"I'm yours," she gasps. "Always—fuck—I'm—"

She shatters.

Her cry rips through the room—raw, high, holy. Her hips jerk, legs locking around her hand as her body arches off the bed. Her pink glow crackles, lightning alive beneath her skin.

Her orgasm hits in a violent tide, her climax clawing up the air until it grips me by the throat. My knees nearly buckle. My lungs seize. My cock throbs with brutal, aching force before spilling in hot, bright spurts in my shorts. I gasp and groan as the pressure explodes from me in a geyser.

My soul claws toward her on instinct, mad with the need to reach her, mark her, fuck her until the fire in my chest finds a home.

She chants my name while her body is a pulsing, living star.

It's the most beautiful thing I've ever seen.

But then, her body jerks once. Twice. Then stills, and I know.

Her magic doesn't crest.

It *detonates*.

Her body convulses, but not in pleasure.

The waves of her power that have always emanated outward suddenly reverse course, hammering into her body with a dark purple aura. Her veins pulse with light. Her back bows, every muscle straining as if pain itself is wringing her spine.

"Aurora," I call, removing my hand from myself as panic takes place over release. She doesn't hear me. She's feeding on her own life force.

"Stay with me, Aura," I demand. *"Breathe."*

But she doesn't respond. Her eyes roll back.

Shit. Shit. Fuck.

"Aurora," I shout again, louder this time, *desperate.*

Her lips part in a silent scream. Her glow turns violent. Wild. Her body jolts, violent and raw, every movement a silent rupture.

My chest crumples under the impact, air gone in a blink.

I don't think—I move.

Surging forward, I scoop her up, sheets and all, then sprint for the shower. Terror rises in my lungs, even as I step in the tub. Still holding her in the bunched-up covers, I flip on the cold water like she's been doing recently.

She lets out a startled gasp when the shower blast hits her in the face. I can see the waves slowing their reverse course, but her body is still feeding on itself.

My tentative idea, the one I'm not sure is a good idea is no longer an option.

Aurora needs to feed, and it has to be tonight.

CHAPTER 21

EATING MYSELF OUT

AURORA

A sheet of cold rain comes down on Talon and I as we walk along the darkened docks, chilling me to the bone. Which, admittedly, helps. A little.

Because fae lords, my body *hurts*. It's not the ache of a good orgasm. Not the soreness that comes with satisfaction.

This is *wrong*. Current rips through my spine. My limbs feel brittle, glass stretched too thin. My skin is too tight. My chest is caving. My ribs are knives, and my stomach is one great screaming void. My curse kicked the door wide, a meal waiting on the other side.

Worse than starving. I'm cannibalizing.

We had to wait for hours. Trapped in that apartment, waiting for nightfall to come.

Every minute dragged. My head split open behind my eyes. My limbs wouldn't stop shaking. And all Talon kept saying was *"Hold on. Just a little longer. I've got you. It's going to be okay, baby."*

Baby. I still love when he calls me that.

I have no idea why Talon's brought me out here. I want

to ask, *why aren't we going to a motel like last time?* But even forming words grates across my tongue, heavy and slow.

My limbs are shaky, useless. My head's pounding with the kind of migraine that feels personal. And under all that?

Humiliation.

I tried to take the edge off. Tried to be strong. Clever. In control of my own body. But I can't even *touch myself* without it turning into a fucking catastrophe. Can't even come without lighting the match of my own slow death. My curse feasted on my orgasm. I was nothing but fuel.

I thought maybe I could handle it on my own. Just once. Take a little pleasure. Take a little power. But instead, I fed it *me*. My own life force.

I've never felt so betrayed by my body, and my list of grudges against it are long and detailed.

This is some tremendous bullshit, and if Mal were here, I would tell her so before popping her in the face with my fist.

I stumble.

Okay, maybe it wouldn't be a very hard punch, but once I get a little dick in me, I'm going to track her down and beat her to a pulp.

I laugh at my own thoughts, but it comes out a strangled rasp.

Talon hesitates. "We're almost there," he says.

Then he wraps his arm around my cloaked body to help me keep straight as we continue. My face turns up into the cold sleet just in time to catch the hot red embers flashing in his eyes as he holds me. Talon uses his other hand to lift the hood on my cloak, so it better shields my face from the light rain.

He's careful not to touch my flesh, and for one brief moment, I let myself believe this is our life. That I get to lean on him. That he gets to hold me. That we're just... together. *Whole.*

The fantasy gives me equal jolts of pleasure and pain. Resentment flares in me. Why does everything between us have to be so witchtitting bittersweet?

Even through the headache, through the haze and burn and emptiness, I keep thinking about what he said. All of it.

The way he saw me. The way he *knows* me. The way he's been watching, memorizing, *aching* for me, without ever touching.

I want to gather every word, every whispered confession and name he called me, and fold them into something solid. A memory box. A talisman. Something I can clutch to my chest when I need strength.

"We're here," he announces, drawing my attention forward.

From the outside, it looks like a condemned warehouse—rust streaks, rotted siding, one half-lit streetlamp above. But the bouncer standing out front tells a different story.

He's big. Bigger and bulkier than Talon. Bald head, tattooed neck. His eyes glow like lit coal.

"You here to play?" he asks, gaze flicking between us.

Talon nods, retrieving his phone. "We're registered."

"Then you know the terms." The bouncer pulls a rune-etched tablet from his coat, tapping the screen. "Blood signature. Both of you."

Talon puts his phone away before he reaches out and touches the tablet with his index finger. There's a small blue spark at the contact.

Under the expectant gaze of the bouncer, I reach out to do the same. A sharp pinprick zings across my finger.

"Magic immunization verified," the bouncer intones. "Emotional consent spell active. No cursed bites. No fertility issues. No dream-walkers without collars. You're cleared." He studies us. "And you understand the Old Pact still holds?"

I hesitate, having no idea what the hell he's talking about much less where we are. "I—"

"We do," Talon says, voice rough.

The bouncer lifts the metal bar behind him and lets it drop with a heavy *clang*. The sealed door creaks open.

"Then the only thing you'll catch in there is heartbreak," he mutters. "Don't say I didn't warn you."

We step into warm, velvet shadows, and music that pulses like a heartbeat.

"What's the Old Pact?" I whisper to Talon as we enter the building. The air is charged enough to raise every hair on my body.

Talon keeps a hand at the small of my back, steering me gently. "This place is a temple to Bastet—Egyptian goddess of pleasure, sex, and safe indulgence. The owner made a pact: anyone entering offers a drop of blood, and in return she grants protection against disease, coercion, and magical corruption. Think of it like divine sanctuary."

A club. A sacred one. Maybe a safehouse for people like me?

Then the scent hits me.

Thick, heady. Sweat and skin and pheromones.

Sex.

It's an incense that thickens the air—tangible, cloying, almost sweet. My mouth waters. My pulse kicks up. Beneath it all, a low bass thrums through the warehouse walls, a second heartbeat vibrating my bones. Moans roll, distant thunder tangled with the wet slap of flesh, a breathless gasp that triggers my entire body to shiver with anticipation.

Lust doesn't just hum under my skin, it scrapes. Sparks. Ignites.

That's when I see it.

A woman in sheer mesh bent over a velvet bench while a vampire laps at the inside of her thigh. Just beyond them, two men kiss with teeth and tongue, one of them trailing glowing runes down the other's chest with the glow of a spell-branded fingertip.

Oh.

This isn't just a club.

This is a *sex* club.

The realization slams into me with a second wave of hunger—deeper, more dangerous. The hunger snarls to life. Thankfully it directs outward, away from my body for the first time since I made my massive mistake.

The warehouse is a den of sensual excess. Draped silks in oceanic blues and greens billow from the high ceilings, giving the illusion of moving water. A chandelier fashioned from mother-of-pearl shells casts refracted light in fluid patterns.

To the left, a sunken lounge area pulses with low music and lower moans. Lovers sprawl across cushions in various states of undress. Some whisper confessions, others grind slowly, hands and mouths exploring.

A server glides by with a silver tray of jewel-toned cocktails, each one fogging with chill or glinting with enchantment. The waitstaff are all human, dressed in corseted uniforms with subtle scalloped patterns—fish scales woven in satin and silk. Every corset, regardless of gender, is cut to showcase as much skin as possible. Tits out, hips bare, and fishnets held up by garters.

Farther in, alcoves carved into the old brick walls host more private performances—a fae couple locked in a tangle of limbs on silk ropes, a human woman bound and writhing with pleasure as her partner teases her with flickering illusions.

I shudder when I catch sight of a vampire kissing his partner before sinking his teeth into what looks like a willing donor on his lap. The memory of the bouncer's words about everything protected for consent comes to mind.

Talon leads me down a corridor to a series of rooms. I glance at the rules posted in ornate gold lettering. Door closed means private party. Open door means come join and play.

Talon directs me inside one of the rooms. It reminds me of the high-end hotel suites I've seen on *Hex Island*, when the cast got to go on a sexy vacation and suddenly everything was silk robes and spontaneous hookups.

This is that, if the producers had taste.

The space is immaculate, the air thin and over-purified, the sheets stiff with the memory of steam pressed into them between every guest. The lighting is low and soothing, tinted in soft sea-glass hues that ripple over the satin walls. Everything carries the faint bite of citrus peel overlaid with the dry crisp of linen. Fresh, not floral. Even the leather ottoman gleams, the kind of polish that screams clipboard inspections and relentless standards.

A minibar stretches across one wall, gleaming with brushed gold accents and crystal handles. Behind the glass are chilled bottles of wine and champagne, glistening mineral waters, delicate chocolates sheathed in foil, and sea-salt caramels lined up like jewels.

Then there are neatly stacked boxes in matte black and pastel velvet, each one sealed and labeled with delicate symbols. Some are obvious—cuffs, plugs, vibrators. Others look like medical-grade tools wrapped in luxury. I don't know what half of them are, and somehow, that feels intentional.

The sign makes it easy to figure out how it works. Open a box or crack a bottle, and it simply goes on your tab.

The bed is sleek, minimal, and unapologetically indulgent. The linens are ice-white and buttery soft, layered with silk throws in coral and gold. The pearlescent and intricate headboard is a curved seashell. Above, a ceiling mirror edged in burnished brass reflects every angle, catching the flicker of recessed lights that move like sunlight through shallow water.

"Undress."

The timbre of Talon's voice causes a shiver to go through me before landing as a pulse in my sex, despite how wretched my body feels.

I try to keep hold of myself, even as I obey him. "I don't know if I can do this." I confess. "I'm too hungry, and last time, I almost killed Merry." I end on a shamed whisper, shutting my eyes tight.

I wrap my arms around myself. I'm running on a fraying edge.

Whoever comes in here, I'm going to kill them. I know it. I have no control. Even with Talon here, there will be no holding back the fangs of my curse from draining whoever walks through that door and into this bed.

"Aura." The way he says my name forces me to open my eyes. "Trust me."

I search his dark molten depths, letting myself relax, just a fraction. "I trust you."

"Good." He nods. "Because you won't be feeding from just one person. We are going to have a little..." he hesitates, "party."

My brows lift a fraction.

That way I'll feed from multiple people. Maybe taking some from several will keep any one person from being drained.

"You thought of this?" I ask.

He nods, a flush coming to his cheeks. "It seems like it could work."

I can't say I disagree. We seem to be trying all sorts of things these days. I swallow hard. Hopefully his plan goes better than my idea did this morning.

Then he pulls out the chains from the pack he brought. We don't have to use the chains, but they are a reminder.

I need that reminder, like a uniform. Dropping the cloak, I push off the loose dress I wore under and take them from him.

The cold jewels find all the dips off my body, causing goosebumps to wash over me. I shudder in equal parts disgust and anticipation. The larger part of me grows with excitement and insatiable appetite, ready to pounce.

Before he can move, I speak again in a lower tone. "I wish it was you. You and me."

He stops, swallowing hard. I follow the bob and drop of his throat. "Me too." Then in a quiet, wistful tone that matches mine, "Me too."

CHAPTER 22

YANKING THE COLLAR

TALON

I patiently wait with the collar in hand until Aurora lifts her hair for me to snap it on.

"So you're her Dom?" a soft voice asks from the door as I finish securing the collar to Aurora's neck, wrapping the long leash around my hand to shorten it.

The question comes from a petite girl with chestnut hair in a messy bun and oval glasses who barely comes up to my elbow. Her conservative sweater and skirt make her look like she wandered in from a librarian conference—and not a single part of her looks uncertain. Just...quietly amused.

I exchange a glance with Aura.

"Yes," I say.

The woman looks between us. "May I...play?"

Aura licks her lips like a starving wolf. She can't wait much longer. Then her expression hardens as if she knows she's about to hurt this girl.

But I won't let her.

I give a curt nod. "But I stay on the sidelines."

She nods, but her eyes drop to the black scales along my chest, and I swear something in her expression shifts like she gets it. At least a little.

She approaches the bed. Aura is already on her knees, one hand lazily rolling her breast, occasionally pinching the nipple. My temples tighten as I fight any bodily reaction. I need to stay vigilant.

The Librarian hesitates, but Aurora doesn't. She surges forward and catches her in a kiss with a needy moan. Their lips glide, tongues dip, and I can tell from the soft sounds and arched backs that it's a *good* kiss. The Librarian startles at first but quickly matches Aurora's heat.

She cups Aura's breasts and plays with the weight of them like she's handling precious things. Aura arches, hips rocking in the air, mindlessly seeking contact. Her need is a living thing.

When they finally break apart, the Librarian's glasses are crooked and her hair has come undone in soft waves. "Whoa," she breathes, dazed.

Then she steps away and starts unbuttoning her blouse.

Aura whimpers, reaching out like she might physically pull her back. I jerk the jeweled leash. Not hard, but enough.

She tries to set me on fire with her glare.

"Be a good girl," I warn.

The Little Librarian laughs under her breath, even as she shimmies off her skirt and blouse to reveal a lavender, lace bodysuit. The color is delicate, but the curves inside it are anything but.

"Room for more?" another voice rumbles behind me.

I turn.

A broad-chested Black man stands confidently in the

open curtain, wearing only slacks that hang low on his cut hips.

I immediately sense an easy strength about his character. It's an open energy in his eyes and smile. His forearms are thick. But it's his hands I notice—big, calloused, worker's hands that aren't afraid to take action.

Aurora will like that.

Behind him, a second figure lingers, a slender man with long, blond hair and bright, too-perceptive eyes. His jawline is knife-sharp. He's likely half-Elf, if not more. Hesitant, watchful. The fae man studies the dynamic like someone used to reading a room before acting.

I nod to them both. "The more the better."

Literally. This division of Aura's feeding may be the answer, but a lot is riding on my bet.

I shut the door to the room. No interruptions now. This is more than enough energy for me to field, and hopefully it's enough for Aura.

I loop the leash once around my wrist, a physical reminder that I'm still the one in control, even as this spirals toward chaos.

Aura's breath is ragged, her pupils blown wide. She's kneeling on the bed, a sacrificial offering, flushed, trembling, barely holding back the hunger I've collared. Her gaze flicks to each of them, ravenous.

The Little Librarian eases onto her back, positioning herself near the head of the bed, legs parted with a confidence that's anything but quiet now. Her fingers hook into the bodysuit, pulling the center aside to bare soft folds already slick with arousal.

"You want to be a good little sub?" she asks, taking the cue from our dynamic. "Come be a good girl and eat this pussy."

Aura crawls forward on all fours, starving eyes locked onto the prize. With a reverent sigh, she lowers her head and licks a slow, exploratory stripe up the woman's cunt.

The Librarian moans, one hand gripping the sheets while the other tangles into Aura's hair, encouraging her deeper.

Aurora groans against her, devouring eagerly like this isn't sex, it's salvation. She sucks on the Librarian's clit, tongue swirling, adjusting to every shiver and sigh like it's her favorite feedback loop.

Hands steps forward and strips off his pants in a practiced motion, revealing a cock that matches his build. Thick. Veined. Heavy.

The man wastes no time, lining up behind her body. His large hand falls on her shoulder, sliding down over her spine, covering her ass for a moment and giving a squeeze before trailing over her hip. Aurora moans at his touch.

From behind her, Hands slides a finger along her seam, and she whimpers so loudly, so desperately, he slides inside her with two digits. Aurora jerks like she's been hit by an electric bolt before melting and writhing on his hand.

"Fuck girl, you're so wet," he gasps as he gives her several more experimental pumps. Then he sticks those same fingers into his mouth, sucking them clean with a satisfied groan.

The Blond man strips silently—his slacks pooling like water at his feet. The open poet's shirt he wears slips off his shoulders, revealing lean muscle, pale and elegant. There's a chain at his throat, a golden pendant resting on his chest.

Hands lines up his cock to Aurora's dripping entrance. As she eats the Librarian's cunt, he pushes inside her in one long, deep thrust.

Aurora chokes on a gasp and recovers instantly, her hips

driving back against him as she keeps licking, relentlessly. The bed groans, bodies stacked in a line of pleasure.

The Blond steps closer to the head of the bed. The Little Librarian, glassy-eyed and panting, reaches out with one hand, fingers closing firm on his cock. He hisses between his teeth but doesn't stop her. She strokes him slowly at first, then with rising urgency, guides him toward her mouth.

He leans over her as she parts her lips, taking him in, her moan vibrating through him.

From my place near the edge, I feel it—that heatwave shimmer from Aurora's power, that ambient magic no one but me knows to look for. It stops rolling inward into her body and moves off her like a fever dream, invisible but heavy.

A sigh of relief goes through me. It's working.

It thickens the air, threading through them, binding as surely as rope, a spell hidden in plain sight.

Their movements grow more desperate, more synchronized. Her magic enhances everything. Pleasure sharpens, arousal heightens. It's working. It's feeding her.

My cock is thick and aching again, but I force myself to focus. This morning's release was more than I deserve. This is about Aurora. Her needs. And I need to stay vigilant, in control, for everyone present.

Aurora tries to take sips, but like a child who's gone too long without water she takes big, unsteady gulps.

I grip the jeweled chain tighter and give it a warning tug. Just enough to make her flinch.

She slows, barely. Still lapping at the librarian's clit, her eyes fluttering shut, and I feel the energy rippling off her in waves. Because there are three of them it is easy for her to drink off them without feeding on any one too hard.

But she's still drinking too deeply.

I yank the chain harder.

Her body jerks, driving her onto Hands' dick with force. He groans and wraps his hand in her hair.

Aurora whimpers with genuine disappointment as she forces herself to ease off. The Librarian arches as her abs shudder. Her hands yank Aura's hair as she comes apart beneath her. Her cries are muffled by the Blond's dick her lips are currently wrapped around.

The first orgasm. A flood of energy rushes to Aura. Librarian tries to squirm away as she rides it out, but Aurora adds her fingers into the mix, elongating the orgasm.

Then the entire bed rotates as Aurora sprawls out and Librarian returns the same treatment, crouched between Aurora's legs, sucking and fingering her toward orgasm. Hands uses the position to make Aurora taste herself on his cock, and she uses her hands to help take him deeper. The Blond slides into Librarian fucking her slow and steady.

The bed is a tangle of limbs and sounds—wet and hot and overwhelming. They fuck and suck and finger each other with rising frenzy, shifting again, and again until Aurora is on her back, her legs spread, mouth open in a moan as they all worship her.

One kisses her throat while another thrusts slow and deep inside her. One hand is in her hair, another between her thighs. Her skin glows with power, her body flush and damp.

She has become the center. The focal point of every mouth, every hand, every cock. They orbit her, lost in the gravity of her hunger, the heat of her pleasure, the ache of her need.

She is divine. And they are worshipping.

And as she feeds on them, I can't help but feel the dark snake of jealousy that's recently arisen.

I wish it were me.

CHAPTER 23

A DRAGON DICK TO HAUNT YOUR DREAMS

AURORA

Everything is too much.

Pleasure, yes. Pressure, more.

The weight of the muscular man's cock in my mouth. The push of the Elfin man's cock stretching me from behind. I am spread, stuffed, worshipped, but it takes everything in me not to give in completely.

Depriving myself has made me reckless.

I want to drink, gorge, devour, consume every pulse of euphoria flowing into me, but Talon's grip on the leash keeps me tethered. He calls me to heel with a single jerk of his fingers.

The muscular man grips my hair and thrusts forward. I swallow around him, drooling as I suck him deeper, his salt and heat sliding over my tongue.

Behind me, I'm filled in long, slow thrusts that shudder pleasure up my spine. I rock between the two men, used and adored and so very full.

The woman with glasses kneels beside me, her fingers working my nipples, then sliding down to rub my clit with maddening pressure. She knows what she's doing. I want to cry from how good it feels.

"Are you going to come?" she asks, voice breathless and teasing.

I want to. Fae lords, I want to. But something's missing. Something just out of reach.

My orgasm coils tight in my belly, desperate to break free, but the frustration climbs higher. There's more sexual energy here than I've ever had access to. I should be overwhelmed. I should be unraveling.

But I'm not.

They surround me. Fuck me. Feed me.

I try to take only enough.

But I'm still starving.

If I hadn't fucking thought to take things in my own hands—literally—I might not be in such dire straits. Maybe the three of them could have satiated me, but I'm running on less than empty even as I drink their life forces in.

Tears sting the corners of my eyes.

Then I hear him. Talon.

"She needs more," he says, low and certain. Steady in the chaos.

And I know, without turning, that he knows exactly what that means.

A pause falls over the room, just long enough for the man with the sharp elegant jawline to glance at him, then back at me.

"Tell us what she wants," the fae man says. He's quiet but resolute.

Talon doesn't move at first. But something shifts in the air. In him. And when he speaks again, it isn't hesitation, it's command.

Talon directs them.

The muscular man lowers onto his back, guiding me to straddle him. His thick cock presses against me again, and I sink down with a gasping moan.

"Go slow, torture her," Talon says with a dark flash in his eye. "Pinch her nipples, *hard*."

He's not guessing. He knows. Every touch I crave. Every pattern I respond to. Every dirty detail I've never said aloud.

"And she wants it in that sweet little asshole." Talon is hard, almost cold in his command. Yet the air turns molten. My heart kicks up to a gallop.

Strong, nimble fingers slide between my legs to spread my wetness up to my rear and my eyes flutter closed. It feels so good.

"She needs to be wetter than that," Talon says flatly, voice sharp and dark with knowledge. "Spread her and spit." There is a ruthless edge to the direction that sends another shock through me before turning into hot liquid on the cock I'm slowly riding.

The woman kneels behind me, parting my ass cheeks with reverent hands, then spits. It hits me like a bullseye, wet and hot. My stomach clenches, and I gasp.

"That's right, baby," Talon says with that same steel tone. "You like it filthy, don't you?"

Only an incoherent moan escapes me as I take in this new side of Talon. The sound of smacking behind me tells me the petite woman and blond man are kissing. Something brushes my thigh—her fist curled tight on his cock.

"Now finger that little asshole until she's squealing," Talon says.

My body involuntarily lurches forward, my thighs spreading wider, allowing the man beneath me to fuck me even deeper as I spread myself.

I twist enough to see the woman smearing the wetness

over my tight ring of muscles with two fingers before sliding one of them in.

"Oh." The sound of surprise explodes out of me as I'm stretched. Then the blond man's finger joins hers in my puckered entrance until I'm moaning. Sexual energy charges the air and I take full swallows of it now, and for the first time, the sharp edge of hunger dulls slightly.

They take turns working me open, teasing me, torturing me under Talon's direction as I'm penetrated from below.

"Please," I whisper. Not to the others. To *him*.

No one else notices the tension that's snapped taut between me and Talon. He knows what I'm asking for.

I've been rejected once, but I can't help it. I want him and I'll take any little bit I can get.

The intensity in his eyes lets me know he's thinking. Hard.

He's considering my ask. What it will cost him. What lines it breaks.

Then his hand moves. Slowly. He reaches down and unzips his pants before pulling out his cock. I gasp.

It's half flesh, half black scales like the rest of his body, but it's ridged. Huge. Heavy. More beautiful than I expected, and more terrifying.

The thing between his legs is going to haunt my every dream.

Scratch that. My every waking moment.

He strokes it in front of me for the first time.

For the second time, he's not just a bystander. Not tonight.

Every command he's given, every way they've touched me, it's him. He's the one guiding their hands, their mouths, their cocks like he would his own. He knows me so well, it's terrifying. And I love it.

"She's going to need you to fill up her ass with that cock," Talon says to the blond one. "Push it in so deep she'll feel it in her throat."

"Fuck," the man breathes under me. Talon's words are affecting him too.

His voice is the only thing guiding me through the fog.

Finally, the other man aligns himself and pushes his cock in. He goes slow—agonizingly so—and my gasp turns into a sob of pleasure.

"That's it, princess," Talon coaches. "You can take it. Take them all."

The moans turn into cacophony.

Talon tightens the chain and everything inside me clenches.

I can't feel his hand, but I can feel his will.

My eyes close as it's all too much to take. Every nerve ending is alight. I'm full. Stretched to capacity in a way I've never felt before.

I miss the murmurs from Talon, but next thing I know, the woman kneels beside me, fingers pinching my nipples again before trailing lower. One hand slides between my thighs, careful not to disrupt the rhythm of the men inside me, her touch finding my clit again.

She rubs in tight, quick circles.

Oh fuck fuck *fuck*.

"Faster," Talon snaps. "Harder. She needs more."

The man below me groans, driving up into me with piston precision. The slim, elegant man wraps one arm around my waist and fucks my ass bent on fusing our bodies together. The woman's fingers never let up on my clit.

My brain melts as my body transcends to another realm. The slick slide of so many bodies pressed to mine is unreal. With three of them to drink from, I begin to feel the beginnings of satiation. But I want to gorge myself.

"Tell me you're my good little girl," Talon says. "Tell them you're mine. You'll always be mine."

The sexual nature shifts as Talon dives into the most private parts of me, wrenching them up to the surface. It's all true, but my throat locks. I don't want to say it out loud, surrounded by all these people pleasuring me.

"I want to hear it, princess," Talon demands, his jaw clenches with anger. "Say it."

But I'm already committed. I always have been his, and he's always been mine, and nothing will ever change that. Even if it tortures us for the rest of our lives.

"I'm your good girl," I sob. "I'm yours."

"That's it, sweetheart," Talon says. "You want to come so hard? You are going to take it all. You're going to be filled and fucked because *I say so*." He yanks my chain, only hard enough to get my attention.

"That's it," he goes on. "Look at me while you come. You know that's the only way you get there. You need me watching you—owning it."

I turn my gaze to Talon's eyes. He stands at the edge of the bed, his hand still sliding along his beautiful dick, my leash wrapped on the other.

That's all I need. My nails dig into the strong chest below. My knees press into the sheets. The moment I have that line of sight, everything inside me tightens. Focus sharpens.

My entire body pulses, shaking. I ride the man below me with desperation, push back against the man behind me, and grind down into the woman's hand.

And I come apart right there in front of Talon, with all

of them watching, touching, helping. I scream through the orgasm, legs trembling, vision white.

And I feast.

A FULL SCALE SHIFT
AURORA

The air outside the club is cool and quiet, with only the sound of our boots on the wet concrete. The others we left on the bed, sleeping like the dead but still very much alive. I checked. Twice.

Talon and I don't speak as we walk. The silence is heavy. The bound-up leash still dangles between us as I didn't bother to take off the collar.

I should be sated. I've never fed like that, from so many at once, but part of me still growls with hunger. Not dangerous, not ravenous...Just hollow.

I wonder how long I have before I need to come and top myself off again. That's how I should think of myself. Like a gas tank that needs to be refilled, but never to the top. Always running on less than full, but it's doable, right?

I'm not the only one left unsatisfied.

I glance at Talon as I shift the pack on my shoulder. He didn't come. Just tucked himself in his pants and helped me set things right.

I was able to use the attached bathroom for a quick

shower, taking a moment for some semblance of normalcy even if I'm not fully sated.

My lashes flutter shut as the echo of Talon's commands still hovers in my ears before etching into my bones. I'll forever be haunted by the fierce expression of possession and need as he slides his hand up and down his dick.

He exposed himself. Even in front of those other people. Something he's never done before.

Talon's right. What we've been doing is too dangerous.

But I can't stop.

I love him. Beyond reason. Beyond sanity.

My heart is so full of him, it's a wonder it hasn't cracked my ribs open.

We round the corner of the warehouse into a long industrial corridor near the Boston Harbor, the salt tang in my nose. Rusting shipping containers line one side. A crooked blue-and-white street sign marks the dock zone ahead.

Talon slows.

So do I.

"What's wrong?" I ask quietly, but my voice seems too loud. A cold mist falls from the sky, threatening to turn into fat raindrops.

From the shadows, figures emerge—too still, too pale, too deliberate. Their eyes glint in the weak light from the flickering dock lamp. Urban leather jackets, boots, dark hoods, they look like they've stepped out of a street gang, not a castle crypt. Fangs bare beneath grins full of malice.

First two, then five.

Vampires.

Mal sent them. To kill me. To punish my father.

"Aura, get out of here," Talon orders, already moving to intercept.

The first vampire lunges. Talon grabs his throat mid-air. A searing hiss fills the night as his palm ignites, turning skin to blistered ruin. He hurls the vampire sideways, spine snapping as it hits the ground.

A snarling female sprints toward me from the left. Talon turns and crushes her with a backhand that sends her sailing into a rusted container with a crack of bone.

My feet are glued to the pavement as I watch in frozen horror as more appear from the shadows.

Three more vampires fall on him. He throws fists, and embers spark off him but there are too many. A fourth pushes his way into the fray. I catch the glint of steel right before a blade sinks deep into Talon's ribs.

Talon bellows, the sound raw and animalistic.

"Talon!" I cry out, lurching forward instinctively. Cold fear is washed away by red hot anger.

They hurt Talon. *My* Talon.

My hand closes around a length of rotted dock wood, splintered but solid. I may be a princess, but I'm also a Lost Girl now.

The words from the tattoo parlor return to me, firming my resolve.

"They'll underestimate you...let them."

"They'll want you to play nice...don't."

I swing wide. The beam connects with the vampire's temple, a sickening crunch echoing through the night. My makeshift weapon snaps in two on contact. As my target drops to the ground, another vamp peels off from the fray and heads toward me.

"Aura, get out of here! Go!" Talon roars before two more vampires slam into his back. It takes six of them to drag Talon down to one knee.

Their hands tear at his skin, fingers prying between his

glowing scales where the knife is lodged. One vampire hisses as he rips a scale free, still pulsing orange at the edges with heat. Blood gushes as Talon cries out.

"Shit," I breathe, dropping the useless bit of wood left as I stumble.

My throat closes as Talon is overwhelmed and the vampire stalks purposefully toward me.

The Rosari aren't combat-trained people. We don't invest in armed forces because we can suck the fight right out of anyone.

All *I* can do is suck the life out of this guy through his dick, but that's not exactly the scene set here, and I'm in no hurry to get in close.

I suddenly wish I had secretly trained in some kind of martial arts all these years instead of working on watercolors, horse riding, and reading books.

Talon slumps forward, fury flaring in his eyes even as his body begins to fail. He mouths to me, "*Go.*"

I don't want to leave him. But I can't help him.

I run in the other direction for a few feet, then glance over my shoulder. He's surrounded now, a blur of fists, claws, and heat.

Then I'm yanked back. The collar cuts into my throat so hard it breaks flesh. A garbled choke escapes me as my hands fly up to my neck.

I reach to unclasp the collar, but the vampire jerks the chain still locked around my throat and drags me down like an animal.

My knees crack against concrete. My palms scrape open. The leash bites deep into my skin.

"Talon!"

The young vampire in front of me stares down at me with a cold green gaze. "You're not as powerful or dangerous as she said." He leans over, yanking the chain to bring my face to his. "Best not to chance it though. Won't let you fuck me to death, even if you are hot."

I feel a pulse. It starts in my chest then drops lower, deeper.

Something in me rises, uncoiling from the center of my being, and I gasp.

Power—sexual, ancient, hungry—ripples beneath my skin. My lips part. The vampire holding me suddenly freezes, eyes wide. His grip falters.

I taste something electric between my teeth.

The world tilts. My power wants out. I don't know what it's trying to do, only that it is trying to do *something*.

A boot smashes into my stomach. A cough explodes from me with equal violence as I double over and cradle my center.

"What the fuck were you doing, witch?" he demands.

When I lift my head, I connect with Talon's gaze. Another two bodies are ash at his feet, but he's still outnumbered and overwhelmed.

My left eye just about explodes from my face as I'm backhanded. I groan, the slippery metallic taste of my own blood filling my mouth, the inside of my cheek cut along my teeth.

A blast of heat rolls over me.

Through my blurred vision, I meet Talon's eyes. They flare with a fiery orange hue, like embers born of fury. The intensity builds, and the orange deepens into a molten, liquid gold, swirling and shifting as if alive. Suddenly, they burst into flames, fierce and consuming, casting flickering shadows across his face.

A growl erupts like an avalanche, shaking the very air as the sky splits open. Wings explode from Talon's back, wide and violent, soaking wet and shimmering with firelight and rain.

The storm breaks as Talon surges upward, dragging three vampires with him. His whole body pulses, orange-lit fissures racing across his scales, glowing like molten fault lines. I watch in horror and awe as heat radiates off him in blistering waves.

Bones crack like gunfire beneath his skin. His spine arches, limbs elongating. Scales rip through flesh in a rapid sweep as if his very skin is being rewritten by fire. Claws replace fingers. His jaw stretches. Horns burst from his skull.

The vampires claw at him, hissing and snapping, trying to drag him back down even as they cry out in a panic.

A whip of his arm sends one vampire crashing into the wall with a wet crunch. Another tries to leap on his back but is smacked away by a powerful wing. Another is incinerated by a blast of fire that erupts from his mouth.

My breath stops. It shouldn't be possible, but there he is in full, complete Dragon form.

He's beautiful. Terrifying.

Talon's tail slams a metal dumpster into twisted shrapnel. Then he turns, unleashing a torrent of flame into the alley. The blast lights up the rain-slick darkness, the way sunlight floods a cathedral at high noon. Vampires scream, their silhouettes writhing in the inferno before collapsing into ash. One by one, he hunts them down without mercy. The fire rolls forward, cleansing the alley of every bloodsucker in his path.

There are more than I thought. So many hidden in the shadows. The sheer number that had come for us makes my blood run cold.

The vampire who yanked my leash and dragged me to my knees tries to run.

With a thunderous flap of wings, massive claws hook under the vampire's ribs, and he lifts, screaming, into the night sky.

For a breathless second, they're suspended above the warehouse rooftops. Then Talon tears him apart midair, flinging his halves in opposite directions. Blood rains down, mixing with the storm.

I stumble to my feet, soaked and trembling, unable to look away. The whole stretch is empty now. No more movement. No more fangs. Just scorched concrete, chunks of charred limbs, and blood seeping into the storm drains. The rain pelts metal and concrete with a steady rhythm, washing it all away.

Movement snags my eye. A vampire slips behind a row of crates, Talon's torn scale and the still-wet blade gripped tight as he disappears.

And then Talon falters.

The flames die in his mouth. His body cracks and shudders, and shifts. Scales retract. Bones shrink.

His massive body drops like a felled tree. One wing folds in. His limbs shudder. Fire flickers, then dies.

And then the shrinking begins. The slow collapse inward. Muscle, scale, bone, folding down into a man.

I break into a sprint, heading toward him unsure of what to do. Even if I got to him in time, he'd crush me on impact.

He hits the ground several feet in front of me.

Fear pierces through me as I run to him. "Talon!"

When the smoke clears, he's human again.

Naked. Bleeding.

I fall to my knees, not caring about the pain. My hands

hover over him. Frustration roars in me that I can't touch him. I can't feel if he's okay.

The half of his body covered in black scales no longer glows with orange fissures. They are dull, dark, drained. Black and lifeless, like spent coal. He bleeds heavily from where the scale has been flayed from his ribs.

He lies there in the alley, broken and burned out.

"Aura," he gasps, lifting his head, eyes fluttering.

Whipping off my cloak, I ball it up and gingerly slide it under his head. My hands still itch to touch him, to hold him.

"I'm sorry, I'm so sorry." I can't tell if my cheeks are wet from the slow, lazy drizzle of rain or from my own tears. Seeing him hurt feels like someone has ripped out my guts and I can't stand it.

"Shhh," he soothes, despite being a broken mess. "It's just a flesh wound. Don't worry, princess."

"Don't worry. *Don't worry?* If it weren't for me, we wouldn't have been out here. This wouldn't have..." My words die in my throat as my senses connect to the nerve endings in my hands. They continue to hover uselessly over his body, but I realize the usual heat isn't pulsating off him.

My heart catches in my throat.

The foreboding orange fissures between his scales aren't there.

I hold my breath as my fingers move of their own accord.

Panic flares in Talon's tired eyes as he realizes what I'm about to do.

"Aura, no," he barks.

But I don't hesitate. I slide a hand over his jaw, cupping it.

There is the scratch of his dark scruff raking over my

soft fingertips. There is the firm, too warm skin that wraps around his jawline that I feel my way along, tracing the square bones there. There is the softness of his lower lip as I brush my thumb over it.

But there is no scalding.

There is no pain.

Just...Talon.

A half-hiccup, half-sob rocks my body as my other hand reaches for him, and I frame his face.

Fear and wonder battle in his dark gaze.

I stare at him in wonder. "You burned off so much energy, you're..."

"Cool," he finishes.

It's true. My hand is warmer than his flesh even as I shiver in the cold pelt of rain.

"Has this ever happened?" My hope is rising too fast, too hard.

Talon shakes his head slowly. "No. It shouldn't be possible."

He looks at me, then down at his own chest, flexing his fingers like he's trying to summon something long-familiar. "I've had power surges before. Flared too hot. But I've never gone full Dragon. That form...Dragons aren't meant to shift that far anymore."

My breath catches. "But you did."

His eyes lift, locking on mine. "And I think I burned out all my fire doing it."

Talon presses my palm to his chest. "Once in a tavern, I heard an old Dragon tale. About burning so hot, so fast, you exhaust your flame forever. Most don't survive it. Those who do...they never burn again."

My heart lurches with equal measures of guilt and hope. "You think it's permanent?"

He swallows hard. "It feels different this time. Like I didn't just *use* my fire...I emptied it. I don't know if it can come back."

He grips my wrist with iron strength, an urgency flashing in his eyes. He's holding onto me for dear life. I can tell reality is slow and hard to hit.

"Aura." The way he breathes my name breaks me into a million pieces, but I don't mind because he can scoop up all the little pieces in his hands now.

"Talon."

Our mouths collide.

CHAPTER 25

A SURPRISE SET OF WINGS

TALON

Aura's lips. Soft, pliant, cold, and utter fucking heaven. How does she taste even better than she smells? The sweet candy notes intensify and darken the more I plunder her mouth.

I want everything, all at once. My hands are in her hair, sweeping over her neck, gripping her face like it's my last lifeline as everything in me comes alive in an explosion of fireworks.

Perhaps I should be worried I've burned out. About what it means. We should be worried about Mal's horde of vampires, but I can't give a single flying fuck about any of that.

I'm finally touching, holding, kissing the woman of my every desire, and there is no space for anything else.

Needing more, I force myself to sit up. Hot raking pain stabs through my ribs, but I ignore it. I can't help the groan of pain, but I gather Aura closer to me.

She puts her hands, her gloriously perfect fucking hands, on my chest and pushes me slightly.

"You're hurt."

I recapture her lips, pulling her to me, unable to give her an inch of space or a moment to speak. "I told you, it's a flesh wound," I say against her lips.

I coax her open, and my tongue meets hers. My groan this time is entirely different. She's utterly edible. I'm going to eat her up. There will be nothing left of her when I'm done.

The silky wet welcome of her mouth triples my desperation for more.

Aurora whimpers as I grip the hair at the base of her skull, angling her so I can kiss her deeper.

I'm going to do so much more to her. A bottleneck of ideas, fantasies, needs, and wants drill into my brain with unrestrained, wild pressure.

In a moment, she is half on my lap where I'm hardening so fast, the rush makes the world sway and my vision blurs.

Or maybe that's the blood loss...

She clutches me close, nails digging in as she meets my frenetic onslaught of kisses with equal passion.

We cling to each other, tasting, devouring, *feeling*.

Only when it's absolutely necessary to breathe do we break.

Still, I drop small, short kisses on her lips, down the line of her elegant neck. I taste salt, soap, rain, and *her*.

"Talon." A laugh bubbles out of her. It's only then I notice her teeth are chattering. Her entire body is trembling, hard.

My protective instincts kick in.

"Hold on," I say, dropping a kiss on the perfect shell of her ear. I gather her closer. Ignoring the pain, my wings expand and I force myself to stand. Aurora's legs encircle my waist, tightening as I shoot us up into the sky with a powerful stroke of my wings.

A little squeal of surprise slips out of her, and I hug her tighter, unable to stop the smile forming on my lips.

With a quick scan, I spot a brick industrial building with open windows on the third floor. I easily push the oversized pane so it swings open wider for us to pass through.

The pain in my side burns, but it's so far down the list of feelings I'm experiencing, it is quickly a dull throb in the background.

The large warehouse is deserted. Tall wooden crates are stacked like forgotten tombstones, casting long shadows. An insignia of a rose with thorns is burned into the sides of all the containers. A few hanging bulbs strung across a central beam flicker softly to life—motion-triggered. The amber glow spills across the concrete floor, warm and golden against the cold outside.

I land in the center of the space and spot an old wool blanket thrown over a crate. I grab it, pulling it over Aurora's shoulders.

The sound of fluttering has me on instant alert. I catch whispers of movements overhead. Bats maybe? I catch a pair of floppy ears and twitching noses up in the rafters. Ah. Flutterbuns. Little half-rabbit, half-bat creatures with horns. It's surprising to find them nesting here, but they won't bother us.

Aurora is still laughing, and shivering. Her cotton candy pink and blue hair has turned dark, heavy with rainwater. I carefully rub part of the blanket over her head.

Her laughter subsides, eyes drifting down to my side.

"You need medical attention," she says more seriously.

"You're right, but I need this first." I grab her roughly and claim her mouth again.

Need builds inside me, stronger than it ever has, threatening to consume me whole.

Aurora shoves me hard enough that I break away. "We have to do something about it," she says before turning to go.

Panic surges as I grab hold of the blanket around her, pulling her back to me with a stubborn *harrumph*.

"Fine." She snorts in fake impatience. "Come with me then." She drags me by the hand over to an office where she finds a first aid kit in one of the drawers.

She hums as she picks through the surprisingly well-stocked kit. Impatience gets the best of me as I brush her hands aside, grab a swath of gauze and quickly tape it over my side.

It'll do for now, but I'm not the only one with damage.

I grab the disinfectant and force Aurora to keep still as I clean the scratches on her hands and knees. All the while, she tortures me by kissing my chest, my neck, any bit she can reach. It feels like an eternity after I'm done bandaging her scrapes.

Finally finished, I hold Aurora's face and taste her deeply and completely. When her butt hits the desk, I don't stop. Picking her up by the hips, I set her on the surface. Stepping in between her legs feels like coming home.

My extended wings flap and stretch with unrestrained excitement.

The blanket falls from her shoulders as I nip and taste down the column of her throat, eliciting the most cock-hardening whimpers and moans. I tug down the neckline of her dress, exposing her full breasts.

Goosebumps rise along her golden flesh as my mouth covers her swell and my tongue swirls around her perfect pink nipple. Savoring the taste of her skin, I'm desperate for more. I squeeze and coax the other breast so it doesn't feel neglected until I can switch and molest that one too. The peaks are already stiff against my tongue, and I flick and nip between sucking and kissing them, worshipping her like I've always wanted to.

"Talon, I..." Her voice chokes up, like she can't get the words out.

"I know, baby, I know," I coo. I yank her dress up, and my fingers find her wet seam.

She gasps. I gulp.

"Such a soft, perfect pussy for me to play with." The words are husky to my own ears as I gently slide two fingers along her sex, spreading the generous wetness that's already there.

She clenches her eyes shut as she holds onto me for dear life. Nails bite into the back of my neck as if she's afraid I'll disappear.

There's nowhere in heaven or hell I'd rather be.

My fingers glide inside her, and we both groan at the contact. Fuck, she's so wet and tight. Closing my eyes, I remember all the times I noted that perfect angle she needed and adjust my wrist up as I give her several shallow pumps.

"Please, please, Talon. I can't wait. I'm losing my mind," she practically sobs.

I think I've already lost mine.

Her pleas are muffled by my kiss, and I reluctantly pull my fingers out of her. I want to stick them in my mouth, taste her, savor her, drown in her cunt if need be, but desperation has taken hold of both of us. We rush to undo my pants and clumsily shove at them. They're barely halfway down my thighs when she takes hold of my hard, hot cock.

"Ahh," I hiss as she immediately pumps me.

Oh fuck, oh fuck, oh fuck. Oh witchtitting fae lords, I'm going to come so fast.

My thighs twitch. My gut tightens. Every nerve feels like it's been rerouted to my cock. I've never been touched until now.

Not like this. Not ever.

I didn't know it could feel like this—hot, sharp, almost unbearable in the best way. She palms me again, and I swear I see black around the edges of my vision.

"I can't believe I haven't seen your cock before tonight," she says between kisses, pushing out that bottom lip in one of her famous pouts. "It's brutally unfair."

I can't comment. My brain is lost in a fog of lust.

She doesn't hesitate—not with the ridges or the thickness. As she strokes my length, I swear I nearly see stars.

"Can you..." She swallows hard. "Can you show me the rest?"

The rest?

Oh.

I clear my throat, feeling awkward. How long has she known? Yet again, I underestimated her.

Relaxing the muscles between my thighs and my cock, my second set of wings expands. They sweep forward, then out wide. Considerably smaller than the ones on my back, but the thin membrane stretches out several feet. The little claw tips at the bottoms twitch from being released, unused to the freedom.

"You're beautiful," she stares at them so lovingly, my chest hurts.

Aurora continues to stroke me, and I curse, because *fuck*, my cock was made for her. I know it's not like any she's seen before. Thick and ridged, the shaft is half-wrapped in black scales that taper off into the flushed head, glowing faintly with violet undertones like embers caught under glass. Her thumb drags along the generous textured length, and my knees nearly buckle. Her breath catches.

Despite the extra ridges and girth, she doesn't hesitate to touch me.

Unable to take anymore, I move her hand away to fight my pants down the rest of the way while she rips off her dress. Underneath, she still wears the jewels.

We both freeze.

Aurora's expression turns grave. "I don't want to hurt you," she whispers.

I tug the chains, forcing her pelvis to meet mine. "You won't. I'm still the only one you can't hurt."

Before she can protest or come up with some other ridiculous fear, I have her on her back on the desk. My body covers hers. The tip of my cock finds her entrance, and I slide in.

The world detonates.

For years, I've imagined this. But imagination never came close. The first clutch of her heat steals the air from my lungs. My vision whites out. Every nerve in my body screams that this is impossible, that I shouldn't be here, shouldn't be inside her, and yet I am.

Now she takes me. She surrounds me. The wall of fire I have carried all my life isn't here to keep us apart. Every breath of hers pulls me deeper into a world I thought I would never reach. The loneliness I buried for years tears open and I can barely withstand it.

For the first time in my life, I am not untouchable. I am not abandoned. I am hers. I am alive.

The heat of her drags the last shred of control I have straight to the edge.

Our cries echo all around us as I work my way into Aura's excruciating tightness.

More fluttering comes from overhead. We've disturbed the natives, but I don't plan on stopping.

"Talon." My name is a prayer and a plea on her tongue.

I brace my forearm above her head, breath ragged, my hips locked tight to keep from slamming all the way in. I want to savor every fucking inch of this.

She's so wet, I slide deeper than I expected, and my body tenses to keep from losing it right there. My cock is wrapped in heat and velvet, and it's better than anything I ever imagined with a fist in the dark.

Then, on pure instinct, my second wings move. They slide forward from where they're tucked at the tops of my inner thighs, unfurling slowly until they wrap around her hips. Thin, almost translucent, they mold to her curves like silk laced with heat. Her breath hitches against my mouth.

She's not afraid. She leans into it. Her hands drift down, fingertips brushing the edge of one wing where it grips her side. My whole body jolts. They're hypersensitive and no one's ever touched them before.

The clawed tips of my wings angle and hook her ass cheeks, pulling them apart.

The sensation travels straight to my core. Tugging her open like that—fuck. It's primal. Possessive. I feel more animal than man.

"Does that feel good, baby?" I ask, knowing all the signs that it does. For a moment, self-consciousness seizes me. She's never been with anyone like me. And fuck, I've never been with, well...anyone.

"Yes." Her nails rake over my shoulders. "Oh fucking fae lords, Talon. It's so good."

Heat shimmers off her in glorious, beautiful waves of power.

She's hungry.

My chest tightens. I've seen that hunger before, from across a room, with someone else under her. But now it's for me. Only me.

A small voice of fear tells me to stop. This might be like when she tried to pleasure herself. If she can't feed from me, she could end up hurting herself.

"I can't stop," I say it out loud, even as I finally fill her to the hilt.

Her body tightens around me, snug and pulsing, like she was made to take me. I bite back a groan that wants to break loose from somewhere deep and raw.

"If you stop, I will *murder* you," she growls.

"Yes, princess."

CHAPTER 26
FUCK UNTIL FULL
TALON

I pick up the pace, sliding in and out. But with my wings surrounding her, I never pull out very far. My claw tips drift and slide deeper between the swells of her backside until they hit that tight ring of muscles.

Aurora braces a hand on my shoulder away and drags me back down as if she can't decide if it's too much or if she wants more. Still, the claw slips in deeper until a screech escapes her.

Oh *shit*.

That was *definitely* a sound I've never heard her make before. Her eyes fly open, begging louder than words ever could. She silently begs me for more.

I push in the other claw.

Her whole body arches, back bowing, tits pressing to my chest, a guttural sound tearing from her mouth that makes me want to fuck her through the wall just to hear it again.

"I have you," I say, and I mean it with every cell. Every thrust pulls her deeper into my body, those delicate wings working on their own, guiding her into the rhythm I've only dreamed of.

The heat builds between us, her power pulsing in time with our movements. I can feel it winding around us, alive, binding us together. It's terrifying and exhilarating all at once. I've never felt anything like this, never knew it was possible to feel so much.

Every nerve in my body is alive. Every sense is focused on how she feels. How she takes me. How I never want this to end.

The room fills with the sound of our ragged breaths and the distant rumble of thunder from the storm outside.

Aurora's eyes are closed tight, lashes still wet with tears or rainwater, I can't tell. I kiss them away, tasting the salt on my lips. Her hands find my face, holding me close as our bodies move in sync.

Her moans become louder, more insistent. "Talon," she whispers, "I think...I think I can feel you." She shakes her head as if that's the wrong word.

I pause, searching her face. Her eyes are wide with wonder, lips swollen from my kisses. "What do you mean?"

She gasps as I rock into her again. "I can taste you."

Despite feeding mere hours ago, heat shimmers off her in glorious, beautiful waves of power. Her hunger bleeds through her skin, sultry and wild. But it's never touched me.

Until now.

At first, I don't feel much. A soft prickle at the edges of my awareness, static brushing across my skin. Then it deepens. Sharpens. Like an invisible tongue dragging down the center of my soul.

A shudder runs through me at the sensation. It's not good or bad, just different. Her mouth is wrapped around my soul and drawing it out in slow, molten pulls. But there's no fear. No strain.

Just...pleasure.

Twisting. Building.

Our mouths crash together, teeth and tongue and heat. Not soft. Not sweet. Just need. It's everything we've been denying ourselves, and it's fucking explosive. Then she gasps. Her eyes go wild with fear.

"Talon," she chokes, shaking her head. "I...I can't stop. I don't want to hurt you. I'm trying, but—fuck—I can't stop."

She pushes at my chest, trying to get away, afraid she'll pull too much, that she'll lose me in the taking. I don't let her out of my grasp. Between pinning her on the desk and my second wings trapping her hips, there's no escaping me.

"You don't have to." Something in me cracks open, and I give. I offer. I lean in, panting against her mouth. "I'm not like the others. I *never* was. Take it. Take it all."

I drive into her harder, my pace shifting, rougher, deeper, matching her hunger as it takes hold. We fuck with the reckless certainty of bodies that have always belonged together.

Despite Aurora's attempt to cage it, it's as if I've given her curse permission to let go.

Her hunger sinks its teeth in, a starved beast that's scented something it can't resist. Aurora's eyes roll up as she claws at my chest, but this time in pleasure. This isn't how it is with the others. Even when she didn't kill them, I've seen what it costs. The way they'd shake. Pale. Struggle to stand.

They always looked hollowed out, scraped clean of life.

But this?

There's no loss. No drain. Her feeding matches the way my body was made to give. And fuck, it feels good.

The longer she feeds, clarity rips away. Heat burns through thought, through reason, until I'm nothing but instinct and the raw need to keep pushing into her. My hips chase the rhythm, the connection, the growing pulse that ties us together. I've never felt more vital.

She pulls, and I pour. Not because I have to. Because I want to. Maybe it's the Dragon in me. Maybe every part of me was made for this. My power doesn't dim. It rises. Builds. Rushes to meet her, answers her as if my body has always known this command.

Or maybe it's because my love for her isn't just deep.

It's bottomless.

Each thrust sends another pulse of energy into her. Dragon magic, soul magic, whatever the hell it is, it's hers now.

She moans again, full-throated and helpless. Her slick heat seizes me with every thrust, tight, pulsing, greedier by the second.

My hands find hers, fingers lacing together above her head. Our gazes lock, and it's like the world falls away. There's only us, only this moment. "Aura." I whisper her name. "I love you. More than life itself."

Her glassy eyes look at me with heartbreaking adoration, and for a moment I don't think I could possibly deserve this gorgeous, clever, stubborn creature. "I love you too. I always have," she says before yanking me down to fuse our mouths together again.

My hand fists in her hair. My wings tighten on her hips. And then we're gone.

The rhythm turns urgent. Desperate. I thrust deeper,

harder, and she takes all of it—clawing at my shoulders, mouth open, eyes wild.

My second wings grip tighter, the tips dragging along her skin, guiding her to me on every stroke like I'm using all of me to hold her right where she belongs.

She starts to unravel—panting, gasping, crying out with each thrust. The room disappears. All I can feel is her. All I want is more.

I give her everything. Every bit of my lust, my love, my hunger. Every secret fantasy. Every starved second I spent watching her feed from men who weren't me. Every time she moaned for someone else while I was locked in place, hands fisted, jaw clenched, *bleeding* for the right to be hers.

Now I am.

She milks me, her inner walls fluttering and grasping. Her breath catches, eyes glazed and shining. She's close. *So fucking close.*

And I know it.

I feel the heat rising in her clenching belly. The flutter of panic at the edge of her climax. Her thighs quiver against mine, slick with sweat. But she grips it in her teeth, refusing to release.

I grab her chin, forcing her to look at me.

"Look at me, Aura. I'm fine," I say, steel in my voice. "I'm here. You take me so well, baby. Now give in. Let go. Take all you need. I've got you."

Her mouth opens, but no sound comes out at first. Just breath, ragged, like she's been hit with too much pleasure to process.

Her brows pinch, lips tremble, and her chest heaves with the sharp upward spiral to her release. Then she drops off that cliff into uncontrollable spasms, her curse, her power sinks into me all at once and it gorges.

My name tears from her throat as Aurora's scream echoes off the warehouse walls.

Somewhere an explosion of wings signals a nest of flutterbuns, or several, that flee from the riot down below.

My release crashes through me, surging straight from the base of my spine and flooding into her with punishing force.

I've never come inside someone. Never been deep inside the woman I loved, at the exact second she came around me. It's too much. Too perfect.

As she pulses, I feel her power weaving, stitching, anchoring to me as it drinks.

When we float back down to rejoin our bodies, both dripping with sweat, a breathy laugh filled with happy disbelief bursts from Aurora. I can't help but smile and laugh with her.

I brush my mouth over hers softly. A kiss that seals our new reality.

CHAPTER 27

TASTING THE DREAM

AURORA

Talon's wrapped around me, armor and shield in one. His blood is still drying on his skin, and his power hums low beneath the surface. More importantly, for the first time since I was cursed, I'm *full*.

Not just sated.

Full.

Every part of me swells with it. Not the desperate hunger that claws at my edges, or the quiet itch that is always present.

This wasn't the shallow fix of a regular feed. I've always been a cracked cup, leaking no matter how much I take in— and Talon just gave me an ocean.

I want more. Not out of hunger, but out of *want*. Out of love. I want him in me again, not just physically, but from a place that says *mine*. Forever.

I blink up at him from where I'm still sprawled on the desk. Our bodies are slick, tangled, flushed with sweat and heat. His wings retract slightly, until they are loosely holding my thighs.

He watches me with that look. That *Talon* look, memorizing the shape of my soul, not just my body. I've no doubt he'd fight the fae lords themselves if they ever tried to take me away again.

My fingers drift across his jaw. "I've never come that hard," I whisper.

His hand curves gently over my hip, thumb sweeping in slow circles. "You've never fed with that kind of abandon." It's not a question.

I shake my head as my throat tightens. "You completely filled me. You made me feel like I wasn't...alone."

His eyes darken. His hand slides higher, curling around my ribs. "You're not alone. You've never been alone."

"Just...separate," I amend.

A grunt of begrudging agreement comes out of him.

"I've always told myself it didn't matter. That our...*friendship*," I use that word instead of calling it the pining, heart-wrenching close-but-not-close-enough rela-tionship, "is enough. That I don't need more to be happy. That I can be independent, alone. A Dragon. You didn't need anyone."

Talon's fingers softly trace down the side of my face, pushing sweaty strands of hair aside. "Before I met you, I was...it was..." his brows scrunch as he tries to think through whatever he is trying to get out, "fine. Sufficient. But then I met you and my whole universe opened and there was so much more. I knew I needed you before I even met you. Does that make sense?" Intensity bears down from his face as he tries to make sense of his own feelings.

I nod. Even when I was young, maybe too young to think about such things, I yearned for the deep kind of connection we share. We can communicate with a glance. We have so many shared experiences, both good and bad. We have little inside jokes.

I kiss him again, softly at first, then deeper, slower. Everything in me reaches for him, not just the part that needs to feed, but the part that wants to *belong*. Me to him and him to me.

When I ease away, I murmur, "I love you, Talon."

Fuck, it feels good to say.

Talon seems to struggle with breathing for a few beats.

"I'll never get enough of you," he growls.

Then he pulls out of me, slow and careful, but his eyes stay locked on mine, molten and reverent.

I gasp at the loss, at the way my body clutches around nothing. But before I can say a word, he's dropped to his knees between my thighs.

"Talon—" I start, but he cuts me off with a look.

"Lie back," he says, voice all gravel and heat. "I need to taste what's mine."

Fae lords help me.

The moment my back hits the desk again, his hands grip my thighs and spread me wide. His mouth is on me in a breath, tongue dragging through my slick folds, starving for more.

"Fuck, princess. You taste even better than I dreamed. *We* taste good together." A rumble escapes his throat, a sound so deep it rattles my core. He groans, eyes flashing up at me dark with need. "You don't even know what you do to me."

I shatter in minutes.

My legs jerk, fists clenching the edge of the desk as I scream his name. But Talon doesn't stop. He groans, devouring me, his hunger fixed solely on my pleasure. His tongue circles, dips, devours, until I'm bucking under him and coming again, harder this time, tears slipping down my temples from the sheer, brutal release.

But still, he doesn't stop.

His fingers slide into me, curling expertly as his mouth returns to my clit, sucking with just enough pressure to make me beg.

"I've always wanted you this way," he mutters. "Legs spread, soaking my mouth, begging for more."

I moan helplessly, already teetering again. His tongue works me with brutal worship. My body convulses again, and I'm crying, shaking, and clutching at his shoulders. I try to catch my breath, but he keeps going. Lapping me up. Marking me with his mouth. His words and his tongue push me right over again. It borders on torture, but still, he doesn't stop.

Not until he's wrung every drop of pleasure from my body. Not until I'm trembling, incoherent, clutching at him. He's the only thing anchoring me to this world.

And even then...his tongue lingers. Worshipping.

Because I'm his to do whatever he wants with. Forever. Nothing can break us now that we've found our way to each other.

WE LEAVE the warehouse in a haze of exhaustion and want. His wings carry us to our apartment and I press into his chest as dawn cracks like an orange yolk over the gray ocean waters. Neither of us says much, but the silence between us isn't heavy. Everything feels lighter.

As soon as we close the beat-up door of the apartment, we resume devouring each other. I have to force both of us to stop before all our clothes come off again.

"We have to clean you up," I insist, referring to his wound. Blood has seeped through the gauze. My bandages came off sometime between the first and fifth orgasm, but my wounds had miraculously closed. Not that I'm surprised.

Feedings always helped heal little cuts or scrapes I'd gotten almost instantly.

Talon continues to attack my neck, hands roaming over my breasts, and over my arms before tangling his fingers in my hair. "Later."

"No," I say firmly. "Now, mister."

I force him off me and toward the bathroom. He leans against the counter as I remove his dressings. As soon as I reveal the exposed meaty parts of him, all the organs in my body clench up, recoiling from the wet exposure of muscle.

"Aura?" he asks.

"Mmm," I say, trying to remain standing though I sway a bit, my head suddenly light and fuzzy.

"You're white as a sheet," he says.

"I'm fine." I struggle to fight down my gag reflex. It's hard to breathe.

Talon gently eases me aside with a firm hand, and I let him, hating myself.

Standing with my back to him as he goes about cleaning his wound, I blink up at the water spot on the ceiling. "Ugh, I hate this."

"Hate what?" he asks absentmindedly, as the faucet runs.

"That I can't take care of you," I cross my arms over my chest, hearing the petulance in my own voice. "You take care of me all the time, and I should be able to do it for you."

"It's my job, Aura," he says. His words are tight as if he's in pain.

"So?" I turn my head to the side, catching him disinfecting his ribs out of my periphery. The healing liquid drips into the sink with intermittent spatters. "You deserve to be taken care of too."

He rips open a gauze packet. I insisted on bringing the comprehensive first aid kit from the warehouse.

There's a low chuckle of amusement that equally pleases and annoys me. He's never laughed much so I enjoy the sound, but I don't appreciate being laughed at. "Baby, you've taken care of me just fine."

The sensual lilt in his tone lets me know exactly how I've taken care of him. When I turn around, he finishes taping up the new bandage.

I drop to my knees in front of him, wasting zero time releasing him from his pants.

"Aura?" he asks, a new kind of strain in his voice that has nothing to do with pain.

"Shush," I say, immediately setting to stroking his gorgeous, scaled dick which quickly hardens under my touch. "If this is the only way I can take care of you, I plan to make sure you are very well cared for." With that, I take him in my mouth completely.

Talon groans and grips the counter behind him. "Oh fuck, Aura."

I can't help my lips curving up as I continue to suck at him until he's quickly and fully hard. I reach down and cup his balls, giving them experimental squeezes until he makes a choking sound that I want to spend the rest of my life replicating.

Talon threads his fingers through my hair, not guiding me, not forcing, just *holding on*. His knuckles brush my scalp as I hollow my cheeks and take him deeper, tasting the salt of his skin, the faint, smoky undertone that's uniquely him.

Satisfaction curls inside me. Though I'm on my knees, it's he who's at my mercy.

The bathroom fills with the wet sounds of my mouth, the rasp of his breath, the soft squeak of his grip tightening on the counter. I glance up through my lashes and catch his expression—jaw tight, eyes molten, fighting the end even as his hips betray him with a subtle thrust.

I trace the ridges of his cock, learning all its eccentricities with my tongue. My fingers drift up his thighs until they meet his balls and stroke them along the delicate folds of his tucked away wings.

"Aura—fuck—baby, I'm gonna…" he pants, voice cracking like he hates how fast he's losing it. He tries to pull back, heroic to the bitter end.

But I growl, low and possessive, sucking harder as I grip his hips to anchor him in place, still stroking that folded wing with the other. I *want* everything.

I break the seal with a pop. "You're not going anywhere. I'm going to swallow every fucking drop."

Orange ember flashes in his eyes, and a moment of fear goes through me. Is he going to heat up? The fear melts away as his eyes turn dark again. His knees buckle, but he grabs the counter in time. I return to my task, sucking and bobbing hard and fast.

His balls draw tight under my palm, and I hum low in my throat, sending the vibration up his shaft. One wing unfolds slightly so I rub the thin membrane between my fingers.

"Fuck—Aura—" he chokes, and then he's gone.

He comes with a roar, hips jolting, one hand gripping my hair. I swallow greedily, every hot pulse of him, moaning around his length while his body trembles.

When I finally let him go, he's panting, his skin flushed and gleaming with sweat.

"Feel taken care of now?" I ask, wiping my mouth with my wrist and flashing him a smug grin.

He stares down at me like he might drop to his knees and propose on the fucking bathroom tiles.

Instead, he hauls me to my feet and crashes his mouth against mine.

He lifts me easily and sets me on the edge of the sink, then turns on the shower, until steam curls around us.

He helps me remove my mostly destroyed dress. When I'm down to the glint of the jeweled chains still hanging in the hollows of my body, he plays with them at my hips.

"If I can touch you and you can feed from me, maybe..."

Then he rips the chains from my body, breaking them away. Jewels hit the tile floor with a rain-like tinkle.

I shiver from more than the chill.

Suddenly I feel free. The freedom I came here to chase. It's here, it's mine, and it's almost too big to keep in my body.

We step under the spray together.

The water scalds at first, plastering my hair to my scalp, tracing rivulets over my curves. Talon soaps his hands and starts at my shoulders, working slow, firm circles down my spine, trying to learn my body with touch alone.

He reaches around to cup my breasts, running his palms over them, then drops to his knees as if praying, licking the water from my navel before scrubbing gently down my thighs.

His worship is frantic and hungry, yes, but threaded with a kind of awe. He's not just cleaning me.

He's claiming me.

I return the favor. Soap slicks his chest, his arms, the muscles of his abdomen. We're careful to keep his bandage out of the water. I run my tongue over his lower abs just to taste the salt of his skin. He hisses and jerks, already half-hard again.

We don't last long.

He fucks me against the tile, hot water pounding down as my palms slap the wall and my legs shake from the sheer intensity.

Later, we stumble to the bedroom, wrapped in half a towel and even less restraint.

He enters me again before we're even fully dry, pushing me into the mattress with slow, deliberate thrusts. I'm sore, but I wouldn't stop even if a vampire burst into the apartment.

I ride him backward, water still dripping from my hair onto his chest. He grips my waist, biting at my shoulder and groaning filth into my ear—how tight I am, how I was made for him, how no one will ever touch me this way except for him.

Thank fucking fae lords, because I don't want anyone else. Never ever again.

At one point, he lifts one of my legs over his shoulder, going deeper than I thought possible, dragging another orgasm out of me. He says he's collecting them.

He eats lobster rolls and greasy fries from the Salty Bastard, while I eat takeout Chinese (I don't have a stomach made of steel) naked on the couch. He feeds me with his fingers. I lick them clean. He watches every movement as though he's seeing me for the first time.

We nap in each other's arms then I wake to his tongue between my thighs again—his version of breakfast. I come against his mouth with a cry that leaves me breathless and boneless.

We laugh. We fuck. We make love. We *touch*.

It's the perfect day. The kind I want to last forever.

CHAPTER 28

WHEN THE DREAM ENDS

TALON

"They didn't go after me. They went after *you*, Talon."

Aurora's legs hook through mine, a lazy knot that holds me close. Her head sinks against my chest, heavy and warm. Her fingers skim over my cold black scales.

One hand props my head, while the other traces along the curve of her back. My fingertips map each ridge of her spine in slow, repeated strokes until they're etched into memory. Our scent lingers around us, and a deep satisfaction has stretched out from the inside of my chest. I know it won't be long before one or both of us goes back in for more. We have a lot of time to make up for.

"They were trying to subdue me before grabbing you," I say.

She shakes her head. "I don't know. They...they seemed focused on you. And then they..." The hand resting on my chest slides down to the edge of my bandage.

I shut my eyes, but I'm assaulted by the memory of them slicing that scale right off my body. A hot anger boils at my core. No one has ever gotten close enough to do damage like that before, but there had been so many of them. I couldn't fight them off.

Their strike had been meant to cut through to get to my heart, to kill me. Then Aurora would have been defenseless.

The thought stokes the heat of my anger even higher, but I let it smolder inside, careful not to tense underneath her.

"I'm fine," I reassure her, dropping a kiss in her hair. "Better than fine," I add before rolling her over onto her back, covering her body with mine.

Her full breasts crush to my chest, but I'm careful to keep my full weight off her. My hips slowly rock, my half-hard cock sliding along the inside of her thigh.

She lets out a giggle as her fingernails scrape along my scalp, sending ripples of pleasure into my brain before spreading through the rest of my body. "You're insatiable."

"Well, if you weren't so delicious, I wouldn't be," I say before dipping down to catch her nipple in my mouth. I suck until her gasp catches, spilling into a throaty moan. Her back arches, pressing her breast harder into my mouth, her fingers tangling in my hair as her body twists beneath me.

"I'm trying to be serious here." She pushes my shoulders, but I don't give her an inch.

"Mal is only going to keep coming for us," she says so seriously this time I release her delectable flesh from my mouth. I raise myself to meet her eye.

"You're right." I can't lie to her. "Which is why I'm going to have to find her and kill her."

Aurora's lashes flutter wide with surprise. She shouldn't be.

"You created a new life for yourself here," I say, propping my elbows so I can hold her face, forcing her to meet my gaze. "You want this life. I see it. And I want you to be happy. So I will do what it takes to give you what you need, Aura. Like always."

She squirms under me, and I know she's thinking of the sex club, of Merry, of all the many people I've brought to her before.

Brows furrowing, she frantically searches my face, her discomfort rising. "It's—"

"*Exactly* the same as it's always been," I interrupt before she can say the word murder or anything like it. "I'm as culpable as you for all the deaths over the years, if not more so. I bring them to you knowing the cost. Mal is not innocent. She lashed out at you as a baby, she carries hate in her heart, and she intends to act that out on you. I'll kill her first. And then you—*we*," I correct, "get to live happily ever after."

Aurora gives me a watery smile. She's still not sure about this, but she trusts me.

"Okay," she says quietly.

"Okay," I echo back.

A thump and a pointed yowl interrupt us.

Lucifer slinks into the bedroom, tail flicking with maximum offense. He doesn't stop at the jacket this time. He hops up on the bed, marches across Aurora's thighs with all the grace of a petty god, and plants himself square on my chest.

His nose goes straight to my collarbone. Sniffs. Sniffs again. Then, with slow, deliberate rudeness, he sneezes. Right on me.

Aurora snorts. "Wow. Rude."

Lucifer's ears flick, unimpressed. He stands, turns in a circle atop my ribs, and *kneads* me once, claws slightly unsheathed, as if testing for warmth. Finding none, he gives a final insulted flick of his tail directly in my face before leaping off with a *huff*.

He circles my discarded coat next, sniffs, and lets out a disgusted *mrrrow*. This time he bats at it like it personally offends him before strutting from the room, tail high, dignity intact.

Aurora watches him go, her brow arching. "He usually tries to crawl inside your coat. Or, you know, aggressively seduce you for body heat."

I glance at the leather draped across the chair, realization creeping in slow. "Because it's warm." Or it used to be. My heat is gone now, or at least dulled enough the damn cat noticed.

"Wow." Aurora shakes her head with mock solemnity. "So he didn't love you. He just loved the heated seat."

"Figures," I mutter. "Everyone wants something."

"Not me," she says, dragging her nails down my chest. "I just want you."

I roll us so abruptly she lets out a yelp. With a quick readjustment of her hips, I have Aura spread above me. "Now, how about we focus on the present moment where you sit on my face?"

The shock that flashes in her features is quickly chased away by what I can only describe as a devious feline-like sensuality. "Fae lords, yes. But when I'm done drenching your face, you better flip me over and fuck my ass so slow I forget how to walk."

It's like the wind has been knocked out of me. Instead of answering, I immediately start delivering on the plan.

~

A SCREAM RIPS me from the dead of sleep. I'm sitting bolt upright in bed before I realize I've moved, unable to comprehend why Aurora is standing by the bed, crying.

Her arms cinch across her chest, chin tucked, eyes wide and wet, her whole frame shrunken in on itself.

"Aura, sweetheart, tell me what's wrong." My brain is a hot buzz of panic trying to catch up. I only remember we passed out after another round of Olympic-level sex.

Aurora shakes her head, tears streaming faster down her cheeks.

Then I feel it.

My stomach drops and twists into a sickening ball.

Aura extends a trembling hand. Along her palm is an angry red burn.

"No." The words slip from my mouth, distant and foreign. The room tilts, narrowing into a darkness that leads straight to hell.

"I got up to use the bathroom." She fights to get the words out. "When I came back, your scales were..."

I follow her gaze.

My scales glow faint orange, like embers reigniting after a long smolder. They'd been cool last night. Cold, even. But now...now they pulse with heat again, creeping up my ribs and over my shoulder.

The fire's back.

I stumble forward without thinking, arms outstretched to touch her, to comfort her, but she flinches.

She *flinches.*

And that does more damage than any wound ever has.

"It's going to be okay." I rush to say. "We can figure this out. I can...I can try to burn off the energy again."

Even as I say the words, a part of me whispers, "*How?*" The situation that caused it had been extreme, dire even. I was under full attack and injured, and only when I saw Aurora get pushed to the ground did it tip me over the edge into the change.

"You said that Dragons can burn out their fire," Aurora points out.

Guilt and frustration clogs my every vein and artery. "It was a story I heard once. Most of what I know about my kind is via stories from other people and books from those who tried to study Dragons, not my actual people." And I've never been more angry that I've been left on my own to figure it out. That I have no choice but to rely on anyone but Dragons to get information. I should have known not to take the bit of information seriously. In the same conversation it was dropped that Dragons have two dicks. I didn't bother to correct them, but it should have given me an idea that they had no idea what they were talking about. But hope is hope, even if it's born of nonsense.

"I thought we had time. I stupidly believed we had all the time in the world. I thought we could *be together*." She breaks on those last words, and something inside me snaps clean in two.

"I can burn it off," I say again, too quickly. Too desperately. "I'll go now—I'll push it out—I'll find something, anything—"

"Talon." Her gentleness stops me. "No."

My body turns numb. My fire hums low and traitorous under my skin. I'm alone again. I always knew I had to stay solitary but now truly knowing what the other side tastes like...

I will die if I can't touch her again. I can't go back to how it was. Watching her. Wanting her.

I can't.

I won't.

"I can't do it," Aurora whispers. Then louder, more panicked. "I *can't fucking do it!*"

I turn back just in time to see her pacing the room like a trapped thing, one hand pulling at her hair, the other clenching and unclenching at her side.

"I can't go back to feeding on strangers like an animal. I won't!" she yells. "It was just going to be us. You and me. No more kills. No more damage. Just...*you.*"

Her eyes meet mine, and they're wild, burning, devastated.

"Now what am I supposed to do?" she demands. "Go fuck some more randos and pray I don't suck the life out of them? Is that how it has to be? Without you, I go back to being a monster."

She's spiraling so fast she doesn't even realize her knees have hit the floor. Her hands cover her face, her whole body heaving with the force of her sobs. "I *felt* you, Talon. I felt your love and...and I was *full*. And now it's gone, and I don't know how to survive without it."

I can't hold her, I can't reassure her, I can't do anything.

Except the thing I've always done.

Protect her.

Even if that means we have to go back to being what we've always been.

I kneel in front of her slowly. Not touching.

Then I speak. Cold. Steady. Razor-edged truth.

"Pull yourself together, princess."

She freezes.

"You'll do what you have to do to survive. Just like you always have." My voice is low, deliberate, slicing through the noise in her head. "You're a Lost Girl now. You're tough as hell. You fight. You get back up. You adapt. That's who the fuck you are."

Her watery gaze meets mine, but underneath, I watch the steel in her begin to reform.

"I don't want anyone else," she whispers.

"I know." My composed response is a stark contrast to the molten sorrow churning inside me. "Neither do I. But we swallow what the world throws at us. Doesn't mean we wanted the taste. Just means we know how to live with it in our gut."

Something flickers in her eyes. Is it the spark of resilience, or a flash of resentment? Resentment at the world, or at me, for not allowing her the solace of despair?

Some part of me wonders if I should let her wallow. Let her drown in grief. But I won't. Maybe it's not about her. Maybe it's because if I let myself succumb to the unfairness of the situation, I'll crack so wide open I'll never put myself back together.

To finally be gifted everything I've always wanted, only to have it so cruelly taken away...it's a hell I don't wish on anyone.

CHAPTER 29

RICHOCHET

AURORA

"Mommy and daddy are fighting, and I don't like it."

I ignore Snow as I unload the glasses from the dishwasher rack, preparing for what promises to be another crazy Saturday shift.

"Yeah, it's freaking me out," Ariel agrees with Snow.

"We are not fighting," I say tightly, not slowing my movements.

I'm heartbroken. It's different.

Actually, heartbroken doesn't even cover it. I had him. For one impossible, perfect stretch of time, I had Talon. His hands, his mouth, his body pressed to mine, and I thought maybe we could finally be what we were meant to be. Then the fire came back, and he ordered us to bury it. Bury the touch, the closeness, the hope. I hate him for that.

I hate that he told us to shove it all down, as if we could. He's just as fucked up about this as I am, and there's no covering it. Not with acceptance. Not with silence.

We are both split open, bleeding, wanting what we

can't touch, and it makes me furious. Because it's not only rotting me from the inside, it's killing him too.

Watching Lucifer curl up on Talon's lap this morning only added to my irritation. Why should that little beast get to be so close to Talon, and I can't?

I've never despised a cat like this before. Being heartbroken is making me a monster...or just more like Snow, who hates that cat more than anyone.

"Ugh, I should have closed today," Rap says, sidling up to the bar with her laptop. Her normally sharp green eyes are dull and bloodshot. Even her rainbow Mohawk is wilted.

"You were the one who provided so many bottles of Jolly Roger rum, boss," Snow points out.

"Which was an amazing wedding gift," Ariel quickly adds when Rap glares at Snow. "I know Goldie and Ted appreciated it."

Rap resumes rubbing her forehead and mumbles a word that resembles "coffee."

I'm quick to jump on her request. When I return with a steaming cup and saucer, my boss grunts a thank you.

"Can I get one too?" another voice asks.

I don't look at Talon even as he stands next to Rap.

I shrug noncommittally even as I turn to head to the coffee pot.

"What did you do to her?" Snow asks Talon even as I pull another cup and saucer. My motions slow.

He didn't do anything.

No, scratch that, he did *everything*. And we can never do it again.

Talon remains silent. I know he's just as twisted and torn about what's happened, but he basically told me to get my shit together. So that's what I'm doing. On my own.

"Take care of her tonight," he says finally.

"We always do," Ariel says a little sharper than normal.

I set the coffee on the bar in front of him. "Leave him alone, guys," I say. "Everything is fine."

"Bullshit." Snow's eyes volley between us.

Even Rap watches us now with a sharp eye. Or as sharp as her hangover allows.

Maybe I should tell them we were attacked by vampires.

But that would lead to too many questions.

The door flings open, and at first I don't recognize the tall, muscular Black man in the purple satin suit. As he nears, fluttering massive false eyelashes and heavy eye makeup, I realize this is Dame Kiki out of drag. And she looks...errr...upset.

"Good, you're here," Rap says, rousing from her goblin slouch over the coffee. "Geanie," she calls loudly.

"Oh this is gonna be good," Snow crosses her arms as Ariel sucks in a breath.

Rap calls for him twice more before Geanie emerges from the back rooms. He slinks rather than walks, as if he's fighting resentment with every fiber of his being.

Kiki pops a hand on her hip and taps her gleaming shoes. "Well?" she addresses Rap.

"Geanie," Rap says in a low, threatening voice.

He pulls at the collar of his shirt, lips twisted as if he's been sucking on an entire bag of lemons.

"We talked about this..." Rap pushes without subtlety.

He mumbles something.

"Come again?" Kiki cups a hand behind her ear. "I didn't hear that."

"I'm sorry," he says louder.

"For..." Rap urges him to go on. She might as well have

Geanie by the scruff of the neck. I almost feel bad for him, but I'm still not sure what this is about.

"For ripping off your wig during Goldie's bouquet toss."

I turn to Ariel for confirmation, and she meets my expression with a solemn nod and a grimace that tells me it got even uglier than that.

Kiki sets her hands on her hips, narrowing her eyes. "You mean before ripping the stems straight out of my hands like a petty little—"

"Kiki," Rap interrupts in a warning tone.

Kiki backs off, clearing her throat of whatever other nasty insults had built up there. "Thank you for your apology, *Eugene*." She says the name with as much pleasure as Geanie's displeasure. "I understand it's hard when you feel you are getting outshined...Well, I've never actually felt that but—"

"*Kiki*," Rap says sharply this time, and Kiki drops it. "Now shake hands and get over this petty bullshit before I cut you both off from the steady supply of free drinks you both so liberally enjoy."

Despite being rivals, both Kiki and Geanie wear a matching open-mouth expression of scandalized shock and fear. Begrudgingly, they shake hands, and Rap nods with evident satisfaction before they part ways.

I feel Talon's eyes on me, compelling me to look at him. It hurts. It hurts to look at him. To remember what slipped through our fingers. Even if it's not his fault.

He sets the empty coffee cup down and leaves to take his spot by the door. The night is about to kick off.

I try to swallow down the pain as I polish the bar top with extra vigor.

"Can I get a coffee to go, sweetness?" Kiki asks, sidling up in front of me with an empty travel mug she's pulled from her glittery tote. "And if you pour a bit of that Irish cream in there, mum's the word. Got a hot night at the Pumpkin Coach Club tonight and I've still got to get glam."

I nod, feeling like a hollow doll as I go about filling the bottom with Irish cream. Kiki will be on foot, and the club isn't far from here, though we've yet to have a girls' night there.

"Pain does funny things to a girl," Kiki says as I pour the coffee. "Can give a girl an insatiable hunger for more...if you know what I mean."

I curse as hot coffee spills over my knuckles. I'm quick to grab a rag and clean up the mess I made. My pulse and thoughts jump erratically. She knows I'm a Succubus, which is terrifying enough, but to be speaking in code about it while everyone is milling about puts my nerves on edge.

"Just don't forget, darling," Kiki adds, her nails cool on my wrist. "Pain is sometimes how we find our people."

Dame Kiki has swept off and out the door with her drink by the time I've swallowed down the knot in my throat. But I can't digest what she's said, because the music flips on at a blaring volume and the lights dim as another magical night at Poison Apple kicks off, and the doors open.

"And here's our resident beauty, Aurora," Genie's voice rings out as the spotlight hits me. I twist and turn and put on the usual show as I do my Lost Girl introduction, but tonight my heart isn't in it.

I'm angry. I'm devastated. But at least I'm full. Of Talon. That knowledge makes everything hurt all over again.

I lean forward, letting my breasts spill dangerously as I

pour vodka straight into open mouths below. Cheers rise, but my focus blurs.

A ripple of warning zips up my spine before I lift my gaze. When I look further into the crowd of gyrating, swaying patrons pumping their fists in time to the music, my attention fixes on a single face. Small. Still. Unmoving.

She doesn't dance. Doesn't drink.

Just watches.

An Asian woman. Hard to place her age—twenty or forty—but her heart-shaped face is carved from porcelain. Electric violet eyes stare back, unblinking.

It's the dimples that betray her. The same as King Kaison's.

Mal.

I swallow hard, pulling the bottle back up. I try to continue my little dance and shuffle across the bar, but Geanie's booming words and the sound of the crowd muffle as panic roars in my ears.

Maybe I'm seeing things?

I turn to look again and she's still there. My heart thuds so hard it bruises my chest.

I've never seen the woman, but I know it's Mal.

The woman in the crowd tilts her head ever so slightly as if to say, *so you do know me.*

It's too much. It's just too fucking much.

All the rage and heartbreak I've felt over the last several hours boils over as I face the one who cursed my entire existence.

Power rises, low and furious beneath my skin. It stretches and pushes its way out of me, reminding me of this same sensation when I faced that vampire on the docks. It's like finding a new muscle I didn't even know I had, so I'm not even sure what it's trying to do.

Until it surges forward.

A crack of pink light arcs from my chest, visible, unmistakable—an aura made of hunger and curse and wrath.

The hunger that has always stayed in my bones, that always has been called via touch stretches out of my body, hungry jaws open wide, directed at *her*.

It slices through the air like a whip of smoke and neon, fast and bright and impossible to ignore.

People cheer. They think it's part of the show. Part of the Lost Girl act.

But this is no act.

I give the curse direction. I give it teeth.

The barest, almost imperceptible raise of Mal's eyebrows makes it appear as if she is more intrigued than afraid.

It slams into her, but instead of devouring Mal, it whiplashes back. That surge of power I sent at Mal crashes into me.

Pain detonates in my chest. My ribs cave inward. My knees smash into glass. Shards cut into my skin but I barely feel them over the hollow tearing through me as everything is ripped out.

The curse takes. Hard and fast and wild.

I thought the pain of cannibalizing myself by masturbation was bad. Compared to this, that sensation was a lover's caress.

I'm emptied in an instant. My vision runs red and pink. My hand shoots out, grasping a stranger's face. My mouth opens before I can stop myself. Power drags into me and I almost choke on the relief. He groans under my grip, pleasure tangled with pain.

My name echoes from somewhere far away.

As my vision clears slightly I see patrons stagger. Some collapse.

Enough sense returns to me that I release the man I've been feeding on. He drops to the ground like a bag of bones.

I have no idea if I've killed him, but I can't stop to check. The instant I stop feeding, my body convulses. The rush that had filled me vanishes, leaving every nerve flayed raw. My skin burns cold, my insides claw at themselves, desperate, empty. The hunger isn't gnawing anymore. It's ripping me apart.

I seize a woman and yank her close. Her scream cuts short against me as more power floods in. It does not fill me. Nothing does.

I am ripped away, hauled through the air.

The searing heat on my exposed waist tells me it's Talon. The blistering touch jerks me back to some clarity.

We crash onto the platform by the front door and he lets me down. My ribs convulse. Pain throbs with a new rhythm.

Talon's mouth moves at my ear, but I can't hear him. All I catch is the thunder of my pulse hammering in my skull, the blood rushing so loud it drowns the world.

Snow grips the table, her eyes wide, as if she doesn't know me. Ariel holds her forehead as she tries to shake off her daze.

Their faces are masks of horror. The people who were my family now look at me like I'm nothing but a nightmare in their midst.

I fed off them.

Oh fae lords.

I hurt my friends.

My throat locks. I cannot breathe. My stomach twists and heaves. Shame crashes over me, heavier than the hunger, sharper than the pain. I clutch my chest, but it does nothing.

All eyes are fastened on me.

The weight of their stares crushes me, pinning me in chains of judgment and fear. My breath stutters, my knees buckle.

They know.

Succubus.

The word pulses in the air. I hear it in the mutters. In the silence. In the recoil of bodies pulling back.

Every drop of hope I carried for the last month drains away.

There's no hiding anymore. No future. I'm a monster exposed, and the way everyone stares at me makes me want to shrivel up and die.

In one moment, I've lost everything, and I may have left dead bodies on the floor of Poison Apple. I'm not sure.

They are going to string me up and burn me. At the very least they'll exile me like Mal. I search the spot where I last spotted the vampire, but she's disappeared.

I'm dragged out into the night by Talon. I've lost everything except for one thing.

The hunger.

"Mal was there." My voice scrapes out like sandpaper as Talon drags me into the apartment. "She was in the crowd."

He doesn't answer. Doesn't even look at me. Just drops to his knees beside the couch and pulls out his old leather bag, seemingly searching for something.

"My curse...it left my body." My breath hitches, my

chest burning with more than exhaustion. "I didn't even know I could do that."

And it happened in front of everyone. I sucked off the entire room of the Poison Apple as I tried to drink some of them dry. The looks of shock on Ariel and Snow's faces burn inside of me. In one stupid, rash moment, I lost my friends, my job, my new life. Because now that it's out I'm a Succubus, no one will want to come within thirty feet of me.

Hell, since my identity as the Rosari Princess was also outed, it may even get back to the kingdom. If it does, there's really no going home.

Still nothing from Talon. He reaches into the bag and retrieves something new.

Black gloves. Fine leather. Unmistakably his size.

When the hell did he get those?

He slides them on and grabs my elbow, hauling me toward the bathroom. The motion sends a scream through my starving body, like every muscle is shearing away from bone. My legs barely work. I'm shaking so badly I'm vibrating out of my own skin. Hunger gnaws deeper like acid, eating me alive from the inside. My vision tunnels in and out.

He sets me on the toilet seat and lifts my crop top so it rests up on the swells of my breasts. My skin prickles with the painful awareness of his closeness, but Talon moves with mechanical precision. There's no hunger in him now. No heat. Just cold, grim focus as he kneels and starts working antiseptic into the burns his hands left on my waist.

I hiss at the sting, but it's nothing compared to the ache gnawing at my center. The real pain is beneath. Deeper, spreading. My soul is devouring itself, cell by cell, thought by thought. I'm an empty pit lined with teeth, clawing for something to fill it.

I fed a little, but not enough. Not even close.

Talon is silent as he digs shards of glass from my knees, his jaw tight. My power used to heal this kind of thing. Now? I'm too empty to knit skin, too drained to even stop the slow trickle of blood down my calves.

"What was Mal doing there?" My voice breaks on her name. Even now, with my body collapsing in on itself, my mind fixates on her. The shape of her. The look she gave me. She did this. She did this on purpose. She must have.

"I don't know," Talon says, clipped and distracted as he tapes gauze into place. His touch is careful, almost tender, but his tone is steel.

"You sound like you don't care." The words come out harsh. My hands won't stop shaking, and their wide-eyed stares keep replaying in my head, as vivid as if I were still standing in that room. There's no room for grace or softness left in me. "Like you don't care that I blew up our new lives in spectacular fucking fashion."

I hate myself for how bitter it sounds, how desperate.

Talon finishes with my bandages and stands without a word. I trail after him into my bedroom, dazed.

My knees buckle under me, vision tunneling as the hunger gnashes harder, meaner, hungrier. Not just in my gut now. In my veins. In my bones. In the hollow of my skull, where thoughts used to be. I can't think. Can't breathe. There's only the need. I'm burning through my own existence trying to stay upright.

Talon opens the drawer like he's reaching for a gun. But it's worse.

The collar.

"What are you doing?" My heart sinks as he holds it in his gloved hand.

"My job." His tone is flat as stone.

"No. I—I—"

"You have to feed," he says, like it's a fact as immutable as gravity. "And we're going back to the club. Right now."

Panic rises sharp and hot in my chest, choking off air. "I'm not going to feed on anyone but you. Never again." The vow anchors me. I've already chosen. I let him inside me, and that choice is carved into bone now. I won't share my body, my hunger, my curse with anyone else, even if it starves me hollow.

For a moment I can't remember if my parents found Talon to protect everyone from me, or me from myself?

Even in their fear of what I'd become, they searched for a solution, spent a fortune to keep me safe. Would they recognize this starving, stubborn creature I've become?

Would they still see their little princess in this Lost Girl covered in piercings and rage? Part of me hopes not. Part of me desperately hopes they would.

Talon's face is unreadable as he closes the space between us, taking off his gloves.

Part of me relaxes as he does so.

He's not planning on making me do anything I don't want to. Otherwise, he would have left the gloves on to haul me off to the club like he threatened.

The collar clips around my neck, and his bare hand holds it, melting the clasp shut.

My pulse beats frantic against the cool band.

"You will," he says. Quiet. Unmoving. Unshakable. "Because you're dying." His grip is unyielding.

And he's not wrong. Something about the ricochet off Mal has thrown the power of my curse...off. It doesn't even burn the way hunger usually does, sharp and bright and urgent. This is something darker. Deeper. It feels like decay.

Like I've poisoned myself.

But I can't go back. Not after *him*. Not after what we had. I won't crawl back into bed with strangers. I won't sink my curse into random bodies just to patch over the hole that keeps ripping open.

I'd rather burn out from the inside than let another stranger touch me again. I'd rather starve than let someone else's energy fill me.

Talon puts his gloves back on and pulls me out into the night.

CHAPTER 30
FORCE FEEDING A HANGRY SUCCUBUS

TALON

The fae leather gloves creak as I drag Aurora by the arm, her shoulder tucked tight against mine. She jerks, but I don't loosen it.

Aurora's power has been tainted, and it's turned on her. She won't admit it, but I can see it plain as day. The energy around her is tinged with black as if she's been poisoned by whatever happened in the bar.

It could very well be that Mal was there, but I don't give a flying fuck about the details right now because the only thing that matters is getting Aurora to feed. Or she'll die.

She may hate me for this, but that's a price I'm willing to pay.

We round the corner toward the club again, the street wet with earlier rain. Aurora suddenly bolts—twisting hard, teeth bared, eyes flashing.

I catch the leash mid-whip, the chain clinking taut between us. My boots slide on the slick cobblestone as she spins back, clawing at the clasp at her throat like she can rip it off with sheer will. Her fingers scrabble, nails scraping skin, frustration carved across her face.

"Let me go," she mutters under her breath, lips trembling as the lock refuses to budge.

I grip her arm.

"Aura, stop it," I snap. "You're acting like a child."

Her eyes flare, and she tries to pull away, but I tighten my hold.

"I am not. You're the one who put gloves on just to drag me along," she hisses. "You're treating me like some kind of prisoner. Let me go."

"You think I want this?" I ask. "You think I'm enjoying dragging the woman I love through the streets like this to force her to sleep with someone else?"

"Then let me go," she bites out, still fighting my grip. "I'm not going to feed anyway."

I turn on her. "I'm not letting you go, and yes the hell you will."

"No, I won't," she shoots back.

A strangled groan of frustration escapes my throat even as I try to suppress it. "You are being such a brat. If you keep this up, I will bend you over and spank you like you deserve. Might knock some damn sense into you."

Her mouth drops open, eyes sparking outrage. "How can you say that to me?"

"Because someone needs to." I step into her space, watching the flare of anger war with the sting I know I just landed. "You think being stubborn makes you strong? It doesn't. It makes you reckless. You latch onto these ideas—*I won't feed, I won't go home*—and even when it's killing you, you dig in your heels to protect your pride."

Her breath catches, but she squares her jaw like she's holding herself together with sheer spite.

"You'd rather die choking on your pride than change course and go home."

Her hand flies fast. The slap lands sharp across my face.

For a second, all I feel is the heat of it. Then the ache catches up.

She stares at me, wide-eyed, her fingers pressed to her mouth like she can't believe she did it.

I roll my jaw slowly, testing the sting. Can't lie—part of me likes the contact.

"Did you burn yourself?" I ask, low. "Did I hurt you?"

Her shock morphs into exasperation again. "Are you serious? I slap you, and you are worried about hurting me?" She scrubs her hands over her face, and I surmise her palm is fine. "Of course you're serious. That's all you know how to be. Protect me. Protect, protect, protect. You've made it your whole damn personality."

"Aura—" I start, but she barrels over me.

"How about after you've been continually forced to *fuck* and *kill* people for the majority of your life, then you come back to me and give notes on how I'm handling this."

My teeth grind. The truth is ugly, but it's ours and I can't deny it.

"You think I'm stubborn?" She glares. "You think I'm the one who won't change? At least I'm trying to figure out who I am. What I want. What living looks like. What about you? Have you even tried to live here? Or have you just been following me around like a shadow, waiting for things to go to shit so you can take me back to the castle where you can control 'the situation?'" She throws air quotes around *the situation*. A way to illuminate how we avoid talking about the ugly heart of what it is she does and what I force her to do.

"If you're not safe, nothing matters," I grit.

"And you think that's enough? You think that's living?" She shakes her head, disgust flashing through her exhaustion. "You're so careful, so controlled. You've never even asked what you're supposed to do when you're not protecting me. You don't even know how to want anything beyond that."

"You think I don't know that?" I raise my voice to be heard. "You think I haven't noticed I don't have a life beyond you? It's my job. Your parents hunted me down because I'm the *only one* who can help you. I bound my fealty to your safety. Maybe if you could go two damn minutes without needing me to swoop in and save the day, I would have some time to figure out what the hell else I should do."

Her breath catches, and I see it, that look. The one that says I've been too sharp, too harsh.

"That's it?" Her arms fold tight across her chest, like she's holding herself together by force alone. "I'm just a job to you?"

I rake my hands through my hair. "Aura, you know that's not what I mean." She's twisting my words around me so quickly, I'm chasing my own wings.

"Well, congratulations," she says, lifting her chin. "Consider yourself dismissed. Go on a vacation, learn how to knit, find something else to do, Talon, because I'm. Not. Feeding."

The logic part of her brain has completely switched off.

She's drowning in grief, in anger, in hunger, and whatever black energy I continually watch stab and sink into her, turning her weaker and paler with every moment that passes. I shake my head. "You have to."

She shoves me with both hands on my coat. I fall back a step, but it's not the strength that matters—it's the rage. "You can force me through the doors. Hell, you can fucking tie me to the bed. But I won't feed. Not from anyone else. Not ever again."

"I'm heartbroken too." That gets her attention. "You think this doesn't wreck me too?" I drop my voice to a low timbre.

Her head jerks back toward me.

"You think it doesn't kill me to walk you into that club and serve you up like a dish to everyone there? To pretend it's fine? To pretend some stranger touching you doesn't slice through my fucking insides?"

Her mouth parts, eyes wide. She hadn't expected that. I hadn't either.

Of all the things I've let spill out, I've never, not once let jealousy get the best of me. But it's always been there. Always simmering, bubbling beneath the surface, turning my stomach.

I never wanted to pile *that* on top of her burdens.

I grab her by the shoulders. "I love you, Aura. I love you so much, I'll drag you into that place with these gloves on and let someone else fill you up because I'd rather die of heartbreak and jealousy than watch you waste away." The words crack out of the deepest part of me, and for a moment, I feel I'll split in two.

Her face crumples. Not into tears, not into softness, but into something worse.

She looks at me like I've ripped her open without lifting a finger.

We stand in silence, our breaths steaming between us in the cold. The leash hangs slack.

When I finally start walking again, pulling her along by the arm, she doesn't fight me as I lead us to the club.

With another quick drop of blood on the enchanted rune, we are inside.

For the second time, I lead Aurora past the main area to the back where I've already reserved a private room.

Once she's inside, I stand at the door looking out for interested parties as much as I'm keeping her inside.

"I'm not doing it," she says behind me, her voice stiff with defiance.

I don't answer.

Instead, I keep my focus trained on the crowd outside the private room—scanning for someone with steady energy, someone who won't scare her or overstimulate her.

Someone I can stomach watching touch her. The list is fucking short.

"This is useless," she mutters.

I turn just in time to block the exit with my body.

She nearly crashes into my chest but pulls back at the last moment. "Move," she orders without meeting my gaze.

The dark, sickly energy seems to have doubled around her from the last time I looked.

"No."

She tries to push past me, clearly not caring anymore if I burn her. I catch her arm in a gloved hand, gently but firmly. Snow was right. Why the hell didn't I get these things earlier?

Aurora's breath hitches, caught somewhere between fury and exhaustion. "You're torturing me."

She might as well have shoved a knife into my chest and twisted. "I'm saving you." I say the words through the guilt and pain.

Then her eyes flick over my shoulder, and I feel the shift before she says a word. Her posture stiffens. Her head tilts, lips curling into a challenge I've seen before and never liked.

"Him," she says.

"What?" I follow her gaze.

The broad-shouldered man with nice hands from last time, is lounging across a velvet couch, a glass balanced loosely in one large calloused hand.

"No," I snap. "No repeats."

"Then I don't feed," she says smoothly.

"Aura—"

She folds her arms. "Your rules, your choice. Him or no one."

We stare each other down. She's daring me to say no. Daring me to push her further. And fuck me, I want to. But I also know what will happen if she goes much longer without feeding.

Her cheeks have become even more sunken than they were outside.

I grind out a breath through my teeth. "Fine."

I step outside, just enough to catch the man's eye and tilt my chin in invitation.

He rises. Smooth. Casual. Controlled. He approaches with measured ease. He's shirtless like last time...that same deep brown skin gleaming under the low lighting. Muscles tight, cut, unapologetic. There's plenty for her to grab onto.

Suddenly, I hate him on principle.

"Hello again," he says smoothly.

I merely jerk my head in a nod. "Not looking for a big party this time. Just an intimate experience."

I'm not sure what Aurora needs, but I'm not willing to have more energy in here than I can handle.

His lips curve up, making him look impish and sexual at the same time. "I'm amenable to that."

I step aside and let him in. Aura has already disrobed and lies back on the bed, naked. This time there are no chains to remind her that not only she is a princess, but that she is to restrain herself.

My stomach churns. This is how I had her. Fully naked, unencumbered. I don't want anyone else to have this.

The collar is still on though, and it will have to be enough to remind her who's in charge.

Her smile is cruel, her lips pursed in defiance.

Nothing good can come from what's going on in her head right now.

Her playmate walks in, an easy grin spreading along his face. "Hello there again, darlin'. You wore me out good last time, and I'd like to test my stamina again if that's alright with you." I didn't notice the slight Southern twang last time. But now I seem to notice every little detail about him. Not for tactical reasons, but because I know watching this is going to hurt.

Aurora smiles and nods from her seductive pose, though there is an imperious air about her now that wasn't there two minutes ago. "I'd like that," she purrs. Her eyes flick to me, and I instantly know what I'm in for. My stomach clenches in anticipation, but we have to stay the course.

She gets up on her knees at the edge of the bed. "What's your name?"

"Sawyer. What's yours, gorgeous?" He reaches out and takes her hand.

"Aurora," she announces.

I suppress a groan, as he kisses the back of her hand in official greeting. She should have at least given him a fake name. Now I'm not sure if I want him to survive, knowing what he knows. This is quickly turning into a terrible idea.

Aurora slides her hands over his chest, fingertips tracing every ridge of his abdomen like she's learning a new language. She moans—loud, exaggerated, and utterly false. She turns her head slightly to make sure I'm watching.

I don't blink.

When she drags her tongue across his nipple, I feel it in my stomach. Cold. Sharp. A blade grating slowly under my ribs.

Sawyer groans, clearly enjoying the attention. And why wouldn't he? Aurora's not just touching him, she's adoring him. The way she palms his cock when he drops his pants, the way she stares up at him under heavy lashes. She's playing her part too well.

She drops to her knees.

And then she starts to suck him off.

Not just a blowjob. A performance. Deep throat. Slow pulls. Her tongue flat, her cheeks hollowed just right. Her fingers curl around the base as she bobs, soft moans slipping past her lips as if this is everything she's ever wanted. As if he is everything.

She doesn't break eye contact with me.

Not once.

I grip the leash until my fingers ache through the gloves.

Sawyer threads his fingers into her hair. She hums. Pushes deeper. Her throat flexes around him, and she makes a show of choking just a little—then swallowing him down again like it's a challenge she's thrilled to win.

She lets go with a pop, lips slick and pink, and plants a kiss on the tip.

Then she pulls him to lay on the bed and straddles him.

He leans against the pillows. She slides up his body like smoke, her back to him, sitting on his abdomen. Wrapping her tits around his cock and letting it glide between them as she fucks him with her chest.

And still, she looks at me.

As if asking, *"Do you regret it yet?"*

I do.

Faefucking hell, I do.

But what cuts deeper is what I don't feel.

No pull of her feeding. No tug of magic in the air. She's not taking anything from him. This is all for me. Every filthy, exquisite second of it is a show put on to torture me.

She wants to punish me.

And worst of all?

It's working.

CHAPTER 31
SPANKING THAT PRINCESS PUSSY
AURORA

Talon can drag me here, he can set me up with someone at the club, he can even make me hook up with someone else, but he can't make me feed. And I have no intention of doing so.

But I have *every* intention of making him suffer. Of torturing him the way I feel tortured.

"I'm heartbroken too," he yelled outside.

The words, his pain echoes in my ears, but my pain is so much louder. He's right, I am being a child about it, but it's the only way I can exert control in this situation. I intend to exert every bit of control over my body I can, and over Talon's emotions because it gives me a modicum of dignity back.

So as I take my partner so far down my throat I gag, I do it to hurt Talon.

I gag because I want him to see it.

To suffer at least a fraction of how I suffer.

Because I am being exactly what I'm expected to be. He should hate it as much as I do. I hate it. I hate me and what I am.

I swirl my tongue around the head of Sawyer's cock and hum low, letting the vibration carry. He groans, loud and guttural. I can feel his restraint fray under my hands. But I don't stop. I double down.

He says something. I don't hear it.

Because I'm watching Talon.

He's a statue by the wall, arms crossed over that broad chest, jaw locked tight. But his eyes are on me, always on me. I can feel his heat from here, a potent mix of fury and arousal.

I pull off Sawyer with a pop and slide forward, my thighs already slick and my breath ragged with my own need. My vision has been blurring in and out. Despite the show I'm putting on, I feel weak and unsteady.

But none of it matters.

This isn't about feeding or pleasure.

This is controlling the only thing I can.

I angle myself above Sawyer, grinding the thick head of his cock at my entrance and sinking down all at once. A gasp bursts from both of us, but mine turns into a loud, obscene moan that echoes off the chamber walls.

"Oh witchtits," Sawyer groans, hands flying to my hips.

"Fae lords," I pant, tossing my hair back and rolling my hips. "You're so big—fuck—no one's ever filled me like this."

I look straight at Talon as I say it.

Sawyer's eyes flutter. "Fuck—darlin', slow down, I—"

But I don't.

I speed up.

I ride him like he's mine to break, grinding down with enough force to slap skin to skin, making sure Talon can hear it.

"You like that?" I pant. The question isn't directed at

Sawyer. "You like watching me get split open on someone else?"

Sawyer moans, panting hard. "Too much—shit—you gotta slow down or—"

But I bounce harder, faster, grinding out every ounce of rage, shame, and heartbreak I've been choking on for days.

This isn't feeding. This is punishment.

My hands slide up my own body, squeezing my breasts, and tossing my head back, I use every iota of power I have left to resist opening the fanged maw of my curse and sucking Sawyer dry.

I'm surrounded by sex, by delicious life force and sustenance that would save me. But I refuse it all.

I know it the moment before it happens.

Sawyer's hands clamp down, his body jerks, and he lets out a strangled curse before pushing me off him, desperation written across his face.

I stumble back onto the sheets as he fists his cock and comes in a hot, pulsing rush across his own abs with a hoarse groan of relief and regret.

I sit there, legs splayed, chest heaving, heart pounding like a war drum.

But I don't feel full.

Not even close.

Because it wasn't Talon inside me.

And because I never fed.

When I look up, I find myself staring down one pissed off Dragon.

I'm not sure what rankled him more—openly taunting him, or not feeding, but his eyes spark with orange embers.

Talon isn't distant and controlled anymore. He's not annoyed or irritated. He's furious. The fissures between his scales glow a deeper red, pulsing like veins lit with magma.

...that's new.

"Again," he growls.

I push myself upright, brushing hair from my face with the back of my hand, defiance still buzzing in my blood even as my limbs start to shake from the drain I refuse to acknowledge. "I can do this all night," I say casually, flicking a glance toward Sawyer. Fully meaning I will fuck this guy all night and never feed.

Sawyer groans behind me, still sprawled on the bed, hand flung over his face. "I just need a minute, darlin'."

Talon doesn't respond immediately, but something shifts behind his eyes, calculating, commanding. "Take your time," he says to Sawyer—voice low, calm, terrifying. "But we're not losing momentum."

He walks across the room without hurry to the minibar cabinet set into the wall. His broad shoulders block the view for a moment, but I hear the sound of a box and packaging unwrapping

When he turns back to me, his expression is unreadable, but his hands are sure.

In his gloved hand, he holds a toy—new and gleaming from just being taken out of its plastic casing. He tosses the wrapper to the floor and walks toward me.

My throat dries, but I raise my chin anyway. I'm still panting from the exertion of what just happened, still trying to pretend I'm not depleted.

"Talon," I warn, but it comes out softer than I want.

"Open your legs," he says.

I don't.

He doesn't repeat himself. Instead, he grabs the leash still attached to my collar and yanks it with a snap, forcing me to the edge of the bed in one brutal pull. My breath knocks from my chest as he shoves my knees up, spreading me wide. I brace myself on my elbows, heart hammering with something that feels like fear and anticipation wrapped together.

I was in control a few moments ago, but I've seemed to have lost all of my ground. And I'm not sure I want to get it back either.

Instead, he looks down at me—those dark, merciless eyes glowing from beneath the veil of his hair—and I can feel heat surge through my core before he's even touched me.

Still, I try to mask it. "What are you going to do?" The words are haughty, a challenge.

He can't make me feed.

The corners of his mouth lift—barely. He sets the toy down on the bed next to me.

Then with one gloved hand, he slaps my pussy.

A sound, stinging jolt that steals the breath from my lungs and sends a sharp, slick heat rushing through me.

I gasp, but it turns into a moan halfway out.

He doesn't stop.

"You want to act like a brat?" Another slap, firmer this time, punctuated by the grip of his other hand anchoring my hip. "Then I'll treat you like one."

The ache between my legs becomes unbearable.

And I realize Talon's not going to sit on the sidelines anymore.

His gloved hand lingers between my thighs, the sting from the slap blooming into heat that races through my pelvis. I try to hold onto the performance, the edge, the anger that's been shielding me all night, but it starts to slip the moment his fingers slide through my slickness.

He's methodical. Unhurried. A Dragon dissecting his prey.

His eyes hold mine. Unrelenting. Brutal. There's no mercy in them now, just purpose.

My hunger claws up through me, thrashing and demanding. Like it knows *this is Talon now.* Talon's gloved finger fucking me open, Talon's scent in my nose, Talon's fury and love and possession pouring over my skin. I want to scream. I want to stay cool.

"Feeling hungry yet?" he murmurs, voice low enough to vibrate in my bones.

I grit my teeth. "Fuck you."

His lips curve with malice as he reaches for the toy beside me. It's long, sleek black glass, curved subtly upward with a flared base.

He coats it in lube from a packet he tears open with his teeth, never looking away from me. His gloves glisten now, frictionless and gleaming.

Then he presses it against my entrance.

It's not him. It's not skin. But it's his hand. His control.

And my body *knows.*

I suck in a breath as he pushes it inside, inch by inch, forcing my body to stretch around the intrusion. I feel every ridge, every slick drag of it until it bottoms out, and I'm gasping, my hands clutching the sheets behind me.

Sawyer shifts on the bed beside me, his chest still rising and falling. He sits next to me, watching the scene unfold with wide eyes, his cock already starting to harden again as he strokes it lazily.

"Fuck," he breathes. "That's hot."

"Give her nipples a pinch," Talon instructs Sawyer.

The man does as Talon directs, his hand reaching out, cupping my breast, calloused thumb flicking my nipple before rolling it in a pinch. I jerk.

The toy inside me is pulsing now with every slow withdrawal and push Talon gives me, and I can't focus on anything else.

Talon kneels between my legs, a priest at the altar of his own destruction.

"Look at you," he murmurs. "Fighting me when your body wants to beg."

I shake my head, lips parting in protest, but the moan escapes before I can stop it.

The collar around my throat suddenly feels too tight. My slick is dripping down between my ass cheeks, sticky and obscene. The toy slides in deeper, slower, angling up, and my vision spots.

I lift my eyes to Talon's bare chest. The open leather jacket frames it like a goddamn gift. His body gleams, skin and scales catching the low light of the room, alive with restrained power. Those perfect, ridged abs flexing with every precise movement, the sharp cuts of his hips leading straight to that line of pants I've wanted to tear open a hundred times.

Now that I know what's under them, I'm hungry to touch, to taste, to claim him again. Like no one else ever has, like no one else ever will.

The need rips through me so hard I forget to breathe.

I want him.

Not just sex. Not just pleasure. I miss his fire, his heat, his *everything*. I want to drink down every shard of Talon and feel full again.

But I can't feed from him. And it hurts me as deeply as I feel the pleasure he is giving me.

Talon fucks me with the toy relentlessly—deep, smooth thrusts, dragging it against every swollen nerve until my vision whites out at the edges. His gloved fingers press into my thigh, anchoring me open as I writhe.

My hands fist in the sheets. I tilt my head back and groan, trying to shut it down, trying to resist the way my power churns, hungry and wild, like a beast clawing at the walls of my flesh.

My hunger turns rabid. A thousand sharp teeth gnaw at the inside of my ribs. My stomach cramps, my skin flushes, my head feels light.

I need to feed. Sex flows all around me. Mine and Sawyer's energy intertwines though I'm at the mercy of Talon. From him, I cannot drink a drop.

No.

No, no, no.

I can't feed. I won't.

But Talon sees it. Sees the change in my breathing. The desperation breaking through my armor. His next thrust with the toy is brutal. Perfect. Cruel.

"Let go," he says softly. "Stop trying to starve yourself just to prove a point."

Sawyer reaches down even as he pleasures himself to join Talon's efforts, rubbing my clit. I gasp, my spine arching off the bed.

"Let me give it to you," Talon nearly begs. "Let me give you what you need, even if it's through someone else."

I clench my eyes shut tight as my senses leave me.

"No," I protest again even as my body riots, twisting and climbing toward that inevitable peak. Pressure coils, sharp and unbearable, right behind my pubic bone as my stomach flexes almost painfully.

Talon's expression goes flat, reminding me of a shark. "Then I'll make you."

CHAPTER 32

BLOODSUCKERS KIDNAP THE PRIZE

AURORA

"Take her by the throat," Talon orders, pushing the other man's hand aside to take over.

The cadence and pressure is as effective as if Talon was in my mind, knowing exactly how to push and punish the twisting upward string of tension inside me.

Sawyer's hand slides up to my throat.

"Higher and harder," Talon tells him.

Sawyer's large hand wraps perfectly so my vision blurs and my pleasure heightens. My control is fast spiraling as my curse licks at all of Sawyer's delicious sexual energy that pulsates so temptingly around me.

I try to breathe, but the air sticks in my throat. My body trembles, my nipples hard against the chill of the room, my cunt stretched wide around the glass toy and desperate for more, and Talon's gloved fingers torturing my clit with perfect roughness.

Before I can protest again, my whole body bows off the bed. A scream tears from my throat as I fall off that sharp, steep cliff.

Sawyer groans near my head, his body jerking. His grip loosens as I feel his hot, wet cum hit my shoulder.

I suck in the flood of Sawyer's need and wanting in delicious waves. I feed, I swallow, I devour as I come hard to the vision of Talon penetrating me, sweat dampening the hair at his brow and intense concentration.

I lose myself to everything, the room sliding and fading out of view.

The collar cuts into my throat with a violent jerk.

"Aura, stop," Talon commands, removing the toy.

I whimper, my hips buck, trying to follow the shaft and sensation.

"Stop," he repeats with the same firmness.

I gasp for air and blink until reality comes back into focus. Sawyer is passed out on the bed. The warm tones of his skin have cooled. Panic grips me as I scramble over to touch his neck, feeling for a pulse.

After a moment, I detect the steady thrum of his heartbeat. I let out a sigh of relief, body slumping.

Then I twist to look at Talon, who stands rigidly at the edge of the bed. His face is a mosaic of emotions—conflict, regret, and a shadow of something more profound.

Suddenly, I retreat inward, wrapping my arms tightly around my body as if trying to shield myself from the world.

"Aura?" Talon asks, his voice noticeably softer, lacking the firm authority it held just moments ago when he seemed so sure of himself.

"I'm cold," I murmur, the words barely escaping my lips. I rise from the bed, the cool air prickling my skin, and begin to dress as Talon sets the room to rights.

We don't speak as we leave the room with Sawyer comfortably situated. We don't speak until we are outside.

We don't take the main roads. Talon guides us through smaller streets, quieter routes where the empty alleys are littered with broken umbrellas and plastic cups. Boston's nightlife has all been snuffed out for the night.

"I'm sorry, Aura," Talon finally says, the words heavy with sincerity. Then his shoulders stiffen, "No, I'm not sorry. You need to feed. I also wish things were different, but they aren't. We have to play the hand we are dealt."

I bite my lower lip, feeling the pressure build until I stop abruptly, forcing Talon to halt as well.

"You were right," I admit, my voice barely above a whisper.

He looks at me, his eyes wide, clearly taken aback. "What?"

We pause near an old park, iron benches slick with rain beneath the jaundiced glow of a streetlamp. Everything smells like wet stone and damp leaves. Boston holds its breath, waiting for us to move again.

"I...I wasn't coping well. I'm sorry." The words taste like ash on my tongue. Not because I don't mean them, but because they cost something. My pride. My armor. The illusion that I could outrun the truth if I just kept being difficult enough.

Talon doesn't answer right away. His eyes search mine, and I hate how gentle they've become.

"I'm not proud of how I acted," I say, arms still wrapped around myself. "I felt...powerless. And angry. And heartbroken. So I lashed out."

His brow furrows, and I expect him to jump in, to soothe, to forgive.

But I don't let him. Not yet.

"I wanted to hurt you because I thought it would make me feel better," I admit, my voice cracking. "And it didn't. I just felt like a bratty little Succubus having a tantrum, and guess what? Turns out even Succubae get hangry and irrational when they're starving."

That earns a blink. Then a twitch of his lip, just the barest ghost of a smile. But he lets me keep talking.

"I know you did what you had to, forcing someone else on me," I say, stepping closer. "Even if I hated it. Even if I'm still furious at the world for making you the one person I want most...and the one person I can't touch."

The ache behind my sternum presses hard again, but I push through it.

"I came to Boston thinking I could rewrite myself," I murmur. "That if I was far enough from the palace, the past, the chains, I could just...be someone new. Independent. Uncursed. A Lost Girl."

I shake my head, laughing bitterly. "But you were right. I can't outrun this. My hunger, my power, my curse, it's part of me. And I need to stop pretending it's something I can shed like old skin."

Talon's gaze sharpens, but I keep going, voice steady now. "That doesn't mean I'm giving up. It means I need to make peace with it. On my terms. Not out of shame or fear or because I want to prove a point."

Talon's jaw flexes. He doesn't interrupt. He listens.

"And what you did tonight," I say, finally meeting his gaze, "letting yourself touch me like that, even through gloves, even through another body, it was dangerous. It was painful. But it mattered." My throat tightens. "Because for a moment, it was just us. And I'd rather risk it all for mere moments like that than go without ever again." I push my hair back behind my ear nervously.

Talon sighs and tilts his head to the sky for a long moment. My insides turn itchy from waiting on him to respond. "My job, my duty, has always been to protect you. But since being here, I've seen you adapt, grow—hell, you've been thriving. And it makes me...ashamed."

I blink. *What?*

Then he steps in close, heat pouring off him like a wave. "You fought for the life you wanted. You carved out a life here, one that suits you. Despite the challenges, despite the steep learning curves and all the broken glass."

My eyes narrow at that as I give his shoulder an indignant shove. "Hey."

He wraps a gloved hand around my waist, the heat seeping through my clothes, stopping me. The gesture is so casual, so intimate, and something we've never done before. "I haven't fought for you like that, Aura. And you deserve someone who doesn't pull back when things get complicated."

Suddenly I'm far too warm all over, but I refuse to step away from his touch.

"I want you more than anything. No, I need you." He swallows hard, eyes searching and pained. "I tried to tell myself if I kept that bit of distance then one day I'd stop wanting it to be me. But it never stops. It just hurts more. So I regret not stealing every small moment I could. Any point of contact." He slides his hand up so it rests along my back. Our bodies aren't quite touching, but we are so close. I'm hovering, floating in his gravitational field, and it feels like coming home. "The pain of keeping you safe far outweighs the risk of your happiness, of the life I've seen spark in you. You inspired me."

He drops his head so his lips hover mine. It's so close I feel heat sizzle across in pleasant little zips of power. The proximity is a luxury, a witchtitting revelation.

"I can't be on the sidelines anymore, Aura. I'm done

pretending you're not it for me. You're my turning point. The before and after of everything I am. We're in this together. When you feed, I'm going to be right there showing you how much I want you. Loving you even with a quarter inch of fabric between us."

"We'll make this work, we'll make *us* work," he says, "Even if it's messy, unconventional, and unfair. It'll be ours."

I nod. "Even if it's not perfect."

His mouth tilts in something that isn't quite a smile. "Perfect's boring anyway."

I huff a laugh. I can still love him. And for the first time, I think I can love me too. Curse and all.

Despite the resolution, I still feel the knife in my heart from losing my friends. "I guess we should move, huh?" I ask.

Talon nods. "It's not safe here, when everyone knows what you are."

"And Mal hunting me down," I add, agreeing. "And it's likely already gotten back home. If we go back, it will cause my parents a lot of trouble." It's probably best if we pick up and move to another town. We can use new names. Though it will be harder with Talon being a Dragon.

Talon slows at my side, nostrils flaring, the collar of his open leather jacket fluttering in the breeze. The molten cracks between his scales are dim, but they pulse once— like his body's bracing for something.

We've wandered into a part of the city lined in rusted chain-link fences. We're still close enough to smell the salt from the ocean baked into the bricks. But it's too quiet, and uneasiness kicks up in my gut.

Shapes peel out of the shadows. Hooded. Casual. Like

locals out for a late-night stroll, except they move too smoothly, too quickly. There's no sound of footsteps.

I freeze. "Talon?"

"Behind me."

The first vampire lunges. Talon grabs him and sets him on fire.

It happens so fast I barely register the scream. Heat explodes in the alley as flame ripples across the vamp's coat, curling denim and skin in the same breath. He goes down flailing.

Another comes in from the side. Talon spins, driving a boot into its chest, sending the creature flying into a dumpster.

But there are more. Half a dozen now. Maybe more.

One charges me.

I scream and swing my fist in a wild motion, but it connects hard with his face. He grunts, more surprised than hurt, and grabs for me again. I elbow him in the side and duck away, but the edge of the curb snags my step. I pitch forward, skin scraping raw as my knee cracks against the ground

Another grabs my arm, yanking me upright with claws scraping skin. I twist and rake my nails across his cheek, shrieking like a feral animal.

I'm not trained. I don't know what I'm doing.

But I won't go down easy.

A blur of black fabric.

Steel flashes.

One of the vampires jerks backward, a dagger embedded in his temple. The other's head whips around just in time to catch a boot to the face.

Snow drops to a crouch beside me in a godsdamn catsuit. Her white hair is braided tight, daggers glinting in each hand like frozen lightning. She slashes one across the chest of the vampire nearest me, then pivots and plunges the other into another's eye socket with terrifying precision.

She's breathing hard but she's calm, eyes like twin ice picks.

"Are you—"

"What the hell are you wearing?" I gasp.

She doesn't look at me. She hurls a second dagger into another vampire's throat and grabs my wrist. "Run."

"What the fuck are you *doing* out here?"

"Not now, Aura." She spins, a third dagger already in her hand.

I look over her shoulder...

Just in time to see Talon go down.

He's surrounded. Overwhelmed. Three vamps cling to his back, clawing at his scales, trying to rip them free. Another wraps a chain around his throat, yanking him backward, dragging him down with brute force.

He sets one alight, but the others don't falter. More chains flash through the dark—around his ankles, his wrists. One clamps his wings to his body.

They've come prepared this time.

He fights like hell, fire bursting from his mouth, searing two clean off him—but there are too many. Five more. Ten. They swarm him, driving him to his knees.

A vampire lunges in with something small and sharp. A syringe sinks into his ribs. He bellows then staggers.

I take a step toward them as Snow grabs me, keeping me from going any further.

Talon drops to one knee. Another vampire steps in and, with a gloved hand, slams his fist into Talon's temple.

Talon collapses.

"No—" The scream tears from my throat.

A blinding pink arc erupts from my chest, seething with raw fury. It doesn't merely whip or curl, it hurtles forward with lethal speed and ferocity. It hits the vampire who struck Talon square in the chest.

I feel it.

Feel him.

Not his body, his *life force*.

I grip the pulse of something soft and vital beneath skin and bone. The teeth of my curse sink its teeth into the center of him without ever touching him.

And then I pull. The hunger lunges, a starving animal bursting from its cage. I rip his life straight out of him, and it funnels straight into my veins. My body clenches, shakes, the rush of it so sharp and immediate it borders on orgasmic.

I gorge. I *feed*.

The vampire drops in an instant. Not burned. Not wounded. Dead. Like his soul has been scooped out of him. Or if vampires don't have souls, whatever animates him.

It tastes as delicious as any other person I've devoured but tangier and honestly...a little dry.

My breath comes ragged, my skin flushed and tight as the energy rushes through me, filling in the cracks that Mal carved in me.

Half of them drag Talon back by the arms of his jacket, leather scraping pavement.

I take a step to go after them.

Snow hauls me around, shoving me down a side alley.

"Let me go!" I scream. "We have to go back! We have to help him!"

"There are too many," Snow says, unrelenting her grip on me.

Behind us, I hear one of the vampires shout, "We've got the Dragon! Leave the girl."

Snow drags me half a block before I shake her off me. I turn and run back to where Talon was being swarmed and drugged. But when I return, there's no one there. Only spots of blood and a few charred corpses left behind.

Mal has Talon.

The realization hits me like a bowling ball to the gut.

She always wanted Talon. It was never about me.

I stumble. My hands shake from hunger and from the sick, terrifying realization of what I just did. What I could do again.

"We've got to go," Snow says softly before taking my wrist again and wrenching me away from the scene of Talon's abduction.

LOST GIRLS ASSEMBLE

AURORA

Snow drags me back to our apartments.

Panic, confusion, and fear swirl inside me, twisting tighter with every breath until I can't tell where one begins and another ends.

I was right, they wanted Talon all along.

"We need to get Ariel," Snow says, coding into the front door of our apartment building. The lock opens with a click and a gasp.

"What were you doing, out in a catsuit, in the dead of night?" I ask, taking a closer look at the tight-fitting, black matte outfit that has nothing to do with clubbing or the Poison Apple.

"Err, new workout routine?" she says, blinking those big blue eyes at me.

I cross my arms. "With daggers?"

A lopsided grin blooms on her face as she unlocks the door to her and Ariel's apartment. "Okay yeah, maybe not the Zumba class everyone else is taking. Let's just say, you aren't the only one who's been keeping secrets."

Ariel is dead asleep until Snow crashes the door open

and flings on the lights. "Wake up girl, our friend needs us," Snow announces loudly.

"What the hell, Snow," Ariel says groggily as she shields her eyes from the overhead attack of light.

"Talon has been taken," she says.

"Wh-what?" Ariel asks, still waking up.

"Talon has been kidnapped by vampires. Keep up," Snow claps. "We need to get Rap and figure what the hell is going on and save his big broody ass."

Ariel throws back the sheets and transitions into her chair faster than I thought anyone capable. She rolls to the chest of drawers and pulls out a black band tee shirt.

"Aren't vampires only hanging in the Midnight Realm?" Ariel asks.

With her back to us, she throws off the silk camisole and tugs on the shirt before going about changing her pants next.

"I've been seeing more and more crop over the last couple months. Not from Midnight, regular Boston people turned into suckheads." Snow whips around to me. "Do you know who's turning them? Who took Talon?"

I freeze, both Ariel and Snow watching me, waiting for an answer.

"Wh-why would you help me?"

Ariel's brow furrows. "Because we're friends."

"Duh," Snow adds.

"But—" My brain short circuits as I try to wrap my mind around this. "But I'm a Succubus. I accidentally hurt you guys, I—" My voice chokes from emotion tightening around my throat.

Snow steps closer, putting a hand on my arm. "Hey, so you're a Succubus. Who the fuck cares?"

"You should. Everyone else will."

"I mean, I don't think you want to fuck either of us to death," Ariel adds.

"Which I find slightly insulting," Snow sniffs, then playfully squeezes my arm.

"We all got baggage," Ariel says. "I mean, look at Catwoman here."

"Hey," Snow snaps at Ariel. Then looking down at her own attire, she smirks. "Okay, yeah, I have some very well-dressed issues going on myself."

Snow turns back to me. "But we need to deal with yours first. Tell us everything."

"Everything?" I say in a small voice.

The idea is terrifying. Legit, fall off a cliff into a pit of sharp rocks terrifying. But they already know I'm a runaway princess. They know I'm a Succubus, and I even accidently hurt them with my power. And they are still here, ready and willing to help me and help Talon.

BY THE TIME we push through the door of Poison Apple, Rap's already there. A full pot of coffee steams on the counter. She has a mug in hand and an alert look in her eye. Between that and the thick eyeliner she sports, I can't help but wonder if she was already awake.

Her eyes land on me. Keen. Calculating. "You said vampires took him?"

"Yes," Snow answers before I can. "Organized. Not random."

Rap's jaw ticks. "I've been hearing chatter for weeks. Bodies disappearing. People turned. The vampire count in Boston has been slow but steady over the last ten years or so, but the last month? There's been a notable uptick." Her brows furrow. "There's also a rise in mage disappearances in the neighboring city. My gut tells me that's not a coincidence."

"A month ago? That's when Talon and I started working here," I say, my voice thin with panic. "When I became a Lost Girl."

Rap's eyes narrow. "Someone noticed you."

"No." I shake my head. "They noticed *him*. Mal wants Talon."

"Mal? You mean Kai's sister?" Ariel asks.

I nod. "Yes, she's the one who cursed me. Kai was right about all of it. She was engaged to my father who broke off the engagement and married my mother a couple weeks later. She was exiled from the Midnight Kingdom by her father, but what no one knows is she came to Realm of Roses. She broke into the castle and she...cursed me." It's hard to force the words out. I've never told a single solitary person in my life. Despite the acceptance I've received, my insides still quake as I lay it all out. "She cursed me in my crib before she was run off. When I had my first...um... sexual experience I...uh... I..."

Ariel touches my arm and gives me an encouraging smile. "It's okay. You can tell us."

I look at the ceiling to blink back the stinging in my eyes. "I found out I was a Succubus. After that I had to regularly feed, and my partners never survived. Talon would take care of the details. He would pick people who deserved to meet their fate." My words are rushed as I try to explain. "But I didn't want to be that way anymore. I came here and tried to get away from what I've done, from what I am. And it's been so hard." The words cracks. I scrub my hands over my face. "If I hadn't come here, Talon wouldn't have been forced to follow. He's been taking care of me while making sure no one else got hurt. And because of me, he's been taken by Mal for fae lords know what."

"That Dragon blood made noise." Rap pours herself another coffee, black and violent. "Noise travels fast. Faster than we realized."

"So where is she keeping him?" Snow demands. "I've been tracking the vampire movement for the last couple weeks, but it's erratic. Hard to pin down."

Ariel pulls out her phone. "What's the pattern? Show me on the map."

Snow begins dropping pins on Ariel's phone.

Ariel analyzes it, chewing on her lip. "Disappearances, feeding dens, drain sites. It's a web. But there's a center."

Rap taps her nail on the map. "If Mal has Talon in one of these old crypts, there's likely power running to it. These aren't Midnight Fae. These are Boston people turned vampire. They aren't going to forego the luxury of electricity. Let me make a call and we can find out which one is lit up." She steps away, already on the phone.

"I'm gonna go shake down Kai. He was an absolute ass to Aurora, but he wouldn't be down with this. If he can help us find out where she is, he'll do it. Even if I have to beat it out of him."

"Love you, babe," Ariel says. "But I'm not sure you've got what it takes to make Kai squeal."

Snow shrugs. "Then I'll get Cinder to step on his balls with her spiky platform boots until he submits." With that, she's out the door.

Rap stays on the phone in the corner, barking orders. Ariel keeps working at her map, fingers flying over her screen, piecing together routes and patterns.

And me?

I sink onto one of the barstools. For a moment, it's just

me and a cup of coffee going cold between my hands. The sun is creeping up, bleeding pale light over the Boston skyline. It's nearly six AM.

My thoughts spiral back to that young vampire sneering at me. *"You're not as powerful or dangerous as she said."*

It was right before Talon went full Dragon, right before everything unraveled. We got swept away by the fight, by each other. But those words haven't stopped bouncing around my head.

Mal told them I was dangerous. Powerful.

But surely, she didn't mean I'd roll over and spread my legs in order to murder them. No, she was warning them about something else. She meant something else.

She knew. She *knew* my hunger, my power, could leave my body. That I could weaponize the curse she strapped to my soul. When my instincts lashed out and targeted Mal, she didn't look surprised. Intrigued? Maybe. But not shocked.

Granted, it ended in absolute fucking disaster. But for the first time in my life, it felt like I had a grip on something real. Something *mine*. What if I could...

What I did to that vampire. That wasn't an accident. My curse can stretch beyond touch, beyond my body. I can *control* it.

Even now, I feel the tether. Like a muscle flexing under my skin. Coiled, waiting. Fueled by fear, by rage, by hunger...and by my need for him. *Talon.*

I jump to my feet when Rap comes back. She shakes her head. "I put some feelers out but most of my contacts have their phones on Do Not Disturb and are asleep right now. We'll have to wait."

"We can't wait," I snap. "We need to go over to that

cemetery and start searching the area. Mal had one of her vampires slice a scale off Talon. Whatever she wants from him, it can't be good. She could be torturing him. Or worse."

"You're not wrong," Rap says, pushing back from the counter. "But we don't charge in blind. We plan. We arm up. We think this through."

"There's no time." The words rip out of me—too loud, too sharp. "They have him now. They took him for a reason."

Rap crosses her arms, gaze narrowing. "And running in half-cocked will get you killed. Then who's going to save him? You're no good to him dead."

I jerk like she slapped me. "You think I don't know that? You think I don't know how dangerous this is? I don't care. I can't sit here and drink coffee while he's—" My voice breaks. "I can't do nothing."

"You're not doing nothing. You're regrouping. You're surviving long enough to fight smart," Rap says, her tone steel-edged but not unkind. "He'd want that."

"That's easy for you to say," I fire back. "You're not the one who left him behind."

"You didn't leave him. They took him. That's different."

It doesn't feel different.

Rap's phone rings. She picks up, murmurs, listens. Her expression hardens as she hangs up.

"There's only one crypt in this area pulling power right now," she says, pointing at the map Ariel's built on her phone. "An abandoned burial site in the old district, under St. Ignatius. City records show a power reroute a few weeks ago. It's too quiet. Too clean. That's your center."

"We should wait for Snow," Ariel says, trying to steady

the room. "She's getting Kai. He'll talk to his sister. Maybe we can avoid bloodshed."

I nod. "Okay. You're right. I'm going to shower and change at my place. Be back in twenty."

"Wait," Rap says, stopping me with a hand on my arm. "Take the stairs around the corner. My place is unlocked. You can shower there. I don't want you wandering off alone when you're this...raw. Stay close. Take any clothes you need."

She thinks she's keeping me safe. Keeping me from doing something reckless.

She doesn't know me well enough to understand I've already decided.

"Thanks," I say softly, meaning it. Because this is the last kindness I can take from her before I walk into the dark alone.

I head outside and walk right past the entrance to Rap's apartment.

I can't risk them. Not for this.

Talon has always been the one to protect me. To drag me back from the edge when my hunger, my curse, my shame tried to devour me whole. He's bled for me. Burned for me.

He's not here to protect me now. That means it's my turn to protect him.

My heart pounding. My hunger roaring. My feet carrying me toward the crypt. Toward Talon.

They'll forgive me later.

If I survive to earn it.

CHAPTER 34

MAL DRINKING MAGES
TALON

I push through the cotton that fills my mind, blinking hard to bring my surroundings into focus.

The world returns in fragments. Cold stone beneath my body. Damp air, metallic and stale. The distant drip of water counts the seconds. I drag my gaze up, and the room comes into view. A wide crypt with vaulted ceilings and carved stone walls, lit by sputtering torches and faintly glowing mage lights. Old bones are stacked into niches.

Pain comes next—low and blooming at the back of my skull. Whatever they used to sedate me was strong enough to drop a Dragon.

With the pain comes an unwelcome stench. Rank. Sour. A reek of decay, steeped in vinegar and sweat. The scent sinks into my sinuses, thick and cloying, a stink no Dragon could mistake for anything else.

The smell of mage powers.

My stomach tightens in revulsion, throat closing against the weight of it. Normally a single passing, low-level mage doesn't make me do much more than wrinkle my nose. Plenty filter through the Poison Apple, but it's never been anything like this.

To my left, a row of mages hang strung up, slaughterhouse refuse on display. Chains bite into their wrists, heads drooping on broken necks. Some still breathe, barely. Others hang silent and sunken, their skin already slackening in death. Bite marks tear at their throats and arms. They've been drained to the marrow.

I grit my teeth as I roll my shoulders, testing resistance. Chains.

Thick, iron, and etched with sigils I don't recognize. My arms are spread and bound at the wrists, anchored to the wall behind me. I yank once—nothing. Again, harder—and fire shoots down my spine.

Magic-reinforced. Of course.

In the middle of the room, a long table is covered in glassware—beakers, flasks, metal instruments. They all shine gruesomely under the cold steel lights that have been set up around it.

Some of the containers hold blood—thick, vibrant, glowing faintly like liquid light. One vial pulses with blue. Another with green. Most are labeled, and I can make out the names of people and...mage levels?

Then I see a bloody, black scale on a large petri dish. My scale. The one those vampires had cut from *my* body.

A figure works at the table quietly.

She's petite, barely a presence in the room. Until she turns around. Her skin is porcelain-pale, her features sedate in a heart-shaped face. Black hair falls in a perfect sheet to her shoulders, and when she tilts her head, the cold lights glint off her fangs. A bloodsucking Midnight Fae.

But it's her veins that stop me cold.

They pulse with color—violet, silver, and searing

cobalt. Magic is alive inside her and trying to claw its way out.

She's not just one of the Midnight Fae, she's something else now. Some kind of magic abomination, but I'm not sure how.

"I was wondering when you'd wake up," she says, her voice smooth, a silk ribbon wrapped around a blade. "I've been interested in you for a long time, and now I finally get to meet you."

I don't answer. The taste of ash and silver fills my mouth. But I know exactly who I'm facing.

Mal. The exiled princess of the Midnight Fae.

She steps closer. Her heeled boots don't make a sound as she walks. Her dress is black leather, built in armored stitches, fused close against her frame.

"Hello, Talon," she murmurs. "I've been looking forward to meeting you for a long time."

"As have I, *Mal*." I speak through gritted teeth.

The corner of her lips twitch before her expression returns to that implacable mask.

"Where is Aurora?" I demand.

One brow lifts. "I don't know. She ran off, I suppose."

That doesn't sound like my girl. Though I pray that's true, that she got away.

"Don't worry, *hot boy*." Another twitch of her mouth that reaches her eyes this time. "That's what they call you at the bar, right? I don't have any use for the princess."

Her fingers brush along the table edge, tapping the beakers with the deliberate precision of someone choosing a specific wine pairing.

She leans in. The stench of mage blood slams into me. Not one kind—*all* kinds.

I clench my fists against the chains. "How many mages

did you have to feed on before you developed their powers?"

She tilts her head in a measured acknowledgement. "More than even I cared to stomach. Especially when there are so many level ones and twos running around, but so few higher-powered treats for me to suck on. But it's worth it." She raises a hand and a ball of purple energy appears in her palm, roiling, glowing and shifting. "For the power." Closing her hand, the energy ball snuffs out. Based on what she's done to Aurora, I know she can do a lot more than a light show in her hand.

The memory of Aurora telling me the vampires seemed like they were coming for me rises in my mind. I hadn't paid the theory much attention then, but now I realize she was probably right.

"What do you want with me? Why do you have my scale?" I jerk my chin toward the petri dish.

Mal pulls up a stool with a terrible screech before she hops up onto it.

"I want you to help me finish what I've started."

"Cursing babies and throwing a fit?" I suggest. It's almost as if I've absorbed some of that Lost Girl sass...for better or worse.

Her eyes darken, and I feel a thickening of power in the room. "Admittedly, leveraging the princess did not go quite to plan."

"If you don't need her, why did you come to Poison Apple the other night? Why did you expose her like that in front of everyone?"

Mal calmly folds her hands. Every sedate, controlled motion is at odds with the chaotic powers flaring from and around her. "I had no intention of outing Aurora, and I had just learned that you were the answer." She gestures to the scale on the makeshift laboratory table. "I wanted to come see how she turned out. When I cursed her all those years ago, I anticipated that she would be burned at the stake or at the very least, cast out of her father's kingdom, hopefully breaking Roland's heart." The first flash of emotion goes through her eyes. But as quickly as it shows, it disappears. "And I also expected her to come into her full power by now."

Full power? What does that mean?

"I'd been warning my...lackeys," she says with some disdain, "to watch out for her when trying to get to you. When they told me she had no concept, no grasp of what she could fully do, I had to see for myself."

"What are you talking about?" I openly sneer at her. "Are you saying the curse was a gift?"

She shakes her head. "Oh no," she says loftily, pushing her hair back with one hand. "But I figured she'd come into the full powers of a Succubus if she'd stayed alive for this long. I was quite surprised when I found her so restrained, so pent up even as she degraded herself, dancing atop that bar." She gives me a bemused smirk of superiority. "And when she saw me, that power tried to bloom, tried to grow the way I expected it to years ago. Of course," she interlaces her fingers again, "when she tried to use her power on the person who cast the curse, it obviously backfired with critical results." She cocks her head to the side. "But boy, have you done a good job cleaning that mess up. It's a pity all these years you've been used as some kind of servant," her nose wrinkles as she spits the word, "to the Rosari's. When you are *so* much more."

My insides coil with trepidation.

"I don't know what you are talking about," I say plainly.

Mal hops down from the stool, approaching me slowly,

craning her neck up to meet my eyes. Her irises are dark—almost black—but shimmer when she moves. Like the magic inside her can't stop writhing.

"You are one of the few Dragons left in this Realm. You are resistant to the influence of others, even my own Vampire thrall. No Rosari can feed on your energy. You are powerful, strong, with independent will, wings, and *fire*." As she describes my qualities, her eyes turn glassy with...lust.

My jaw tenses. My gaze flits to the barely breathing bodies in the corner as I realize why I'm here.

She grins now, a smile that still doesn't reach her eyes but shows off the gleaming vampire fangs. "And I would very much like a taste."

FINDING THE POWER AND THE VILLAIN
AURORA

They took him.

Mal took the man I love from me.

All logic, all fear has burned away. What's left is singular and sharp, a diamond-hard truth I can't escape. He is *mine*. And I won't burn the world to get him back.

I will devour it.

"You've always saved me, Talon," I whisper to the empty stairwell. "This time, it's my turn."

The narrow staircase winds downward beneath the old church, each step slick with centuries of damp. My boots skid once on the wet stone, but I don't falter. I can't. The air is heavy with mildew and incense and something older.

My power gathers and swells the further I descend. It's different now. It's not breaking free of me in panicked bursts, lashing out wildly. It's rising because I call it. Because I want it. Because for the first time in my life, I'm not trying to choke it down.

I feed it fear. I feed it fury. I feed it every breath I take as I descend.

The curse doesn't slither in serpent twists. It doesn't coil anymore. It waits.

A mouth. Open. Starving.

I feel it now, gnashing beneath my ribs, pressing against my bones. Not trying to hurt me, trying to answer me. My hunger. My curse. The same thing. It aches to be fed.

For once, I don't fight it.

I aim it. I shape it. I sharpen it.

I become the thing with the mouth, the thing with the hunger, the thing ready to bite back.

The arched doors at the base of the stairs blow inward, not from wind or force, but from my unleashed hunger. Power arcs from my skin in jagged streaks of pink light, licking the hinges, prying the heavy wood open with a sound like cracking bone.

The catacombs stretch before me, yawning open, cold and slick and thrumming with quiet violence. Not Mal's. Mine.

I step forward, my cloak trailing behind me, my collar still locked around my throat, my hunger bared beneath my skin.

Power pulses under my skin, a second heartbeat. It hums through my ribs, licking along my spine. My fingers twitch, aching with it. My mouth waters with it. My curse isn't inside me anymore. It's riding just beneath the surface, eager, obedient.

The double doors at the far end blow open on another blast of my hunger. Candles gutter to life in ripples, bending toward me.

The vampires rear back, snarling. One lunges. Another bares fangs.

I don't flinch.

Hunger moves faster than thought.

A crackle of pink arcs from my outstretched hand in an open maw that crashes down on the first vampire. It sinks in, deep. Ripping. Feeding. His eyes go wide with terror and rapture as his life tears free of him in streams of light and heat, flowing into me.

It feels...good.

Not like Talon. Not like love. But like quenching a thirst I've carried in my marrow for years. Like filling the hollows I thought were permanent.

The vampires hesitate now, then come at me anyway.

Their skin withers, pleasure and life ripped from them in luminous streams of soul-light that pour into my veins. Their mouths stretch open in silent moans before they collapse, brittle and lifeless.

More vampires surge forward, drawn by instinct, by rage, by the overwhelming scent of power. Some rush to kill me.

Others...don't.

They falter. Stumble. Their pupils dilate.

They want me. They can't help it.

My skin glows now. Not just with magic, but with *heat*, with *need*, with every ounce of hunger I've ever felt and now let free.

I become something radiant. Otherworldly. Sensual.

My hair lifts on an unseen breeze. The very air around me pulses in rhythm with my power.

They can smell me. Taste me.

And they come, helpless to resist.

I open my arms, and my power arcs again—out, out, snapping through the dark with jaws, biting into flesh, into bone, into magic and marrow. The curse works through me, but not against me. It doesn't take from me. It takes *for* me.

Silken power slides through my veins, weight and warmth filling every empty corner inside me.

They come faster now, drawn in by hunger, by instinct, by the scent of death wrapped in sugar.

Some try to kill me. Some try to kiss me. All of them fail.

Their bodies wither beneath the weight of my need. Their souls pour from them in shimmering ribbons, pulled into the hungry maw of my curse until there's nothing left.

I walk forward, the air parting for me, the last of the vampires breaking against my power.

I've waited my whole life to stop hiding. To stop starving. And I'll feed on this entire fucking world before I let them keep him from me.

THE CHAMBER where they are holding Talon isn't what I expected.

It's worse.

Stone walls press close, slick with mildew and shadow. Candles flicker in old iron sconces. The air is wet and metallic, soaked with the scent of blood and damp rot. A table at one end gleams with steel instruments and broken glass beakers, each of them sticky with drying crimson. Magic residue clings to the surfaces with a static that makes my skin crawl.

And in the corner…

Bodies.

Some slumped in chains. Some crumpled in heaps, lifeless and used up. Then I recognize one of them. The level one mage who created smoke ribbons in the club to impress a girl the other night. Though now, his sightless eyes stare up at the ceiling. He's sunken, bloodless.

Then I recognize another one. She had been floating quarters at the bar. Now her head is twisted at an odd angle, dried blood at the puncture marks on her neck. Were all these people mages?

My stomach turns.

I scan the bleak surroundings until my gaze lands on Talon.

He's been strapped to a vertical stone slab—arms bound wide with iron cuffs, legs locked at the ankles, chest exposed. His head hangs forward, chin resting on his chest, his body limp beneath the pull of gravity.

He jerks, just slightly, as if trying to lift his head.

Clinging to him, a small, dark-haired parasite of a woman.

Mal.

She's latched to the front of him, her fangs buried deep in the crook of his neck. Her fingers claw into his waist, bare feet braced on his thighs like she climbed him, climbed my Dragon, and is now *feeding* from him like he's a fucking wine fountain.

His blood trickles from the corner of her mouth, glistening red-black. Her eyes flutter half-closed in ecstasy.

She's *gorging* on him.

I start to gather my hunger before I remind myself what happened last time. I grab her by the hair and yank her off Talon. She crashes into the table, glass shattering, liquids colliding with sizzles and smoke leaving an acrid stench in the air.

I stand between her and Talon.

Mal lifts her head, licking her lips as she rises to her feet with a slow, languid grace. Her small frame makes the gesture look almost childlike.

"You came," she murmurs, her voice soft and infuriatingly mild. "I had a feeling you would."

Black scales form on her skin, creeping like armor up her neck from the collar of her dress. Fissures glow orange beneath the surface, pulsing with light, as if something volcanic writhes beneath her fragile form. Sparks spit from her fingertips—mage magic, stolen and unstable.

"What did you do?" I demand, fists clenched, every part of me trembling.

Her mouth slowly splits into a terrifying grin as she takes in the scales on the backs of her hands.

"You should know better than anyone, Aurora," she says, still grinning when she meets my eye. "You are what you eat."

And she's eaten Dragon.

Talon hangs there, pale and broken, his chin tipped forward, skin slick with sweat and blood.

I rush to him.

But I'm not sure he even sees me.

His eyes flutter open, dazed, unfocused. His lips part like he wants to speak, but nothing comes out.

Blood still drips from the puncture marks on his neck. The orange light between Talon's scales has dulled and dissipated. I touch his chest gingerly, confirming my fear. He's cooled.

I whirl around when Mal steps closer. She's not afraid. Not rushed. She knows. She knows I can't touch her. Not now. Not with her skin blazing and my power unable to sink its fangs into her.

"I regret it, you know." Her voice stays soft, a lullaby against the scream building in my chest. "Punishing you for your father's sins. I thought it would satisfy something in me. But all it did was waste time." Her hand drifts lazily through the air, sparks trailing from her fingertips. "No matter. I'll correct the mistake soon enough. He'll know the pain of losing everything. Like I did."

Fuck. I instinctively reach back to touch Talon. His arm is cold, but he groans at the contact. He's still with me.

Hang on, baby, I've got you.

"But you could have your life back."

"What are you saying?"

"I'm saying," she says, toying with the words, "I could take the gift back."

"Gift?" The word curdles in my mouth until my lips twist.

"No more hunger." Mal speaks so evenly, as if she's completely in control of everything. "No more deaths on your conscience. No more shame. No more strangers. No more feeding. And I could make you more. Like him." She gestures to Talon. "Like me. Then you would be free to touch who you want. Free to love who you want. Without burning. Without fear."

The offer hits me square in the chest.

No more hunger. No more bodies. No more curse. No more strangers in dark rooms. I could touch Talon without gloves. Kiss him without restraint. Love him without fear. I would be just a regular girl in Boston working at the bar with her friends.

For one aching, terrible heartbeat, I want to say yes.

Mal sees it in my face. Her mouth curves with indulgence. "We could take them all down together. The Rosari who kept you locked away. The Midnight Kingdom who cast me out. Wipe the slate clean. Build something new from the ashes."

But I see Talon's Dragon power burning through her

veins like poison. She's not free. She's trapped by her hate of my father, my parents. She's living in the past.

"I've already been building something new," I say, my voice soft but steady. "Without burning the world down. Without becoming like you."

Her smile falters. "You think this life you scraped together matters? You think those girls care? You think he —" She gestures to Talon like he's nothing, like he hasn't bled and burned for me. "—can save you from what you are?"

"No." I lift my chin. "But I can."

For the first time, I see her clearly. And I don't envy her. I don't hate her. I pity her. "I don't want to tear it down. I want to build something better. I already am."

All kindness falls away like a veil dropping until hate gleams from her eyes. "Then starve, little princess."

She turns. Walks away without fear, without hurry. Because in her mind, she's already won.

And Talon hangs by a thread behind me.

CHAPTER 36

HOT BOY NEEDS HEALING
AURORA

Talon will be all right. He has to be.

"Mal got away," I say. Back at Poison Apple, my heart flutters like a hummingbird that is unable to land. I can't sit. I can barely breathe.

Talon is laid on a cot in Rap's office since getting him upstairs would be too tricky, even with all of us trying to move him.

With some cleverly used towels I arranged as a buffer, I got Talon's arm over my shoulders and helped him stagger out to the entrance of the crypt. Not without leaving with some angry red burn marks from when I buckled under his weight.

But when I emerged into broad daylight, I found myself met with Rap and the crew who jumped into action, helping me get Talon in the van they came in. They also gave me hell for running off on my own. I didn't argue with them. Hell, I could barely hear them through my terror for Talon.

We couldn't take him to a hospital. They can't treat a Dragon with skin that burns, but Rap said someone who can help is on the way.

"What is Mal planning?" Ariel asks, her fingers nervously playing with the lens on her camera. Sunlight blasts through the massive skylights, feeding the live tree at the center of Poison Apple.

"She's planning on being a bitch, that's what," Snow snarls as she storms back and forth.

"Not helpful," Rap says dryly from where she leans against the bar.

"She wants revenge," I say as I hug my body.

Everything Mal said runs through my head on a loop.

We could build something new.

You could have your life back.

I could take the gift back.

Never did I imagine I'd get to face my tormentor, and now that it's happened it's almost more than I can process. I rejected her offer, but I can't dismiss the possibility that I could somehow get free of this hunger.

"We're here," Cinder announces as she sweeps through the front door, letting rays of sunshine in. A vampire walking openly under the sun? Then I remember Snow and Ariel debating something about it being connected to her blood magic.

Behind Cinder comes the fast-strutting Fairy Godmother, Dame Kiki Eleganza.

"Where's the hot boy?" Kiki asks without preamble.

Rap directs her to follow, and I'm close on their heels.

Kiki pauses, turning to me. "You want to help him, honey? I need some room to work, and he's gonna need a whole lotta calories when I'm done with him. Order some food for everyone while you're at it. It's on Rap."

"Hey," Rap protests.

Kiki shrugs. "Don't be a stingy scrooge of a boss."

"I've got it," another voice comes from behind me. I turn to find myself face to face with King Kaison Charming. Mal's brother.

"You," I sputter in anger.

Kiki and Rap leave us to go help Talon.

"You thought this was my fault? Well, it's not. It's your stupid sister's fault. She ruined my life. Did you know that?" The words tumble out of me faster and faster. "Did you know that she's turning people into vampires and thralling them? That she used her magic to curse me as a baby? For something I had nothing to do with? I didn't ruin your family, but your sister ruined my life. She tried to suck Talon dry and now she has absorbed some of his Dragon abilities. She is still set on destroying my family for what happened. She has to be stopped." I gasp for air after I finish my tirade.

"You're right," Kai says quietly.

That stops my fury cold. "What?"

I was expecting a fight.

I was preparing to hit below the belt to make sure he knows just how misplaced his judgement was.

I was not expecting...agreement?

"She's..." Kai runs a hand through his silky black hair in open distress. "Mal is out of control. I remembered her as a child, as one reveres an older sibling, but I see now how she's lost it."

"We stayed in town after the wedding," Cinder says, "to investigate the rise in vampire activity in Boston. She came to the Common World when she was first exiled, but she settled on the East Coast a few years ago. You're right, she's been turning people into vampires and thralling them into doing her bidding."

"Which would be abducting mages and sucking them

dry to absorb their magic powers," I inform them as I cross my arms.

Even the implacable Cinder reacts to that.

"W-we didn't know," she says, looking between me and Kai even as his expression hardens. "The power to thrall is a trait of the royals, but absorbing mage powers through blood..."

"Isn't that what happened with you?" Ariel points out. "You both can walk in the sunlight, but that happened after Kai drank your blood, and you have mage powers."

The couple studies each other, exchanging some silent communication.

"That is what happened," Kai says slowly. "I can't believe she'd do this. She's turning people, using them, draining mages, cursing babies." He swings an arm in my direction. "She's practically become our father." Something dark flashes in his eyes as his jaw tightens.

Kai turns to me. "I'm sorry about what I said before. I'll do whatever it takes to help you."

I step back. "I don't want your help."

Cinder encircles Kai's arm in her hands, leveling me with a look of resolve. "Well, you've got it anyway. Mal can thrall others, but *I* can break that power."

"Blood magic," Snow murmurs somewhere behind Cinder with what sounds like new respect.

"I won't let our kingdoms go to war," Kai continues. "The Midnight Realm will do everything to aide the Rosari princess and the Realm of Roses." With that, he bows to me.

I swallow back the myriad of feelings that have stuck in my throat like a toxic lump.

"Thank you," I say through numb lips. My royal upbringing kicks in, and I know I will do whatever it takes to stop her from hurting the Rosari Kingdom and my parents.

Oh fae lords. I rub my forehead. "My parents, I need to warn them."

"And tell them what?" Ariel asks. "You don't know what Mal's planning."

My lips thin. "I don't, but I have to tell them she's coming for them. And that she's gorged herself on Talon's blood."

"Oh." Snow perks up. "Are you gonna use that courier system between Realms?"

I sigh, my shoulders sagging. "I was actually hoping you would let me borrow your phone." I hold out my palm to her.

Snow's brows scrunch together. "But the Realm of Roses is like Midnight, isn't it? No tech allowed?"

Kai and I exchange a look.

"Tech was forbidden in Midnight when my father ruled," Kai clarifies. "That has changed, though I doubt it will become popular anytime soon. But it is *very* nice that I don't have to smuggle batteries in using my various cavities anymore." He grins.

"The Rosari can have tech, they just prefer not to," I say as Snow puts the cold device in my hand. I've rarely used one of these, but I remember my training.

"What does Talon like to eat so I can order food?" Kai asks quietly.

"I've got this," Snow announces, throwing an arm around Kai steering him away. "Have you had the pleasure of frequenting a fine dining establishment called The Salty Bastard?"

"Snow," I hear him say even as I walk away. "I drink

blood. But even if I didn't, I don't think I'd eat at a place called The Salty Bastard."

"Don't act so high and mighty," Cinder counters coolly. "You've technically sucked on actual salty bastards."

"Ew," Ariel says while Snow makes retching sounds.

"Gross, babe," he says, though I can hear his smile.

I force myself to pass Rap's office where Talon is, and head to the break room. I pull up the phone and type in the number etched into memory. As a princess, I'd been given many means of communication should I ever need them. I just haven't wanted to use them...until now.

The phone slips in my sweaty palm as it rings.

The call opens with a video and two people staring at me.

I give a little wave. "Hello, Mother. Father."

CHAPTER 37

GOING HOME AGAIN

TALON

Waking up to a drag queen healing me was only a little less of a surprise than realizing I was going to live.

"There ya go, hot boy," Dame Kiki coos. "Right as rain. You just need a little rest, a truckload of food, and you'll be breathing fire in no time."

The Fairy Godmother gets up from her kneeling position next to me, and I realize I'm lying on a cot in Rap's office. My boss is standing behind Kiki, arms crossed, expression tense.

I feel...wrong. Like my body's been stitched together with thread too thin to hold. The heat inside me is gone, not smothered, but distant, buried under layers of cold ash. My limbs ache in ways no healing spell can fix, and my chest feels hollow where the fire used to burn. But I'm alive.

"Aura?" I ask, my voice cracking.

"Just outside," Rap assures me. "I'll get her."

"We'll give you two some space." Kiki winks. She's about to follow Rap when she pauses at the doorway. Kiki's acrylic nails tap the doorframe a moment before looking back at me.

"Loving someone is hard," Kiki murmurs, eyes soft now, her usual sassy attitude giving way to something older, weightier. "But you two…I've never seen a bond like it. It's not tethered—it's *interwoven*. That kind of love doesn't come around often. And once it locks in? Baby, not even death can unfasten it."

I try to absorb her words, but my head is too foggy and I'm too anxious to see Aurora. Before I can ask her what she means, the Fairy Godmother has gone.

Aurora sweeps in, and I struggle to sit up.

"Stop," she orders, pushing me down with her bare hand against my chest.

"Guess I've cooled off again," I say, my hands instantly closing around hers.

Fucking fae lords. I bring up her hand and kiss each of her knuckles. I revel in being able to touch her again.

"It won't last," she says gently.

"I know," I say in between kisses. It's why I have to take advantage of every moment we have.

I have to be pushed beyond the physical brink to cool to a touchable level. Some part of me is already thinking of ways I can achieve this in the future.

"Stop it," she says.

"What?"

"You aren't going to hurt yourself just so we can touch."

I scowl at her, even as I pull her on top of me.

"I don't think the cot can—oof." She lands on me hard, but the makeshift bed holds underneath us.

I wrap my arms around her, laying my cheek on her head. Aurora nuzzles in, and all of our limbs naturally seek and find the hollows and swells between us until we fit so perfectly, I'm certain we were made for each other.

We breathe in for several breaths, just holding one another. Assuring ourselves this is real.

"I'm the most self-involved person in the world." Her words are muffled against my chest.

I crook my head to try and catch her expression, but it's hidden.

"Mal must be after me," she says in a parody voice. "Oh, she must want to finish the job. She must want to kill the princess." She snorts. "What kind of narcissist am I?"

She lifts her face so she can look at me. I see her frustration, her regret, as if it was written on her forehead.

I brush the back of my knuckles along her cheek. "We both thought it."

She shrugs, still agitated. "We've spent so much time focusing on me, when you are a true wonder, a true..." She searches for the word. "Specimen."

I can't help but full-on grin at that.

Aurora rolls her eyes. "Oh fae lords, now this is going to your head."

I pinch her side and she yelps before swatting my chest. The simple delight of getting to touch her and tease her like this will never lose its novelty. People take for granted those little points of contact.

"You said it, not me." Then I frown. "But they did go for you. You were targeted as well."

"To take me out. Turns out Mal expected me to use the *gift* she gave me against her." She throws air quotes with her fingers even as she tries to remain wrapped around me. Then her expression darkens. "And I finally found a way to use it."

Before I can ask what that means, her fingers clutch at my chest. "I called my parents."

I can't help but massage her hips. Somewhere deep inside me, I already feel the whisper of my fire kicking up. Our time to touch is limited. "What did they say?" I ask.

"Well, for one thing, they said the only thing keeping them from coming after me and dragging me home by my now pierced ears was the regular letters you sent them, updating them on what was happening." Her eyes narrow.

"Did you want them to come after you?" I ask her pointedly.

She pouts even as she shakes her head, knowing I have her.

"I didn't tell them...*everything*," I say.

Unable to help myself despite all we have to discuss, I pull her down and kiss her. Tangling my hands in her hair, reveling in the taste, the feel, of her.

The heat inside me is rising quickly. Time is slipping through my fingers. I grip her tighter until she's plastered to me and I'm delving deep into her mouth, finding my favorite spot in the universe. The one that makes her groan and claw at me like she can't get close enough.

The door creaks open, breaking us apart.

"Hey guys—whoa," Snow says, shielding her eyes. "When you're done banging in your boss's office, we've got food here."

"What?" comes a sharp exclamation from Rap somewhere behind her.

"We aren't having sex," Aurora says, sitting up, though I don't let her get far.

Snow drops her hand, nervously looking between us as if still expecting to find our privates exposed.

I sit up despite the soreness in my muscles and fatigue. My stomach lets loose a vicious growl at the thought of food. "Food would be good."

~

EVERYONE IS EATING and chatting amongst themselves at various tables, giving me time to refuel at the bar with Aurora.

After five lobster rolls and three sides of fries from The Salty Bastard, I almost feel like myself. *Too much* like myself. The heat hums under my skin again, deep and steady, licking along my ribs and tightening my chest. I'm aware of it now the way a man is aware of an old wound waking up in the rain. Familiar. Inescapable.

Aurora reaches out to touch me and I step just out of her grasp. Her eyes widen before I look down pointedly at my bare chest. The faint orange glow between my scales has returned, flickering softly beneath my skin like coals in a dying hearth.

"You're all better," she says with a smile that doesn't reach her eyes. Her fingers curl into her palm before she tucks her hand to her body.

That small, careful gesture guts me more than it should.

I swallow against the tightness in my throat. I want to reach for her. I want to draw her in, kiss her slow and deep until we forget all of this, but that's not possible.

Now that I've regained my strength it's time I share what I know, and there doesn't seem any use waiting until we're alone anymore. Apparently, everyone in this room knows the score, and I can't think too hard on how that makes me feel.

I clear my throat. "Aura," I say, "I overheard Mal's

vampires while I was chained up." The memory is still sharp, still sour in my gut. "They were preparing to leave soon. Tonight, I think. They said something about fire covering the sky."

Aurora stiffens. "What does that mean?"

The chatter around us quiets.

"I don't know. But it can't be good." I push away the empty food cartons. "They weren't just talking about a few of them. They've been gathering more. A lot more. Not just a handful like the ones in Boston."

"She's planning to take a horde of vamps into the Realm of Roses." Aurora's words come out hollow, but certain. Her gaze drops to the table, and her shoulders draw tight, like she's bracing for a hit she knows is coming.

"What?" Kai shoots to his feet, chair scraping loudly against the floor.

I don't flinch at his outburst.

I'm still not used to the King of Midnight sitting here like an ally, but as Snow pointed out, he paid for the food and stopped being an asshole to Aurora. That earns him...a sliver of respect.

Maybe.

Rap's phone rings, and she barely glances at the screen before taking it and striding off with it to her ear.

"But the Rosari can drain vampires of their energy, put them to sleep," Kai says, frowning. "Vampires wouldn't get far. Why would she bother?"

"The Rosari aren't fighters," Aurora says, her voice sharpening. "They can drain the vampires, sure, but it's not like snapping fingers. It takes time, effort, proximity. Meanwhile, Mal has likely trained those vampires to rip people apart. There would be a lot of bloodshed."

"The vampires are a distraction, a means to an end." My

jaw tightens at the memory of Mal's teeth sinking into my throat. "She's not just bringing a squad of bloodthirsty idiots, she's bringing an army she's thralled. They've been turning people. Stockpiling. Preparing to flood the borders with bodies, overwhelm the Kingdom by sheer numbers so she can get what she's really after."

"My parents." Aurora's hand curls into a fist on the table. A thrum of protectiveness rushes through me, visceral and immediate.

"To kill them," I confirm. Because that's what Mal has wanted all along. To punish those who rejected her, who got her exiled. And she needed my blood to help her do it.

"Well, how do we know when she's going to make her move?" Snow asks, tapping a fry against her lip. "If we've got time, we can come up with a real plan—"

"We're out of time." Rap's voice slices through the conversation. She crosses back to us, sliding her phone into her back pocket. Her face noticeably pale beneath the armor of dark eyeshadow and matte lipstick.

"Vampires are already flooding the Realm of Roses," she says.

"Shit." That came from Cinder this time.

"She's going to waltz past the chaos and kill the King and Queen," I say. "Because she drank from me. She believes my blood has made her immune to Rosari powers. The Royal guard is unarmed except for their feeding abilities."

"I called them." Aurora's head whips up, a wild panic in her eyes. "I warned my parents. I told them Mal was coming for them. But I didn't give them enough warning. They aren't prepared."

"Is that true?" Ariel looks from face to face. "Is she immune from Rosari powers?"

"If she's been gorging on mage blood and absorbing their powers," Cinder says slowly, "then it very well might be the case. But who knows what aspects of Talon's fae abilities she's taken on."

I share a look with Aurora. Silently, we communicate that no matter which ones she gets, it will be bad.

"Well, sounds like we better go find out," Snow says, standing up in a ready position. "I got to change real quick, and then I'm good to go."

"I don't have time to wait." Aurora pushes to her feet as well. "I have to go now." She raises a finger at Snow. "And you are going to have to explain the catsuit and daggers eventually."

All eyes turn to her.

Snow laughs nervously, eyes darting between us. "What? I took a Halloween costume too far and now it's just...useful."

"Going by way of the border would add at least an hour to the trip," Rap says, slowly. Then she walks to the tree, resting a hand on the bark. "What if I told you there was a shortcut?"

"Oh, ho, ho, boss lady," Kai says, rubbing his hands together, "I've always liked your style."

"You can't go," Aurora protests, crossing to Rap.

Rap's brows raise in surprise before her expression flattens. "Oh. Is that right? Well, I'd like to see you try to stop me. Or them for that matter." She nods toward the rest of the group. I follow her gaze and see what's written on their faces. They don't plan to be left behind.

"She's right," I add, standing. "This isn't your fight."

"Of course it is, you numbskull." Snow rolls her eyes.

"Family fights for family," Ariel says, lips thinning with determination.

Aurora and I have another one of our silent communications as we both realize the same thing. There's no stopping our friends. Or rather, our new family.

"It's time to go home," Aurora says.

And though I've been wanting her to say those words for the last few months, they only fill me with dread now.

~

WE STEP through the secret portal Rap opens in the massive oak tree, leaving behind the uneven hardwood of Poison Apple to arrive on lush green grass.

Fresh air hits me first, clean and rich with flowers, the kind I remember from childhood. A sky spread wide and endless above. For a breath, the Realm of Roses is as it should be — open, green, untouched.

Then the dream shatters.

Smoke curls up from the village below, thick and black against the night. Flames snap across rooftops, spitting sparks into the air. People run through the streets in chaos, their shouts breaking into screams that pierce the fields around us. A woman stumbles, clutching a child to her chest, before vanishing into the crush of bodies. A man falls, dragged down by pale hands, his cry cut short.

Vampires.

Above it all, wings blot out the stars. A massive shadow glides over the Realm of Roses, and fire rains down in a burning arc. Mal.

"She grew wings." Aurora repeats the words, but they come out numb, disconnected.

"And she can use my fire." I grit my teeth.

"We'll help the villagers," Ariel shouts to be heard,

already rolling toward the village despite the uneven grassy terrain. "We'll put out the fires and get people to safety."

"Care for assistance with that, and maybe a push?" Kai offers. Ariel waves him on, and he takes the handles of her chair before racing forward to the village with vampiric speed. Rap gives us a curt nod and sprints after them.

"What do you say, Cinder?" Snow asks, tapping the daggers along the belt of her catsuit. "You kill the thrall on anyone Mal is forcing to do her dirty work, and I'll stab any of the ones who are just here because they wanted to party?"

Cinder side-eyes Snow. "Done this before, Snow, darling?"

Snow shrugs. "It's good to have a hobby."

With that, they charge toward the village.

"We've got to get to my parents," Aurora says. "They aren't going to stand by while the village is terrorized. They'll sacrifice themselves to try and stop her."

I rip off my jacket, already in a run. "I'm on it." My wings extend, and with a few powerful flaps, I launch into the air.

Aurora calls my name, and I turn. Her jaw trembles, her eyes dart between me and the fight ahead, panic and hope warring in them until it's all I can see.

"Talon, try not to hurt her too badly," she yells up at me.

I cock my head to the side, not understanding.

"She...she says she can break the curse." The expression of hope and dread tells me she debated even telling me.

My heart soars out of my chest with a hope I didn't know possible.

Mal could undo what she's done?

Aurora could be free?

Terrified screams send my heart plummeting right back down to earth again.

I nod and fly off, already knowing I have to stop Mal at any cost. Even if that cost is me and Aurora.

CHAPTER 38

THE CORPSE OF LOVE ATTACKS

AURORA

It doesn't take long to find a horse and saddle up. I mount and take off toward the castle, keeping wide of the village chaos. Two vampires whip their heads toward me, fangs flashing as they break into a sprint, their feet pounding against the earth in a blur of speed.

I pull the power into me, grip it tight, and aim. For once, I don't fight it. I let it surge. Heat builds in my chest until I can barely contain it, then I release. The blast tears free in a rush of searing pink light, spearing into the vampires mid-stride. Their bodies jerk, limbs contorting as if yanked by invisible hooks. I scoop the life force out of them, devouring, feeding.

Delicious.

Patting the side of the horse, I urge them faster until we've raced through the gates of the castle.

As I approach, my eyes turn upward to see my mother and father standing on a balcony above the gates. They aren't hiding. Even from here I can see their fierce expressions. My mother's dark blonde hair is braided back under her crown and I see the glint of determination in her matching gray eyes. My father holds her arm in his as he grimaces at the monster flying directly at them.

My mother finds me first. For one impossible breath they soften, relief breaking over her face as if my return alone is enough to steady the world. My father's arm tightens around her, his own lips lifting in the ghost of a smile. They're glad to see me. Glad I'm alive. The love in their faces steals the air from my lungs.

Then their relief evaporates. My mother's hand flies to her mouth, my father's smile twists into horror as their gaze lifts to the shadow bearing down on them.

My chest aches with how much I still love them. All the distance, all the resentment, it burns away under the fire in Mal's wake. Whatever else I've become, I am their daughter, and I would die to keep them alive.

"No!" I jump off the horse as Mal sails on massive wings, with fire beneath her skin.

She looks nothing like the woman she once was. Skeletal wings beat against the night, heavy with muscle and corruption, dragging her bulk through the air like something pulled from a nightmare. Black scales stretch across her bloated limbs, glowing fissures pulsing underneath with molten hate.

I understand that kind of hate.

One moment with Talon, brief and bright and stolen, ripped away so fast it left me raw and seething at the world. But what simmers inside me is nothing compared to the thing above me, the full-grown beast of heartbreak left unchecked, left to rot and fester in isolation until it twisted into this. Mal is not just angry. She is the corpse of love, animated only by spite.

Ice crystallizes in my veins as I stare into a possible

future for myself. What I'd become if I let this grief curdle inside me until nothing human remains.

But this could never happen to me. Hiding my secret had begun to kill me from the inside. Mal let exile and heartbreak rot her soul until she embraced it. I refuse to let that happen.

Even when I cannot control what I am or what the world throws at me, I can still choose. I can break rules to claim my own life. And I have help, from Talon and my Lost Girls, true friends who choose to love and support me no matter what I am. I built a rich, exciting, fulfilling life even with heartbreak and pain rooted smack dab in the middle of it.

Time crawls with painful clarity, and I can plainly see the hate and glee gleaming from the burning embers in her black eyes as she breathes in deep, her mouth open wide, fire sparking at the back of her throat.

She releases her breath, and flames spew out toward my parents. My heart lodges in my throat as panic sends a rush of white-hot needles through my brain.

I'm going to watch my parents die, and there's nothing I can do to stop it.

A dark shape barrels through the sky and slams into Mal's side with bone-shattering force.

Talon tears her from her path in a spray of black scales and shrieking rage, sending them both tumbling through the night sky.

Heart still hammering, air snags in my chest as the Dragons collide, claws tearing, teeth sinking into flesh. Blood arcs across the stars. Talon's wings beat once, hard enough to shake the trees below, sending them both spiraling higher, locked together in a brutal grapple.

His scales catch the moonlight in brilliant flashes of

obsidian and fire, but Mal—gods, Mal is wrong. Her shape keeps changing, shifting, struggling to hold together beneath the weight of what she's become.

I rip my gaze away only when movement below draws my attention.

Vampires. More than I can count, surging from the burning village like ants from a cracked nest. Feral. Hungry. Thrall-bound and mindless as they make for the gates. For the castle.

For me.

I step forward, planting myself between them and the people I love. Between them and the threshold they will not cross.

"You better back the fuck up," I warn. I feel my eyes light up with power and my hair lifts, defying gravity. "Because I'm a Lost Girl and I will eat you alive." I grin, my lips curling upward without humor.

They don't listen, rushing toward me anyway. *Witchtitting idiots.*

My power pours out of me like a hungry maw with fangs made manifest. Pink arcs tear free from my chest and slam into the first wave, sinking invisible teeth into flesh and bone. I rip their lives free without thought, without mercy. Souls unravel in ribbons of light, pouring into me, feeding me.

It's not like feeding from Talon. It never will be. But it's enough. Because I control it, it doesn't control me.

The next wave breaks against me. I open my arms to meet them.

Power crashes outward again, cracking through the night like jaws snapping shut. Vampire after vampire drops in my wake, their bodies falling in a fast-growing pile, their souls flooding the void inside me that craves even more.

I step over a corpse without slowing.

Above me, Talon roars—louder, fiercer than I've ever heard him. Fire rolls off his wings as he collides with Mal again, their claws raking, their teeth sinking deep. They fight, gods above a burning earth, locked in a bloody struggle.

Smoke claws at the sky. Fire devours rooftops. Screams cut through the night, and the stench of blood and magic burns in my throat.

Rap is in motion, barking orders as she hauls villagers from burning homes, her hair wild in the firelight.

Ariel maneuvers her chair with ruthless efficiency, weaving through the wreckage, owning the terrain. Her voice rings, reassuring but sharp over the din as she drives people toward the gates where Rosari guards fight to hold line against the vamps.

Kai carves his way through the chaos with precision, shielding civilians, pulling survivors from the smoke, cutting down any vampire stupid enough to cross his path.

Cinder breaks thralls with precise bursts of blood magic, unraveling Mal's grip on the vampires one by one. Confusion flashes in their eyes as control breaks, and then those freed turn on their captors—adding to the chaos, the bloodshed, the hope.

Snow fights like something feral. Daggers gleam. Her smile is all teeth and satisfaction as she cuts through Mal's army with vicious precision.

My friends hold the line.

I continue to stand my ground but the frenzy of battle is already calming.

"Aurora!"

My mother's voice cuts through the smoke and chaos. I turn to see my parents rushing down from the castle gates, guards flanking them. My mother's dark blonde braid has come half-undone, ash smudging her cheek. My father's crown sits crooked, his royal robes singed at the edges.

They're *alive*.

For a breath, I can't move, can't breathe. My heart lurches, a ragged sob tearing free before I can swallow it down. I missed them so intensely. As I stumble forward on shaking legs, I become a child again, desperate for the safety of their arms.

My mother reaches me first, her hands frantically checking my face, my body, searching for injuries. "My darling girl, you're hurt," Her fingers ghost over the burns on my arms, tears streaming down her face.

"I'm okay," I whisper.

My father pulls us both into his arms, and for a moment I'm not a cursed Succubus or a Lost Girl or even a woman who's killed to survive. I'm just their daughter, held safe between them.

It's what they always wanted. For me to be safe.

"You came back," my father says, his deep voice rough with emotion.

"I'm sorry," I sob into his chest. "I'm sorry I ran away. I'm sorry I brought this here—"

"No." My mother pulls back, cupping my face with both hands. "This was never your fault. And you left to find yourself. Talon has kept us apprised in letters, telling us how you've grown, how independent you've become. And just look at you." Her eyes trace my piercings, my chopped hair, the confidence that sits on my shoulders even through the exhaustion. "You found who you were meant to be."

My father's hand rests heavy on my shoulder. "We should have let you go sooner. Should have trusted you to find your own way."

Cries echoes from the village, followed by the crash of a building collapsing.

My parents' heads whip toward the sound, and I see it, the weight of crown and duty settling back onto their shoulders.

The vampire horde has dwindled, but it's left the wounded and dead to be tended to.

"The people—" my mother starts.

"Go," I say quickly. "They need you."

My father hesitates, searching my face. "Will you..."

"I'll be fine. Go help our people."

My mother kisses my forehead, quick and fierce. "We love you, Aurora. Always."

My father squeezes my shoulder once more. "Always."

Then they're running toward the village, their guards forming a protective circle as they race to help with the rescue efforts. My mother turns back once, our eyes meeting across the smoke and distance. She mouths "*I love you,*" before disappearing into the chaos.

I stare after them for a heartbeat, until an agonized screech turns my attention up again.

Mal's shape is breaking apart. Wings glitching between forms, scales splitting to show pulsing veins of raw, unstable magic. Her mouth opens wider than it should, spilling fire in crooked spirals. Her eyes burn black-red, unfocused, furious, blind with hate.

Talon tears into her again, claws raking down her spine, teeth sinking deep into her wing joint. Mal shrieks, and the sound vibrates through the stones beneath my feet.

She crashes to the ground.

Hard.

A crater blooms beneath her ruined body, dust and fire curling around her like smoke from a pyre. Her wings flap once, then fall still. Her chest heaves with breath she shouldn't have left.

I break into a run toward the collision. My heart pretzels up into knots and sweat breaks out across my body. Is she dead? If she is, I'll be stuck with this curse forever. The prospect turns me cold.

As I approach the crater, Mal's head turns.

Her gaze slides past, fixing on the figures rushing up behind me. My friends have come. A rush of air precedes Talon landing on the ground. Scratches carve jagged paths across his chest, raw and bleeding, but his stance is iron. Red rivulets drip from his hairline and well along his cheekbones. The shine of raw wounds that make me ache to reach for him, but he's still upright.

Mal's lips curl, blood staining her teeth. "Little brother."

Kai doesn't move. He watches her with the kind of horror only family can feel. "Mal, what are you doing? You have to let this go. You can come home now." Wetness rims his eyes.

Mal turns her disfigured, half-bloated face to the side and spits. "I have no home. And I'll make sure everyone knows my pain. You and your friends will suffer, they will know the pain I've endured for years. I won't rest until you all bleed and break." She looks at Snow, Rap, Cinder, and Ariel, as if memorizing their faces. Already envisioning how she'll make them pay.

Kai's throat works but no words come out.

Mal laughs. It's a broken sound. Then she lunges—not at Kai. At Cinder.

"No!" Kai shouts.

On instinct the curse rips free, a beast unleashed that

wraps Mal in pink light. It hits her, stopping her in place, but I realize my mistake too late.

"Aura, no!" Talon yells.

My power ricochets off her, slamming her back a step but slamming into me twice as hard. The curse turns on me with the full brunt of a deadly beast. The cavernous emptiness inside me tears wider, edges burning and infected, a wound that eats deeper with every breath.

It's like at Poison Apple all over again, except worse. I've grown stronger, and my power strikes deeper.

My muscles lock, clench, tremble. My hunger gnashes at my insides. I...need. I need so bad.

"You think to hurt me?" Mal says with affronted disbelief. "Why, you little slut, you are too hungry to do anything else but *feed*." The word is sonorous, loaded with magic as she pointedly looks between me and Talon. Then she laughs, a horrible sound that cements the pain and emptiness writhing inside me.

Her eyes glow red with malice and magic. Energy crackles around her, building fast, savage. She's working up toward something catastrophic.

Talon's hand flashes to Snow's belt, pulling free one of her daggers with a practiced twist. In the same breath, the blade drives clean and hard through Mal's chest.

Her laugh dies in a ragged choke.

Shock slams into me. It happened so fast. Too fast. My brain can't catch up to what it means, but my knees buckle until I stagger.

My hope shrivels into a tiny black ball that decays as quickly as Mal's life.

Blood bubbles from her lips as she looks down at the dagger buried in her heart before turning to Kai. "Little... brother..."

Kai doesn't flinch, though his face crumples with anguish. "This has to end, Mal." His voice breaks. "It ends with us."

Cinder seizes his arm, anchoring him as his whole body trembles beneath her grip.

Mal's hand spasms, clawing weakly at the air. Her gaze snags on me with all the hate and blame I've embodied for her since I was a baby.

Her body gives out, folding in on itself, hitting the earth with a dull, final thud. Her body crumpled like a goddamn afterthought. The grass around her drinks up her blood.

I stare.

My heart slams against my chest, but I can't tell if it's grief or fury or fear.

"Aura, I had to," Talon says from somewhere far away. "I'm sorry. I'm so sorry."

The words don't land. They drift around me, muffled, as if the air itself has swallowed them up. My fingers are numb, my legs heavy, and yet my heart hammers so hard it makes my vision pulse white at the edges. I can't move. Can't breathe.

That was it. That was my chance. My tiny, shimmering thread of hope.

She said she could undo it.

She *was going to*. If she lived, she would have been imprisoned, and I would have found a way to bring her around. Even if it took years, there was a chance. A chance I'd be free. Talon and I could at least be together by choice, not because of this fucked up arrangement that forces me to be with everyone except him.

But now she's dead.

The curse—the one she draped over my crib like a noose—is carved into my bones forever.

I'm never going to touch him without consequence. I'm never going to stop feeding. I'll always have to fuck to survive. Always have to tiptoe the edge of murder just to stay sane.

Nothing's changed.

My throat tightens, glass lodged there, cutting deeper with every breath. My hands curl into fists, nails biting crescent moons into my palms, trying to hold myself together with sheer force of will.

The ache in my chest spreads outward, crawling in sharp fractures through my ribs, my spine, down into my stomach where it twists into a knife's edge. Everything inside me pulls tight, raw, frayed. I'm so tired. I've fought so hard to be someone new. To be who I want to be, only to come home exactly as I left.

But I'll survive this too. Because I have to.

I'll feed again. I'll keep going.

"You have to feed," Talon says, closer than before.

He stands next to me. Like always. Steady, unshaken. Ready to hold me through the worst of it. Ready to catch me when I break.

Not literally of course.

The emptiness inside me yawns wider, a canyon with no bottom. Cramps wrench my stomach, and my jaw aches from holding back the scream clawing up my throat. Every inch of skin pulls taut, ready to rip under the pressure. I'm not sure if it's the curse chewing away at me or my own certain fate.

"Aura, now," he adds quietly but firmly.

A numbness spreads through me. I must be in shock.

I nod, knowing he's right. I know this drill. The hunger already threatens to pull me to my knees. It's in my teeth, my throat, my chest—gnawing, gnawing, gnawing. I can bear it. I've borne worse.

The ground trembles under my feet. Grass blades lift, shimmer. From Mal's corpse, something red and wrong slithers out, a living scream.

Power.

Dark. Furious. Wild.

It snakes out of her open mouth, her chest, her eyes—streaks of red lightning flaring outward in veins against the green grass. Not aimless.

It's coming for me.

It slams through my bones, splintering me from the inside out.

CHAPTER 39

THE POWER OF TOUCH

AURORA

The cursed magic breaks through my spine, my ribs, sinking sharp teeth into every nerve.

The air disappears.

It's not just pain—it's *hunger*. Amplified. Multiplied. Multiplied *again*.

My lungs seize. My throat convulses. My eyes burn. I can't scream. I can't even breathe.

Hunger threads through every muscle, guiding bone and nerve, answering a need that doesn't belong to me but feels carved into my marrow. Thought dissolves. Will shatters. Craving is all that's left.

The body moves. Not from choice. Not from thought. Just hunger pulling the strings.

"Aura?" Talon asks, his voice tight with panic.

I'm already reaching for him.

"Aura, don't," he says, scrambling back. My curse whips out of me with an invisible maw with drooling fangs, and sinks into him. And it feeds.

Talon stiffens under the attack.

Not close enough. I need more. Oh fae lords, I need every piece of him. I'm empty, caving in on myself. My insides scrape raw, curling tighter, tighter, until I can barely breathe. He is salvation and I drink like an addict, gorge on his life force.

Every cell in me shrieks for more of him. Not just his magic. *Him*. His fire. His soul.

I gorge myself.

A harsh guttural sound rips from him as his head whips back in pain. I know I took too much. I would have killed anyone else from just that but there is so much more of him. Ancient, powerful Dragon energy, and I must have more.

My hand finds his face.

His bare skin.

"Aura, no." His voice cracks, fear splitting through the pain in his eyes. He scrambles back, hands raised. "Aura, stop—don't—"

The curse doesn't listen.

Neither does my body.

Something inside me unspools, and whips out. It lashes through the space between us and hooks into him.

Talon jolts, eyes going wide as the drain begins.

His life—his fire—is flowing into me, and it's everything.

Every part of him calls to me: the molten fire that lives under his skin, the ancient thrum of power that no one else could ever match. I need it. I need him.

He tries to pull away, but I'm faster. My hands find his jaw.

His body arches as he cries out. Not a grunt. Not a cry. A full-bodied, pain-ripped scream that tears down to his soul. A similar sound rips from my own body as blistering pain sears across my palms. I scream, trying to yank my hands back, but I can't. I am tethered to him, siphoning, consuming. But the drain doesn't stop. I clutch harder. I'm latched onto him with both hands now, frantic to drain him even as I yank him tighter, burning, blistering, but still pulling, always pulling.

Flames erupt. The fire quickly eats away both our clothes, hot enough to disintegrate even his fae leathers.

Then my arms catch. Skin splits. But I *feed*. My power opens its mouth and takes big deep swallows, devouring. I feel the energy repairing my arms even as they burn, a sick cycle of healing and destruction that can only lead to one end. Will I burn to death before I suck him dry?

My body is fire and need, drowning in a hunger that burns through bone and thought and love.

"Aura, stop," he chokes, but it's too late.

I'm tethered. Anchored. Devouring.

He's burning me alive. I'm draining him dry.

Flames crackle along my arms. I smell my own flesh cooking, but I can't let go.

Not when he tastes like this, not when he fills me so completely even as it all drains away. I'm a sieve, and his life force is draining away into me.

My skin rips open, and somewhere beneath the pain, I feel myself knitting back together, healed by the very life I'm stealing.

He groans again. The sound is low, guttural. His legs give out. His hands slam into the ground beside me, clawing for something to hold on to. Heat pours off him in waves as his power spirals out of control.

His body starts to glow from deep within. More orange fissures bloom across his ribs, his neck, his thighs, like magma breaking through rock. His breath comes in ragged bursts.

I sob, the sound swallowed by fire and power. My hands shake as they sear, skin peeling from muscle. And still I don't stop.

I'm still empty and I can't resist him filling me over and over.

But it's killing us.

Talon's heartbeat stutters again, then flutters like wings failing mid-flight. His scales dull further, paling from obsidian to soot. The light in his body gutters like a candle about to go out.

And still, I hold on.

Still, I feed.

My arms are fire. My chest a furnace. My throat a clawing void. I'm crying, I think. Or maybe it's just the burn in my eyes as his magic pours into me in uneven pulses, his strength hemorrhaging straight into my marrow.

He looks at me with that same unflinching devotion that's never once wavered.

There is no rage in his face.

No betrayal.

Just heartbreak.

The kind you can't scream through. The kind you can't fix. The kind that's always been coming.

His lips part. A name, maybe. A prayer. Maybe a final breath.

My hands convulse. More screams tear from my throat, warped and feral, the sound of a soul splitting down the center.

I'm killing him.

I'm healing from the fire with every breath I steal, but he's unraveling under it.

And still I can't let go.

Because this is the last time I'll ever touch him.

I want to say his name.

I want to tell him I'm sorry.

But we don't need words. We never have.

Even in our worst moments, our eyes said what our mouths never could.

Every time I was with someone else, I found his eyes. Letting him know, silently, *I wished it was you. It was always you.*

Throughout our days together I looked at him like I loved him, because I did. And he returned that look with such intensity I felt it burrow under my chest where his love took permanent residence. Even if we couldn't touch. Even if I had to keep sleeping with other people. We loved each other more than most people were capable of and even in our last, tortured moments, in the culmination of our worst fears, we still loved each other more than anything in this world or heaven above.

And he'd look back.

With that same fierce, steady love that split me open every damn time. No jealousy. No resentment. Just that quiet, endless promise: *I'm here. I'll always be here.*

We spoke with glances. With silence. With everything we couldn't afford to say out loud.

And now, as I kill him with the very power that cursed me, we speak again.

I'm sorry.

I love you.

I didn't want this.

It was always you.

As if knowing there is no stopping the end for us both now, his hands find my waist, bringing me closer. Even as the fire climbs higher, devouring me inch by inch. His scales flash once more before flickering out.

Let the fire take me.

Let it take us both.

My lips meet his, and flames consume me as I finish devouring him.

CHAPTER 40

MATED TO THE DRAGON

AURORA

My lips press to his, burning, blistered, ruined, but I don't care. I want him to be the last thing I taste. His mouth. His pain. His love. All of it. If I'm going to die, let it be like this—devoured and devouring. Together.

He kisses me back.

Gods, he *kisses* me back.

Not weak. Not fading.

Fierce. Feral. Like he's choosing me, even as everything unravels.

Our mouths slide, clash, part—nothing soft, nothing delicate. It's grief and surrender and love, all crushed between our teeth. His hands tighten at my waist, as if the fire won't take me if he holds me close enough. Maybe the hunger will stop.

But it doesn't.

My body is still starving. My skin still smokes. I can feel the last threads of my soul fraying.

And then...

Deep inside, where the curse coils like a second spine, *something cracks*. A flash. A break. A spark.

His fire flares, bright and wild. Not recoiling from me this time.

Reaching.

The heat that should sear me now *recognizes* me. It curls around my bones like silk. Slides across my skin like breath. I feel it rise through him—an ancient, unstoppable tide—and instead of burning me away…

…it *sears into me.*

Like it's always belonged there.

Something threads between us. Not magic. Not hunger. Something older. Truer. A tether of fire and soul that latches on and *roots.*

I gasp into his mouth as the connection coils tight *inside* me. A low hum starts in my belly, then pulses outward, curling around my spine, my ribs, my throat. I feel *his* power, wild and molten and *endless*, not filling me, but *fusing* with mine. Melding. Matching.

My body's still begging, but not from emptiness.

From *completion.*

My curse buckles. Then it breaks.

The hunger implodes in on itself, folding around his fire like a lock finally finding its key. I'm not draining him anymore. I'm *holding* him. Taking *with* him.

And gods—it's too much. It's perfect.

Talon jerks, a raw cry ripping from his throat as his back arches. Orange light erupts from the fissures across his skin, his power reborn in real time. His Dragon reignites.

And this time…

I don't burn.

I *rise.*

I clutch his jaw tighter, tears slipping past my lashes.

His scales flare against my arms, but they don't hurt. They *sing*. My body hums in sync with his. My magic wraps around him like a second skin.

We are one force.

One breathless, bound thing, stitched together by love and fire and the gods-damned pain of it all. Bare flesh against flesh draws us only closer together.

He blinks at me, his eyes dark and shocked. "Aura?" he whispers.

"I'm still here," I breathe. "You are too."

Talon shudders. A sound leaves him—part sob, part growl—as if his very soul is breaking open under the weight of what we've become.

Then the light inside him *erupts*.

His breath catches. His spine arcs beneath my hands. Fire pulses beneath his skin, then *pushes outward*, blazing brighter with every heartbeat. Magic snarls to life, ancient and untamed, and it no longer fights me. It *lifts* me.

His eyes snap open, molten gold and wild wonder. "I can feel you," he rasps, voice barely human. "Everywhere."

"I know," I whisper, stunned. "Me too."

His scales bloom back to life—not in patches, but in a radiant, unstoppable wave. Fissures blaze along his skin like magma veins, lighting up the dusk. The earth seems to *tremble* beneath him as his body begins to change.

I don't let go.

For the first time, I *don't have to*.

Bones stretch. Wings unfurl. A tail arcs behind him, carving wind. Fire roars through the grass as his true form rises. Not a man, not a monster, *a god on wings*.

And I'm still *touching him*. Arms around his neck, cheek pressed to scales that once would have seared me into ash. Now they hum with power—but *they are mine to hold*.

His Dragon is massive, obsidian and flame, crowned in horn and fury, but none of it frightens me. I see *him*. My Talon. Lit from within. Alive. Whole. *Mine*.

He roars once, an echo that cleaves the sky.

We launch.

The world *drops* away.

Wind lashes my face. Fire curls around his wings. The night swallows us whole as Talon surges upward, higher, faster, *free*, and I ride him without fear.

My thighs grip him. My fingers curl into his neck. The heat of him sears through my clothes, but not my skin. I feel it all, every beat of his massive heart, every rise and fall of his wings, every gust of air that breaks against my body as we climb past the treetops and into the stars.

We don't speak.

We *burn*.

Together.

Bound by something deeper than magic. *Fated*. Made. Claimed.

And for the first time in our cursed, star-crossed, barely-lived lives...

We fly.

BACK TO WHERE WE STARTED
TALON

I land soft enough that our feet barely leave a dent in the grass, but my arms don't loosen. I keep Aurora wrapped up in them like she might vanish if I let go. I don't intend to let go. Not now. Not ever.

The moment we hit solid ground, I know exactly where we are.

The creek where we first met.

I flew here on instinct.

That quiet, sacred place with its soft green banks and glittering water. The dapples of moonlight through the high trees. That moss-covered boulder in the stream where this madness started. Where I first saw her and wanted her in ways I didn't understand.

I fold my wings. My body shifts again. Back into human skin, and our flesh pressed together is the absolute best feeling this life could ever offer.

"You went full Dragon again," she says, breathless.

"I feel like I could do it again," I tell her, unable to stop the grin pulling at my mouth. It's a rare thing. I've never felt so light and free in...maybe ever.

Her eyes brighten, and I swear my hoarding instincts sharpen to dangerous levels. I want to keep her looking at me like that forever. I want to gather every version of her smile and stash them somewhere only I can touch.

I shift her in my arms, still holding her like she belongs there. Because she's mine. And I never have to let her go.

I cup the back of her head and lower my mouth to hers still afraid this is a dream. Her lips are trembling. So are mine. Fear. Awe. Hunger. Relief. All of it tangled up in something that feels bigger than words.

My fire still burns under my skin, alive and humming, but it doesn't hurt her. It wraps around her. The hunger I thought would gnaw at me forever, has gone quiet. She fills it. Easily. Entirely.

We kiss.

Not rushed. Not desperate. Slow. Certain. The kind of kiss you give when time has stopped counting. When you know one kiss will become another, and another, and you have all the space in the world to take.

My hands frame her face. Her fingers slide into my hair. We breathe each other in like it's the first breath after drowning.

I laugh against her lips. A real one. She laughs too.

"I can touch you," she whispers.

"It's perfect," I say. And for once, there's nothing brooding left in me to argue.

We collapse to the grass together. Limbs tangled. Hands roaming. Not frantic, curious. Possessive. Like I'm relearning her piece by precious piece, and adding every inch to my hoard.

I roll to my back, pulling her over me. Her palms on my chest, my hands skimming under her thighs. No rush. No need to feed. Just this. Just her.

The hunger doesn't claw. It's quiet. Satisfied.

My fire doesn't threaten. It holds.

Her hands explore like she's rediscovering me, but I'm memorizing every touch. I'm the one hoarding this.

She straddles my hips, her slick heat dragging against me, and I groan. Loud, wrecked, wanting.

Gods, how are we already this desperate?

My hands cup her ass, guiding her. Slow. Teasing. Drawing it out because I can. Because I want to.

"I don't need you," she says, smiling.

It hits like a punch. I freeze, looking up at her. Is she...

"No, not like that," she huffs, rolling her eyes and swatting my chest. "I don't need you. I'm not hungry. I just *want* you."

Relief crashes through me so hard I almost laugh. I almost roar. Instead, I grin slow, wide, dangerous. "Thank the fae lords. Because I was ready to tie you up and throw you in my Dragon's cave and never let you out even if you begged."

Her eyebrows waggle. "Oh. Kinky." She laughs in a carefree way I'm instantly addicted to. Yet another new sound I've inspired. I'm going to find and cause dozens and dozens more.

Aurora reaches down and lines us up. I hiss as the head of my cock drags against her—wet, ready, perfect. My fingers twitch on her hips, but I don't thrust. I wait. I let her take me.

She sinks down, inch by inch. Stretching, claiming, filling herself with me in slow, shaking increments.

Her mouth drops open. "Oh—fuck."

I grit my teeth, watching where we're joined, heat pulsing through me like a heartbeat. "You feel like a dream," I groan. "No. Better. You feel like home."

She moves in slow, steady rolls of her hips. Torture. Heaven. Her chest brushes mine, nipples grazing the edge of my scales. Not burning. Making her moan. Making me harder.

I surge up, kissing her again. Because I need to. Because she's mine, and this moment is mine, and I'm taking all of it.

Her hands curl behind my neck, anchoring us together like she's afraid I might fly away. As if I could.

"Do the thing," she whispers.

I swallow hard. "I don't know what you're talking about."

She groans and rocks her hips, squeezing me tighter. "Come on," she whines. "I want it."

I push up on my forearms, searching her gaze, finding nothing there but hunger and joy and want. Then I'm up, standing, holding her, her thighs braced around my waist. My lower wings extend before wrapping tight around her hips like a band.

She gasps. I feel it everywhere. The drag of my talon-tipped wings tracing over her ass, spreading her open, dipping into her tight hole.

I thrust, deep, smooth, filling her until she gasps again.

I fuck her like she's mine. Because she is.

Sweat beads on her skin, slicking us together as I move harder, faster.

Foreheads pressed. Breath shared. Shaking. Tethered.

"I love you, Talon. You are mine, no matter what. You've always been mine, and I've always been yours."

"I love you, Aura. So fucking much. Always yours," I groan, hips stuttering. "Fuck, I'm close—"

"Give it to me," she pants. "Give me everything."

I do. Harder now. Deeper.

She breaks first, moaning, clenching, coming around me with a shudder that drags me under too.

I bury myself to the hilt, roaring her name as I spill inside her. Heat. Life. All of me, anchored in her.

And when we still, I don't pull out. I stay. I keep her close.

Because she's mine.

Breathing together. Alive. Whole. Loved.

TAKE YOUR PIZZA TO GO

TALON

Lucifer stretches out in the patch of sun on the wood floor of our new apartment. A puff of black fur floats from his body into the air with the movement. He seems well situated, but I know the second I drop my jacket or sit down, he'll be all over me. His own personal heater.

Though I've come to appreciate the attention, and the feline is always careful not to touch my bare skin and is incredibly adept at avoiding getting burned.

If only he was better at missing my nuts when he jumped in my lap, that would be ideal. But I've had enough wins to last me a good long time. No use getting greedy.

"That's the last box," Ariel says, dropping it on our new kitchen countertop with the rest.

Aurora and I got the keys to our new loft at the top of an old industrial building, the kind with exposed steel beams and pipes that hum faintly when the water's running. We have roof access now—perfect for when I want to stretch my wings without taking the long way around. The light here is better too, the sunlight pouring in through the massive windows like it's trying to fill up every inch of the space with warmth.

It didn't take much to convince her. Just a few well-placed arguments, and a long afternoon of edging her into agreement, both literally and figuratively. We're staying. We're building something. Might as well have a place that feels like it.

Gone is the mildew and cloying candle stink of the old apartment, replaced now with the clean scent of fresh paint and wood polish. The long brick wall is weathered but solid, full of that lived-in charm Aurora calls character. Opposite it, a wall of tall windows frames the daytime view of Back Bay. The buildings, sky, and water layered together in an appealing mosaic.

It feels like a start. Maybe even a good one.

"Thank you, Ariel," I say sincerely.

"Hey, we helped too," Snow protests from the large slate gray couch she's currently sunk into next to Cinder and Aurora.

"Only the hardest workers get pizza," Kai says from the ground where he puts together a small bookshelf with impossibly small screwdrivers.

A cry of protest arises from the couch.

I keep it to myself that I still think we should have got lobster rolls from a certain food truck. When I suggested it earlier, I got a number of pillows to the head with vocal protests that I can't reward their help with food poisoning.

"As much as I like that idea," Ariel says to Kai, "I think you risk being stabbed by Ms. Stabby McGee over there if you try to hold out on her."

True to Ariel's word, Snow plays menacingly with one of her daggers.

"Don't forget, your parents are coming to visit next

weekend," I remind Aurora because I know she will. I mentally make a note to get magnets so I can put it up on the fridge where she'd be hard pressed to miss it.

Relations between Midnight and the Realm of Roses have turned a new corner as Kai and King Roland forged a new relationship on the blood-soaked Rosari ground that day.

And Aurora's parents were as ecstatic to have Aurora home as they were grateful for all our efforts to protect their land. They quickly realized how Aurora had changed. How she yearned to be new, to live differently. So while she may be the heir to the throne, they agreed to letting her live her way for a while.

In sin. In Boston. With me.

Though I did get a stern side talking to from her father, who said if I didn't continue to protect his little girl's heart with the same vigor I'd always protected her with, he'd tear my wings off himself. Then he patted me on the back with a fatherly look that made me feel warm in places I didn't know I could.

"Are your parents really cool with you staying in Boston?" Ariel asks.

Aurora grins. "They know I'm happy here."

"You sure you don't want to go back to all your other friends in Realm of Roses?" Snow tests.

Whatever seal Aurora had been kept under had broken after that night with Mal. The royal court practically came crashing down on her with warmth, gratitude, and not a little inappropriate curiosity. Thankfully, no one was stupid enough to outright ask if she had any connections to the secret beast of the castle or the disappearances. I'm not sure who was more of a threat on that front, me or Aurora's father.

Aurora was overwhelmed by all the attention she got, but happy that the glass around her had been broken.

"I'm glad I'm not seen as some ice princess, or worse, some monster." Aurora looks at me with the same dazed expression she's had in her eyes since that day. "But my people are right here." She reaches around the girls as best she can, and squeezes them while stretching out a toe to put on Ariel's arm, including her too. Ariel pinches her calf and earns a squeal.

"Alright, everyone take your pizza to go, because I am also hungry," Aurora announces, standing and lightly slapping Ariel's knee. "Starving, in fact," she says, grinning wickedly at me.

Snow rolls her eyes even as she grabs an entire box. "Fine, bang it out in your new place. But I'm coming back here to this swanky joint to watch the next episode of *Hex Island* when it drops Thursday. And you can't stop me."

"Yep," Ariel nods, as she steals a cheesy slice from Snow's box. "If you are going to have a place this cool with all your princess rule, you have to host *Hex Island* nights."

"I'm in." A small enigmatic smile curves Cinder's lips. "If that's...okay." She adds, looking at Aurora with sudden uncertainty.

"I'd love that," Aurora says, warmth softening her expression.

Cinder bumps her fist against hers as Kai sidles up to me. "Talon. My guy. My man. Hot boy of the hour." Not sure I love his joining in on the nickname, and somehow making it even worse. "While the women watch their petty TV dramas, maybe we can have some manly time. Drink beers. Or hunt...something." He scratches the back of his head, clearly at a loss for what other manly activities there are.

"You can come watch too, Kai," Aurora says, her lips lifting with quiet knowing.

"Oh, thank the fae lords," he says, clutching his chest. "I'm dying to see that douchebag Viggo fuck it all up for the house in his attempt to get with Chastity."

I shoot him a hard look, and Kai straightens. "Please, that idiot Ricky is going to lose the whole pot on rando girls he keeps sneaking out of the house to meet with."

A grin creeps up Kai's face as he realizes I'm in just as deep with that shitty show.

As soon as the door closes behind them, Aurora jumps me. I easily catch her.

"Feed me, I'm hungry." She pouts dramatically before attacking my neck with nibbles, licks, and kisses that send blood pumping into my fast-hardening cock.

"What happened to your table manners?" I tease. "Are we expecting several courses this evening, madam?"

Her eyes glitter. "As long as I get them from you. I'll eat it all up."

I pull back, letting a moment of seriousness settle between us. "Are you sure this is what you want? Me? Forever? Because I know you'll always have this hunger crop up and maybe you aren't used to—"

"Sleeping with only the person I love?" she retorts, pushing aside the pink hair that fell in her face. "Oh no." She waves her hand in fake dread. "Yeah, no. You are all I've ever wanted," she says more seriously. "Sure, in an ideal world, you could touch people without burning, and I wouldn't have to feed on sex to survive." She focuses on my sternum, deep in thought and shrouded in vulnerability. "But of all the scenarios I'd ever considered a dream reality, I still think this is my favorite one. You fill me up in all the ways. With your love, with your..." She pats me through my pants, causing me to jerk. "But you still always encourage my independence. You help me be the most me I can be. And that version, a version I love, is only possible with you in my life. That's only if you are okay being enslaved to a lifetime of my hunger." A bit of uncertainty creeps into her eyes.

"You can't enslave the willing," I point out before kissing her in that way I know makes her knees weak and her panties wet.

In the kiss, I try to return all the confirmation that I'm in this for as long as she wants me. No, fuck that. Even if she gets tired of me, she'll have to suck it up because I love her too damn much.

When I release her, she licks her plump lips, pupils blown wide and unfocused. Her eyes narrow with slow intent, a spark of mischief glinting as she drops to her knees, unzipping my pants along the way.

Oh fuck, she's going to—oh *fuck*.

I jerk as she takes me in her soft, hot, wet mouth. My fingers find my way into her hair where I hold on for dear life as my Succubus princess girlfriend literally tries to suck the life out of me through my dick.

When I get that familiar rush of tingles up my spine and I'm on the verge of exploding, I yank her to her feet and strip her naked. My wings extend from my groin and wrap around her waist as we fall onto the couch. I slide into her tight, welcoming heat until we both groan and buck with need.

"Welcome home, baby," I whisper.

I feel her smile against my ear. "Best home ever."

～

Visit Holly's website to download the bonus epilogue!

A Lost Girls getaway to the Realm of Roses... as shadows of Snow's past rise to the surface.

https://hollyroberds.com

TASTING RED

Want more of the Lost Girls? Enjoy this peek into book 1 of Tasting Red

"Why did you call me here?" I ask, though I know perfectly well why the grizzled old son of a bitch sent for me. I spin the titanium ring around my forefinger with my thumb.

He frowns under his thick beard, across from me at the wooden table. He pushes a pint of ale over before grabbing his own. I don't pick up the mug, but the man shrugs and takes a swig.

How did I end up here? For most of my life, I've lived on my terms with no consideration for anyone else. Not even the women I sometimes let in my bed. I follow the jobs that bring the most money and that has served me perfectly well until now.

"It's been a long time, Brexley," he says.

Nineteen years, if one were counting. And for nineteen years, I've felt the ghostly shackle, tying me to someone else. Nearly two-thirds of my life, waiting for the shoe to drop.

"Not long enough," I say gruffly, finally grabbing the mug and taking a healthy swallow of the stuff. I hate to admit the shit is good. So I don't.

I've done everything I could to be free of social ties. There is no place for me among mage, man, or fae. But today is the day my only marker is called.

I owe one being a favor in this entire world and he has summoned me here to the musty backroom of his tavern. Boxes pile high around the room, surrounding us. He named the joint *Sam's*, though his name is Jameson. I never asked who he named it after, and I still won't ask.

The drizzle kicks up a heavy mist that clings to the windows. The cold seeps its way into my bones despite my knit sweater and leather jacket. On a shitty day like this, I'd normally be at home by the fire with a book. But this old son of a bitch has me by the balls.

"You owe me, Brexley," Jameson starts, as if he expects a fight.

I wipe my mouth with the back of my hand. "I'm aware, you old bastard. Just tell me what you want so we can get this over with."

His calloused fingers drum on the manilla folder next to him before sliding it over. "I need you to take care of her."

His tone tells me he doesn't mean take her out for lunch and shopping. He must have been keeping tabs on me to know what kind of business I'm in now. Or maybe he's just a sadistic son of a bitch, and I could be a florist and he'd still give me the same mission.

I push the mug away, despite wanting more. Drinking won't make this problem disappear. But once my only debt is paid, I won't have anything hanging over me. I'll truly be free.

I flip the folder open to a picture and a single page of

details: name, occupation, home addresses. But I didn't need any of that info. I instantly recognize the older woman in the photo. I've seen her many times—on billboards, commercials, packages of food, enamel pins that people stick on their jackets.

A dry snort escapes me. "You've got to be joking."

The old bastard doesn't crack a smile, doesn't move a muscle.

Fuck me.

I run a hand through my already unruly silver hair. "Grandma. You want me to go after Grandma from 'Grandma's House?' The face of the most popular household brand, and one of the most powerful witches known to the world?"

Jameson repeats himself in slow, steady words. "You owe me." Coiled tension is locked up behind his dark eyes and in the set of his broad shoulders. Blood lust shines out from his face. This is business from his past. But I don't ask questions, and I'm not about to start now.

I study him, observing how he's changed since I last saw him. Even more gray strands pepper his black hair and beard. His scowl has only deepened with the years, multiplying the lines at the corners of his eyes. He must be nearing his fifties, but under his flannel shirt vest is a body still packed with the sturdy muscles of a heavyweight boxer.

Once upon a time, I considered this man to be like a father to me. He quickly dispelled me of that notion with an unholy vengeance. He taught me the truth. Dependence is death. Don't buy into the lie. You don't need others to survive in this world. It is a gilded lie that ends with getting stabbed in the back.

Or, in my case, a set of claws raked across my face.

But finally, I'm given the opportunity to dissolve my last tie to another being, and this is my chance. As one of the most beloved celebrity icons, this also may be my chance to get killed.

My fingers wrap around the cold handle of the mug, suddenly thirsty. "She won't be easy to get to. And afterward, I'll be hunted like an animal."

His chair creaks with a loud groan as he leans back with a smirk. I've already accepted his terms. "Good thing you're used to it."

So he does know my business.

I shoot him a cutting look over the edge of the mug as I swallow the rest of the amber liquid.

"After all," he folds his arms across his chest, "you are the Big Bad Wolf."

My grin is half-grimace. "And that is very bad news for grandmas right now."

~

Head to Holly's website https://hollyroberds.com to find out what happens when Red and the Big Bad collide at grandma's house

TRACKING SNOW

Preorder the next Lost Girls book now, and we'll return to
Poison Apple in 2026.
Reserve Your Copy Now!

Available for preorders on Amazon and hollyroberds.com

LOVE THIS BOOK?

ENJOY MORE BY THIS AUTHOR

**Vivien woke up with no memories and a terrible thirst for blood.
The Grim Reaper must destroy all blood suckers.
The reaper dogs just want to get pets and loves in between fetching the souls for the Afterlife.**

Read this COMPLETE trilogy and you'll laugh, you'll cry, you'll absolutely die.

Vegas Immortals: Death & the Last Vampire

*Available on Audio and Kindle Unlimited

WANT A FREE BOOK?

Start your Lost Girls obsession for FREE!
Hooking Tink—my sizzling novella starring Tinkerbell and
Captain Hook—is part of my bestselling Lost Girls series...
and you can download it free right now! Visit my website
https://hollyroberds.com/hooking-tink/ to grab your
copy now!

Acknowledgments

Thank you to my assistants, Leah Crowell and Tara Volpenhein who are ever supportive, and keep me going even when things are ABSOLUTE chaos on my end. I could not, would not, want to do this without you.

Thank you to Sarah Urquhart for being my writing and life buddy most days through a computer screen away! Your company makes the trip so much more pleasant.

Thank you to my editors Theresa Paolo, Havoc Archives & Athena Franks for catching all my MANY echos so I don't sound ridiculous.

Thank you to Emily for plying me with bourbon and food during our coffee working date. I cried, I bitched, and you helped me through the editing process which is a bit of a hallway through hell, but boy is it better with a friend.

Thank you to Amanda, Anna, and (of course my evil PA) Tara who inspired the most heinous of ideas by putting wings on Talon's dick when we met at Getting Witchy With It NOLA. Y'all are diabolical, but ya got me! And now we have this (waves hand at document on computer).

To my special reader fan group, *Holly's Hellions* – you are the best, most enthusiastic, and loving readers an author could ask for.

To my Patrons – you guys are the most insane power squadron and you rocket me up when I share the behind the scenes nonsense and snippets of whatever I'm working on. And thank you for not being upset when I fall off the planet for bits at a time as I dive into writing or working my butt off until I don't know which way is up. I hope to always spoil you and keep you forever.

Thank you to l'husbun. You are the love of my life and beyond supportive. You watched and experienced the long ugly slide of me losing time to my deadline and you never complain. You take care of me so sweetly and I never lost gratitude for the life we have together.

A Letter from the Author

A Letter from the Author

Dear Reader,

Thank you for reading!

There is more to come! Ariel, Snow, and a Rap retelling are all in the works, and I can't wait to continue sharing this world with you. You're enthusiasm, DMs, reviews, and support is what keeps this series going and I hope to deliver your wildest, spiciest fantasies.

Want to make sure you never miss a release or any bonus content I have coming down the pipeline? Make sure to join my Patreon: Holly Roberds Books

And definitely sign up for Holly's Hotspot, my newsletter, and I'll send you a FREE ebook right away!

You can also find me on my website www.hollyroberds.com and I hang out on social media.

Instagram: http://instagram.com/authorhollyroberds

Facebook: www.facebook.com/hollyroberdsauthorpage/

And closest to my black heart is my reader fan group,

Holly's Hellions. Become a Hellion. Raise Hell. www.facebook.com/groups/hollyshellions/

Cheers!

Holly Roberds

ABOUT THE AUTHOR

Holly Roberds is an Amazon Top 40 Bestselling Author of the Vegas Immortals and Lost Girls series, known for badass heroines, gut-busting laughs, and spicy romance. When not writing, she's playing Dungeons and Dragons, sinking her teeth into her husband's very bite-able arm, or enjoying a "Holly Happy Meal" (prosecco and espresso) at a vibey coffee shop.

For more sample chapters, news, and more, visit www. hollyroberds.com